Research
Housing

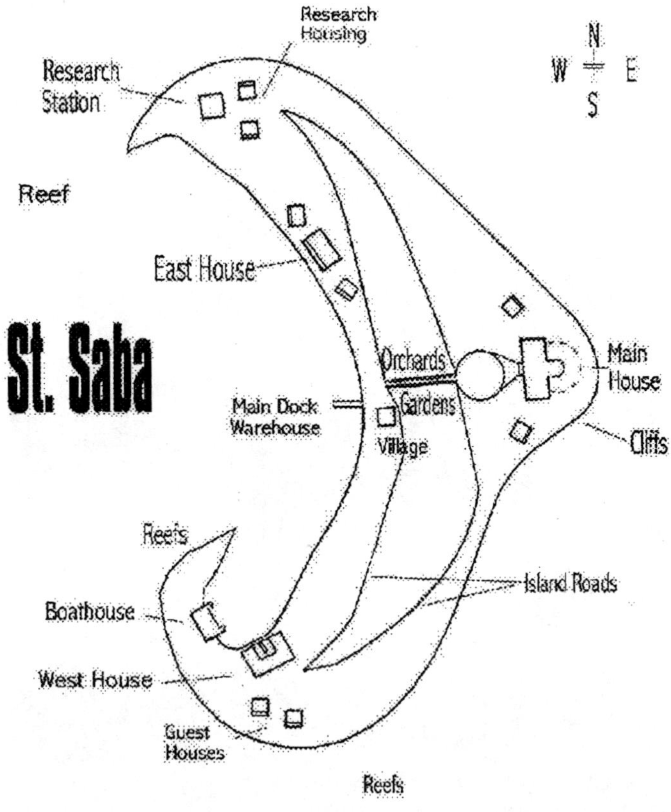

Research
Station

N
W —— E
S

Reef

East House

St. Saba

Orchards

Main Dock
Warehouse
Gardens

Village

Main
House

Cliffs

Reefs

Boathouse

West House

Guest
Houses

Island Roads

Reefs

Edge Of Paradise

It was so lovely she could almost feel the ache inside her shrinking to more manageable proportions. The trees over her shoulder rustled softly in the breeze. She felt at peace with herself and sighed contentedly.

Stars glistened in the sky. Her father told her when she was a little girl that a star was born when someone we loved died. Those left behind only had to look up to see the shining stars and know their loved ones were safe from harm. She'd always cherished that story and knew that her son was up there now, forever safe from pain. He was sheltered, surrounded with her parents and grandparents as well, a comforting thought.

The beach became more littered with boulders and the bank to her right rose higher, but she kept walking, mostly looking at the stars, drifting effortlessly in their hazy nebula. Clouds sailed suddenly across the moon, making the beach dark and mysterious.

She heard strange banging noises and light beams reflected, once off the clouds, then again along the shore. She thought she could hear the murmur of voices, but couldn't be sure. This side of the island had only the big main house with its guest houses perched high on the cliff and they were supposed to be vacant. She must have been mistaken. It was probably the wind.

A large boulder appeared in front of her but she was distracted by the moving light and sounds. Her foot wedged between two rocks, so she ducked her head and reached down to extract it.

Suddenly, she was grabbed from behind.

"What the... ?" She started to yell, but a hand clamped over her mouth while she was pulled roughly to the ground. Struggling to free herself and trying to scream, she was told by a man's whisper.

"Hush. You won't be hurt but stay very still. Your life may depend on it."

What They Are Saying About
Edge Of Paradise

***** An exciting thriller that will keep your adrenalin pumping! I could not tear myself away from the story! I had to know what would happen next! Here is an author that I am proud to recommend to everyone! *Mary Higgins Clark fans should especially consider this story!* *****

Detra Fitch
Huntress Reviews

Wings

Edge Of Paradise

by

Lynda LaPorte

A Wings ePress, Inc.

Encore L'Amour Romantic Suspense Novel

Wings ePress, Inc.

Edited by: Lorraine Stephens
Copy Edited by: Sara V. Olds
Senior Editor: Lorraine Stephens
Executive Editor: Lorraine Stephens
Cover Artist: Pam Ripling
Cover Photo by Lynda S. Burch

Wings ePress Books
http://www.wings-press.com

Copyright © 2002 by Lynda Burch
ISBN 1-59088-923-1

Published In the United States Of America

June 2002

Wings ePress Inc.
P. O. Box 38
Richmond KY 40476-0038

Dedication

This book is dedicated to the loving memory of my father, Eugene Ritcher, who was proud of any and all of my endeavors. His unconditional love and support made me who I am today. As far as he was concerned, I could've been an astronaut and walked on the moon. And by publishing this book, I would have put him on the moon!

Thanks to my mother, Anna Ritcher, for instilling in me the hunger and passion to consume the hundreds of books, that I have devoured so avidly each year. Thanks to my sister, Pat Ritcher, for diving into my first manuscript and MarySue Roberts for the support and the incredible photography through the years. Hats off to my MORWA writing and critique group, who taught me the professional honing skills I would have been sadly lacking.

And last but never least, thanks to my husband for allowing me the time and energy to recreate myself once again.

Somewhere in the Caribbean

Good grief, Lori. How dumb could you be to get in this predicament? She asked herself for the umpteenth time. Out in the middle of the night with the dog, Jake, on an open boat in the storm-tossed Caribbean. Realizing the danger they faced, Lori continued to chastise herself. *Stupid woman!*

Even in this mess, Lori knew Hugh's survival meant she must find help from the big island. Then go back and rescue him. Simple as that. She knew the blood she'd found on the cave floor was his and knew his life depended on her, and her alone. After spending almost twenty years without him, she wasn't about to let him disappear from her life again. *No way!* She would fight, tooth and nail if she had to.

Normally, during night boating conditions, judging the distance to islands or rocks by a white breaker line would be easy, but tonight visibility was pushing zip. Nada. Fifty feet max, if she was lucky. Not much help there. Only the gauges and sheer guts would keep her alive tonight. She rose up on her toes, her body tense.

Beginning to get freaked, Lori turned on the radio knob to alert St. Thomas of her whereabouts. The radio did not work. She didn't know why, but it was every bit as dead as the phones on the private island from which she'd just escaped.

She heard gagging and felt unusual warmth on her feet in the cold rain. When she looked down, she saw Jake shivering and throwing up. The large Rottweiler she'd wedged in beside her for his safety, puked on her feet for thanks.

"That's okay, boy. If I had the time and energy, I'd join you."

So far, each time the boat headed directly toward an islet full speed ahead, lightning appeared to give her the warning she needed to veer south around it.

The wind and the rain continued to slash at her face. If she crouched low enough for the windshield to protect her face, then she lost even more visibility. Standing stiff at the helm with both hands on the wheel, she struggled to increase control by speeding across the wave tops.

It was hopeless trying to wipe the rain off her face. She needed goggles desperately, with windshield wipers. She laughed at herself. *You foolish woman. There are wipers on the windscreen in front of you and they are positively useless in this downpour.*

A stiff tension knot at the back of her neck magnified tenfold. Freezing and scared, she was determined to make it, no matter what bleak prospects confronted her.

Lori felt as though she had been fighting the boat for days. She peeked at the clock, and realized she'd been in this mess for twelve of the longest minutes of her life. She groaned. The Rottweiler sat up and barked in response.

Sparing a glance at the dog at her feet, Jake appeared more alert after the purge. She wondered if he'd been drugged too, but didn't have time to think about anything other than survival. First, they had to make it back in one piece to the port city of Charlotte Amalie.

Maybe this was a bad dream. A very bad dream and she would wake up in her own bed. But she didn't need to pinch

She could hear voices over the sound of the boat, but not enough to recognize them.

Without the advantage of high tide helping to slide them into the entrance, Lori shoved Jake toward the crevice but couldn't get him in with the vest on his back.

"Damn." She spluttered, not wanting the dog out of the vest yet. But she couldn't see how to get him inside any other way. She shoved the spare vest inside the opening and unlatched his vest before pushing him through the crack. Spotlights extended light around to this side of the rocks now, so she quickly kicked herself into safety, too.

Free of the vest, Jake was treading water inside the small circular opening of the standing stones. "Shush, Jake. Quiet boy." Lori thanked God for his silence.

She remembered a ledge during high tides. Since the tide was low, it should be dry. If she could get Jake and herself up on it, they would be out of the chilling water and could rest until daylight. Lori waited for a lightning flash to illuminate the rocky ledge a couple of feet above the water line.

She swam back to the opening and thrust the spare vest out it, hoping whoever was out there would find it. Then go away.

She tossed the dog's vest up onto the ledge. Struggling with the heavy dog until his big feet achieved enough of a grip to claw his way up while she shoved his rear end, which in turn sank her deeper into the water. It would have been funny but her sense of humor was rapidly diminishing.

After that, getting herself up was a piece of cake. She collapsed beside him, gasping for breath. Lori barely had the strength to take off her vest. The narrow six foot ledge would be long enough. Positioned on her side, she hugged the dog to her until they fit snugly. She adjusted the vest under her head then laid back down. Jake licked the salty water off her face and shivered beside her. She snorted, "Some paradise, Jake."

She tried to look at her hands in the darkness enveloping them. Abrasions on her hands she had not been aware of receiving, burned sharply from the salt. Even her broken fingernails hurt. Every single part of her anatomy screamed bloody murder at her. It even hurt to breathe.

The cold hard rock made a most unforgiving bed.

Her breath, raspy in her throat, gradually slowed down to a constant pace. Their combined body heats slowly warmed them. Lori, both physically and emotionally exhausted, could not control her mental state. Her overactive mind would not allow her the release of sleep she so desperately needed. She reviewed each memory in bright vivid detail, in a kaleidoscope of sights, sounds and emotions, marching before a brain she couldn't turn off.

One

Three months earlier,
En route to St. Saba Research Station.

I need to get a grip on this nostalgia jag and nip it in the bud. Otherwise, I'm never going to make the connecting flight to St. Thomas. She glanced at the watch her son had given to her for her birthday last year and bit back the grief that the glance solicited. Lori looked at the row of monitors displaying arrival and departure information. "Oh, no! Gate one-forty four and I just left twenty-two. Twenty minutes before my connecting flight leaves. I'll never make it. I should have taken a direct flight," she huffed as she wheeled her carry-on-bag in front of her and sped down the concourse as rapidly as possible.

Lori skidded to a stop at the next security entrance, looking at a mob of people. A detour to the restroom was called for now. No telling how far to the next one. Exiting the rest area, she spotted a mother with a sleeping infant in her arms having trouble arranging her bags at the x-ray machine. Lori blindly hurried forward, dragging her own bag. "Here, let me help. I'll pick up the one you dropped." And leaned down to retrieve the woman's fallen handbag.

"Umph" Her wind was knocked out when a tall, tan trim man tripped over her bag. He had extended his arms for balance and knocked her to the floor.

"Excuse me. I'm sorry. I didn't see you." He reached down to lift her back into an upright position. "Are you all right?"

"My fault. I didn't see *you* either." Lori waved off his help and chuckled softly, straightening her clothes. His voice stirred a chord of memory.

When she reached to the floor to pick up her bag and place it on the belt, he also grabbed the handle to help her. A *frisson* ignited between them like a jolt of 220 amp electricity. For the first time she looked up into his face and saw a devastating pair of tiger eyes staring at her from a hauntingly familiar face. The memory of that face tugged at her heartstrings like a passionate violist.

She groaned. *Not him. Not here. Not now, I don't need this now. My heart has had enough.* She shivered at the golden glow, dropped her gaze first and bolted. Heading through the x-ray portal, she quickly gathered her bag and ran toward gate 144.

He yelled to a startled crowd. "Lori? Lori-i-i!" He stood immobile. His feet were nailed to the floor, a hand outstretched toward the disappearing woman.

Like a frightened rabbit she scurried toward her plane. The sound of her name echoed down the concourse and she covered her ears to shut out the sound.

"Lori. Lori Paige. Nah, couldn't be. This woman looked too fragile, an injured look in her eyes. Not my Lori." He spoke aloud but no one listened. He was denying the evidence of his eyes and the pounding of his heart. This time he whispered her name to himself, stunned at the vagary of chance. He shook himself back into reality and stiffly marched to his gate.

He had work to do. Again.

~ * ~

Settling into her seat, Lori's heart finally started to slow down. That little jog to the gate had her heart fluttering. *I must be more out of shape than I realized.* The disturbing thought that she recognized those eyes, that voice, that chiseled face, and that lean firm body kept her heart racing frantically. But it was not possible that it could be Hugh. Not remotely possible! She needed to get control and calm down.

Focus, Lori. Focus on the future. This Caribbean research grant was for healing. She took a deep breath and tried to blow away the pain of Nathan's death and Nick's betrayal of their marriage vows. But her thoughts returned to the man with the golden eyes.

That particular tiger-eyed man had walked out on her a lifetime ago. Allowing those memories to surface, generated a distinctly warm pang to her gut, a definite visceral thrill from her college years. Totally unsolicited, a whole floodgate opened, pouring out memories like an invading army...

~ * ~

She remembered the class as the beginning, a simple summer class to get out of the way. When lo and behold in walked the sexiest man with absolutely the most exquisite musculature. He displayed powerful virility, clad in a muscle shirt, shorts and sandals, and took the seat next to her. Who would ever have dreamed that a class on Cuba and Castro's communist influence on Central America could make such an impact on anyone's life, let alone hers?

It wasn't long before he was borrowing a pencil or paper, or buying a cup of coffee to pay back all the borrowing. Eventually sharing study time in the library, he became bolder. His looks set her heart fluttering and made her sizzle. Then one day, out of the blue, he picked up her hand, turned it over, kissed it and scraped

11

his teeth along her palm. Lori shivered to her core at the memory.

That day was the beginning of a summer of passion that Lori fought hard to forget ever since. She guessed it was her naïveté that drew him to her, or perhaps it was simply pheromones, one or the other. It was certainly *her* most exciting summer ever. It created such boundless energy, and as a result, undoubtedly she achieved the easiest 'A' in her entire college life.

Hugh was an ex-Marine whose last posting had been Marrakech, Morocco. No wonder he'd been exceedingly fit. By the end of summer, Lori, too, was "fit as a fiddle," as her dear grandmother used to say.

Giving her heart, body and soul to first love was as easy as opening a door, and ended as hard as that identical door slamming shut on the very same heart. Sitting in that class, listening to radical information spouted by some Castro and Che' Guevara trained students made Lori aware of an entirely different world. As Hugh opened her heart, she expected it never to end, but it did.

She was totally unprepared for that, and shocked at the arrest of several of her classmates, a surprise finale to class that summer. They had been charged with burning an American flag at Washington University and some kind of political rioting and plotting.

But that was nothing compared to what she felt over Hugh's desertion. On the day after the arrest, it was if he simply disappeared from the face of the earth. Nowhere could he be found. *Nowhere.* He had finished his final exam, got in his car and drove out of the parking lot right out of her life. No 'goodbye.' No 'nice knowing you.' No 'see you around.' *No nothing.* That was the absolute hardest reality she'd ever had to endure, until now.

It *couldn't* have been Hugh in the airport, could it? He was definitely *not* calling her name. It was just a man of similar stature with the same startling tiger's eyes and he was most likely a figment of her overactive imagination. Since she'd been in such a memory blitz on the flight down, probably, *any* man would have looked like him. Besides who knew how Hugh had aged? Lori told herself, he could be a great big fat man by now, not that slim trim tight figured man at the airport, and she told herself to push the thoughts of him from her mind once again.

But her efforts were fruitless. She was inundated with memories of Hugh. They were sensations she had denied to herself for way too long. They felt good and they felt bad.

Two years after his disappearance, Hugh suddenly reappeared, finding her even though she'd married, changed her name, had a son and found a new job. One day out of the blue Lori answered the phone at the Zoo's pathology lab. She'd been immersed in work when Hugh Richmond's velvet voice asked her. "Hello Lori. Could you possibly meet me for lunch today?"

A jolt of adrenaline shot through her to the tips of her toes. He didn't have to identify himself. She recognized his voice as though she'd talked to him yesterday. She wanted to say, how dare he think she wanted to see him again, let alone talk to him, but her tongue simply said. "Where?"

"Sunshine Inn sound okay?"

"When?" She felt betrayed by her own mouth, but she went. She had to know why he left her like he did. She needed answers. Then she could pack him away and forget him. Forever.

At least by then, she'd learned to stand her ground. She would never allow him to throw her life into shambles again. Never. In fact, no man would ever have that power over her again. Or so she thought.

At that time, her son Nathan was six months old. Her life had assumed a normalcy of work and family. Usually, she was so tired that she fell asleep as soon as her head hit the pillow. Lori's exhaustion kept her from having the full color dreams that she used to have, and for that she was thankful. It had kept her dreams of Hugh to a minimum.

She had learned a wonderful technique of turning off her brain at night when Nathan was just a baby. When she was in medical school pathology training, she'd had to deal with baby autopsies, turning her vivid imagination on full blast at night in her dream world. She often had bad dreams about all those poor babies.

A hypnotist had taught her how to empty her mind of all thoughts, relax parts of her body and begin counting backwards from 100. If at any time a thought popped up, she would shut it down and start counting backwards from 100 again. It worked very well, achieving an alpha state or something like that, teaching her a control over sleep that she had never achieved before. It allowed her to sleep without the wretched fears of an excessively imaginative mind.

On her way to meet Hugh for lunch at the Sunshine Inn, a popular Central West End restaurant that served healthy food, Lori almost turned around and returned to the zoo. But by the time she crossed Forest Park, her heart simply took control. Her lofty aim was only to seek answers to questions, and refusing to attach any more importance than that, Lori walked into the restaurant with a smile on her face.

When she saw him, it felt as if the earth had dropped from beneath her feet. She wanted to run to him and throw her arms around him, but she stood there, trying to breathe.

"Hello Hugh," Lori said. *Where have you been all my life?* Was what she really wanted to ask him?

"Lori, you look wonderful!"

Outwardly calm, she walked to a table at the front window, wanting this meeting to be in full view of the world, not a sneaky little private luncheon tryst. Seating herself and facing him was another story. It was hard for her to sit quietly and wait for him to speak and it was considerably more difficult not to reach across the table to touch his face. But she was a married woman now. And a mother.

He looked so lean and pale, but maybe that was just her imagination. She had waited long months for an explanation. She could force herself to wait a little longer, right? Lori wondered if she looked as flushed as she felt. Her face felt like it was on fire.

Staring into the face of the man who was, at one point in her life, the most important human being in the world, she absorbed his features hungrily. His face had matured into chiseled good looks but he looked older than his years. He was more gaunt than that summer but his remarkable eyes were still his most dominant feature. Today they shone with a particularly bright penetrating golden glare. Gazing into them made Lori want to escape from their view. They were a lion's stalking stare directly before pouncing on its intended victim.

Lori sat, waiting for him to speak first, but the waitress intruded on their joint perusal of each other. She ordered a Caesar salad, and ratatouille with a wheat roll. He copied her order, and when they ordered tea at the same time, both smiled, finally breaking the ice, their eyes locked on each other.

As the waitress left the table, Hugh reached across to grasp her hand. He took the right one, the one without the wedding ring. Lori attempted to pull it back into her own possession, but he wouldn't allow it. He stroked the back of her hand with his thumb, sending delicious sensations up her arm.

"You have the softest skin on the face of the earth."

She wanted to blurt out. *Sure, that's why you ran out on me, creep.* But she bit her lip instead.

"Lori, every day I've been away from you, I've been trying to get back. When I left, I went back to Washington. At first I thought I didn't need you. I fought with my heart every day. I've been around the world, but every single day I've thought of you and what we had. I had no idea it would take me this long to come back to you."

"Wait a minute! I haven't heard one single word from you in almost two years, and now you just waltz in out of the blue expecting me to fall into your arms. You must be crazy. And I must be crazy for listening to you. Oh! I'm outta here!" Lori tried again to jerk her hand away to leave, but Hugh refused to let go.

"*Please* sit down, Lori and let me explain. I'm doing this all wrong. I need to start at the very beginning." Inhaling a deep breath, he began again.

"I need to tell you something. I work for the United States government. I worked undercover that summer trying to get close to some young communist infiltrators on your college campus. I couldn't tell you who I was. And I certainly had no intention of falling in love with you, but I did. I've regretted my lack of honesty ever since."

"An ex-Marine?"

"True. And everything we felt was true. The problem was with me. I told myself that it was a summer fling and when my work here was over, I could walk away. With some good memories of great times, I'd be off on my next assignment. But it didn't work that way."

"I was sent to New Orleans after a quick trip to D.C. because I needed to identify a couple of characters I'd seen with the students who were arrested. They were part of a terrorist group. It was complicated but we managed to round up the whole group. I had infiltrated them and could identify their contacts. Then I had to make statements for testimony in several different states."

"We'd built quite a case against them, and they were only well trained kids. Most were less than 21 years old, but lethal. Kids or not, they had a hit list of local prominent businessmen. The list contained presidents of a number of major multinational corporations around the country, which they were trained to take out one way or another."

Lori, mesmerized by the sound of his voice had many doubts and many more questions. Before she could voice them, the food arrived and she politely thanked the waitress.

"These kids were terrorists and thought I was a disenchanted Vietnam vet. That's where their gullibility let them down. They couldn't accept any philosophy other than their own. They were dogmatic commies from the word 'go'."

"I don't care about them. I want to know why, in all this time, you never called me. I had so much pain to get over. I had to get on with my life. I'm married now, you know, and a mother. What good does all this do now? It's too late! Much too late!"

Lori hadn't touched her food or even picked up her fork. She'd been so distracted. *At least I managed to get control of my own hand again, thank you very much.*

"But I love you, Lori. I've *always* loved you."

"Hugh, you just think you love me. Nothing convinces me you even know what love is. All it would have taken was one call. One simple call, that's all, just one."

Ignoring her comments, he continued to plead his case. "Next, before I had an opportunity to see you, I was sent to Iran. I was at the U.S. Embassy in Tehran when it was taken over by soldiers of the new regime. It was like Vietnam all over again. All hell broke loose. One moment, the political climate was a little uneasy and then--Boom! The fireworks started. I was almost captured a dozen times in Tehran. If it hadn't been for some brave Canadians hiding us and protecting us in the cellar of their embassy we would have all been killed. It took months to get out of that cellar, and much longer to get smuggled out of the Mid East alive. It seemed like forever."

"Each and every time I faced danger, I swore that I would get back here to tell you how much I loved you and to ask you to be my wife. It was the worst time in my life. I needed you to look forward to. I *need* you now."

"But Hugh, you're not listening, I'm *already* a wife to a great guy and a wonderful father."

"All I want to know, is what you have as good as what we had together? Can you look me in the eyes and tell me that?" Hugh demanded. "What we had was *special*, and you know it!"

"Hugh, I...I can't do this," lowering her eyes from his fanatic gleam. "And the operative word here is *had*."

"Look me in the eyes, damn it and tell me you don't love me. That you never loved me. *Tell me right now and I'll leave!*" His voice increased in volume with his impassioned plea.

Diners in the restaurant turned, taking notice of the couple sitting in the window booth, and made Lori feel uncomfortable.

Sitting quietly for a few minutes, Lori tried to gather her thoughts and absorb what she heard. After all this time, he *had* loved her. She struggled hard to maintain her control. *If* what he said was true, *if* only she had been patient, *if* she had waited for him, she could have had the love of her life. But it was too late. No matter what he said or did now, it was too late. She could never take Nathan away from his father. Even if she carried a burden of lost love for the rest of her life.

Nick didn't deserve to be treated like that. When she married, it was for life, a lifetime commitment to each other. That is what marriage was all about, wasn't it? The bond that was between

Nathan and Nick would only grow stronger every day over the years. She could not and would not allow Nathan to be jerked back and forth between parents like a toy. Divorce did that to kids. No two-way yo-yo game for her son. No way.

Hugh didn't know her very well at all, if he thought she could just turn around and walk away from her life like that. She looked up into his magnificent tiger eyes. Her own eyes filled with unshed tears, Lori gave Hugh his answer.

"Hugh, I *did* love you. But *I can't* and *I won't* throw my life away. You haven't asked about me or my son or my job or any of the things that are important to me! You don't know me. You don't even begin to comprehend who I am. And I don't know you. My son will grow up with a real father, not a weekend dad."

Refusing to accept that answer, Hugh kept pushing. "I don't want to be caught out there alone without you. I will not accept 'no' as an answer. I can't!"

He paused and then began again, "I need you. I need *both of you* to make my life complete. Tell me that you will at least consider what I'm asking of you, *please. I love you and I can wait a long time!*"

Lori's only response was a nod as she rose from the table.

"Lori, I'll be waiting for your answer. I'll wait for you, as long as it takes." He whispered as she walked away from him.

Two

Thinking back on that miserable summer of Hugh's sudden reappearance, she remembered losing weight and developing an ulcer. But she never gave in, not to anything, not even to herself. As her resolve strengthened, she convinced herself she was doing the right thing. And once again, without warning, Hugh simply disappeared from her life. As Lori pushed her past behind her yet again, this time she succeeded in forgetting the man at the airport and forced herself back to the present.

Flying high over the clouds, countless waves of grief gently washed over her, succeeding in cleansing away endless months of anguish. First, the death of her only child and then the double whammy of divorce. Surely there was nothing else in store for her immediate future, please God. Her heart could only bear so much. *Lori Paige, get a grip on yourself girl. No more tears. I won't allow it. I can't allow it.*

The infant in the next row and the soft fluffy clouds evoked long ago memories of soft smooth skin of her own newborn son. What a delightful tender thought. She could almost smell that wonderful clean baby scent and leaned her head against the airplane window. She felt the muscles in her face form a smile and looked at her reflection to confirm it. It was probably the first genuine smile on her face for a long, long time. *Good, maybe the smile is a sign of returning to the living world. Even though Nathan had been long past babyhood, I could never forget the scent and feel of an infant.*

Leaving the most miserable Midwest winter of her life, Lori looked forward to a solar healing of her weary soul in the bright shining sun of the Caribbean. She admitted it. She was solar powered. She needed sunshine like some people need exercise and she needed it *now*. Which reminded her of Nathan's personality and ability to spread sunshine just like that old black and white cartoon, throwing bottles of sunshine happiness at grumpy people. Sighing, if only happiness could be bought in a bottle.

Lori couldn't wait to sunbathe on a brilliant white beach under a warm Caribbean sun. *Sounds like absolute bliss*, she thought, feeling lucky to land this job. Her boss knew more people in his field, than she could meet in a lifetime. As a select member of a national task force that reported to the U.S. Surgeon General, a contact had told him about this terrific research opportunity for which he encouraged Lori to apply. And if her research yielded definitive answers, she could publish, which she hadn't done lately.

She decided when she reached Charlotte Amalie, to send her boss a telegram or some flowers. *Yeah, I like that idea*, and smiled once again to herself. It seemed smiles were coming easier today. Hallelujah.

Looking out over the shimmering blue ocean, countless little coral atolls slid into view. The plane cast a long shadow upon the land and water passing below. Her final destination would not be much larger than these.

The private island of St. Saba was a five mile long crescent-shaped islet, with a protected lagoon within the crescent. Its highest area was two hundred and fifty feet above sea level, on the opposite side of the crescent from the lagoon, with steep cliffs falling straight to the sea. The widest point was one mile, but most of the islet's width was a half mile.

After the short flight to Charlotte Amalie, St. Thomas, capital of the U.S. Virgin Islands, she'd catch an intra island boat that regularly ran supplies and mail to the islands. Enjoying the wonderful blues and greens of the water unfolding an endless panoramic view, she speculated on the mortality phenomenon of the water life that she was going to explore. She hadn't snorkeled or scuba dived in such pristine water for a long time but her swimming skills were excellent. *Besides, it's like riding a bike, you never forget how, right?*

Approaching the airport, the town displayed a pastel splash of buildings against a verdant tropical forest backdrop overlooking an endless azure sea. She spied a breathtaking rainbow beginning at the old colonial town and ending west out at sea somewhere. *Amazing.* Where in the world did that come from? It reminded her of the triple rainbow she saw the morning of her son's death and felt a sharp pang in her chest.

For some reason she expected pirate ships with tall masts to sail into the harbor, instead of the pretty congestion of cruisers and sailboats docking there. A number of brightly painted fishing boats headed back to port.

The aerial view blocked signs of modern life. The trees hid the power lines and typical towers of twentieth century progress. Lori couldn't see vehicles on the roads as the airplane swept in a large loop out to sea before swooping in like a big bird to land at the airport.

Lori wouldn't have been surprised to see a horse and buggy draw up to the plane and wait for her to disembark. This island was simply enchanting and she felt time change as she stepped in to a slower, calmer world.

But the illusion was spoiled at the airport. The workforce arrived in a multitude of assorted vehicles and scattered to attend to their various duties almost before the plane came to a complete halt. A loudspeaker from the quaint white stucco terminal directed the passengers to an open veranda on the side of the building where Lori joined the queue forming to wait for luggage.

Entry to this easternmost outpost of the United States appeared sketchy to Lori. A customs official checked her ID with little formality before stamping her travel papers and telling her to have a nice stay.

Employees at the airport appeared more British than American, dressed in khaki shorts uniforms designed for the temperate climate. Lori checked her watch. Barely after noon and the sticky heat made her wish for another layer of clothes underneath her sweatshirt and jeans. Saint Louis had been cold when she left.

Huge fans overhead stirred the air but as soon as she stepped into direct sunlight the temperature felt stifling hot. *Well, sunshine is definitely a major part of the appeal of these West Indies, Lesser Antilles chain of islands*, she thought.

She'd studied the location situated east of Puerto Rico and lying between the Caribbean Sea and the Atlantic Ocean. The three islands and fifty islets remained fairly unpopulated. Tourism bolstered the economy, with cruise ships regularly docking at the fine harbor loaded with cash and plastic carrying tourists.

Lori helped load her baggage into an old green dented taxi waiting in line. After telling the driver that she needed to go to the harbor to catch a boat, she settled into the back seat with a yawn. Maybe this weather was already having an effect on her.

Everyone she'd seen so far *had* been rather slow moving. Only the taxi was fast, and it moved like Speed Racer. It traveled a minimum of eighty miles an hour on a smooth packed sandy roadbed covered with crushed sea shells. Trying to get a glimpse of the speedometer, she sat up straight in her seat and held on for dear life. The taxi windows were wide open, blowing hot air in her face. Lori could taste the strong salty smell of the sea.

Opposing traffic appeared to be separated by a fairly safe distance. Ha! Must be a divided highway. Lori laughed to herself. At least a head-on collision seemed out of the question in the near future anyway, so she settled back in the seat, absorbing the sights flashing past.

The taxi driver drove one handed with his arm resting on the seat back. He spoke with a clipped British accent. "Historically, the Virgin Islands were discovered by Christopher Columbus on his second voyage in 1493 and were named by him. In 1666, the Danish West Indies Company colonized and controlled the group for the next hundred years or so. After that they were administered by Denmark until the U.S. purchased them for $25,000,000 in 1917. A strategic price for providing a U.S. location for a sizable Navy presence, don't you think, ma'am?"

She didn't tell him she'd already done research on the island chain long before her trip. Instead she said, "I hope to find plenty of time to explore all the islands."

He continued his dialogue. "There is a lovely fifteen thousand acre National Park on St. John. The park encompasses two-thirds of the island and contains a treasure trove of two hundred and sixty species of plants, a hundred bird species and vast undersea coral gardens."

The small port city sprawled lazily around the bend with the crystal water sparkling in the background. It appeared all roads lead straight to the harbor. The concrete block and stucco buildings were light pastels for reflecting heat from the strong sunshine, which reminded her she would need a hat for the boat ride.

Leaning forward in the seat she asked, "Where can I buy a hat and get a late lunch before I catch my boat?"

"There is an open market across from the port authority, ma'am. Also, some good al fresco dining areas along the dock's boardwalk. The food is a bit pricey, but quite good, ma'am."

"But what about my luggage?"

"We drop it off at the boat first, then you can take your time shopping and eating. The O'Tarbutton boat usually departs at four o'clock for its evening run."

Startled, Lori asked, "How did you know which boat I was catching?"

"Easy ma'am, it is the only boat that puts out to sea on Tuesday afternoon. All the cruise line ships are in port Monday, Wednesday, Friday or Saturday. The fishing fleet goes out early in the mornings or late afternoons. Most of the private boats are weekend boaters. And pardon me, but you don't look like a military type, ma'am." He flashed a big smile over his shoulder with gleaming large white teeth set in his dark face.

She smiled back, having forgotten about small communities where everyone knew everyone else's business. It wasn't like living in a suburb to a big city like St. Louis where there was at least some degree of anonymity.

In the narrow city streets houses or garden walls bordered the road beds with lush tropical trees and shrubs providing lovely bursts of riotous colors. The bougainvillea displayed shades of bright fuchsia to dark red. Trailing over walls, across hillsides, and along fences, flowers everywhere blazed dramatic colors.

There were many trees and plants Lori did not recognize. Hot house plants in St. Louis grew in tropical profusion here, Australian Schefflera umbrella trees, rubber trees, eucalyptus trees, oleanders, and figs. A cornucopia of flowering fruit trees bloomed in abundance providing a visual and sensual bombardment.

25

The harbor spread out before them when the taxi turned right and followed the long coastal road toward the docks. The central part of the deep aquamarine harbor dedicated to business bustled with marine activity in every direction.

Boat shops with docks stretched out into the water, bounded on both sides with every possible form of water craft. Lori smiled again, enjoying the sights as the taxi approached a large building that housed an open market area, as she swung her head back and forth attempting to absorb the sights.

Small nautical shops and restaurants edged the boardwalk across from the docks and looked like a good place to lose herself for a time. The taxi passed them by and continued to an interesting looking ramshackle building made of gray weatherbeaten wood. A hand painted crooked sign hanging over the pier, announced it as the home of the O'Tarbutton Line.

Line of what? Lori wondered. It looked rough to her, and what a name. She got out of the taxi and helped the driver gather her belongings and load them on a cart outside the door. She pushed open a screen door that had so many holes in it that it couldn't possibly keep out anything, except maybe a large dog or a horse.

Inside a perky young brunette in cutoff jeans and a red plaid shirt tied off above her bare midriff yawned, leaning against the counter. She looked up from a magazine she'd been leafing through. "Can I help you?"

"Yes, I'm Lori Paige. I have a reservation for a trip to St. Saba this afternoon and I was wondering if I could check in my luggage before I do a little shopping?"

"Sure, put it on the cart at the door. The boat sails at four, so be back or it sails without you. We have deliveries to make."

"I already have it on the cart and I'll be back in time, thanks." She smiled at the bored looking young woman. "Bet it's kinda quiet around here for a young girl like you."

"If you only knew. But it picks up when the big cruise boats come in with their horns sounding. Then this whole place starts bouncing." She rolled her eyes and grinned back at Lori. "Boy, what I'd give to work on one of *those* boats!"

The taxi driver recommended his cousin's restaurant Amalie's Place, so first Lori found a shop and wired flowers to her boss back in St. Louis then headed for the open market. Colorful salespeople were busy weaving straw hats and baskets. Jewelry and other items made from seashells were being strung. A cacophony of sound vibrated as they hawked their wares loudly.

Fingering through sari scarfs and tropical print fabrics she quickly chose a T-shirt and a couple of different straw hats. Lori discovered prices suddenly started falling if she moved away from the vendors.

After putting on a multicolored straw hat with a brim wide enough to protect her face, she sighed in relief in the cooler T-shirt. She crossed the street to Amalie's Place for a light meal.

A large breasted woman leaned over the counter and asked, "What do you want to eat?" in a deep contralto voice.

"What's good?"

"The best 'kunk' chowder in the Carib. You will like it."

"All right. I'll have a bowl."

The local wonderfully thick rich dark stew was distinctly spicy and made her eyes water. "More tea, please!"

"Ha, you like it I see. Told you so."

"Yummy. I love it. It's wonderful." Pleased with her first culinary choice.

Lori watched the time and the traffic in the harbor and simply vegetated for a while. Examining her surroundings, she spotted charming hotels blending into the natural landscape on the slopes of the island.

Strolling back down the boardwalk, and swinging her shopping bag, she meandered back toward the office. She chuckled to herself when she saw her bags exactly where she had left them. *Hmm, low crime area.*

Pushing open the screen door, she walked into the dark interior blindly. It took a few seconds for her eyes to adjust to the dim light. She announced in a singsong voice. "You who. I'm back!" Lori expected to see the young lady again.

"I can see that, and for a lovely lady like you, I will wait any day. I am Captain Jerrod O'Tarbutton, the proud owner of this line. And I'm *very* glad to meet you. You must be Miss Paige, I'm thinking?" The man behind the desk grinned, approving her dark golden hair and shining blue eyes. She was petite but perfectly proportioned, with a great complexion, smooth with lightly pinked cheeks and slightly full lips. Just right for kissing, he thought, and no obvious makeup to slide off of either. Her age was looked just right, too, late thirties maybe.

Lori blushed as she took the hand he offered to her. Now she knew where the 'Line' came from on the sign, because this blue-eyed man, holding her hand too long, was definitely full of good old Irish blarney. She was afraid he was going to kiss her hand the way he raised it.

Smiling into his heavily tanned face with laughter wrinkles crinkling, she knew she'd better watch out for this guy. He had way too much charm. It stirred up feelings she was doing her best to ignore, and put her body on full alert.

"Sorry, am I late?"

After he checked her hand for signs of wedding rings, he was even more enthusiastic. "No, of course not. I was just waiting to see if you're as pretty as my daughter said. I'm thinking she should've used better adjectives. Let me be the first to welcome you to our own little part of the U.S. and please call me Jerrod. We are informal on the islands. We are all great friends here, and since you are going to be seeing much of me, what may I call you?"

"My friends call me Lori, but why would I be seeing much of you?"

"Because I have the contract to deliver mail and essentials to St. Thomas' outer islands. So anytime that you need anything, just whistle and I shall surely come a'running with it! If you get my drift?" He winked at her and raised a sexy eyebrow simultaneously.

Finally, retrieving her own hand from his grasp, she said dryly. "Thanks, I think."

She shook her head at his sexual innuendos. He couldn't be that old, but he surely came across as an old roué. Lori wondered how many times he had used *that* line before. She followed him outside and down the pier to an old dirty white fifty-foot Hatterras.

The boat was large and squat looking, wide in the beam and loaded with all sorts of boxes and bundles tied down to the deck cleats. He placed her luggage inside the cabin.

"You are welcome to ride on the bridge with me or stay here in the cabin. But please ride with me for I've specially ordered a beautiful sunset just for you."

"You're incorrigible. You know that? I guess I'll ride up with you but *only* for the scenic views." Lori couldn't help grinning at him anyway and pulled her sweatshirt back on over her head.

"I'm thinking that you'll like the ride." The captain grinned magnificently over his shoulder at her. "*And* thanking me for many a time to come."

Lori plopped on a bridge chair, feeling on top of the world. Exhilarating in the feel of the wind and sun on her face, she gazed into the vast expanse with islets dotting the water near and far.

She watched St. Thomas fall behind as the boat headed for the open Caribbean. Water gleamed a brilliant glistening green then turned blue as the water depth changed.

A school of five bottlenose dolphins leapt, jumped, splashed and raced with the boat. They grinned, ridiculous grins at the boat passengers as though they shared a common joke. Lori hung over the side and gaped in delight at them.

Captain Jerrod said, "I ordered them to follow us just for you."

"Oh, malarkey. They'll follow any boat. It's all a game to them and you know it."

"Well, you can't blame me for trying. They have been following me for years. Same five. I think they know my schedule. If I've been fishing, I share with them a bit of my catch, so they know me, I'm thinking."

"I'm sure they do. They are very social animals. They live in pods or family groups. Will they follow us all the way to St. Saba, do you think? I'd love to get to know them."

He simply shrugged his massive shoulders, keeping his eyes on the water. Lori took a few minutes to look him over while he was preoccupied with piloting the boat. His blue black hair was thick and shiny under a Chicago Cubs baseball cap which looked out of place on the ocean, but each to his own taste. His eyes were much the same vivid blue as the sky above, drifting with few clouds. His well-tanned features were ruggedly handsome with a wide generous mouth made for smiling.

He was not a tall man but seemed bigger than he was. He was four or five inches taller than she was, with a powerful barrel chest and muscular arms. He looked exceptionally strong for his height. He seemed very comfortable in T-shirt and faded jeans worn almost white in some areas. The jeans fit him as snug as the blue T-shirt stretched across his broad back. The shirt was imprinted with the bold letters 'NO FRIGGING IN THE

RIGGING!' Whatever that meant, Lori thought. His feet were comfortably encased in scruffy old tennis shoes with no socks.

Catching her looking at him, he raised an eyebrow and winked again. She felt a tiny stomach flutter, surprised at herself. Maybe she really was coming back to life, after that long empty spell.

To change the subject in her head she asked him. "That was your daughter back at the office? She's a lovely young lady, but I bet you've got your hands full with her. The young men probably like her too much."

"Yeah, and she wants to leave and go work on a cruise ship, for God's sake. A flippin' love boat, no less. She needs to go to college, not party twenty four hours a day!"

Recognizing a sore subject, Lori changed it by asking what he knew about her destination.

"Well, it is classified as an islet, and St. Saba is one of the few inhabited year round. All of the owners are seldom there at the same time. They have other homes in Europe, and when they arrive they bring a whole household with them. You should see the stuff they drag in with them, you wouldn't be believ'n it! Most of the full time residents are caretakers, gardeners, maintenance people and families. Thirty people or so."

Lori noticed that his brogue appeared and then disappeared from his speech when he talked, making her curious about him.

"There are three large houses, but only one of them is occupied right now. A writer fellow lives in one of the guesthouses at East house. That's the closest house to the research station. Main house is mostly closed now, has been for at least a year."

"Some Laurents must be too busy making babies, I'm thinking. The youngest ones are newlyweds, only been married for five years. The older ones are not in the greatest of health. West house has other Laurents living there, been there forever.

They also have guests from time to time. There is an artist in residence at one West guesthouse, and he's been there awhile, too." He glanced at her to make sure she was paying attention.

"Each big house has two guesthouses. Then there is the research station with two cabins, and ten cabins in the village with a warehouse. It's very quiet there, most of the time. The most exciting it gets there, I'm thinking, is when a hurricane comes roaring through. Then everything gets closed up and they gather at the main house. Or they head back to us at St. Thomas depending on the size of the storm."

"Hmm, sounds wonderful."

Shocked, he asked, "A storm?"

Lori chuckled "No, the solitude, I'm thinking," making mock of him.

"Now, where was that you hailed from? New York or some such place?"

"No, I'm from St. Louis and the most water there's the mighty Mississippi, or down at the lake but I doubt I'll miss it here." She couldn't keep from staring mesmerized by the gentle swell of waves surrounding them.

"What lake?" Jerrod quizzed.

"Oh, sorry. The Lake of the Ozarks. Midstate. Missourians love it. Not as treacherous as the river,"she mumbled.

One bright rippling shine directly ahead created an arrow of light pointing straight into the sun. The sun seemed to grow larger every second as it began its incredible descent from the western sky. The vision was incredibly calming. Her heart rate slowed so much, that she could hear each individual beat. Lori rested her chin on her hand and lost herself in the sight. She felt enveloped in this singular moment. She knew she'd be seeing many sunsets out here but somehow it seemed that this first one would last forever.

She forgot to talk. She forgot to think. She simply was. And that was enough for now.

Staring at the sudden rapid fall of the brilliant orange sun into the sea, she suddenly realized she was holding her breath. In that one exquisite moment before it dropped, the clouds in the sky flared brilliantly with rose light. Then, just as quickly, the arrow of light was quenched like a candle flame.

A gentle nudge from the captain brought her back down to earth, reminding her of the rest of the world.

"Don't forget to breathe, pretty lady. I was thinking, you might be needing mouth to mouth about now." He smiled broadly at her with one raised eyebrow.

Laughing at him she said, "I think not, sir. But wasn't it lovely?"

"Aye, a sight for sore eyes, I'm thinking." Jerrod looked only at her and enjoyed what he saw. Her golden hair lost its highlight when the sun went down. Her eyes looked sad to him.

Drawn back to reality, Lori asked him. "How long have you lived here in the islands?"

Captain Jerrod's expression grew more somber. "I came here with my children ten years ago. Julie was just a little tyke then, but already getting into trouble back in the old Chicago neighborhood where drug pushers on every street corner sold to kids. Geez, she mimicked selling stuff on the street when she pretended, can you imagine that?" He shook his head.

"I worked on the lake and docks all my life. So when my wife was dying, she made me promise to take Julie and Joseph away from big city sins, good Irish Catholic girl that she was. Joe is two years older than Julie and off to college in Florida now, a good boy.

"My wife, she wanted us out in the islands with lots of sun and fresh air and not too many people. She wanted to be able to look down on us and see clean sky and blue waters. She picked the location. So here we are. Population a couple of hundred thousand on the islands, give or take."

"Sorry to hear about your wife," she murmured. "But I like the way she found to protect you all, even after she was gone. You've never remarried?"

"Hadn't met the right woman 'til now." He pierced her with his penetrating bright blue gaze.

"WHOA. Mister, you move way too fast. And assume way too much." She snapped.

"Pardon me, ma'am." The Captain doffed his baseball cap at her. "But you're the first real lady to pass my way in a long time that appeals to my finer senses. And you are available, aren't you? I mean... You're not wearing a wedding ring, or anything. So, I'm thinking, I know that I like you..."

"Well...just don't move so fast. I have no intention of being pushed into any kind of relationship right now." She broke eye contact with him.

"Sorry, I'm not usually a pushy type, believe me! I'm a very shy guy." He batted his thick-fringed eyelashes at her.

"Yeah, and I'm Little Orphan Annie."

"Well, I've only the best intentions. That I'm promising you."

"Mmm. We'll see. We'll just have to see." Lori withdrew into herself and crossed her arms. She knew that talk was cheap with some men. She had definitely been burned and would prefer to withdraw from the fire, thank you very much.

Three

Night fell quickly in this part of the world. One minute it was daylight, and it seemed the gray blue black merged into a blur of dark. Darkness closed in and before she knew it the sky blazed, suddenly brilliant with stars. The stars glittered in a diffuse and somewhat different pattern. Turning to Jerrod, she asked. "Is there a good library at Charlotte Amalie?"

"Sure, if you ever need books from there, let me know and I'll pick them up. I can get anything you need and bring it to you on the next trip out."

"Thanks, I should be able to get most of my research over the Internet, but anything else I need, I will certainly be sure to call. By the way how do we communicate with St. Thomas from St. Saba?"

"There is a phone with a satellite uplink at the main house on the island, and most calls are made from there. I'll be leaving you my numbers so you can reach me if you need me."

"Well, I have a cell phone that I'll use to network my laptop with the lab's computer back home. I'm depending on it as an integral part of my research. So I can probably call you. *If* I need you, mister."

"Oh yeah, I keep forgetting everyone with their little pocket phones. If only the world would learn to solve its problems, instead of wasting time coming up with more newfangled gadgets, I'm thinking. Me, myself, I'm waiting for one of those buttons on my shirt that I tap and tell it, 'Beam me up Scotty.' Now *that's* a gadget worth waiting for." His wide smile warmed her inside and out.

"I can guarantee that you'll be calling me much sooner than you think. You may perhaps find your life on this island to be desolate without me, I'm thinking."

"Ha. You are full of yourself, *I'm* thinking! I am a *very* independent person, you will find out. I doubt that I will be having much time to be pining for you, Captain Jerrod O'Tarbutton. But thanks for the random thought."

Lori decided that he would be borderline insufferable if not for that roguish grin of his. She bet he had been a pirate in a previous life, and just kidnapped whomever he chose.

"And what kinda research do you do?"

"Hmm? Oh, I have a research grant to find out why there are large blocks of certain kinds of fish showing up dead. Fish mortality anomalies."

" Oh that sounds like fun. Not! As Julie would say. Do you get to eat them?"

"Heavens no!" She snorted, disgusted at the thought.

"Well, how does that work? Are you a vet or a marine biologist?"

"No. I work for a veterinarian at the St. Louis Zoo. That is, I did." She frowned. "I trained in pathology to study disease mechanisms in animals. Why they get sick. Why they die. Stuff like that. Lab work: tissues, cellular, hematology, histology and pathology."

"Sounds like a lotta gees to me!"

She laughed at his expression and clasped her arms around her as the temperature dropped since sundown. The potent smell of the salty air overwhelmed her nose and caused her to sneeze. The wind in her face gentled.

A small island appeared in the darkness before them. It didn't rise very high out of the water. *And obviously why they evacuate in a bad storm,* she thought.

The bow nose spotlight created a luminescence on the pounding surf. The gentle waves out at sea now piled up, rolling across the shallowing water and crashing in a cacophony of sound louder than the sound of anything else. Manmade or otherwise. She watched as a long curving white beach came into view, glowing with a light of its own. In the center of the beach a concrete dock took shape before them, a single post on the end with a light, swinging in the breeze.

Village lights twinkled through the trees. A lone dog barked in the distance, giving notice to the approaching boat. Jerrod sounded his boat horn twice, answering the dog.

A small vehicle raced through a fringe of trees bordering the beach. The miniature jeep type cart screeched to a stop. A thin young man and an enormous black dog jumped out of the vehicle and bounded down the dock.

The Captain maneuvered the boat to coast into the dock, making it look effortless to Lori. The man waved and ran to catch the first rope that Jerrod tossed to him, tied the lines, then hopped on board.

"Benjamin, here, will be your assistant at the station. Benjamin Franklin Adams, this is the Miss Paige, you've been dying to meet. He goes to college in Charlotte Amalie but had to come back to the islet to help take care of his grandmother this winter. She fell and broke her hip, but she's up and about now. He'll be a great help to you, I'm thinking, since he has worked at the research station every summer for four years. Or is it more, Benjamin?"

"Four, Captain. I'm very pleased to meet you, ma'am. You can call me Benjamin or Ben, if you'd like. Forget the Franklin, please. I was born in an electrical storm, and my grandmother

37

had a brainstorm." Benjamin announced, a shy welcoming smile in his handsome black face. He extended his arm and gripped Lori's hand with his very large hand.

"I brought the station's golf cart to load up your luggage and take you to your quarters. I hope you don't mind. It's your vehicle to drive while you're here. There are real jeeps at each big house but the rest of us only have carts."

"Thanks, Benjamin, I appreciate you doing that for me." Lori picked up her things, exhaustion suddenly overwhelming her.

Before she stepped off the boat onto the dock, the alarmingly huge black dog with a brown face and markings sat staring at her. He growled deep in his throat, but not loudly, more of a grumble. He was the largest Rottweiler she had ever seen in her life. She stepped off anyway, offering her hand for him to smell.

She told him, "Hello there, old boy, how are you?" as though the dog was human. She squatted down to his eye level, which was not very far for her to go, and rubbed behind his ears. He stood up immediately on all fours and began wagging his stubby tail.

The Captain and Benjamin both stood dumbfounded, with their mouths wide open, momentarily speechless. Finally, Jerrod said, "Never ever in my born days have I *ever* seen that dog take to anyone! He never lets *anyone* touch him, let alone pet him. Amazing. If I hadn't seen it myself, I would never have believed it. He's the most independent dang dog. Thinks he owns this island, and I guess in a way he does. He always had the run of the island. He meets every boat coming in. He hears us coming. Everyone here feeds him, that's why he's half horse, but he only puts up with people. Like Benjamin here, giving him a ride down to the docks." Shaking his head, Jerrod took off his ball cap and scratched his head, staring at Lori.

"I've always been able to get along with animals." She shrugged her shoulders at them. "Just born with it, I guess.

Delivered my first set of puppies when I was three. My dad said I was a natural born vet, but I couldn't see myself going to college for all those years. Animals seem to like me, maybe because I like them. By the way, what is this brute's name?"

"Uh, he's Jake. Benjamin, close your mouth before you catch a fly in it."

Benjamin grabbed up a couple pieces of luggage then followed Lori and Jake across the dock toward the cart.

Jerrod picked up two more and groaned as he straightened up. "Geez, woman, whatever have you got in this one?"

"That's the one with books, didn't know what my source of reading literature would be, so I brought a supply with me. Sorry, I'll carry it if you can't manage it." Grinning impishly back at him over her shoulder, she knew she'd issued a challenge to his masculinity.

"Humph…no problem, no problem at all," he muttered under his breath.

As they placed the bags in the back of the golf cart, Lori turned around to Jerrod before getting on the front seat.

"Thank you for a lovely ride and all the help."

She extended her hand and when Jerrod grabbed her hand with both of his, Jake began a low grumble.

Startled, Jerrod let her hand go much faster than he intended. "Now Jake, this pretty lady is a friend of mine too, and I wouldn't be hurting her for nothin', okay?"

He reached inside his pants pocket and took out a rumpled dirty business card. "Here, Lori, take this. It has both my numbers, home and office. Call me anytime. I mean it. You may get lonesome out here for a friendly voice."

He started walking back toward the dock and turned around. "And do you think you could go to lunch with me Sunday? I'll give you time to settle in, but I've got some great places to show you, and Sunday is my only day off, okay? I'll be here every other day with mail and deliveries, but most likely won't be stopping by the research station." He talked fast, hoping to keep her from telling him no.

She looked at him thoughtfully. He *was* very appealing. "Well, I guess if you don't get too pushy. Promise?"

"Promise, cross my heart. Bring swimming gear. I'll pick you up at ten sharp. Rain or shine." Heading down the dock, he whistled, shoving both hands in his pockets.

"Captain, I'll be back to take the mail and packages up to the warehouse after I settle Miss Paige in," Benjamin called out, starting the cart. "After I've done that ma'am, I'll bring the cart back to your cabin, then walk home."

The engine was almost silent, making a kind of purring sound and had strange looking panels on the hood and roof.

"Benjamin, you can call me Lori, please. What powers this cart? It's so quiet I can hardly hear the engine at all." She looked over her shoulder to see where Jake settled himself right behind her. He had jumped on and squeezed himself between the luggage and two seats. "Is it electric?"

"No, ma'am. It's solar powered. The batteries recharge daily. Electricity is needed for too many other uses in the houses. They each have generators. I modified most of the carts several years ago as a science project, so we wouldn't waste fuel." He told her proudly, "I have one more to go."

"I can see you're going to be a valuable asset to me at the station. I can't wait to get started, but tonight I need to crash. I'm so tired, I could fall asleep on this cart."

She could have sworn that Benjamin blushed but with his dark skin, it was hard to tell. He was a shy kid, but she meant what she said.

"I'll just get your stuff to your cabin and show you around tomorrow. I'll be back at ten to let you sleep in, if you need to. I've laid in a stock of food in your pantry. You have a small complete kitchen in your cabin, even a microwave. I didn't know what you liked so I brought the basics. Anything else you need, we can pick up from the warehouse tomorrow. Will that be all right?"

"Sure, Benjamin, sounds fine." Yawning widely, Lori realized she wasn't even watching her surroundings. She must be more tired than she thought. Oh well, she had a year to explore the island. She yawned again.

They approached a small cluster of buildings at the northern end of the crescent island. The research station buildings sat on a curving point of land surrounded on three sides by water. Amazed, Lori looked up at the stars and out at the water.

Total silence reigned except for the soft crescendo of the waves against the shoreline. No city noises. No signs or sounds of mankind. Just peace and quiet.

If this place couldn't heal her wounds, then *nothing* would. Maybe this place could erase all her battle scars, given time.

They unloaded her bags for the last time and took them into the cabin. Jake followed them in the door and curled up on the fireplace rug.

Benjamin said, "Never, ever saw that dog go in a house before. He must really like you. I'm sorry, ma'am, I haven't unpacked any of the crates that you sent to the lab yet. I was waiting for you."

"Thanks, Benjamin."

"For the ride?"

"No, I mean yes. Just thanks for everything."

"Yes'm you're welcome. Coming Jake?"

Jake glanced at him, dismissing him, and yawned.

"Guess not. If you need anything, or need help, there's a bell hanging on your front porch. Just ring it like crazy and people will come. It is kind of like an alarm. Each location has a different sounding bell. Or if you don't like being way out here by yourself, I can come and stay in the other cabin."

"But if ol' Jake stays here with you, you'll be safe as you can be. He's the smartest guard dog there ever was. The closest house is one-half mile up the hill beyond the trees. If you head through the trees, you should be able to see the lights. See you in the morning."

"Uh hum, thanks. Goodnight Benjamin." She closed the door and checked out the dog lying on the rug. "Night Jake."

Lori unpacked her overnight bag lining up vitamins on a kitchen shelf. She wasn't very hungry but grabbed an apple, and took her evening vitamins. She walked around the cabin trying to shake off jet lag, then looked in the fridge for breakfast. Satisfied that she wouldn't go hungry, she showered and fell on the bed, asleep almost instantly.

~ * ~

Bright morning sunshine flooded the room. The first thing Lori did, was hurry outside to the beach. The warm Caribbean sun tingled her skin and with arms outstretched, she spun around ever so slowly.

On this northernmost tip of the island surrounded on three sides by crystal clear aquamarine water and an empty pastel blue sky, Lori felt on the brink of something... Something dramatic.

On the brink of discovery... Like she was on the edge of paradise.

She forced herself back indoors to examine the cabin. Obviously she'd found the bed comfortable because she felt remarkably well rested. Picking up her watch, she was shocked to discover she'd slept around the clock, which she hadn't done in ages.

She made up the white rattan bed, took a quick shower and dressed in a pair of khaki shorts with a white blouse and sandals. The creamy yellow bedroom with heavy yellow lined curtains would block out the brilliant light, but she'd been too tired to close them last night.

She almost tripped on Jake lying at her feet, watching her move around the cabin. "Oh Jake, I forgot you. Are you hungry? Need to go out?"

He looked up at her with his big brown eyes, stood and stretched. She opened the front door for him and watched the dog run out toward the surf. Lori left the door open to let the breeze in and leaned against the frame.

Blue sky. Blue water. Ah, blue heaven maybe... And thought, *this place is great.*

Every window had a view and all but the kitchen and bath had six foot high windows. The ceilings except for the kitchen were nine feet high and white ceiling fans hung from them. Even the porch had a fan. White rattans with green and yellow tropical print cushions furnished the interior and exterior. Woven rugs added color to the polished wood floors. The furniture was arranged with views in mind.

Lori's stomach growled, reminding her how long it had been since she'd eaten, drawing herself away from the sunshine and back inside to the small efficiency kitchen. She poured a glass of fruit juice then pulled eggs and bacon from the refrigerator.

She knew most people abhorred the idea of fat in their diets but Lori had learned a diet that worked for her. Dr. Atkins low carbohydrate diet had trimmed her down after childbirth when she'd been a whopping two hundred pounds. at delivery. That same diet kept her weight manageable ever since. If her weight began creeping up, she cut back on carbos and exercised more.

She grabbed a handful of morning vitamins and downed them. As a firm believer in vitamins, she'd lowered her cholesterol one hundred points with rose hip Vitamin C, natural Vitamin E, and garlic tablets. She added a very good multivitamin with minerals and plenty of antioxidants. She'd inherited a history of heart problems from both parents who had died of heart complications at early ages. On constant guard for any danger signs, she kept to the regimen that worked for her. Even after the stress of the last year, she was disgustingly healthy.

Noticing a large dry dog food bag in the cabinet, she poured a portion in a large plastic bowl and went out to call Jake. He came bounding in from the waterline and let her pat him on the back while he wolfed his food.

She brought her own breakfast outside to eat on the porch. "Why would anyone eat inside when they could sit on this wonderful veranda and enjoy the beautiful vista before them," she asked the dog. Jake sat beside her and watched her eat.

She knew she was going to have a heck of a time keeping her mind focused on any work until she got used to this place. The view alone was most distracting. Quietly sitting, mesmerized with the action of the surf, she forgot to eat. If Jake hadn't been there to nudge her hand, she probably could have sat all day long in that very same spot.

Jake needed water. So Lori took his empty bowl inside and rinsed it out to give him fresh water. Before she could take it back outside to him, he used a paw to pop open the screen door and walked right in.

"Well Jake, just make yourself at home." She could have sworn that dog grinned at her. "You old rascal, used to getting your own way aren't you?" He wagged his big rear end and lapped water while she rubbed his ears.

She walked back outside and stepped down onto the sand, putting a hat on her head. Jake followed her out and then ran down the beach, disappearing into the line of waving palm trees. Lori looked at her watch and automatically converted the time to St. Louis time. She reminded herself to think in terms of time, both here and now. Benjamin would be coming for her soon. Her thoughts drifted to her son and the void his loss created but she worked hard to push the pain into a manageable position.

She walked around the point of the island, following a row of small tiny seashells that had washed in at high tide. The water line had receded eight or ten feet from them. The fresh salty air opened her sinuses and made her sneeze, but the briskly blowing breeze was warm and humid. She inhaled and felt it penetrate her every pore.

Lori kicked her sandals off and walked along the hard edge of the water line where the sand had a firm feel to it. The warm, wet sand squished between her toes and made her want to play in the sand like a little girl. She wanted to sit right down and build a sand castle.

Boy, she was not sure if this place was good for her or not. Already she'd fought off a need to be lazy, and now she was regressing to her childhood. *Get a grip, Lori.*

She strolled around the point looking at the three buildings of the research station. Their location completely exposed them to the elements.

A few large trees on the west side at least would provide minimum relief from the western sun, but the white concrete block buildings were built to reflect light. The roofs were white. Surrounded by pure white sand the entire station was dazzling like snow in the morning sun. The central research building was the largest and had some kind of air conditioner and a generator shed next to it.

As anxious as she was to get to work in the station and set up her lab, she knew she needed to get acclimated and learn her way around first. She parked herself on dry sand, searching the horizon.

Birds sang behind her and gulls fished in the lagoon. The water changed color at the edge of the coral reef that protected the lagoon.

Jake barked and ran out of a clearing in the trees wide enough for the cart to drive through. Looking around behind her cabin, she saw her cart parked on the other side, exposing it to sunlight most of the day. Hmm, she hadn't heard Benjamin bring it back last night. *Must have slept really sound.*

Jake came up to her and pushed her over in the sand, wanting to play, nudging her with his massive head. Lori laughed and pushed his head back. "Be good Jake. Benjamin's coming and I don't want to look like a sand crab when I meet people."

Before long Benjamin appeared, loping down the same path that Jake had, wearing a broad grin on his face. Lori waved at him as she got up and dusted the sand from her clothes.

"Ready to go?" He asked her when he reached her. "I'll drive today if you don't mind." They walked to the cart and got in beside Jake, who had already parked his carcass there. Benjamin grinned at Jake and said, "I think that dog even understands French, 'cause I *know* for sure he understands English."

Jake barked at them and they both laughed.

Benjamin drove back up the path and after a bit it forked off into two paths. "The right leads down to the main dock and the village and warehouse. It also goes to the East house which is the closest to you. We'll go that way first. Right now there is no one in the big house and only one guest cottage at East occupied by a writer. The left road leads to the Main house."

The roadway entered a clearing where a large white ranch house sprawled low to the ground. It had an unusual blue roof, exactly the same shade of the water in the lagoon. The roof corners tilted upward to give it a distinctly oriental flair. There were few windows on this side of the house. Large red double doors were flanked by two six-foot tall Chinese funerary concrete dogs.

Benjamin stopped the cart and led her around a sidewalk to the rear of the house. A wonderful Japanese garden ran the length of the house and slightly lower than the patio it bordered. The garden was in miniature with bonsai plants, so that the view of the water was not impeded. It had tiny carved statuaries, bridges and ponds. The entire back of the house had patio doors leading from each room to the patio. *Yes, definitely oriental*, she thought. "Now I know why they call it the East house. Very nice." She told Benjamin.

"There are two guest cottages." He pointed out the two small cottages set off a distance from each edge of the big house on an angle that were noticeable through the tree tops by their matching blue roofs.

"A writer lives in the one closest to the station, but he keeps to himself most of the time. He burns the lights a lot at night, so I guess that's when he's writing."

Lori walked in closer to peer into one of the patio doors and saw mostly shrouded furnishings. "Kind of spooky looking with everything covered in sheets."

"Everything gets cleaned and oiled once a month, whether we have guests or not. Just to make sure that everything is maintained, and the wood doesn't dry out. Just like the gardens and patios are maintained daily. That's why a full time group of people live here year round, to take care of the whole island."

"Whew, they must have a quite hefty maintenance allotment for that. I can't imagine what that costs." Lori was impressed. Someone must have big bucks.

Jake followed them around back, then disappeared quickly down the beach. Benjamin led her back to the cart. He explained how the warehouse on the island worked.

"When you need anything for your kitchen, you just go to the warehouse and pick up what you need. It's like a grocery store. Lots of fresh fruit and vegetables, fresh fish, frozen meat, some canned goods, dried goods and foods like beans. What you use that we don't grow, gets replaced on the next shipment."

"Then how do I pay? Do you check out like the grocery store?"

"No. Mary Lou runs the warehouse, and people here on the island use it as part of their pay for working here. We grow our own fresh stuff, and we catch our own fish here. If there is something she doesn't have, then she'll order it for you, on the island account. If it's not something far out, she can usually get it. Just ask her. She's been taking care of the warehouse for fifty years. She's my grandmother. You'll like her."

"I'm sure I will, Benjamin. But I don't get paid by the owners here. You know I've got a government research grant to pay for all my expenses and your salary, while I'm here."

"Don't know about that, ma'am. All I know is, anyone who stays at the station uses the warehouse, just like the rest of us. Always have done it that way." He shrugged his thin shoulders at her.

"Well, I have lots of chemicals and equipment either here or on the way, and I am paying for all of them, one way or another, on my account."

"Yes, ma'am. Our next stop is the Main house, and all three are empty there right now."

"I'm confused about the warehouse economics, but I guess you're not the person I need to talk to about that." Lori wiped the frown from her brow, so far finding the island both unique and charming.

Four

"Miss Emily is the main keeper for the island, in charge of everything for all the owners. She bosses the whole bunch of us, including the cousins in the West house. I'll take you to meet her today, too. She's always at the Main house during the daytime, uses it as her office."

They drove on southwest toward a large palm tree lined, circular driveway. The circle was intersected at the top and bottom with a road. At the top of the circle sat a magnificent two story white brick mansion. At the center top of the circle a widely spaced double avenue of Australian Schefflera trees bisected the circle, heading straight down the long hill toward the beach and creating an utterly dramatic view.

The white house capped with a white roof stood on the highest point of the island, commanding a natural dominance of its surroundings. An intricate formal English garden grew all the way around the house. Two gardeners were busy trimming and shaping the landscaping and hedges, which were of all sizes and shapes.

"I can't imagine leaving a house like this empty. It is so perfect."

He smiled getting out of the cart to knock, with the shining brass lion's head knocker, on the front door. A tall thin woman opened the front door, dressed in black bombazine with lace collar and cameo broach. She looked as though she had just stepped out of a Victorian novel. Right down to ugly black brogues.

"Miss Paige, this is Miss Emily Moore." Emily waved Ben back. He nodded and turned away with his hands in his pockets and stepped off the porch.

"Welcome, Miss Paige. Please come in."

Lori felt out of place in her shorts. She fought a need to curtsy, and choked back a laugh. Instead she said, "Thank you." And looked around in the dark coolness of the interior.

The foot thick walls had ceilings at least twelve feet high. A hand carved, exquisitely graceful staircase rose from the center of the hall and split in two. Lovely dark woodwork shone everywhere, on floors, walls, and the ceiling. White rugs were scattered on the bare floors. Peeking into the formal rooms, she noticed the lovely antique furniture upholstered in various white fabrics. The windows were also draped in white.

Lori followed the housekeeper into a huge oval shaped solarium kitchen. Copper pots and pans glowed, reflecting light from the three curving walls made entirely of windows and glass ceilings. The built-in fixtures had shining copper hoods and fronts.

A fireplace large enough for Lori to stand in and still not touch the sides or top, dominated the room, except for the view, of course. The interior walls and fireplace were white brick. The wood floor and cabinets gleamed with polish and smelled of lemon.

She had never seen such a kitchen. A fifty-foot long space filled with organized work areas, islands and ovens centered on an enormous table. The table had twelve chairs around it with room for at least twenty. There were several sitting areas too, each with its own white rug. In a corner a desk was completely surrounded by built-in bookcases full of cookbooks and five drawer file cabinets.

"This is the most wonderful room I have ever seen in my whole life!" Lori exclaimed. She walked over and looked through the glass at the white paved courtyard. Beyond the low brick wall surrounding the courtyard, the land disappeared at a cliff overlooking the sea, creating an illusion of floating above a moving ocean.

Out on the brick patio Jake was busy scarfing a bowl of dog food. "Why, there's where he ran off to," Lori said.

"That dog is a glutton, but he was late for his breakfast today. By the way, I am Emily Moore, and if I can help you with anything please let me know." The stiffly formal woman smirked with a distinctly proprietary air about her. "I enjoy seeing people react to this room."

"It must be bliss to work here. Why cooking could become my passion, if I had this atmosphere. It's wonderful. I love it." When Lori was impressed, she tended to babble. "Jake spent the night in my cabin, that's why he was late for breakfast, but I *did* feed him."

"Jake spent the night *in your cabin?* He does not make up with strangers, and that dog never, never goes inside *anywhere, ever.* He has been trained not to."

"Well, I don't want to get him in trouble. He's perfectly welcome to stay with me, whenever he pleases. He's great company. But he *did* spend the night in front of my fireplace. I like his company and he likes me, too."

"Well, that is quite astounding. I guess there is a first time for everything. If he ever becomes a problem, you must let me know."

Miss Emily opened a door out of the kitchen and led Lori out onto the patio. Jake charged up to Lori from a now empty bowl, skidded to a halt at her feet, then sat in front of her until she scratched his ears. He made a throaty sound and gave her a silly lopsided grin before he raced on around the house and out of sight.

"That dog is his own. Never did see him go after a pet or let someone touch him. You must be a special powerful person." She looked at Lori with new eyes, sizing her up. "He guards this island as though it was his own, and everyone feels safer with him here."

"I did wonder about how I go about paying for food here?" Lori shrugged as she asked.

"You don't. Not as long as you are a guest here. And when you work at the station, you are a guest here. House rules." She said firmly when she saw Lori about to protest. "Please consider them a tax deductible benefit of the owners. They certainly do."

"Well, I do think it's excessively generous of them, but I accept nonetheless. I guess I don't have many alternatives though, do I?"

Emily graciously led her back to the front door where Benjamin waited outside patiently. Jake sat in the cart waiting to resume the tour. Lori thanked Miss Moore for sharing the special kitchen with her, and told her if she needed anything, she would be sure to make her requests known.

"Benjamin, where did you go? How could you stay away from that wonderful room?"

"I knew Miss Emily prefers to show it off herself. Besides I wanted to talk to my Dad. He was working out in the front."

"You should have introduced me. I need to meet everyone here."

"Don't worry, you will. You just won't meet them all the first day. Too confusing. It's hard to miss anyone on an island this size. Now we're off to West house."

"Why doesn't the owner live in the Main house, Ben?"

"Miss Laurent prefers the smaller more intimate setting of the West house. There are no stairs there also. You will like her. Everyone on the island adores her."

They started around the other side of the circle drive and down the road toward the village but then turned left bypassing the village for now. After a couple miles a big white rambling hacienda style house with a red tile roof came into view. The entry and windows were covered with arches. The landscape plants were cacti and succulents and very western. Hence the name, Lori mused. The house was U shaped and opened to the lagoon side of the island. The two guesthouses had matching roofs and both were on the south side of the house and faced the Caribbean.

Jake again jumped from the cart and headed around the house. Benjamin led Lori to the front door and rang the doorbell. A neat looking woman with a severe bun in a short black maid uniform with a ruffled white apron opened the door wide to let them in.

Benjamin introduced her as Miss Marion, and they followed her inside to meet the island matriarch. Lori absorbed her surroundings as they were led through a spacious vaulted living room furnished in a casual western style, with hardwood floors and more white area rugs.

A window wall opened onto a partially covered patio with numerous hanging flower baskets. A long lap pool was the centerpiece of the informal brick patio. Across the beach the lagoon glittered in the late morning light.

The maid led them under the shaded portico into a corner of lush container plants where lovely blooming flowers surrounded a seating area of comfortable lounge furniture. The soft sound of falling water tinkled from a wall fountain.

An elderly white-haired woman in a white peasant blouse and full white skirt sat in the cool comfort of the shade, sipping a tall frosted glass of tea.

"Welcome, my dear. You must be the new resident at the research station. Pardon me for not getting up. I am Genevieve Laurent and you're to come visit an old lady anytime you please. Call me Miss Genny. Would you like some tea, my dear? Bring fresh iced tea Marion, for all of us. Benjamin how is your grandmother doing?" She quickly rambled with a soft French accent.

"Fine, ma'am. She's getting around very well now. You can't keep her down long. She's too stubborn."

"And you, young lady, tell me all about yourself. Your last name is Paige. Do you have French heritage? Is that your married name? You are here to do research on some fish problems, I understand? Everything here is at your disposal. If you would like to swim laps in the pool, please feel free to do so.

"At the boathouse a boat is at your disposal for exploring or collecting samples or for whatever you wish. Benjamin can show you which one to use. If you are not able to handle the boat, I am sure Benjamin or one of the other men can pilot for you. My two grandsons are often here, but today they are away at Christiansted on St. Croix, taking care of family business. Do you play bridge, my dear?"

Marion brought the tea and sat down with them. She poured the tea offering sugar, lemon or sweetener.

Lori took hers plain, and sipped, "This island is such a paradise." She hurried to speak before Miss Genevieve started rambling again. She'd been blocked every time she attempted to insert an answer. Lori couldn't help but enjoy the old lady anyway, even the way the maid Marion was included in the visit.

"No, Paige is not my married name. My great, great something grandparents were French settlers in the Midwest in the 1800's. I can probably handle the boat, we'll see. I plan on doing my swimming in the lagoon by the research station. Thanks for the offer of the pool though. And yes, thank you, I do play bridge, but I've got to get to work." She was torn between being sociable and her eagerness to begin the research.

"Nonsense, young lady. Everyone has to *make* time to play, right Marion?" She was smiling conspiratorially at her nodding maid/companion. "It is good for the soul. And you must take every weekend off. I insist. And now I think that we need some lunch. Doesn't all this lovely fresh air make you hungry?"

Jake strolled around the house as Marion headed for the kitchen. He walked the length of the pool and as he sat at Lori's feet he burped, nudging her empty hand until she responded by scratching his ears. She and Benjamin made eye contact and giggled at the dog.

"Hello, old boy, been eating again?"

"Oh my. You made a conquest there, I see. He's happy as long as he is fed. But he can also be quite aggressive if he chooses not to like a person, or he thinks that they do not belong on his turf. *And the whole island is his turf.* He is one of God's wonderful creatures, aren't you Jake?"

Jake woofed in response to Miss Genevieve's question making everyone laugh, while Benjamin almost choked on his tea.

"My granddaughter lives here too, and will be joining us for lunch. I want you to meet our guests. One is an artist and paints lovely watercolor seascapes that he sells in Charlotte Amalie and abroad."

"Why, I know, we will have a lovely dinner party Saturday evening. Marion will enjoy preparing it, I will enjoy planning it and everyone will be sure to be here for it. Oh, I do so enjoy a good party, don't you my dear?" Her eyes were sparkling in anticipation.

Lori didn't have the heart to refuse, so she nodded. Benjamin rolled his big black eyes at her and almost made her giggle again.

Marion came out to set the table with place mats, sterling and bone china dishes, and asked Benjamin to help her carry out the food.

"Miss Genevieve, how did your family come to St. Saba?"

"We have owned this island for more than a hundred years. We have been doing business in the islands for two hundred and fifty years. First our ancestors were in sugar cane on St. Croix and later they added rum production. Now we also own an oil refinery there. My boys are in charge of production here, and my cousin Jacques' children run the international end of the business in Paris. We all share this island, a condo on St. Croix, a lovely apartment in Paris, and an estate in Montpellier on the southern coast of France. Now tell me all about yourself, my dear."

"Well…there's not much to tell. I'm a research biologist with a specialty in pathology, recently divorced. I'm on a year long sabbatical from the St. Louis Zoo and I'm looking forward to this research." She intentionally left out the more painful parts, like the husband that walked out on her after the funeral.

"Any children, dear?"

"No, my son died last year in an accident." She felt obliged to answer but kept it short, mumbling and looking down to hide her suddenly brimming eyes.

"I am so sorry, my dear. There is nothing harder to bear than the death of a child. I know. My son and his American wife died in a plane crash very young. If it had not been for my wonderful grandchildren, I do not know what I would have done… But they gave me a reason to go on."

"Yes, my grandmother always said that. She lost several children. Very hard." Lori spoke disjointedly, trying to keep her composure and wondering at the tears. She'd been dry of them for so long she thought she'd lost the ability. But since the flight down here, she'd been bombarded with maudlin tears.

Benjamin and Marion came outside loaded down with food. They carried a great platter of chicken salad on fresh buttery croissants and individual bowls of wilted fresh lettuce with a hot bacon dressing. There was a large bowl of fresh fruit for dessert. The food looked delicious, and Lori was suddenly ravenous.

A tall, lovely brunette (aged somewhere in her thirties if you could get to the person underneath the makeup) appeared out of one of the side patio doors. She was dressed in a colorful dramatic caftan with very high-heeled sandals, and her hair was twisted in an elaborate chignon.

Strolling languorously in their direction, the sex kitten seemed intensely aware of attention focused on her. She looked like she would have preferred an audience entirely of men, but practiced daily for anyone.

Miss Genny smiled as her granddaughter joined the group and introduced her to Lori. "Sheree, this is our newest addition to the island, Miss Lori Paige. She will be with us for the next year doing research."

"Hello, Miss Paige." Sheree held out a limp hand and looked her over from head to toe and automatically dismissed Lori as a person of very little consequence. Then she sat down gracefully and began an extended process of examining her perfectly painted long red fingernails.

"Hello, Miss Laurent," Lori responded in mimic, feeling the chill coming off this woman, and looked her over in the same up and down manner and decided *that is one spoiled brat whose main value in life is vanity.* Lori immediately turned her attention back to Miss Genny and proceeded to ignore the tall cool 'princess'.

"Is not my granddaughter beautiful?" Miss Genevieve asked, obviously charmed. "She looks exactly like her mother." The old lady beamed, while Sheree preened.

"Beautiful." Lori repeated and caught Benjamin and Marion exchanging smiles.

Miss Sheree frowned, not knowing whether to accept the accolade as a compliment or something else. She picked at her lunch while her doting grandmother urged her to eat, as if she were a child.

Lori enjoyed the wonderful meal and complimented Marion on the chicken salad with cashews and water chestnuts. Everything was so tasty. She could've eaten twice as much, but knew she would have looked like a hog, especially compared to the minute bird-like portions Sheree ate. After shaking hands and thanking Miss Genevieve and Marion for the lunch, she promised reluctantly to attend the Saturday night party. Then escaped with Benjamin and Jake.

Benjamin pointed out the boathouse as they walked past the south wing of the southwest styled house. She saw it nestled on the southern end of the lagoon in a protected area. A sandy beach curved out and extended past it creating a natural breakwater. The waves weren't nearly as strong down on this end of the island, which would make it easier to bring water craft in or out. Jake escaped, running up the road out of sight.

"Whenever you're ready to try out the boat we'll go."

"Thanks, Benjamin, but I need to set up before we start collecting samples. We have tons of work to do." *Humph. From the looks of her fingernails, Miss Sheree looked like she'd never done a decent day of work in her life.* And *probably would never need to,* Lori thought wryly.

"Next stop is the village and the warehouse." Benjamin said, starting the cart, this time without Jake as a passenger.

As they drove north, cultivated fields and vegetable gardens blew gently in the breeze. The surrounding trees provided a windbreak. A multitude of fruit trees bloomed and floral scents wafted delightfully inland, mixed with the salty scent of the sea.

They approached a building much larger than the others. The entire white concrete block village was spaced in two parallel rows, with a small tree lined street between them. Near the tree line above the beach, numerous brightly painted fishing boats lay keel up with nets stretched out between them.

Entering the windowless warehouse, they passed Jake lazing in the shade next to an empty bowl. Benjamin and Lori looked at each other cracking up with laughter.

"Now I know why Jake is such a King Kong Rottweiler, Benjamin."

Inside the cool building baskets, displaying fresh fruits and vegetables, bordered the aisle. A walk-in refrigerated room for eggs and perishables, was across from a long row of freezers lining a wall. It resembled a grocery store more than a warehouse, with dry goods and canned goods stacked neatly on shelves.

Near the back of the warehouse, in an office area enclosed with counters and file cabinets, sat an elderly gray haired woman with skin the color of polished mahogany. Perched on stools behind the counters were two more women. They looked up expectantly as Benjamin led her to them.

"This is my grandmother, Mary Lou Adams. And Joliette and Denise Greniere. This is Miss Lori Paige."

"Pleased to meet you, Miss Paige. Don't mind me if I don't get up, but I stay off my hip as much as I can. Let Benjamin show you around and if you have questions come back and talk with us. If there's anything special you need, let us know and we'll order it in."

Lori greeted everyone and started wandering around with Benjamin filling a shopping cart. There was a great variety to choose from and she had no problem getting everything that she needed. When she passed the fifty-pound size dog food bag stack, she and Benjamin busted up, laughing all over again. She suddenly realized that she already laughed more in two days than she had in the last two years. This place *had* to be good for her.

She went to the office area to check out and told Mary Lou how impressed she was with Benjamin and just knew that he would be a great addition to her research. Then she thanked them for their help.

The touring finally over, they returned to the research station with the cart loaded down. Jake raced the cart across the island and beat them to the station.

After putting away her groceries, Lori and Benjamin headed to the main research building. She was anxious to see the lab's potential.

The building consisted of a primary room thirty-feet by thirty-feet with windows halfway down on three walls giving a superb view of the sea. The lab was the northernmost building on the island. Two window walls had lab benches against them and two rows of benches running parallel with them.

She noted plenty of storage with shelves under the cabinets and shelving on the entire back wall that wasn't taken up by doors. Doors led to a bathroom, darkroom, computer room and a storage room with a refrigerator. Lori explored the area, poking her head into every area, checking out the lab while making equipment layout arrangements in her head.

Boxes of all sizes were stacked neatly on top of one cabinet row. Lori proceeded to sort the little ones containing chemicals and dyes and carried them to the back shelves. Two sinks were built into the counter tops at each end of the window walls and the centers of the central bench rows. She asked Benjamin to begin unpacking the larger boxes of equipment.

Lori then ran over to her cabin and picked up her laptop computer to draw a plan for the lab.

"Benjamin, we need an area for necropsy of the specimens. And an area to process the tissue samples. One to embed the processed tissues in paraffin and a microtome work area to slice the samples. Next we must allocate space for the automatic stainer for standard staining of the slides, and plenty of space for any special stains."

"A microscope can be set up in the computer room in the back where lighting could be dimmed, reducing eye strain. This main room is way too bright, but there's absolutely no way I can have any claustrophobia problems in this open lab."

Printing up the plan Lori taped it on the wall at the front doors. She spotted old Jake with his nose to the glass so she let him in. At first he wanted to play with the peanut pellet packing material but soon grew bored with the piles of white stuff and lay down at Lori's feet for a short digestive nap. She could hear his tummy rumbling.

They finished unpacking the larger pieces of equipment, set them up then inventoried the shipments received against the order list. The only piece of equipment that hadn't come in was a small cryotome unit for frozen specimen samples. The chemical and dyes stockpile needed to be unpacked, alphabetized and safely stored.

"Benjamin, I don't know what experience you have with chemicals, but some we will be handling are dangerous. We need to be cautious. Use gloves and always wear safety glasses. Many of the chemicals are toxic and since medical aid is limited on the island, we need to be very careful."

Lori decided to stow the more dangerous chemicals in the storage room, after she found the keys for the door. Benjamin told her that most of the buildings here on the island were never locked, which seemed strange to her.

"There must also be a lock on the lab door, some of these chemicals only cause diarrhea or nausea but some are much more potent, okay? We each can have a key. Aren't there children running around loose on the island?"

"No ma'am, they are kept at one house while their parents work. When they're school age, they go to school during the week at Charlotte Amalie. They live with relatives there, usually grandparents, since island marries off island."

"Well some of these chemicals are controlled substances, so they must be kept under lock and key anyway."

Lori began to wind down and lose energy and decided to end work for the day. She sent Benjamin home until tomorrow morning at nine and returned to her cottage.

She didn't make it.

Before she reached the door blue water beckoned to her, so she and Jake galloped down to the water line. She kicked sandals off her feet and tossed them high onto dry sand.

Jake ran in circles, excited to have someone to play with in the bright afternoon sun. She picked up a stick and threw it for him to retrieve it and return it to her. The sun shone brightly in the late afternoon sun. She breathed in deeply and felt a surge of energy all the way down to her toes as though she were plugged into a solar socket.

Lori sat on the sand and started digging her toes in, counting the waves coming in until she lost track. Jake came back and nudged her on the shoulder. She grabbed him by the neck and tried to pull him down beside her, but it was like trying to move a mountain. Lori laughed and gave up, got to her feet and headed back to her cottage, hungry for food again.

She went inside to her kitchen and began preparing a yummy Chinese chicken salad even though she'd had chicken for lunch.

She started the chicken cooking in the microwave and took a quick shower. Lori took her dinner outside on the porch to watch the sunset.

She filled Jake's bowl with fresh water and ignored his food bowl until he put his head down on the decking and looked at her with very pitiful eyes. She felt bad eating in front of him and went inside to partially fill his food bowl so he could eat, too. Maybe it wasn't particularly good for him to eat that much but it certainly didn't appear to hurt him. At any rate he appeared to get sufficient exercise.

The island at her back, she sat on the edge of this Caribbean shelf. Looking north toward the open vista of the Atlantic Ocean, she turned her rocker to face the glorious sunset and sighed.

Five

The peace and solitude were a wonderful balm for her weary soul, and she enjoyed every minute of it. Jake wolfed down his food and disappeared up the trail, heading for his other dinners, she thought humorously. Passing time watching the late evening sky, with its constantly changing kaleidoscope of cloud colors, she reluctantly forced herself inside to read.

A couple of hours later, Lori decided to take a moonlit walk on the beach. She had forgotten to ask Benjamin if she could walk the entire perimeter of the island. Oh well, she would just walk until she got tired and then walk back. Turning all lights off except a small light in the kitchen, she closed the screen door and left the house.

It was immensely quiet out here. On the edge of the world-- out of real time and space. The only sounds were night bird noises, and the sound of the incessant waves rolling to shore.

She walked along the water line barefoot, feeling the waves gently washing over her feet. Time stopped as the clouds danced across the face of the moon. The old man in the moon shrunk as the moon marched higher in the night sky.

It was so lovely she could almost feel the ache inside her shrinking to more manageable proportions. The trees over her shoulder rustled softly in the breeze. She felt at peace with herself and sighed contentedly.

Stars glistened in the sky. Her father told her when she was a little girl that a star was born when someone we loved died. Those left behind only had to look up to see the shining stars and know their loved ones were safe from harm. She'd always cherished that story and knew that her son was up there now, forever safe from pain. He was sheltered, surrounded with her parents and grandparents as well, a comforting thought.

The beach became more littered with boulders and the bank to her right rose higher, but she kept walking, mostly looking at the stars, drifting effortlessly in their hazy nebula. Clouds sailed suddenly across the moon, making the beach dark and mysterious.

She heard strange banging noises and light beams reflected, once off the clouds, then again along the shore. She thought she could hear the murmur of voices, but couldn't be sure. This side of the island had only the big main house with its guesthouses perched high on the cliff and they were supposed to be vacant. She must have been mistaken. It was probably the wind.

A large boulder appeared in front of her but she was distracted by the moving light and sounds. Her foot wedged between two rocks, so she ducked her head and reached down to extract it.

Suddenly, she was grabbed from behind.

"What the…?" She started to yell, but a hand clamped over her mouth while she was pulled roughly to the ground. Struggling to free herself and trying to scream, she was told by a man's whisper.

"Hush. You won't be hurt but stay very still. Your life may depend on it."

Her heart beat erratically in her throat and she wanted to scream but instead she quit struggling. She thought she could hear Jake barking in the distance. If he came looking for her, she would be all right. And this couldn't possibly be a rape, not on an island of this size. She tried to assure herself.

She twisted her body, attempting to look at whoever held her so tightly. But he was dressed in dark clothes and blended in with the shadows cast around them.

He whispered vehemently. "Do not talk. Voices carry a long distance over water."

Lori could only nod her head mutely but tried staring up into the face of her assailant. While he held his hand firmly over her mouth, she reached her own hand down and checked the ankle she twisted, but it seemed fine. She could hear faint sounds further down the shore and shivered as the sand beneath her lost its heat for the day. She felt the combined pitter-patter of their heartbeats between them.

The man stared straight into the woman's face to see whom he held in his arms. The moon shot a bolt of light onto her features. Her eyes widened when the breeze blew her dark golden hair all around her head. He groaned aloud.

"Dear God, is it you? Lori, how can it be you? It *was* you at the airport. Why did you run?" He hissed.

He withdrew his hand from her mouth and gently traced her face with his fingertips. He touched her lips and put both thumbs over her eyes, shutting them from his sight, rubbing them ever so gently. His hands, which by now were shaking, stroked down her arms and took her hands in his. He lifted them to his mouth, kissing their backs softly before turning them over to kiss their palms.

"I should have known it was you when I touched your skin," he murmured.

Lori had gone stiff when he began touching her face, but could hear her pulse pounding in her ears, louder. Her breath caught in her throat as he kissed her palms. She tried desperately to see his eyes in the darkness. She was afraid to move and yet she felt like putty in his hands.

His hands began a journey of their own back up the underside of her arms before they roamed under her shirt. She thought her heart would burst.

"Hugh?" It was the only word that she spoke before his lips claimed hers.

She kissed him back with an urgency that matched his own. She placed her hands along his face and felt the linear planes of his cheekbones. Running her hands down across his back, she felt the tightening muscles. She picked his shirt out of his waist and placed her hands on his bare back and pushed them below his belt.

He gasped and palmed her breasts in his hands, making her squirm with desire. He gently leaned her back on the sand and she pulled him to her needing to feel his hard body over hers. He began unzipping her shorts, greedily holding onto her mouth and breast. She didn't feel the chill of the evening air, only the hot searing heat of his body covering hers.

He pulled his own pants off quickly, giving her no time to help. But she spread her legs wide to eagerly claim his passion. He entered her so slowly that she finally grabbed his hips and pulled him to her wanting these sensations and this moment to never end. He didn't move, holding her tightly to him.

She wanted to move. She *needed* to move. She tried to thrash around but he held her firm to the ground. She started to moan deep down in her throat, but he covered her mouth again and shushed her, filling her fuller and fuller. She began the crescendo of mounting waves of pleasure and with each breath that she drew, the waves kept rolling higher and higher, demanding release. Finally after what seemed like a lifetime, he stroked her harder and harder building to that moment of shared glory, forever binding them, one to the other.

They lay there, exhausted on the damp sandy beach, but neither withdrew from the other. Their hearts slowed to a more normal pace and they shifted slightly so that he bore his own weight.

She held on tightly to him, speaking no words, thinking no thoughts.

Just simply being... Sharing his warmth... Lori was content, eventually drifting off to sleep.

Six

Lori woke up to morning light with a gentle lick from Jake. She was startled to find that she was in her own bed and wondered how in the heck she had gotten there. *Was it only a dream? Did she dream that exquisite mindless passion? Could it be possible that Hugh is on this island?*

She thought she vaguely remembered him saying. "Tell no one that you were on the shore last night. Say nothing about me. I'll be back in a few days and we'll talk. I love you. I've always loved you, Lori, my love." But was that a dream or just wishful thinking? She turned over and tried to go back to sleep, and wondered why Jake had awakened her. And where had he come from?

She put her hand on her breast and felt more than a tingle in her lower gut and knew it had been no dream. If it was, then she should patent it. Because surely it was the best she'd ever had.

Hmm. Hugh Richmond back in her life again. Delicious. What did destiny have in store for this time around...?

She drifted back to a dreamless sleep, her body, soul and spirit in dire need of renewal. Comfortable at last, she waited for the future to unfold, knowing whatever it held for her she was ready. Umm... She was *more* than ready.

When Lori woke again a couple of hours later, she knew, by the quantity of sand in her bed and the sand washing off in the shower, that last night was definitely a reality. Not to mention the fact that her body was superbly sensitive in the aftermath of that intense lovemaking session.

She had many unanswered questions, but if fate had drawn them together after all this time, then at this point in their lives everything *had* to work out, right? This convergence of their bodies and souls must have a meaning above and beyond chance or fate, *right?*

Emerging from her shower, she found Jake waiting patiently by the kitchen cabinet where his food was kept, and fed him.

"Jake, you old rascal, where did you come from? The front door is closed and locked. And you can't lock doors now can you? I don't quite remember coming back to the cottage and going to bed. I must have slept deeper than I have in ages, but I guess you can't answer my questions, can you fellow?"

She sat on the front porch heartily stuffing herself with a breakfast of eggs and bacon, and enjoying every minute of that crystal clear morning sunshine. She'd learned the hard way that each breath and each day is precious.

Jake ate then bolted out the front door on his way to his breakfast rounds.

With only an hour before beginning work with Benjamin, she started back down the beach in the same direction as last night. She walked the eastern side of the island toward the cliffs, watching the gulls swooping into the sea for breakfast.

Lori wasn't exactly sure where her walk had so precipitously ended, somewhere before the cliffs rose too high perhaps and in the area where the boulders littered the beach. But in daylight it looked empty and perfectly normal. There were plenty of large boulders where they could have lain, but there were no signs that they had.

Returning back to the lab, she wrestled with all the questions running through her head. She decided to quiz Benjamin about everyone on the island she hadn't met, hoping to find at least a few answers while she waited for Hugh to return and fill her in. Her mind was in a turmoil and it was difficult to focus on her work. Right now, work was a priority that demanded her full and undivided attention.

She and Benjamin dove into the unpacking work with a vengeance. The shelves on the back wall were beginning to fill with various chemicals, until the mountain of unpacked boxes began to shrink. The larger drums of alcohols and formalin were placed in the secured closet. Lori paused to look around for sprinklers in case of fire, but there were none. Several fire extinguishers were mounted around the room. She checked to make sure there were chemical extinguishers too, just to be safe.

Satisfied there were as many safety features in place as possible, she pumped Benjamin for information. He didn't contribute much more than she already knew though. He did tell her that both the other guests dined often with the Laurents at the West house since Miss Genevieve loved to entertain.

Finishing the chemicals and inventory, they started on the general lab stock and glassware after a quick lunch at Lori's cottage. She'd served and a big bowl of French onion soup on which floated melted mozzarella cheese.

Eating their lunch outside, she asked. "How far away is the closest island?"

"There are lots of islets around but the closest one that is inhabited, besides St. Thomas is a military base at Culebra, Puerto Rico. St. Croix is fifty miles south and the island of Puerto Rico is less than thirty. Lots of them have been inhabited

71

over the centuries by pirates and even shipwreck survivors. These islands have provided history with great hiding places for the pirates of the Caribbean to lie in wait for the Spanish armada and other treasure fleets."

"Every sailor in these parts for hundreds of years has hunted for treasure at some time or other. It's almost a national pastime. When you go to Charlotte Amalie, someone is always trying to sell treasure maps to tourists. Beware. As a kid I personally dug up half this island looking for treasure."

Lori laughed at his mischievous expression while her mind went off on another tangent. She had way too much on her mind now without adding treasure hunts. She and Benjamin continued their work until the lab began to look complete.

"Benjamin, this place is lookin' good here. We've accomplished a lot already. Tomorrow, let's celebrate by taking the boat out to look for some of these dead fish. How does that sound? What is the weather forecast for tomorrow?"

"Sun, sun and more sun. The weather is usually good this time of year. We should be fine. Do you have any idea where we are going?"

"Well, I have coordinates and some documentation to research tonight to see if we can narrow down the search parameters. We may have to spend some time searching, but we can handle that, don't you think?"

"Yes, ma'am. Sounds good to me."

"I'll pick you up at nine at your village with your gear and we'll drive down to the boat house together."

Lori swam on the lagoon side of her beaches. She paced herself in the calmer waves that the lagoon protected. She leisurely swam back and forth. Jake barked off in the distance when a boat horn sounded. Before she got out of the water, Jake appeared. He ran up and down at the beach's edge, and kept pace with her splashing in the water's edge. She almost choked at the silly grin on his face.

Wishing she didn't have to get out, hunger reared its ugly head and forced her to lead Jake back to the cabin to feed them both. She baked lemon pepper grouper and steamed fresh broccoli with lemon dill sauce and carried it out to dine al fresco and read the reports before retiring early.

The drive to the village in the morning breeze after a wonderfully restful night made Lori sigh in bliss. A fast moving low front that produced rainfall during the night turned everything sparkling fresh in this tropical paradise. She listened to the birds singing merrily in the trees and wanted to sing along with them.

She giggled to herself and wondered at her carefree attitude. Oh well, she'd been taking one day at time for a long time now. It was just that it had been so long since she felt this happy. And even in some undefined way, complete. *Yep, I'll take it today, no questions asked, thank you.*

Benjamin climbed aboard. Jake came running, chasing after them until Lori stopped the cart, giving him a chance to jump on, too.

"I guess we're having company today, Benjamin."

Jake barked a woof at them.

They drove to the other end of the island, past West house and parked in a clearing close to the boat house. Unloading their gear and the lunches that Lori had packed for them, they walked a path over the dunes to the boats sheltered there.

Jake beat them to the door and sat panting, waiting for Benjamin to open it for them. The big dog barked once in anticipation and ran around in a tight circle.

The door opened to a building with over a forty-foot ceiling with four slips. Two large cruisers perched on lifts partially out of the water. There was one empty slip, and one launch tied and riding the gentle waves. The dock was made of concrete and sat quite high out of the water, to account for high tides, she guessed.

The building was jam-packed full of all sorts of equipment hanging on the walls. A couple of old boats were suspended way up high in the rafters. The entire back wall of the boat house was open for the boats to get in and out of the slips.

They went directly to the open launch and tossed in their gear. Jake leaped into the boat and woofed at them. Laughing, they untied the launch. Benjamin boarded and turned on the blowers to clear out gas fumes before starting the engines.

The boat was a thirty-six-foot Carver Express, just like the River Patrol patrolled on the Mississippi, with a pair of powerful inboard engines. Lori was familiar with this type of craft but knew she'd need plenty of experience with open water and sea waves.

Benjamin started the engines and backed the boat out of the slip. Lori jumped on board and checked the various boat gear, echo sounder, radio, compass, radar, spare spark plugs, life preservers, oars, inflatable raft, flares, all the necessities for safety.

She had brought along her emergency med-pack in case one of them got friendly with a nasty critter but since today they were only snorkeling, she hoped for the best.

"Where do we go today, Miss Lori?"

"I'm not going to tell you again to just call me Lori, okay Benjamin? Hmm? Today we'll sightsee, so I can get a feel for conditions and populations. Let's start with the closest reef and see what we can, okay?"

"We don't have to go far for that. Our island has its own reef on the west, south and southeast sides. It swings around in a partial circle. The safest passage out of the lagoon is northwest. Then you don't have to worry about any damage to the reef or the boat. We'll go to my favorite spot, and drop anchor a safe distance from the coral."

"Great." She adjusted her hat while the boat picked up speed and sat in the chair next to 's. Jake sat drooling beside her. She put her hand on his head and ruffled his ears. Watching carefully where Benjamin took the boat, she could see the passage clearly through the water below her.

Looking back at the island, she could see the line of trees pointing to the majestic setting of the Main house. The village roofs, the blue roofs of the East compound and the West big house's clay tile roof contrasted with green. The majority of the structures were hidden by foliage. Turning around to look north, she could make out the white buildings of the research center sitting much more exposed on that curving spit of sandy beaches.

Taking the boat out in a large sweep south, Benjamin headed almost due south of the island for about a mile then anchored the boat, after carefully checking the location. They both took off their T-shirts and put on their masks, fins and snorkels. Lori checked the cloudless sky before dropping overboard, and waited for Benjamin to lead the way.

The water depth was twenty feet and sparkling clear. An abundance of blue angel fish schooled in the water above the many colorful species of coral. Tan bushy soft coral, green boulder coral, yellow crenellated fire coral, and the more common greenish-brown brain coral covered the floor. She spotted a large staghorn coral and several huge grooved brain coral growths.

She saw purple iridescent light blue tube sponge, thick bushy, knobby candelabra sponge, and gray pointy warts on pillow stinking sponge, hanging over tan lettuce leaf coral. She dove down under the water to get a closer look at tan sea rods swaying around a nearby group of snappers.

She watched a spotted eagle ray glide over a sandy plain on the edge of the reef, where underneath a colony of garden eels withdrew back into their burrows as the ray reached them. It astonished her how so many sea creatures were completely aware of the predators around them.

Snorkeling could become a passion for her if she let it, and Lori swam until her legs felt like lead weights. It was time to head back toward the boat to check the weather and recover energy. Raising her head, she looked around for the boat and found Benjamin a hundred feet or so away. She waved and pointed at the boat and took her time returning to it.

Swimming slowly back, she enjoyed watching the schools of silversides darting en masse in a swirling bob and weave pattern as though they were all connected to each other by strings. Even when a Nassau grouper loomed just a couple of meters away they drew together and headed straight for him instead of scattering in fear, and successfully evaded the predator.

Reaching the boat, Lori pulled herself up the ladder into the boat and collapsed on the deck. Jake licked her salty hands until she pushed him away. After taking dropping her mask and fins, she retrieved her hat and plopped it on her head. She grabbed her water bottle out of the cooler and drank thirstily.

After Jake watched her drink with such attentive interest, she took an empty bowl and drained liquid from the melted ice for him. Lori hadn't planned for him on this trip, but she might as well get used to his presence, since it looked like he was going to be a definite participant here.

She prepared lunch when her breathing returned to normal. Benjamin had reached the boat by then with a huge grin on his face and his mask pushed back on his forehead.

"Wasn't that great? There are dozens of reefs around these islands, and each one is different from the rest. Did you see that black and white sea lily sitting on top of the pillar coral? She was in the shade of that big elephant rock." He wiped his face with a towel, his breathing barely laboring.

"Yes, I did. I thought they hid in daylight and were active at night. Did you see when the big ray floated by the sandy spot? All the little garden eels popped back in their holes until he was past."

"Benjamin, I could actually hear a parrotfish rasping his teeth, chewing on chunks from a coral head. I should have taken my camera or a video cam. The colors of the reef are so dazzling. It's so easy to be distracted by the jewel tone appearances of the tropical fish that you almost forget to look out for the less dramatic species."

Benjamin nodded and grinned in response and helped to set out the picnic paraphernalia. Lori had packed lemonade, water, Colby and baby Swiss cheese chunks, slices of ham rolled around dill pickle spears, hot mustard, fresh broccoli with spinach dip, saltine crackers and fresh strawberries. She served a plate to Jake and was flabbergasted when the broccoli disappeared, too, although his eating habits should not surprise her by now.

They both ate almost as fast as Jake and decided to rest before moving onto a different location. Lori applied more sunscreen to her face and slipped back on her T-shirt over her tank suit before she lay on the deck for a brief nap. Jake sat on the captain's chair on guard duty, and after about an hour, he woke Lori with another lick on her face.

"Jake, you rascal, are you my alarm clock now?" She sat up stiffly and looked around the sky checking for signs of bad weather. The radio would have announced any storm warnings but it never hurt to be on the alert. As a light sleeper she would have heard any weather warnings, anyway.

Benjamin was already standing at his seat starting the engines. He bowed and gestured for her to take the wheel, then doffed his cap at her with a big grin. She stood at the helm and listened to his instructions, carefully watching the waves and the sky for any sign of changing weather.

He gave her a heading for some cays, partway between their island and Botany Bay just on the northwest point of St. Thomas. There were old shallow wrecks with abundant sea life for them to explore.

The three traveled in silence to their destination with only the breeze for company. The small bare cays had little greenery, made mostly of rock, jutting up from the sea. They were a strange granite type of rock not at all common to this area.

Just below the surface of the water were several sunken ships that had the unfortunate destiny of colliding with those huge rocks. The rocks were as out of place as the shipwrecks on the bottom. Volcanos just did not form rocks like that very often.

"Where in the world did these rocks come from? They look like our Elephant Rocks in Missouri, only darker."

"Nobody knows. There are more like them over on the northeast side of St. Thomas and over by the British Virgin Isles, too. Probably geologists can give you that answer." Benjamin shrugged.

They put on their gear and snorkeled over these manmade artificial reefs teeming with marine life. Lori wished she had her scuba gear to go down and explore the wrecks closer but knew she needed to build up her stamina and swimming skills a bit more before attempting that. Swimming laps in the lagoon would prepare her.

After a couple hours of extensive snorkeling among those uniquely foreign boulders, they were both too exhilarated and exhausted to do anything but swim slowly back to the boat and set course for home.

Seven

A strange uneasiness presented its unwelcome face as Saturday dawned. A premonition of something about to happen gripped Lori and gripped her hard. She tried her best to shake it off, telling herself it must have been a residual carry over from a bad dream. Lori looked nervously around the bedroom, expecting something unusual to catch her eye, to jump out at her.

Stretching, she walked into the living area to greet Jake but he wasn't on the rug in front of the fireplace, or anywhere else in her cabin for that matter. She scratched her head. She knew Jake had been locked inside the night before, just like every other night since she arrived.

"What the heck's going on here?" She remembered the night she ran into Hugh on the beach. That night *she* ended up in bed and *Jake* had been in here with her the next morning, *with the door locked just like today.*

"I'm not a sleep walker and I am definitely not going crazy, but something *is* going on here that I just don't understand."

After fixing a breakfast omelets, Lori carried it to her favorite dining spot outside on the porch. She picked at the food and pushed her fork around on the plate, not sure what exactly was causing her anxiety, other than the missing dog.

Sitting and worrying didn't do her any good. So she went inside and lathered herself up with sunscreen and slid into her one piece black maillot swimsuit that fit like a glove, then put on a large floppy brim sun hat and dark sunglasses.

It was time to work on her tan and explore the beach that bordered the island and quit fidgeting around the house. She didn't take a towel, shoes or watch since the day was entirely free until this evening's dinner party.

Lori started on the backside of the island again just for curiosity's sake, she told herself. As she walked the fine sandy beach on the lookout for seashells, tiny hummingbirds flitted between the colorful red flowers and yellow stalks of palicourea, and the roselike blossoms of cocoplum. Mockingbirds bounced their noisy voices off the huge broad leafed elephant ear philodendrons and lacy ferns that grew in the shade of mahogany, Manilkara and white cedar trees.

The lush vegetation created a cool inviting breeze that beckoned to her from across the dunes from the hot sandy beach. Today was going to be the hottest one since she had arrived. Before the day was over, she knew she'd be seeking the cooling temperatures of the water.

She bent down to retrieve a sand dollar that had washed in whole and put it on her head under her hat since she didn't have a pocket. She looked around her to make sure that no one caught her using her head for once and laughed at the thought. Then with wonder she realized it had been at least two days since she had felt the stabbing mourning pain *or* the misery of Nick's betrayal. Thank God for small miracles…

When the shoreline became rocky, she plopped herself down on a soft sandy spot to soak up some rays before the sun headed west over the cliff behind her. Before long she was so hot and sweaty she couldn't stand it anymore. Dropping her hat with its treasures to the sand, she ran into the water and began swimming laps, just far enough out that the surf didn't pound her to shreds. She kept watch on the island, looking for something to catch her eye... Or answers to the questions in her mind.

Finally, she pulled herself from the water and collapsed on the beach where she left her hat. Lori rested, while the sun dried her skin to tiny salt crystals. Jake came loping down the beach and parked himself next to her, drooling and panting.

Lori knew that she wouldn't get answers from him but she asked them anyway. Getting no response other than a sloppy lick, she brushed the sand off herself and ambled toward the rocky shore. Her mind skipped to unanswered questions in an intricate dance collage.

She shivered, entering the shaded portion of the shoreline directly below the cliff. The area was more rock than sand. Some boulders were enormous, and nestled back along the cliff wall. The cliff wasn't perpendicular, but angled steeply backward toward the top some two hundred and fifty feet.

Shading her eyes with her hands, she couldn't see the big house from this position either. The cliff was steep and it looked extremely difficult to get up or down that wall, and at high tides she realized most of this part of the shore would be impassable. She picked her way gingerly amid the jumble of sharp rocks, while Jake leapt and ran ahead of her.

Looking behind her, the sandy part of the beach was more elevated along the shoreline here and then rose again toward the sandy beach south of her. Evidently, the eastern islet edge bore the brunt of bad hurricane weather coming out of the Atlantic because the beach had worn away in the middle.

When she reached the smooth white sandy beach again, she sat down and viewed that rocky stretch of shoreline from a different perspective. All she could see was the angled cliff, a dip to a jumble of rocks and then more sandy beaches on the other side.

Jake sat down at her side and tilted his head at her.

She put her face up to his and said. "Just curious old boy, and you know what curiosity did to the cat?" He licked the salt from her face and made her grimace.

"Thanks," she said dryly. "I needed that like I needed a hole in my head."

Lori dawdled, enjoying the warmth of the sun now that the high part of the island no longer blocked the sun rays. The West house cottages snuggled into the tree line set back above the beach. A warm breeze blew on her face. She cut across, walking over the rolling grass dunes that protected the boat house and the curving island's southern end.

The packed sand beach on this side of the island offered a more level surface. So Lori picked up the pace and began power walking toward home. The 'hungries' were beckoning her home since swimming always gave her appetite a firm wake up call.

Lori waved through the trees at people she could see on the Laurent terrace. But since she would be seeing them this evening, she kept walking up the beach. She didn't see a sign of any other island residents though. The clean empty beach displayed only a single set of human footprints, followed by Jake's.

Jake stayed at her side all the way home and went right to the kitchen for a late breakfast before he disappeared once again. After eating a large tuna fish salad on a bed of lettuce with sliced fresh tomatoes, Lori flopped on a chaise lounge on the porch to read more research articles until she drifted asleep.

Stretching when she woke up, she went inside to treat herself to a long cool Sunflower bubble bath. Her skin felt a little tight from the sun today and she hoped that she would not glow too pink this evening and look like a tourist. Heaven forbid that she'd look like a Midwesterner on vacation in paradise.

Standing in front of the full length mirror, she slopped lots of lotion all over and eyed her body critically. A nice, crisply defined tan line began at the top of her legs. Luckily there was no sunburn afterglow, just a nice golden tan. Her shoulders and arms were tan enough for short sleeves or even sleeveless.

Her face had a touch of pink on her cheeks, but that just meant that she wouldn't need any blush. She normally didn't wear much makeup. But in this company, she certainly didn't want to look like a country bumpkin. She usually just wore black mascara and a teal eye shadow, but for this occasion she added lipstick and eyeliner.

Grumpily examining her hair, she decided it would just have to do. She'd had it cut short before she left St. Louis and wore it up and away from her face then fringed flat around her neck. She pulled a fringe of bangs down toward her eyes and lifted the top higher. Her hair had already picked up highlights since her arrival, shining with an extra golden glow. She tucked it behind her ears, judging the effect in the mirror.

Having brought little in the way of party clothes, she dug through her closet to find a jade silk tunic with a matching mid length skirt. She added a gold belt and sandals, jade ring, earrings, jade and gold bead necklace, and a jade bangle. Presentable, she hoped. Glancing in the mirror one more time, she pulled off the jade earrings and bracelet. Instead she put tiny gold balls on her ears.

"Better." She told herself. The bangle would be in the way for playing cards anyway. She knew that never in her lifetime could her jewelry compete with Laurent jewelry. Lori just bet that Miss Sheree would be decked out to beat the band.

She felt rather silly driving a golf cart to a party, but on the bright side, at least parking shouldn't be a problem. She bounced up the path passing the East house where a light was shining in the guesthouse closest to her. Pulling into the courtyard at the West house and parking among several other golf carts, she didn't feel so out of place. Yet.

Jake waited for her as she got out of the cart and led her to the front door. Lori ruffed his ears and told him, "Thanks for the escort, old boy, but I don't think you were invited to the party." He sat at the front door and watched her ring the bell.

Marion greeted her at the door and led her through the house to the patio. By the time she stepped through the patio door, Jake had raced around the house, crossed the patio by weaving through the crowd and skidded to a halt outside the door. He met Lori and led her over to the dinner guests.

A silently stunned audience of guests witnessed the event. Only Benjamin in his starched white shirt and black slacks and Miss Genevieve did not look startled.

Lori was embarrassed by all the attention and walked with Jake at her side to greet her hostess. Most of the guests had gathered at the end of the patio to view the stunning sunset. Thankfully, the sunset was such a dramatically perfect picture that it drew eyes back to the rosy glow and away from Lori and her unusual 'date'.

"Thank you for inviting me. I am sorry if Jake crashed the party."

"Do not worry about it dear. He usually attends, but at a distance." Miss Genny was amused. Her eyes sparkled. "I am so happy to see you again. Please sit here by me for a moment and keep me company. You look lovely, my dear, you positively radiate health. I think you must be settling in here quite well? Have you met everyone yet? No matter, we will let Benjamin take you around and make introductions in a bit. First, would you like a drink?" She nodded to Benjamin.

"Yes, thank you. A glass of wine would be fine, Benjamin." Lori finally got a chance to speak. "I'm doing wonderfully here and Benjamin is such a superb assistant. I don't know what I would do without him."

"Thanks, Benjamin." Lori took the wine glass from him when he approached and would hold it for the evening, pretending to drink. Lori surveyed the group gathered here, recognizing the few faces that she'd met previously, but there were more people than she anticipated. The whole island must be attending. Jake sat at her side, panting after his race around the house. She certainly could feel people looking her over.

A dozen white clothed tables with chairs were arrayed around the U-shaped patio, on forty-five degree angles with the pool. The tables and pool were set with floating candles and flowers. Lights twinkled in the trees and bushes. Soft classical jazz music played in the background. Jake left her side to get a drink of water but returned immediately to his former position.

"He accompanied us on the boat yesterday." Benjamin told Miss Genny, nodding his head at Jake.

"Well, he does like a good boat ride now and then." Miss Genny said smiling. "I am glad that you have him out since you are by yourself. If you ever find yourself lonesome, you just come to us and stay for a while. We would love to have you, my dear. Now Benjamin, see that she meets my grandsons and everyone else. And see that she has a good time. Now run along my dear and mingle with my guests. We shall talk later." Miss Gen patted her on the arm, then shooed her away.

Lori rose gracefully from her chair and wandered with Benjamin from group to group, having a hard time keeping names matched to the right face. She met Benjamin's father and his grandmother again, and Miss Emily, but many of the other faces blended to a blur.

The grandsons would be difficult to forget, since they fawned over her with truly French manners, they acted like two little boys fighting over her with exaggerated old world courtesy that was quite silly.

Jon insisted she must have a plate of hors d'oeuvres. Then Gerard freshened her wine, which she had not even tasted yet. She thought that Gerard was a bit foppish and too fussy for her taste, but both were extremely handsome men. They were tall and dark, with dark hair, sunken dark brown eyes, roman looking features and exceptionally friendly smiles.

The Laurent pair eagerly pushed Benjamin out of their way. He just shrugged and smiled, like he was used to it and drifted into another group, but kept an eye on her.

Jake was not so easily pushed out of the circle. He followed at her side as she wandered from group to group. If either of the Laurent men attempted to touch her, and they were definitely 'touchers', Jake growled deep in his throat. Not loud, but loud enough for them to be startled and withdraw from her.

Lori smiled as she patted Jake's head. "It's all right, old boy. Be nice to the gentlemen."

The Laurent men, exchanging uneasy glances with each other, proceeded to keep one eye on the massive head of the protective dog.

They remained by her side though, giving her lots of undivided attention, even when that attention was neither necessary nor invited. Lori was too gracious to send them away, though she would like to. Her face felt frozen in a permanent fake smile.

"Have you met our resident painter yet? Let me introduce you to him. Oh, Steffan, come meet our scientist. Miss Paige, this is Steffan Georges. Steffan, this is Lori Paige. Pretty, isn't she?"

Jon's blatant compliment made her blush.

The rotund little man about Lori's height took her hand and stepped back to study her. Jake didn't blink an eye at the man as big around as he was tall. Steffan tilted his head as if eyeing her for canvas.

"Hallo. Have you ever had your portrait done, my dear? You would make an excellent subject. There is much intelligence in those beautiful eyes, yes?"

Before Lori could withdraw her hand Sheree cut in.

"But Steffan, you promised me that I would be your model for your next portrait series." Sheree smiled brilliantly at her audience, expecting and receiving adulation as usual.

Lori wondered how some women did it, knowing that she would never in a million years have the knack. Suddenly Lori stiffened, her eyes wide, not at the skimpy black mini dress Sheree was wearing, but at the sight of Hugh on her arm. Hugh? Wherever had he come from? And why in blazes was Sheree holding on to him as if she owned him?

"Ah, our beautiful sister at last, on the arm of our resident writer. Now we are truly complete. The party may begin. Darling, have you paid your respects to Grandmere? You look exceptionally radiant tonight. Miss Paige, have you met our writer?" Gerard asked, kissing his sister's cheek, while she kissed air at him.

"Miss Paige, this is JeanPaul Richaud." Jon introduced Hugh.

Hugh stepped forward, bowed over her hand, continental style, and said loud enough for only Lori to hear. "Play along for now." He pressed his lips warmly to her hand.

She couldn't help but play along. Lori was too shocked to utter a word. You could have bowled her over with a feather. She caught Jake looking from Hugh to her, tilting his head.

Sheree laid claim to his arm again when he moved back from Lori, and cooed in her shrill voice. "Isn't he just too wonderful for words?" Smiling provocatively up at him, Sheree batted false eyelashes, heavy with mascara.

"Absolutely." Lori agreed in a dry voice, never taking her eyes from his golden stare. She hungrily examined him, wondering at the game he was playing. She was trying her best to ignore the brilliant blaze of diamonds around Sheree's throat. The brilliance made her feel like a doe caught in headlights. No wonder she had a distinct aversion to that woman.

Hugh was so handsome, so elegant, his chiseled features heartbreakingly familiar again in the blink of an eye. He'd reentered her life as abruptly as he'd left it, damn him.

Gerard took Lori by the arm steering her toward a table, causing Jake to growl again. He dropped her arm quickly and put up both hands. "I give. I won't touch her again. You old grouch."

"Isn't that absolutely adorable? Jake has found himself a date, after all these years. I think that's the cutest thing I have seen in a long time, don't you JeanPaul?" Sheree remarked cattily.

"*Oui*, he is quite grand." Hugh responded with a heavy French accent, more so than the Laurent men or the painter.

Lori quickly responded. "Yes. He is very loyal. And where are you from Mister Richaud?" Raising her eyebrows at Hugh, she thought. *Meow, to you too. Witch! Pull in your claws and I'll retract mine.*

"Our JeanPaul's from Montreal, a French Quebec Nationalist, a true loyalist." Sheree answered before Hugh had an opportunity.

Jake followed them to a table and sat at her side keeping a watchful eye on Lori and the party around them. At least seated, she could set her wineglass down and not have to pretend to sip. She wasn't crazy about dry white wine and drank minimally anyway. Most of the time she pretended to drink to be sociable.

Four men and two women were a bit much, she thought. *Particularly* that *woman. She certainly rubs me the wrong way. No doubt about that.*

Somehow, Sheree managed to proclaim ownership of Hugh. Body language said it all, and Sheree was doing everything but leaning into his lap.

Lori seethed. To outward appearances, she was cool as a cucumber, but internally, she was biting the inside of her jaw.

"And what are you here studying, *mademoiselle?*" Hugh asked her, displaying a natural curiosity for the lovely woman seated across the table from him.

"I am here doing research on mortality anomalies of various aquatic species in the U. S. Virgin Islands." Lori answered, blowing him off, intentionally vague and cool, and refused to look him in the eye.

"Umm, I see." Even though he didn't understand at all.

Sheree seized control of the conversation from then on, and saw to it that as the groups broke into bridge tables, *she* did not have to share Hugh with other women.

More men played cards than women. The rest of the women tended to sit in conversation groups and mingle with each other.

Lori's bridge partner was Jon. She apologized to him ahead of time for being rusty, but in the end she played sharp cards. They won against every team they played.

Once, when it was her turn to sit out, she went to the bar to get a glass of Perrier and a slice of lime. Hugh managed to get her alone for a moment. He whispered that he would come to her cabin later tonight and explain everything.

She looked into those tiger eyes over the edge of her glass, not saying a word and sipped her Perrier.

At the buffet break, Lori filled her plate from the magnificent spread of food Marion had prepared for the party. There was smoked salmon, steak tartar, cold lobster bisque, pheasant under glass, and countless fresh salads. A beautiful display of fresh fruit and a creamy chocolate mousse made her wish for a doggy bag, which made her want to giggle.

Poor old Jake, laying there with such a mournful expression on his face caused Lori to put extra meat on her plate so she could at least slip him some under the table.

If she ate around here for long, she would be adding inches in the wrong places. If only she was as tall as Sheree, she would never have to worry about weight again. Obviously that was out of the question, unless someone would put her on the rack and stretched her four or five more inches. She sighed. It was jealousy making her remorseful about her height, anyway.

After she and Jake finished the plate full of the sinfully delicious food, she groaned and forced herself to return to the card games. She managed to enjoy the evening in spite of Hugh.

During the last hour of the party, as after dinner drinks were served, all of the candles and lights were doused. The guests sat in the moonlight, watching the stars and sharing quiet conversation.

It was a lovely finale to the evening. Lori thanked and hugged Miss Genny for a beautiful evening that she had thoroughly enjoyed. Surprisingly enough, she meant it. She and Jake said their formal goodbyes quietly. Instead of departing through the house, she slipped around the house with her faithful escort at her side heading for home and hoping to make a less obvious exit than entrance.

Strange how she already thought of St. Saba as home. She had to put most of her life in storage in order to come here. Her wonderful *'ex'* had sold their home out from under her. Almost overnight, life as she knew it, was instantly erased. A few words in front of a judge and Whammy! The rug got pulled out from under her feet.

Good old D-I-V-O-R-C-E, just like in the song. Nick expected her to just be pleasant about it all. Sell their home and walk away like two adults. No raised voices. No fights. No stress. Hah. Slime ball.

No wonder she felt so insecure when it came to men, her average had not been that great now had it? And tonight Hugh hadn't added to her confidence either.

At least she had this chance to come here and accomplish something positive before deciding what to do with the rest of her life. Lori sighed as she got ready for bed.

It felt like she had wasted her life until now. She hadn't recovered from losing Nathan, then Nick.

Feeling a little blue and a whole lot rejected, she put on an oversize T-shirt and slid into bed, wiping her wet, blue eyes.

Eight

Waking up confused and disoriented, she didn't know where she was, and felt her heart racing. Bad dream, maybe? No, she could hear Jake, prowling in the living room, which was unusual for him. Lori threw back the covers and headed to the front of the cabin and was startled to see a shadow outside her door. Jake stood a silent sentry, not barking, just staring at the door. She put a hand to her throat and went to his side.

"Lori, let me in. It's me, Hugh," the voice hissed.

She glanced back at the microwave timer light. It glowed 3:04. She went to the door and told Jake, "It's all right, boy." Jake took one look at her and silently slipped out the door as Hugh came in.

Wide awake now, Lori remarked scathingly. "Are you sure it's not JeanPaul? Or maybe it is someone else, someone fresh and new." She mimicked Sheree's brittle voice.

She turned and marched to the kitchen creating a distance between them. Her heart pounded loudly at his presence. She was sure he could hear it too. She ground her jaws together in a bout of tension.

"Jealous, darling? She's nothing to me, absolutely nothing." Smiling, he followed her to the kitchen and put his arms around her waist. He drew her to him and pulled her hips against him so he could feel her body molded against his arousal.

"You are so beautiful, even in the middle of the night. I love you and I missed you. Did you miss me?"

He nuzzled her neck and kissed the pulse points on her throat. He picked up her hands and began kissing every finger, every knuckle on his way down to her open palms.

She withdrew her hands and placed her palms against his chest with every intention of pushing him away but she could feel his heart racing just like hers.

"Well, why in the heck would I be jealous? Well, let me see. You enter my life with a beachside abduction. Disappear just as quickly. *And* then you reappear on the arm of the most beautiful woman on the island who has definitely staked *her* interest in *you*. *With* a false name, I might add. No problem that I can see, can you?" She ticked them off with her fingers, counting the reasons.

Hugh smiled a dazzling sensuous smile, and his exceptional tiger eyes began their predatory glow. He told her. "God, I love you." He inserted himself between her legs, straining his rigid body toward her.

Her eyes widened. Her mouth opened with a short gasp. It was suddenly hard to breathe. She only got out "I... I" before he voraciously claimed her mouth. His kiss lasted an eternity. Her arms reached up around his neck to hold him closer and fervently kissed him back with equal passion.

His hands began a constant roaming, setting her on fire. Her breath grew ragged in her throat and her need for him grew so strong that her only thought was for now.

In one swift move he pulled her cotton panties down and lifted her to the counter top while he dropped his own pants to the floor. He entered her with a force that denied nothing yet claimed everything.

His eyes blazed a golden fire as he pulled her off the counter, holding her weight against him. She moaned deep in her throat, almost a growl, throwing her head back and clasping her hands together behind his head.

He lifted her up and down, repeatedly, and demanded. "Look at me. I want to see your eyes. I want to see your face. I want to see…e…e…you… " He demanded of her with increasing force and magnitude.

His strength and power overwhelmed her, bringing her to that brink, that high mounting spiral of ecstasy that only he could climb with her. Gasping together, their mutual releases were so hard and long that Hugh staggered from the intensity and had to lean back against the refrigerator to support their weight.

After catching his breath he carried her to the bedroom and gently laid her on the bed, careful not to break their fragile connection.

Lori quivered like a mass of jellyfish, so weak she could not have made it to the bedroom by herself. They lay entwined, their hearts pressed together strumming an erratic beat.

Slowly they reentered the land of the living and came back to earth, each holding on to the other for dear life, and savoring that sweet moment.

They fell into a dreamless sleep and woke up to the joy in each other's eyes. This time they made love very, very slowly as though they had all the time in the world, taking the time to enjoy every second and shutting out all else…

~ * ~

Finally, in the predawn light and still wrapped in each other's arms, Hugh began to talk softly. He stroked her bare back.

"I couldn't believe my luck at finding you here. I knew a scientist from the States was coming and that the name was Paige, but I didn't know the spelling, gender or more specifics."

"Of course, you crossed my mind at the briefing. But the last time I checked, and *I have checked,* you were still firmly attached to Nicholas Sherman. The odds against finding you here were phenomenal. I still can't believe it!"

"I'm here on assignment. I've been working with Interpol, trying to backtrack a drug smuggling operation in France that finances European terrorists. So far the trail ends here in the U.S. Virgins. All information I've uncovered points me in the direction of *this* island, but I've run up against a blank wall."

"The other night on the beach was the closest I've come to finding out anything, and needless to say, I was distracted from my job." He smiled and squeezed her gently to his chest.

"Because of my language skills, I assumed the name of a little known French Canadian political science writer and took my position, right after Christmas. I needed to be close to the residents and get to know everyone's habits. I must admit,on the surface,this island appears to be the paradise it is.

"But I also know in my gut that I'm in the right place. Which brings us back to you. There is *very real danger* here, if I'm right and I know that I am." He told her firmly. "I don't want you to be here when I expose whoever is in charge of this."

Lori sat up sharply. "You've got to be kidding. I just got here and you are ordering *me* out? I am *just as committed to doing my job as you are and I am definitely not going anywhere!*"

"Look, don't get your dander up, I'm just trying to protect the woman I love, okay? I need you to trust me on this, now that I have found you and you're finally free. You *are* free, aren't you?" He grabbed her with both hands. "I mean you're not married or engaged are you?" Hugh sounded worried.

"Yes, I am free. Do you think I would be where I am now if I were not?" She asked him, straightening her back, ramrod stiff.

"No, Lori my love, believe me. I, of all people, know how loyal you can be. And how hardheaded and stubborn as a Missouri mule. Please don't force me to use the 'powers that be' to get your grant yanked. Because I can, you know, whether you like it or not."

She jumped up from the bed, put her hands on her bare hips and told him in the most threatening voice that she had ever used in her entire life.

"Don't you dare. Don't you ever threaten me. I am not your typical terrorist scum bag. But I will fight you tooth and nail, and with anything else I can think of, to keep you from taking me from this place. I have just as much right to be here as you do, maybe more. At least *I* am here honestly. I will expose you for who you are rather than accept you pushing me out."

"Lori, calm down. I am not threatening you. Be reasonable. I am trying to protect you. I must know that you are safe. I have to be able to do my job without the fear of anyone getting to you. We are talking about a serious criminal element here. Not college kids gone bad. You understand me?" Putting both his hands on her arms, he wanted to shake some sense into that pretty head of hers.

"Nothing is more important to me than you, *nothing*. Do you understand? I am not ever giving you up again, not ever, for any reason on earth. I have waited most of my entire life for you. You belong to me. *Now and forever*, you got that?"

His tawny eyes glared into hers. "And you had better get used to it, because it is a fact of life."

She stood back and stared into his eyes for the longest time in dead silence, listening to the sound of his heavy breathing. Finally, acknowledging what she saw there, Lori sighed and meekly traced his face with her hand.

"All right, I'll do whatever is necessary, if you just let me do my job until you tell me the danger is close. Then I'll go to Charlotte Amalie until it is resolved, okay? And you have to promise me that *you* will stay safe for me, too." Lori spoke softly and could not resist a smile at the reflected image of his taut derriere in the mirror behind him.

"Jake will help take care of me, you know. He is quite protective, too. I must come across like helpless baggage to the men in my life right now. I think we have just had our first fight and I lost." She shook her head. "Never thought that I could give in *that* easily."

She disengaged from Hugh's arms, and headed for the bathroom to brush her teeth.

"Well, I want you to trust no one, not even Jake. Just me. Got it? You have a phone, don't you? I'll need the number. And no matter where you are, keep it with you. On the beach. In the boat. Wherever."

"When this goes down, I'll call you and warn you to get out. Just do it. No questions asked. No matter what you are doing, where you are, just make an excuse to take the launch and go straight to Charlotte Amalie. Don't take anyone with you. Go alone. Remember to trust no one. Not Benjamin. Not anyone." Following her to the bathroom, he continued his monologue.

"Go to Hotel 1829 on Government Hill. Ask for Charlie at the reception desk. He'll be on the lookout for you and will keep you out of harm's way when the operation goes down. Then when it is over and the island is safe, I will come back for you. Promise? Is that a deal?"

She watched him, leaning against the frame of the bathroom door, with his arms crossed and so casually naked, that she had to giggle. "Uh huh. Wish I had a camera to record the more memorable moments of my 'Caribbean sabbatical.' What a photo album that would make." She waltzed back to bed, jumped in and pulled the covers up to her chin. Her eyes crinkled with laughter.

He tried to stroll insouciantly back to bed, but Lori burst into peals of laughter before he made it, delighting in his presence.

"You know you have the sexiest butt for a man your age?" Laughing again.

Leaping back into bed beside her, he growled.

"Laugh at me, will you woman?" He snuggled his hard taut body up against her soft one. "I've got all day to make you pay for that. I can teach you to respect your elder."

"No sir, I wouldn't think of it. Nosirreebob, wouldn't dare think of it." Giggling, yet again, her eyes shone with mischief.

"*Bob*, who is Bob? How dare you speak of another man in my bed?" He raised his brow, growled ferociously at her, then pounced on her, like a cat on a mouse, making her squeal with laughter.

He placed his mouth firmly over hers to squelch her joyful laughter, and finally succeeded in quieting her down, his roving hands in perpetual motion. He stroked her soft smooth skin, drawing her to him.

She lost the ability to laugh, let alone to breathe.

This time when they woke up they were sated, but also ravenous. Hugh almost cleaned out her cabinets and the fridge of all edible food. He was a bottomless pit, a black hole in the cosmos. Lori watched in awe at the volumes of food that he consumed.

The only food he didn't eat was Jake's dog food, which reminded her of Jake's disappearance when Hugh arrived. She placed food and water out on the porch, but the dog was long gone, already making his morning circuit.

"Thought I'd better put Jake's food out before you eat it, too," she teased Hugh. "That dog is certainly an enigma. If he were a man, he would stand alone, kind of a doggy style 'the Duke'."

"Hugh, that night at the beach, did you let Jake in here when you brought me back? I don't remember much, must have been exhausted." She almost blushed. "But he woke me up the next day and I was confused about him."

"Yes, he escorted us most of the way, then came inside when I brought you to bed. He sat at the door of your bedroom. Watching to make sure that you weren't hurt, I think. After he saw what good care I took of you, he quit growling at me and curled up on the rug in front of the fireplace when I left. You have made *two* remarkable conquests on this island as far as I can see. But that's because you, yourself are remarkable."

"You flatter me, kind sir. My power over Jake is something I was born with. Albeit, my power over you is of quite another sort."

"Oh no. You were born with that, too. No doubt about it."

"Well, I don't know about you, kind sir, but *I* need to bathe and me thinks you do, too."

She crooked her finger at him, led him to the shower and commenced to wash him thoroughly. She washed her hair, slipped on a clean T-shirt and tossed one to Hugh.

Raising his eyebrows, then frowning, he asked, "Aw, do we have to?" petulantly like a little boy.

Lori tilted her head at him, hands on hips and asked. "Haven't you had enough? You insatiable man."

"Never." He announced adamantly. "I could eat you alive and not have enough of you." He meant it and hugged her tightly.

"Well, we have all day and we need to talk. We do not seem to be communicating verbally. If you know what I mean, hmm?"

"Yeah, all day… " His golden tiger eyes glazed over at that thought. "Besides, I don't want to come or go from here in the daytime. I don't want anyone to know about our relationship. To protect you. At night I think I can probably slip in or out and even no one next door would be the wiser. But in daytime this

position is totally exposed out here. So remember that, please."
He gave her an extra squeeze.

"Okay, I'll be good, if you will be good." She stretched her
arms high, tilting to one side and then the other in a stretching
motion.

He watched the play of her breasts against the cloth of her
shirt and the motion of the shirt sliding up and down her legs and
licked his lips.

"Oh, don't do that, if you *just* want to talk. Go sit in a chair.
No, better yet, 'Come sit on my lap said the spider to the fly.'"
He grinned irrepressibly. "So we can talk."

"Only if you can behave for a while."

She watched him nodding foolishly, then went to him and
curled up in his arms. She'd finally come home. And it felt so
damn good. Safe... That was it.

Snuggling in Hugh's arms as he rocked in front of the
fireplace, looking out at the surf rolling gently to shore, Lori felt
safer than she had since she was a little girl. She remembered
her Dad giving her that same feeling of security.

Isn't it funny how happy such a simple thing as arms around
a person could feel? Or maybe it just has to be the right arms.

From a distance she heard Jake's bark, which reminded her
of something. "Hugh, I think the only times I've ever heard Jake
bark out loud, is whenever a boat is coming to the island.
Remember on the beach that night, Jake barked? He must have
heard a boat although I didn't hear one. Did you?"

"Uh hmm." Hugh thought about what she'd just said.

Immediately, a boat horn sounded, not too far away.

"Oh, no...o...o!" Lori wailed. "I forgot." She jumped up and
ran for the bedroom, digging in the closet for her swimsuit,
towel, hat and swim gear, throwing them out onto the floor.

"What in blazes is going on here?"

"I forgot. I made a date for today."

"You made a date? With whom?" He demanded of her.

"With Captain Jerrod to go snorkeling at some secret dive site of his."

"When did you make this date?"

"Tuesday, on the way here to the island."

"Geez, Lori, that man must move fast. He just meets you to bring you here and you agree to go out with him this weekend? What do you know about the man?"

"Not a lot." She admitted and shrugged.

"Are you crazy? Did the taxi cab driver ask you out too?" Hugh asked her acidly.

She grinned up at him impishly as she pulled up her black racer back swimsuit. It fit her perfectly and left nothing to the imagination.

"No, but the cabby did take me to his cousin's for lunch."

"*Are you nuts*? Woman, you and I are going to have a talk about this. You are *entirely* too trusting. And can't you at least put on clothes on that cover you sufficiently, for God's sake." By now he paced around the room, ranting and raving, and waving his hands over his head.

"Just kidding, he didn't actually. Well, he did, but not the way it sounds. I'll explain later. I'd better go, don't you think? Rather than let him show up here looking for me? I'll take Jake with me. He would probably go anyway. Give me a kiss and I'll be back as soon as I can. Wait for me?"

Lori gathered her gear after throwing on a coverup. She went up to him on tiptoe and kissed his stiff lips. Hugh glared at her.

As she headed for the door, she stopped put her hat and told Hugh softly. "I love you." Then raced as fast as she could for the cart to drive to the dock.

Nine

Jumping out of the cart almost before it rolled to a stop, Lori waved at Jerrod. Jake sat waiting patiently on the dock, apparently for her.

"Hi. Sorry, I made you wait. Late night, last night. Miss Genevieve had a card party and I slept in." *Boy, did she ever! Whew!* She tried to feel a little guilty for one itsy bitsy, teeny tiny moment. *Not!*

"I was thinking that you were backing out on me." Jerrod looked at her with one eyebrow raised and led her down the dock to the boat.

Jake followed at a more leisurely pace. Reaching the end of the pier, he ran and jumped in the boat before either had a chance to board the boat themselves.

She chuckled at Jake's maneuver. "Nope, wouldn't be thinking of it," mimicking Jerrod with her fingers crossed. "See my newest friend? He's been my escort since I arrived on this island. My best friend, aren't you, old boy?"

She ruffed up his big brown ears. Jake looked up adoringly at her, with a big sloppy grin on his face.

"My, oh my, you do have a friend at that."

"Where to today, Captain?"

"I'm wanting to show you my secret wreck that has become a wonderful base for a reef. By a little islet not very far from here.

It isn't on the diving charts around here, so there aren't any tourists. Come on up to the bridge with me. Just put your gear down there and we'll cast off."

He directed her to untie the lines on his command while he went topside, where the engines idled. Jerrod kept one eye focused on her to see what she was doing. He watched her smear sunscreen over her exposed skin and replace her coverup.

Jake followed them up and sat in a chair with the wind in his face as Jerrod accelerated the boat out of the lagoon. The dog's face made a silly grimace with the air flow. Lori watched him for a minute and burst out laughing, wishing yet again that she'd brought a camera. She had one back at the cabin, but so far kept forgetting it.

Jerrod inspected her with admiring eyes, joining her in laughter.

"I was thinking that I would hear from you this week, but I guess you were too darn busy to be lonely."

"Jerrod, I've met most of the residents and almost have my lab in shape. It's wonderful here. I love all the sunshine. And everyone is so friendly. Benjamin is the best. We've been out in the boat snorkeling once, and soon we'll have to be out collecting our specimens. There's so much to do and learn about."

He liked her bubbling positive attitude. Actually, he liked a lot about this woman. Jerrod found himself staring at her appraisingly, frowning and puckering up his weatherbeaten face. She had this marvelous healthy glow about her and looked strong, but somehow fragile and helpless. Although she was small, her curves were in all the right places. Her legs were long and perfect and he had to keep himself from drooling, like Jake over there.

"What?" She asked, seeing him eyeing her with a funny expression on his face.

"There is something about you that is different, I'm thinking. Can't quite put my finger on it, but I see it. You look happier, or something. Mmm."

He took one hand off the wheel, took her glasses off and then took her chin in his hand, staring into her bright eyes and seeing the yellow flecks in them for the first time. "Hmm... I'm not sure what. But whatever it is, I like it. Yes, I do."

After he directed his eyes and hands back toward the boat's navigation, Lori checked the compass to see the heading was due east from the island.

"Look, Lori. The special attraction I ordered for you has arrived." He waved in the starboard direction.

She smacked him on the shoulder. "You did not. But stop, I want to swim with them, please?" She was delighted that the group of dolphins was keeping up with the boat.

"No, I think they'll be following us to our destination and you can swim there."

"Are you sure? I don't want to miss a chance to get to know them." Lori hung off the side, waving and calling to them.

"They'll stick with us, I'm thinking." Rather sure of himself, his handsome face smirked under his ball cap. His eyes crinkled and he smiled guilelessly at Lori.

"I cheated. I fed them every day this week so they would follow me, and I haven't fed them yet today. They will stay with us. We don't have very far to go."

She smacked his shoulder again for good measure. "Come on, guys. I promise we will feed you if I have to feed you the Captain's food. You old cheater. You should be ashamed of yourself taking advantage of poor animals like that."

"Yeah, well, it's working and you've got *me* to thank, I'm thinking."

"Well, I'm thinking you are full of blarney *and* bull. Thank you very much."

"Why is it I'm never appreciated? All I do for people. No one ever is grateful, I'm thinking. Humph."

"You poor thing. To be taken advantage of like that. How sad." Lori said with mirth, trying hard not to laugh at his woebegone expression. Fake though it was.

Jerrod steered hard to port around a jumble of large rocks sticking out of the water about five hundred yards out from a cluster of atolls. Jerrod kept an eye on her tanned legs and anything else he could see under that darn baggy shirt while she persisted in hanging off the boat, calling to the dolphins.

The waves pounding on the rocks loomed immense and quite dangerous to Lori. She watched him guide the boat past the rocks to a quieter area amid the atolls to drop anchor. Palm trees blew in the wind above a pretty little beach on one of the tiny islands.

"Is that where we're heading?" She pointed at the beach. Gilligan's Island, maybe, and 'tee-heed' in her head.

"Yeah, later for lunch, but now I want to show you this. In the rocks. You are a good swimmer, aren't you? I just assumed you were." He pointed back toward the rocks and looked worriedly at her.

"Sure, but I don't feel confident about scuba diving until I've built up my stamina a bit more. After a couple more weeks of swimming laps, I should be ready." Lori frowned, concerned with those huge rocks foaming hard in the aftermath of the waves pounding them.

"You'll be okay if you just stick like glue to me. When the tide is high like this, there's an easy groove to slide through and watch the wave makers from a hidden spot in the rocks. Down in the middle of that pile of rocks is the old wreck I was telling you about."

"It's a great place to dive when you get below the surface waves. It's not very deep and I can show you some great sights if you can hold your breath. You've gotta see the arches formed by the boat ribs. It's fantastic."

He took off his jeans, T-shirt and hat, exposing a wet suit bottom underneath, and grinned to see her finally strip off her coverup and show some skin.

Lori ignored his typical male lecherous grin and busied herself, putting fins and other gear on. She patted Jake on the head and told him, "Be good boy." Then she slipped into the water feet first off the lower back deck.

She swam fifty feet from the boat when she felt a gentle nudge from behind her. Thinking Jerrod was getting fresh, she turned around quickly to fend him off and was delighted to find herself surrounded by the dolphins. Ecstatic, she cooed and talked to them, holding her hand out in front of her like she had with Jake at first. The smallest one butted her hand with his snout then stood perpendicular out of the water chattering.

She reached over and gently stroked his belly and he immediately flopped on his back, exposing more of his tummy for petting. Lori laughed and petted him until a larger one nudged her other hand wanting his turn. She rubbed each of them in turn, talking back to their chattering and clicking.

Jerrod treaded water, astonished at her fearless success with the creatures. He had been feeding them for years and they had never gotten that close to him. Shaking his head in amazement, he told her. "Let's swim to the rocks from this side and when we get closer to them, I want you to stay right beside me."

As they swam toward the rocks, the dolphins accompanied them, either leading, following or on each side of her. Lori reached down and grabbed a dorsal fin when the biggest one glided under her and got taken for the ride of her life.

The dolphin pulled her under the water and worried Jerrod until they burst out of the water in front of him. Lori was laughing and gleefully yelling "YEE...HAW!" at the top of her lungs.

When they were close enough to the rocks she let go, patting the biggest one on the head. The dolphins circled keeping close. Jerrod stopped her, and took his mouthpiece out of his mouth, so he could talk to her.

"Take my hand and stay close, there's a small opening we're going to slip into. Once we're safely inside the rock, the waves will lose their power. There is good sized area enclosed like a pocket. It will be hard to hear in there because of the noise of the waves bashing against the rocks."

"I'll show you the little peepholes worn in the rocks by pointing, just like we were scuba diving. After you've seen enough up there, I'll lead you lower and lower. Then we'll dive down to the bottom to a cave, so you can see out. But don't go in the opening."

"Outside, the wreck sits twenty-five feet down but we're only going down about fifteen. Are you comfortable with that? We won't stay down long, just enough for you to view the reef that wreck has become. Stay alert. There are often barracudas after floundering schools of fish caught in the turbulence, so do not put your hands out of any of the lookout holes. I don't want them bit off as fish bait, understand?"

"Yep. Lead on Captain." She saluted him while treading water.

She held Jerrod's hand as he counted the waves and then led her inside what looked like a crack in one of the big rocks. But it opened up much larger inside, and below she saw darkness. Once inside the noise was overwhelming. No wonder he'd given his instructions outside the rocks. She followed him to the closest hole where he pointed.

Some water came in through the holes but the brunt of the waves crashed into the middle of the rocks. She could see the turbulence like being behind a glass wall. It was wild water out there. That old ship had never had a chance.

He led her to more peep holes where small colorful tropicals were caught up in a typhoon of tumbling waves. Diving down gently for short periods, the peep holes exposed her to a virtual explosion of color and light.

The reef below them opened to a vista of arches and tunnels and points and valleys. Virtually every single square inch was covered by coral and other species of aquatic life. Plunging deeper to reach the bottom viewpoint, was a tunnel large enough to swim through.

Viewing the wreck from there was like witnessing a living undersea cathedral. Lori's mouth would have fallen open if it hadn't been firmly gripped around her snorkel mouthpiece. She was not prepared for such a display of dynamic force and majesty all rolled into one. Exploding back up to the surface, needing oxygen desperately, nevertheless Lori yelled at Jerrod between gasping for deep breaths.

"We've got to come back here and scuba dive. It's…it's incredible, unbelievable. I love it. THANK YOU."

He smiled at her and mouthed. "Had enough yet?"

She shook her head at him. He followed her back to each of the looky holes one more time, and would have been grinning except he couldn't. Jerrod led her back out through the crack that allowed them portal to this special kind of underwater paradise and found the dolphins waiting for her. He knew that they were not waiting for him.

Lori played with them all the way back to the boat, catching a ride on first one and then the other. They chirped and chattered and twittered to each other with Lori clicking and sounding right back at them. Jerrod watched her play and looked up to see Jake hanging his head between his paws over the boat wall, watching them.

She didn't want to get out of the water. She was having too much fun. Nevertheless, she was tired, almost bone weary. It had been a short night and already a long day. But she was exhilarated, too.

What an absolutely perfect day. It could have been improved upon only if she shared the swim with Hugh, and felt a moment's disloyalty to Jerrod.

When Jerrod pulled her the last step into the boat, Lori impulsively kissed him a big smack on the cheek. "Thanks Jerrod."

He wryly put his hand to his cheek. He'd been hoping for more. Much more. After all this place was a special load of ammunition in his books and not to be shared with just anyone.

"Before you do anything else, Jerrod--feed the dolphins."

Lori helped him carry up the buckets of fish from below and toss the little fish to the big ones, while Jake kept his comical watch. Lori maintained a constant stream of chatter about all that she'd seen.

Jerrod remained silent, nodding his head at the appropriate places, listening to and enjoying the sound of her voice. Raising anchor, he took the boat to the more protected western side of the little islets and brought the boat in close to the shore of the largest atoll before dropping anchor again.

"We can eat here on the boat or go to the beach for our picnic, your choice."

"I think today I'd rather eat on the boat to keep Jake company."

"WOOF!"

"Sounds like confirmation, I'm thinking." He had to laugh.

"Can I help?"

"Nope, today you are my guest. Er, both of you. Good thing I brought plenty of food. I hadn't counted on your majesty there.

But I will be glad to provide a feast fit for royalty, since I've already provided the entertainment."

Lori combed her hair back from her face with her fingers, then placed her hat back on her head as Jerrod went down below to bring up food. She followed him to the galley to find some fresh water and a bowl for Jake.

Jerrod set out a platter of fresh veggies with a ranch dip, and a dish of sliced spicy little sausages with a strong horseradish dip that brought tears to her eyes. She made a plate for Jake and nibbled some herself while she watched Jerrod light a fire on a small hibachi grill.

When she stretched out on a padded bench, she could not keep from yawning. The warmth of the sun and the gentle rocking of the boat almost put her under. If Jake had not given her a gentle nudge on her hand, she would have drifted off to sleep.

Forcing herself to sit up, the sizzling sounds and smells of food on the grill made her mouth water. That was probably why Jake got her attention, too.

Jerrod served delicious shish kebabs of beef, mushrooms, onions and corn on the cob slices, all marinated in lime juice. He poured them each a frozen Margarita. Lori's limit was one. The food was a heavenly delight to her taste buds and she told him so. Jake of course, simply inhaled his portion.

After she ate, Lori stretched lazily and laid back for a cat nap hoping to rejuvenate and catch some more energy from the sun.

Jerrod stretched out on his side on the opposite bench with Jake between them on the deck. He kept his line of sight focused totally on her, absorbing every detail of her body from the tip of her toes to the top of her brow in the shade under her hat, slowly perusing her.

Mesmerized for an hour and a half, he wanted to touch her so badly that it hurt. Instinctively, he knew that now was not the time, especially not with Jake present. He called softly to her and went topside to take her back home.

She'd thanked him over and over when he returned them to St. Saba but Jerrod left feeling very frustrated.

Ten

Lori hurried back to her cabin, anxious to spend more time with Hugh. When she went inside it was empty. She knew it the moment she entered. Even before she closed the door behind her. The cabin vibrated with emptiness.

She asked anyway. "Hugh?" but received no response. Where could he be? He said he would not leave in daylight and it was at least an hour until sunset.

She walked through the quiet, feeling more alone than ever, touching things that Hugh had touched. Strange how the presence of one man could fill a void in one's life. And his absence created a yawning hole, a pit of epic proportions.

Lori believed herself to be impervious to any permanent masculine presence, yet in a matter of days her reality flip-flopped. She knew that she never wanted to be so alone, ever again.

Depressed. Exhausted. She took a quick shower, washed the salt out of her hair and sought the comfort of her bed. Seeking oblivion that only sleep could provide, she erased all thoughts from her head and crashed completely.

She woke up after dark hearing a sound at her door. Jumping up and hurrying to the door, thinking it must be Hugh, she was disappointed to find it was only Jake. Letting him in, she overreacted to his coming home by giving him more than his share of attention, food and water.

She welcomed the distraction that the dog provided. He curled up in his spot and promptly started snoring and twitching in his sleep. She watched her big, ugly, adopted dog for a while. And smiled at his dreaming from the white wicker rocking chair where Hugh had held her so comfortably only hours ago.

She rocked and contemplated how that man had the capacity to put her on an emotional roller coaster with such remarkable ease, and leave her dizzy. She forced herself out of the rocker to poach a couple of eggs for a light meal.

~ * ~

The open front door let in the brilliant sunshine and the fresh salty breeze as Jake bounded out the door for more breakfast. She began work early. She and Benjamin finished unpacking and arranging the lab space, except for the last few stragglers that had not arrived.

Lori needed to restock her kitchen pantry and fridge. She arranged a trip to the warehouse with Benjamin, after lunch. She thought perhaps she would run into Hugh somewhere, but she was disappointed.

She threw herself into her work for the rest of the week, immersing herself in the myriad details of laboratory life. They began collecting normal specimens of the various fish species that had been reported as unnatural deaths.

She discussed with Benjamin the problem of excessive high mortality rates could possibly be caused by a volcanic heat vent where enough variables in temperature could allow a disease to manifest. Or even a food shortage. Neither explanation was likely to affect such a varied population nor kill them all at once. But it was an enigma to them.

Perhaps the water temperature could heat too fast but then all of the species in an area would be killed. Not select ones. Also the satellite imagery should have picked up any thermal anomalies if venting was occurring and the reports should have reflected it. Surely something else must be going on.

It was an intricate puzzle needing to be solved. Her first priority after she set up the lab was to establish a baseline of normal samples that would create a standard on the cellular level. After netting the live fish, which in itself was quite a challenge, she taught Benjamin how to help her with the fish necropsies.

They must take samples of every organ and carefully place identifying labels on each species. While on the boat, they placed the tissue samples in a formaldehyde solution in small baggies to 'fix' them for at least twenty-four hours before processing. After returning to the lab they would continue the many steps necessary to get the tissues ready for the final microscopic stage.

Following the fixation period, back in the lab, Lori sliced the larger tissues uniformly to 1/2 centimeter and placed them in perforated plastic capsules before dropping them into an ethanol solution.

She explained to Benjamin how the tissue processor took the samples through correspondingly higher percentages of alcohol to water during an overnight period. The procedure dehydrated the tissues to prepare them for infiltration with xylene and then finally hot paraffin.

After the tissues had been fully infiltrated with the hot paraffin, they would be placed strategically to embed them in a capsule. More hot paraffin would be added to cool quickly and hold them in place. Little paraffin rectangles in plastic cassettes quickly grew into piles. Benjamin examined the embedded samples of paraffin blocks, carefully turning them over to inspect them from all sides.

Lori proceeded to show him how they were placed in the microtome, an instrument with an exceptionally sharp blade that could slice the paraffin blocks into 4 to 5 micron sections. Ben was impressed with the infinitely fine slices that were floating on a hot water bath.

He thought they were perfectly clear cross sections of the tissues and organs, which was exactly what they were. She smiled and mounted the sections on clear glass microscope slides that she had prepared previously, and set them in racks to dry.

Benjamin fascinated, never left her side, eager to see what the next step would be. She processed the slides in a reverse order of the same chemicals, xylene and alcohols, in order to deparaffinize them.

When she began to rehydrate them in the exact reverse order, before staining with the standard Hematoxylin and Eosin stain preparation, Ben understood the chemical dynamics of the processing. Soon he was nodding his head in anticipation of the end result.

He was completely dumbfounded by the clarity of the cellular structures when the full staining technique was completed. The cells' nuclei were stained blue. The cytoplasm of the cells was all crisply pink. She checked the slides under the microscope after they were cover slipped with a synthetic mounting medium. Then she presented Benjamin with the finished products of normal organ tissues for over a dozen tropical fish species. He was hooked and wanted to spend all his spare time studying the slides.

The serum samples were labeled and sent to the hospital lab in Charlotte Amalie that Lori had made arrangements with, since her lab was not equipped for that type of analysis. She had high hopes that her histotechniques would solve the puzzle for them.

Now they simply had to wait for another sighting of dead fish before they collected any more samples. Lori planned on using everything at her disposal to solve the mystery of deaths. She was confident of her skills and explained to Benjamin how different chemical reactions produced differing results could help identify foreign matter in the tissues. That was why they had so many chemicals stockpiled.

The entire fleet at Charlotte Amalie had been advised to report any unusual sightings by radio to the warehouse here on St. Saba, even the military presence were on alert. The plan was then she and Benjamin would go to the reported coordinates to gather samples.

Lori passed time teaching Benjamin how to operate the equipment. Training him first in the safety procedures was a natural prerequisite for her. Now that he had a working knowledge of the process, she needed him to get comfortable with the direct operation of the process, so that when the time came, they could work more efficiently as a team.

Ben was already accomplished with the skills of autopsy work because he'd taken dissecting classes in college. He was a quick study, and only needed to be shown a procedure once before he mastered it.

She was more than gratified with his work. In fact she had to force him to quit work at the end of the day. He wanted to spend countless hours at the microscope in the computer room, sitting in the darkened room, staring at the cells. She teasingly told him he was going to wear out his eyeballs if he was not more careful. She was pleased to share any and all of her cellular anatomy and histotech books with him. Benjamin absorbed knowledge like a sponge.

Every day that went by with no signs of Hugh, forced Lori to put him out of her mind. She tried not to allow his presence or his absence to dominate her psyche. Here again, the man had simply vanished without a word.

Where had he gone and why? So much for him never leaving her side again. Lori grew more and more depressed as time went by with not a word or a sight of that man.

She was tempted to ask Benjamin if he knew of Hugh's whereabouts but remembered Hugh's warning to trust no one, not even Benjamin. But it was increasingly difficult to keep from questioning every single person that she ran into about Hugh, or rather *JeanPaul,* she told herself mimicking Miss Sheree's sharp voice.

She sighed to herself and went to swim laps again in the lagoon. Swimming was such a mindless function, taking all her oxygen just to breathe. Lori and Jake played stick retrieval on the beach before her evening swim. She noticed herself sighing a lot more lately. Not a good sign.

Thanks, Hugh, as she wiped a tear from her eye, determined more than ever not to give in to self pity. And she thought her tear well had been depleted a long time ago.

Lori's suntan progressed to a lovely golden shade and the sun created a mass of gleaming lights in her dark blond hair. Her face had tanned lightly from the reflected light off the clean white beaches and shining water in spite of her hats. The daily swimming regimen had slimmed her body.

But where the heck was Hugh?

Jake, her most constant companion, only left her for his rounds to collect meals all over the island. He had been coming to the lab and watching them work. His big brown eyes in his brown face expressed an intelligence that somehow acknowledged her talks to him.

But no matter how much she talked like he was human, he could not possibly replace Hugh. She admitted to herself that she needed him. Her life would be incomplete without him, so where in blazes was he?

She kept her cell phone by her side religiously, more because she hoped Hugh would call than for protection. Lori had no fear of this lovely island paradise and couldn't imagine anyone here putting her in danger.

Lori and Benjamin continued their exploration of this spectacular archipelago set on the edge of the sparkling Caribbean. She had never seen the many shades of blue and green as these waters offered.

Nor could the diving be equaled anywhere else. The astonishing variety of the underwater world and the incomparable colorful marine life of these barely submerged realms was amazingly unspoiled by the crowds that usually take over such sites. Lori hoped they would always remain as pristine and without pollution.

They explored Jimmy's Surprise, off St. Croix where Lori spotted horse eye, and cralle jacks schooling around the wondrous offshore sea mount. They swam to the large pinnacle that rose to within sixty feet of the surface was densely covered with lacy sea fans decorating its western slope. Unusual shaped barrel sponges perched on a rocky eastern ledge. Lobster, grouper, and nurse sharks hid in crevices. The fish were so fearless that some of the large gray angels followed them gulping at their scuba exhaust bubbles. Their skinny faced countenances with lips protruding, tried to catch Lori's bubbles, and made her spit out her mouthpiece she was laughing so hard.

Lori and Ben explored Rust Op Twist, Salt River Canyon West Wall, and Cane Bay Drop Off. Snake eels, octopi, eagle rays and hawksbill turtles kept them on guard. Lori learned to dodge the large green morays, barracudas and manta rays. The coral formations, picturesque ridges and countless sightings of ancient anchors, sunken wrecks, caves, tunnels and arches in abundance enraptured Lori.

If only every job offered such diversity. Lord, but she could get used to this kind of lifestyle. Here her occupation seemed more play than work. It seemed that she enjoyed all the pleasures of leisure instead of work. Instead of drudgery, it felt more like a wonderful extended vacation.

Every time she went diving, Lori felt guilty, definitely enjoying this way too much. Already she couldn't imagine returning to St. Louis with three-month-long cold winter and the seemingly endless rainy days of spring. In fact, spring there would only start about now, with flowering spring bulbs and emerging green of the grass.

It made her shiver just to think of all those dark dreary days without sunshine. But every day that passed without a word from Hugh made her believe that St. Louis would still be her final destination when she departed this glorious place at the end of her sabbatical.

Better to ignore that for now, Lori had lots of time before it was over. Think of it later. Be a Scarlett O'Hara. Right?

Knowing that she should not, Lori and Jake took a walk past Hugh's cabin several weeks after he disappeared. From all appearances it looked deserted, vacant. She looked in the back windows on the opposite side from the beach and hopefully away from prying eyes.

She came away more disappointed than ever. There was no sign of him. She was determined to discover what was going on, one way or another. She began to plan an excursion to Charlotte Amalie to talk to Charlie in a week or so, if she had not heard from Hugh by then.

She would take control of her own destiny.

Lori refused to let Hugh's absence affect her more than it already did. After all, she was her own person. She could be anything that she wanted. Lori decided she did not need anyone anymore. She had been there, done that. *Get tough, woman.* Let her life be dictated to by outside forces? *Not anymore. Pay attention.* She told herself.

Eleven

Deciding to become more sociable, Lori walked the beach every evening after her swim, hoping to run into the island inhabitants and play detective. With Jake's companionship for protection, she transformed into a brazen woman, and flirted boldly, when she ran into any men on the island. She couldn't wait to make her way to West house to pump Miss Genevieve for info. The talkative woman would surely have information that Lori craved.

Lori encountered every single person on the island except Hugh, of course. The fat little artist was determined to get her to pose for him, and she had finally agreed. Arrangements were made for sittings to begin next week in the late afternoon sunshine.

Jake remained her bodyguard, although surprisingly he had never growled at Stephen. But she couldn't see the painter as any kind of threat. Obviously, neither did Jake. But Jake continued to give the Laurent men a good dose of fear if they invaded Lori's space too much. Lori held back her laughter to see those men jump.

Finding out that Sheree had suddenly left St. Saba, was definitely one thing she did *not* need to hear from Miss Genny. She wanted to grind her teeth in annoyance and howl at the world to release the pent up jealousies that raged within.

Instead, she smiled and chatted with Miss Genny for over half an hour, making pleasant conversation with the charming old lady. It was not her fault that Lori was jealous of her too perfect, too tall, and too skinny granddaughter.

Making excuses for not attending an upcoming card party on next Saturday, Lori's thoughts roamed far away. Maybe she should leave too. She planned a trip to the Bahamas as an interlude away from this place, maybe Nassau. Or maybe she would just go to Charlotte Amalie and explore on her own.

She simply needed to get this place in perspective. Get away and be objective about it all. Get control of herself and her life again. Be positive. Quit the internal whining to herself all the time.

It was a good thing she didn't have to pay much attention to Miss Genny's rambling monologues. Her own internal dialogue already perked up her defenses. She made her goodbyes to Miss Genny and promised it wouldn't be so long before her next visit.

Lori walked with a strong purposeful stride across the length of the island back to her cabin. This time she didn't even look sideways at Hugh's cabin when she passed it and felt quite pleased with herself.

~ * ~

Time crawled until her trip. Working with Benjamin in the lab, she did her best to shore up her lagging self-confidence. Every day she looked in the mirror and denied her need for Hugh. Out loud. Determined to go it alone from now on.

A stray thought kept nagging her to remember something important, but for the life of her, she couldn't remember what. She jogged her memory for that odd information to surface since she arrived. It would simply have to come to her in its own way, since she obviously couldn't force it out by dwelling on it. She didn't even know if it was related to her research or to the missing Hugh.

One morning she discovered either she'd been misplacing items or her memory was failing her. She woke up and couldn't find her laptop computer anywhere in her cabin. She'd have sworn it was in her living room last night. She told Jake that she must be losing it, mentally. Before making breakfast she jogged over to the lab and found it on a desk in the back room. Picking it up, Lori specifically did *not* remember leaving it over here at the lab.

She wondered if she were getting Alzheimer's which reminded her of her grandfather who used to call it 'Old-timers', and remembered Gramps with a smile.

She had loved that wonderful loving strong bear of a man with an oversized heart of pure gold. He had died exactly one month before her grandmother more than nine years ago. Her grandmother simply couldn't live without him and died of a broken heart. A large lump formed in her throat, God, how she missed them.

Too many are gone... but no time for that now. Lori shoved it into the recesses of her mind.

She returned to her cabin to pack for her long weekend away. Captain Jerrod was picking her up and taking her to Charlotte Amalie on his regular Thursday route. He sounded eager to see her when she called and asked him for the ride. Lori knew she could take the launch but felt more comfortable this way. More independent.

She explained to Jake that she was going away for a few days and wonder dog that he was, she was undoubtedly sure that he understood perfectly... Silly old dog.

"Now Ben, if you get an alert on fish mortalities, you promise to call me on my cell phone. I'll meet you at the coordinates, one way or another, okay? Promise? It would be my luck to go to St. Thomas and miss a call. If I have to rent a boat

I will get there. I plan to be out on the water at least part of the time anyway."

"Yes ma'am, I promise. You know Miss Genny is very upset that you're not coming to her party Saturday night? She enjoys having someone new to entertain. Also, she thinks you should take the launch."

"I will be here for other parties. I just need to get away for a bit, Benjamin." She was shrugging off the question like snake shedding old skin.

"I'm looking forward to exploring as much of the main island as I can. I'll save St. John for another trip. I'm going to meet with the lab personnel at the hospital tomorrow to establish blood chemistry norms so that we can set up a computer program to kick out any abnormals. Also, to determine standard tests."

"Besides, you need the boat, just in case. I'm counting on you. You'll need to bring our supplies if we get alerted. Otherwise, I'll play tourist. Is there anything that you would like me to bring you back from town?"

"No, I can't think of anything, but thank you for asking. Have a good trip and I'll see you when you get back. Don't worry. And don't forget, don't waste money on treasure maps. Even our island was reputed to be a hideout for a pirate. Supposed to have tons of hidden gold, stolen from the Spanish, discovered here in caverns hundreds of years ago. At least that's the story we grew up with. There is probably a similar story for every island. So save your money."

"Well, I don't have time to treasure hunt, but thanks for the warning. I know I can count on you." Lori smiled gratefully at him and patted his shoulder.

Jake's bark carried from across the island and the boat horn sounded in reply. Placing the cell phone in her pocket, she picked up her laptop and bags ready at last to catch her ride.

"You use the cart anytime while I'm gone, Benjamin." She called as she flew up the hill waving at him.

~ * ~

Last night she'd shared a particularly lovely evening with Captain Jerrod. He was a very sweet man, both gallant and an old world charmer. Jerrod had gone out of his way to make her feel special and had insisted on taking her to dinner to celebrate her visit to St. Thomas.

When he picked her up at the hotel, he'd brought her a lovely bouquet of fresh exotic flowers. He took her on St. Peter Mountain to the Mountain Top, which claimed the invention of the first banana daiquiri and had a remarkable sunset view. After cocktails they returned to her hotel to dine at Entre Nous. There they gorged on an exquisite meal of lobster poached in champagne, a wonderful endive and radicchio salad, fresh sauteed vegetables in local herbs and a sinfully rich triple chocolate cheesecake.

On St. Thomas, Lori woke up in Blackbeard's Castle after a great night's rest. This morning she groaned, burying her head under a pillow when she remembered the succulent dinner with all the calories she'd scarfed. She was learning eating habits that were almost as bad as Jake's. She stretched and put on the hotel's white monogrammed robe and walked over to the window. The view was a spectacular one.

The island glowed like an emerald and the harbor sparkled in the bright morning sunlight. At least five cruise ships were docked with countless boats of all sizes moving about in the splendid crystalline waters. From this viewpoint, numerous little islets dotted the azure sea and disappeared into the horizon.

The water changed color from every shimmering shade of blue to green. Looking past the outer edge of the hotel's swimming pool where the landscape fell away, the city was displayed in the distance.

She hurriedly dressed in shorts and white blouse eager to get out and about. She grabbed some informative tourist brochures on her way through the lobby. This hotel was one of St. Thomas' most famous sites. It had been built in 1679 as a watchtower to scan for pirates and enemy ships, supposedly by Edward Teach, the infamous Blackbeard himself. It had been both his lookout and hideaway, according to history. Almost everything here was a multifaceted history lesson.

The hotel was situated on the very ruins of Fort Skytsborg, a 17th century fort, at the top of the ninety-nine steps (In actuality a hundred and three, Lori counted them on the way down). The steps had been laid in the mid 18th century to the summit of Government Hill, made from brick that had originally been used for ballast in the holds of Danish sailing ships.

Lori spent a full morning with the hospital lab staff, reviewing data on the samples that she sent them. They correlated data into charts and graphs for comparison in the future and established norms. She was quite pleased with the results.

Jerrod had made her promise to dine again with him and then scuba dive with him before returning to St. Saba. He was such a pleasant man that Lori felt remarkably comfortable in his presence.

Although he was full of Irish blarney, she felt he had nothing to hide from her. No secrets. No deception. Just a warm sincerity. She liked him more as she got to know him better. He had such a sincere quality, Lori felt that she could trust him, which was more than she could say about Hugh right now.

Humph...she wondered where in the world he was right now. She'd like to give *him* a piece of her mind. That JeanPaul, or whoever he was, deserved to be dragged through the streets behind a horse or better yet an ass.

The taxi driver again relayed historical information as they traveled past the pastel colored buildings. "That's the Grand Hotel. What is now the Virgin Island Museum was once Fort Christian and dates to the 17th century. Would you like me to stop at the Visitor's Center, ma'am?"

Showing him the stack of brochures, "First I'll explore the West Indian Company Dock. Second, I'll make my way to Havensite Mall then I'll make more decisions over lunch." The Mall sat half a mile east of town and offered a great view of the harbor and the cruise ships in port.

The streets were named gades and many had undecipherable Danish names that were remnants of the island's historical past but the map pinpointed locations for her.

This trendy part of town provided everything anyone needed for some heavy duty-free shopping. Lori had a hard time keeping her money in her pocket, there were so many good buys, but she wanted to find a nice spot to eat and gawk at the tourists. She didn't want to load herself down with packages at the beginning of her jaunt.

Taking the Paradise Point Tramway to a complex seven hundred feet above the sea on Flag Hill provided Lori an ideal vantage point to view what seemed like the entire Caribbean. Visibility extended for miles and miles into the sparkling distance. There were lots of tourists to watch so she settled down for lunch.

Lori ate a perfectly grilled tuna on a bed of Bibb lettuce with a wonderful smoked ranch dressing and downed three glasses of iced tea while she perused the information. It was a difficult decision to decide what to do next. Charlotte Amalie offered a variety of guided tours. A flight seeing tour covered St. Thomas and St. John on a forty minute flight. Hmm, she'd call them about schedules first thing tomorrow. Probably too late to work in today, anyway, she told herself. Even submarine rides were available for non-snorkelers or families to ride one hundred fifty feet down a reef. She kept thinking that Nathan would have loved this place but pushed that thought away to deal with later.

"Too much to see and too little time. Today by land. Tomorrow by air and sea. Sounds like a plan." She told herself ruefully. She found herself talking to no one way too much lately.

She glanced around at the diverse crowd surrounding the gift shop. A smaller cruise ship docked while she was eating and extended its gangplank for departing tourists. Finished with lunch, Lori walked over to a lookout telescope viewer to get a closeup of the busy waterfront after she paid for lunch. A plenitude of colorful flags and the beautiful sleek lines of the ships in the harbor drew her eyes and she tried to identify the countries they represented.

Suddenly, a tall brown haired man walking with his hand on the back of a tall, slender, splashy, glow worm green-dressed woman with an enormous black wide brimmed hat, entered her the scopes focus. *Gad. I despise that color.*

For some inexplicable reason Lori continued watching, as if instinctively she recognized the couple, and did not return to scanning the crowd. After reaching the busy thoroughfare, the woman made sure to firmly grasp the man's arm in a repulsive possessive manner that seemed even more familiar to her.

Lori gasped. It certainly looked like Hugh Richmond and Sheree Laurent.

"Damn, that man. Damn and double damn." She cursed to herself furiously.

When she looked again, they were lost in the crowd and suddenly the game of people watching didn't seem so fun after all.

Deflated emotionally, she descended on the tram paying little attention to the dynamic panorama of the Caribbean spread in all its glory before her. She knew it was there but it just didn't register. Over and over she kept repeating to herself, "It wasn't him. It wasn't him."

Lori halfheartedly joined a bus sightseeing tour of the island, hoping to pack in as much as possible in a short period of time. The open air bus was festive and the tourists were friendly. She sat stiffly on top of the bus with her sunglasses and hat jammed on, determined to enjoy herself. She refused to acknowledge the possibility of Hugh with that witch.

Many lovely buildings and historical sites were pointed out by the guide: Fort Christian, the oldest building on the island, and Emancipation Garden. They passed Hotel 1829, where she planned to go later, Government House, Seven Arches Museum and beautiful eye-catching 18th and 19th century churches.

Market Square was a wonderful local market with an exotic supply ranging from fruits and vegetables to local herbs and spices. A half mile west of the center of town, a colorful harbor village retained a West Indian feel. The tiny little houses and streets belonged to another era, and only needed horses and buggies to set off its perfection. Picturesque soft pastel houses with picket fences charmed the tourists and added a delightful blending contrast to lush overgrown trees in profusion that provided shade for the village.

The tour bus jaunted cross country to a famous overlook known as Drake's Seat where Sir Francis Drake was said to have watched ship movements in the area hundreds of years ago. The overlook viewed Magens Bay, one of the prettiest beaches that Lori had ever seen. Drake's Passage and the British Virgin Islands stretched eastward with a hundred islands in sight.

Lori and the other tourists scrambled for their cameras to memorialize the impressive vistas. She couldn't resist joining the crowd at the overlook, caught up in the Kodak moment.

After making a reservation for an early flight seeing tour in the morning, and signing up to join a diving group after that, she detoured to Hotel 1829 on Government Hill. Lori intended to pry information from Charlie about Hugh. She had to know what was going on and where he was.

Lori militantly marched up to the reservation desk, standing until she got the young woman's attention.

The hostess checked her out as another casually dressed tourist and took her time fiddling with the long reservation list.

"Excuse me, miss, but I'd like to speak to Charlie. Now." She spoke quietly but forcefully. Lori was not in the mood to be ignored by *anyone* today. Certainly not by this little whipper-snapper.

Startled, the hostess looked up with big brown doe eyes and stammered "B...b...but he's not here right now. Can I seat you at the bar while I check on him? He should be back soon. Or would you rather have a table? I have a small table I could seat you for dinner, then I can send him to you when he returns?"

The young lady, suddenly helpful, amused Lori at her turnabout in attitude. She did not know who Charlie was, but whoever he was, got the girl's attention back on track anyway. Checking her watch, she decided to sit for dinner and maybe the queasy feeling in her stomach would go away.

"The table please. And I'll wait."

"Who shall I say is waiting, ma'am?"

"No name. Just send him to me."

"Yes, ma'am, right this way."

She led Lori to a small alcove with a table for two beside a window on a courtyard where musical sounds tinkled from a fountain. Exquisite exotic floral fragrances wafted gently through the open window.

Seating herself with a sigh, Lori inhaled deeply the rich aroma of food mingling with the scents of the flowers. She shook her head ruefully, always surprised that food could be so appealing even though she had been on a temperamental roller coaster ride today.

Just the possibility it *could've* been Hugh with that witch, set her jaw to clenching and her imagination running rampant. On the remote chance that she could have seen them coming off a cruise ship was impossible odds. Of course, look at the odds that they could end up on an island in the Caribbean together. She should know better than that.

Better yet, what were the odds that she would find Hugh here after all those years? It was just her imagination, pure and simple. A tall man and that horridly ugly chartreuse dressed clinging, cloying woman, could be any couple, right? Right?

She ordered a tall glass of Rum and diet coke, not a very sophisticated drink. But then she wasn't in a very sophisticated mood either. Tonight she was in the mood for a drink and not a pretend drink. Dinner was a typical Caribbean fare to challenge her taste buds. She studied the menu and settled on spicy yellow rice and beans, which she ate sparingly. A yummy blackened grouper seared to perfection. Sauteed button mushrooms and squash. And a tart green apple crisp to die for. Lori sat back after attacking the food and took the coffee cup in both hands to sip cinnamon cappuccino.

Eating lately always managed to remind her of Jake, her traveling gourmet companion. She already missed Jake's company. She even missed talking to him. She hadn't had a dog since she was a child.

Nick would never allow it. He hated animals in the house or yard. Too messy. She only had one pet in her marriage, the cat she had when she married him. He thought cats wouldn't live long, so he didn't think he would have to put up with it for long. But that old siamese had fooled him and lived for eighteen wonderful years.

Ha. One of the few times he didn't get his way. Nick was such a manipulator. Funny how she had never seen that until the marriage was over. Even the divorce had been orchestrated by him like the maestro conducts the St. Louis Symphony.

She shook her head and, in retrospect, admitted to allowing Nick the control. She could've taken a stand on any number of issues, but didn't. She simply gave in rather than stand up for herself and what she wanted.

Well, never again. It would be her way or no way next time. Hmpf, if there was a next time. No more railroading, overbearing men for her. Ever again.

Reflecting on her failed marriage, forced the pain of Nathan's loss to bubble to the surface in her deliberations. For that's how she looked at his death. Losing him. That chain of events that put him out of her reach forever.

The drunk that lost control of his vehicle, yet emerged unscathed.

The automobile accident that traumatized Nathan's brain.

The coma that he lay in for three incredibly slow and endless weeks.

The grim foreboding atmosphere of the sterile yet smelly hospital.

Her husband's short daily visit to the hospital on his way home from work.

Her constant vigilance at her son's side holding his hand, talking to him soothingly. Only leaving his bedside to go home to shower and change.

The doctors' poor prognosis. The longer her son stayed in a coma, the worse his recovery chances had been.

She read to him, told him news of his friends, and talked, talked, talked to him. She wouldn't give up. It wasn't her style. She could be tenacious. She almost lost her voice, and had to speak in whispers for days but continued talking anyway.

Finally, twenty-two days after the crash, he opened his eyes, alone with her in the middle of the night, and said only four words.

She would never forget his gravelly voice saying, "Mom, let me go."

Sometimes she could hear it still in the wind around her.

Holding his hand, with tears choking her voice and heart, she told him. "I love you… Nathan… I love you."

But he was gone, just like that. He was gone. She lost him… To the other side. Life lost… Death won.

Lori walked out to a brilliant morning where three rainbows shimmered in a perfectly clear sky, and the last one ended at the Gateway Arch.

What did it mean?… What could it mean?

She was numb. It was over. Her life would never be the same. Lord, was she ever right.

With tears in her eyes yet again, threatening to spill over, she sat and waited. Waited for Charlie. Waited for confirmation that Hugh was okay. She needed to know. His job and cover be damned. Sometimes people were more important than their work. Honestly, people were *always* more important, weren't they?

Lori allowed the tears to flow down her cheeks. She couldn't stop them if she tried. Letting the pain squeeze her heart, she tried her best to be optimistic about the future. Everything would be all right, wouldn't it? The worst had to be over now…surely.

For the first time, Lori realized that Hugh had not asked her about her son, not once. Oh, Lord, just like the last time. How in the world could she have a real relationship with that man if all that she could share with him was superficial sex?

Yes, the sex was good. Okay, it was great. All right, it was the best she ever had. She could admit that to herself but was that *all* that they had? Lord, what had she gotten into? As her grandmother used to say, "Out of the frying pan and into the fire." Maybe they had grown too far apart over the long years separated from each other, to ever truly come together now.

Lori bowed her head and her shoulders over the small table, glad to be in a secluded nook of the restaurant and away from prying eyes. She tried her best not to succumb to tears so easily. Blurring maybe. Full flowing tears, no. In fact, she had shed so many buckets of tears over the last year, she'd thought her tear wells had surely run dry.

Taking a deep breath and shaking off the overwhelming doubts bombarding her overactive mind, she sat up straighter in her chair and prayed her wait for Charlie would be over. Soon.

Shortly, a portly dark-skinned man with shiny smooth black hair limped toward her, leaning on an elaborate cane of carved wood. Seating himself at her table's other chair, he sighed and held out his huge hand to shake hers before he spoke.

"Madame, I understand that you are waiting for Charlie. I am at your service. I hope you do not mind my presumption of sitting with you. But I am not wholly recovered from a leg injury and I must rest these weary bones. How is it that I may help you? I trust that your dinner was superb? Are you enjoying your stay here on our islands?"

She shook his hand and bit her lip. Lori was at a loss for words. She was uncomfortable with being here. She didn't know whether she should use Hugh's real name or his alias, so she would use neither. Lori didn't know how far she should trust this man and she hadn't thought this through enough. But Hugh had given her Charlie's name as the only person that she could escape to safely. So she decided to lay her cards on the table.

"Charlie, I was told to come to you when I received a warning to get out. Do you understand?" Lori was intentionally cryptic.

"But, have I missed something? Have you been alerted? Is it going down now?"

On guard, losing his formal way of speaking, he fell into the lingo of the trade. Confused, the man called Charlie sat up paying more attention now. He was no longer the casual soft-spoken islander. His eyes darted, encompassing his surroundings and searching the shadows cast in the courtyard. His entire attitude grew more alert, less laid back and on guard. He grabbed for his cane as though it were a weapon.

"No, I am sorry. I didn't mean to misinform you. I just wanted to know if you were aware of me and if I could count on you for information. I mean, you are the only contact he has given me, and I wanted to know, well, I *need* to know if he is okay.

"The last time I heard from him was weeks ago. I don't know what happened to him. He wasn't where he said he would be, then he just vanished and I have not heard from him since. You see, I know you are not meant to hold my hand. But I thought that I saw him today coming off a cruise ship with a woman. I think I am beginning to imagine things because *I just don't know*. I know that I have no right to expect answers. I know that his work is important and I don't want to create problems, but is there anything at all that you can tell me? Please, is he all right? Can you at least tell me that?"

There was a long pause.

God, she hated sounding so needy and weak. It embarrassed her to sit and beg like that. She sounded like a lovesick teenager. Lori had never felt this helpless before or so distracted. And she blamed Hugh for putting her in such a despicable position.

Charlie sat there for a few moments digesting what he had heard. One hand rubbed his upper lip and stared into her beautiful blue eyes. He had been briefed with a very accurate description of her and still that did not do her justice. She was a lovely woman, and did not deserve the pity that he felt for her.

Ultimately, it was impossible for him to give her any real information, even if he had all the answers, which he did not. He was only here to offer a safe house. He was out of the business actively and could only promise her safety when the time was right. Hopefully, she had not compromised his position by showing up ahead of schedule.

"Tell you what, Miss Paige, you give me the address where you are staying here in town. I will check around and if I can determine that he is okay, I will leave you a message at your hotel. It will say 'Your reservation is confirmed for your dive Sunday with Sea Trade.'"

"Does that sound reasonable? That is the best I can do. I cannot imagine that he is not okay. He is an exceptionally experienced operative. But I will look into it for you. It would be best if you did not come back here until it is time. I do not wish to be inhospitable, but you must understand my position. Please be careful and be patient. Dinner is on the house. It has been an honor to meet you."

He stood using his cane, bowed to her formally over her hand and limped from the room.

Twelve

Lori looked forward with anticipation to the flight-see tour of the big islands. The bright sparkling day lightened her mood. At least the fantastic weather in the Virgins was consistently superb, day after day after day of heavenly sunshine. This place didn't seem to generate clouds like the Midwest did, or maybe the trade winds simply blew them all away. Optimism was her forte. She needed this sun.

Coming out of the shower with one towel wrapped around her head and a huge white one around her body, she spotted the message light blinking on her telephone. And made a mad dash for the phone. Retrieving the message, she waited tensely until she heard the confirmation message exactly as Charlie had proposed last night. Thankful, she hung up the phone with a sigh of relief and fell back onto the bed.

She knew absolutely nil about Hugh's whereabouts but nevertheless didn't feel quite so isolated since she'd met Charlie. He inspired confidence and capability in a simple five minute conversation. It was an illusion of security perhaps, but she would take it.

It *was* all she had, unless she wanted to count on the words of a man who was such an expert at disappearance.

As she did with most that she attempted, Lori threw herself into the tour with an eager attitude and a smiling face.

Exchanging first names with the other five passengers, she strapped herself in for the short flight.

The pilot kept up a running informative commentary as the small craft flew over the town of Charlotte Amalie heading east from the small busy airport. Flying low over the east side of town on a hilltop stood the tower of the pirate Bluebeard built for his only love, Mercedita. According to legend, after having discovered that she had been unfaithful to him, he killed her and sailed away never to be seen again.

Seems like every notorious pirate lived here at one time or another, Lori thought.

"Here are some of St. John's magnificent aerial views of the lush mountainous vegetation and the exceptionally fine beaches of the National Park which covers two-thirds of the island. The capital at Cruz Bay is a typical lovely Caribbean town on the right with its stunning bay. Caneel Bay is a most famous resort built in the fifties by Laurence Rockefeller. If you stay there take plenty of plastic. Lots of lovely dive sites wait to be explored at a leisurely pace or the frenetic pace of the cruise ship visitors," the pilot informed them.

"Look on the eastern side of the island for the meeting point of the Caribbean Sea and the Atlantic Ocean where they merge in a dynamic blend of greens and blues. There the water depths change at the underwater mounts of the British Virgins and the rest of the Leeward Islands off into the distance."

The pilot pointed out Sir Francis Drake Channel, bordering Tortola, and the small chain of islands, streaming toward Virgin Gorda, that reminded her of all the old pirate movies that she'd seen. A big old pirate ship with taut canvas was all it needed to make it picture perfect.

The plane swept back toward St. Thomas and Lori kept her nose pressed to the window searching the numerous cays and countless bays that the mountainous little island offered.

Back at the airport she waited for Billy Bob's transportation to take her to the marina. From there they set out on a six-pack boat for a day's diving with William Shell, a retired navy Captain catering to small groups. She joined four other divers going out that day.

The plans were to dive at Cow and Calf Rocks, the Lobster Bowl, and weather permitting, a secret hideaway spot. Lori wondered if it was the one where Captain Jerrod had taken her.

It sounded like more than a full day's worth of diving to her, not a half day. *Bet that will wear me out and make me sleep like a baby. Maybe I'll have time for a quick nap before dinner with Jerrod so I won't fall asleep on him.*

Captain Billy told them, "U.S. Virgin Islands lie at the edge of a huge underwater shelf that extends eighty-five miles from Puerto Rico before dropping off into the Atlantic Ocean to the north and the Caribbean to the south. It was part of those geologic plates grinding together that formed the volcanoes that lifted most of the islands out of the sea. And some of the islands were formed over time by extensive reef systems in the area."

The captain took them through the safety procedures and proper diving rules of etiquette that divers should adhere to preserve the reefs. "I know you've all heard it before but we must constantly reiterate the main rule of diving. Be sure to take only pictures and leave only bubbles."

Lori couldn't wait to dive in and explore

On the way to their first dive they spotted a dolphin group following a cruise ship's wake and Lori told the others about swimming with some of them.

The captain explained. "We'll use Cow and Calf Rock to start the dives and test the skills of the divers. It is a relatively easy dive of twenty to forty feet deep with plenty of caves, tunnels, and ledges for detailed exploration. Stay together and in sight of each other at all times."

Getting acclimated to the gear, Lori found the dive as easy as taking a walk in a park, underwater park anyway. A huge eight-foot long barracuda coasted by her while she peaked in a large cave and startled her, but mostly she just swam slowly and absorbed the colorful underwater surroundings.

Since it was an easy dive it didn't take too long to view and get back to the topside, ready to go on to the next site. Captain Billy stayed down until the last diver came up and made sure everyone was okay.

Getting back into the boat with all the gear on was much harder than getting out, but they finally were off again to the next site. Everyone had seen the giant barracuda and wondered if it ate tourists for breakfast. They enjoyed a good laugh and Lori loosened up enough to join in.

The next series of dives became increasingly challenging and displayed soft colorful corals that dominated the reefs. Basket starfish in the daylight had their multiple arms tightly intertwined. Anemone fish nestled among the folds of the host anemone and a giant tube sponge dwarfed one of the nearby divers. Countless banded butterfly fish swarmed past a bizarre one ton mola mola that was absolutely immense even for that enormous species.

Lori found porkfish cohabiting a reef crevice with their cousins, the yellow and blue striped grunts. The schools of horse eye jacks were on a reef prowl searching for food.

To Lori's delight the school of dolphins showed up and must have recognized her as their swimming companion. It was much easier to ride them submerged with air tanks. At least this time she could breathe.

The other divers were astonished at her daring camaraderie with the big fish. They scrambled to snap pictures of her exuberant rides through the clear waters.

Finally wearing her out, the dolphins carried her back to the boat knowing unerringly where she needed to go. She laughingly spit her mouthpiece out so that she could talk to them and scratch each of their underbellies when they rolled over for her. They stood up in the water and walked backwards, chirping, tweeting and whistling at Lori before they swam away from the reef.

The divers applauded Lori, wearily taking off her gear, while they gathered on the boat thanking the Captain for a great finale to the day. Lori was accused of being planted aboard with the divers as part of the entertainment.

"No, I am not part of the dive. I have never even seen Captain Bill before today. Really. I am not and never have been a paid performer."

But the others divers were not convinced. "Look. Here's my driver's license from Missouri. And my diver's C card with my old Missouri address. But can you send me copies of your pictures to St. Saba, U.S. Virgins?"

"Oh yeah. Sure lady, you just happen to live here now?" one of the men said.

"Look people, believe it or not. It really doesn't matter. I'm here doing research. I played with them before. They know me I guess."

Captain Bill who had remained quiet during this grinned. "*Do* you want a job?"

"No! But you can refund my money if you want to!" She grinned right back at the man.

Lori did wonder how the big fish recognized her in the water with her tank and diving gear on though, but enjoyed every second of their swim. She was glad the secret dive location wasn't the one Jerrod had shared with her. It was a nice wreck but it simply didn't compare.

~ * ~

After a quick nap and shower, Lori stood before the mirror on the back of the bathroom door examining her body critically. Her body looked better now that she had toned up with swimming since arriving here in the islands. *In fact it could pass for a younger woman, if you looked through gauze*, she thought.

Her tan wasn't all over since she didn't have the nerve to tan nude. She squinted her eyes, mentally erasing the faded silver stretch marks from her lily white belly. Although it was firm now, there was no escape from that fifty-six-inch pregnancy waist-line. And only sixty-two inches tall, she thought wryly.

She rubbed the stretch marks gently, her only physical acknowledgment of the existence of her son. She wouldn't erase them if she could. It would be like denying Nathan's life. And it would always serve to remind her of him, no matter what.

She was ravenous again. How could she be? All she did was eat. This place had a tendency to do that to her. Of course, she was much more active here than in her old job in St. Louis, where she worked in a lab all day long.

She picked up her cell phone and checked the battery. She carried it around with her everywhere, just like Hugh had told her to do and it had not rung one single time.

"The story of my life," she chided herself gently. "Waiting for someone to call my number. And the lucky caller is... Ha." Well, at least she arrived at this wonderful place completely on her own and could depart in the exact same manner.

She dressed in a dark golden silk sleeveless sheath and slipping on a heavy gold chain necklace, golden tiger eyes stud earrings and a tiger eye scarab bracelet to match. She left the gold ring on and added her tiger eye ring, carved, of course, in the shape of a tiger. Could be that she had a thing for tigers, hmm? *Wonder why?* she asked herself.

When she opened the door, Jerrod stood with his mouth wide open. He gulped like a teenager and stuck his hand out with another bouquet of lovely exotic flowers again.

"You are stunning, I'm thinking." He came in the room and took her hand and twirled her around so that he could see her from all sides.

"Yes, ma'am. I surely am glad that you have come to me here. Come to *be* here. That color sets off your sun kissed hair and your golden skin. Wow. It's proud I am to have you as my date this evening. I just don't do justice to you." His sparkling blue eyes and his roguish grin were in full force, at least a hundred watts.

"Oh, I don't know, you look fairly good to me. Rugged. Handsome. *And* definitely full of blarney. But a woman likes to hear a little compliment occasionally. I am starving so please tell me that we don't have far to go." Tilting her head, she checked out the width of his big strong shoulders and the dark hair curling over his crisp white shirt collar.

"That straight little dress does nothing to hide your curves. It makes my hands itch."

"What? Your *hands* itch?"

"Yes. To get my hands on you. Um, it's an old saying. Don't mean it. Well, yes I do, but I know not to push you, right?"

Jerrod saw the fire in her eyes and wanted to keep from getting her temper up, even if he did like fire in his women. It showed strength, and a challenge he couldn't resist. He bowed to her, pointing at the door and couldn't take his grin from his face.

"I'm taking you this evening to a pricey little place on the eastern end of the island at the Grand Palazzo Hotel. You will like its elegant renaissance architectural style nestled on Great Bay overlooking the island of St. John."

"You sound like a tourist brochure!" She pointed a finger at him.

"Well, I did study one. Just wanted to impress you." He scuffed his foot like a kid.

She decided to give him a break. But he was right. The charming, warm service of Caribbean hospitality, and the fantastic view matched the setting of this grand old place.

Lori stuffed herself to the gills with a sumptuous huge shrimp cocktail and a cold dill salmon mousse salad. She moaned when they brought out a shrimp scampi so rich, it was swimming in a rich garlic butter sauce, served over a bed of brown rice. The next course was a delightful fruit and cheese plate with hot Brie.

The dessert tray presented was so elaborate that she had to pass it up. She simply couldn't choose. Besides she was so full that she had trouble breathing.

Jerrod, the courtly gentleman, relished catering to her every need. He enjoyed the many admiring looks cast her way. Who could blame them? After all he could not take his eyes off her either. She was a great looking lady when she'd come to St. Thomas but she positively bloomed since then, and he was crazy about her.

He was ready to move to the next level with her but he was not sure how to proceed. He'd been too far removed from the dating game. His strong instincts couldn't be denied for long. Aching to hold her close, he felt like a teenager in severe lust. With her he definitely needed control because his hands *did* itch to hold her. He would admit it to himself anyway.

Lori, oblivious of the strangers' stares, was quite aware of Jerrod. He was so very non-threatening and easy to be with. He made her laugh and she knew that quality was important in any relationship. Funny, but she began looking at him in a new light. Warm, intelligent and handsome in a very rugged masculine way.

His features were as Irish as they come, dark curly hair and heavy brows, a strong Roman nose and a generous smile that lit up his face like a spotlight. His dark suntanned face contrasted starkly with the crisp white shirt and his vivid blue eyes.

There was much strength in that man, and not just physical, she thought. He exuded strength, character and dependability. She thought it was funny how you could instinctively trust some people when you first meet them. Jerrod... Benjamin... Miss Genny... Hmm...

Brought out of her reverie, she took her hand from under her chin when he refilled her champagne glass again. Reaching to cover her glass too late, she asked him, "Captain, if I didn't know better, I would think you are trying to get me drunk. But you *wouldn't* be doing that now, I'm thinking, *would you?*"

"Of course not. I'm thinking, you looked thirsty after all that food that you just put away."

She choked on a mouthful of champagne while laughing, then threw her napkin at him after she wiped her mouth. "You rogue." She retorted when she managed to get the words out.

"But I do not *like* a dainty eater in a woman. Seriously. A woman who picks at her food has no appetite for life or anything else, I'm thinking. Too prissy for my taste. *And* too cold. I mean it. Brrr. That kind of woman makes me shiver."

He shivered and made a face to make his point. "On the other hand *you* eat like you mean it. Like you love food *and* life."

"Thanks a lot. Make me sound like I eat like a horse."

"Would you like to take a walk around the point to help settle your dinner and make room for dessert? It is a lovely night, I'm thinking. No moon 'till dawn, but the sky will be full of exquisite stars and the evening will be as enchanting as you are." His eyes gleamed in anticipation of a cozy walk and with *no Jake* on guard this time.

His wonderful wide smile was inviting as sunshine is to a sun worshiper.

The walk down to the eastern end of the island exposed them to a chilly breeze blowing off the Atlantic. Lori shivered at the sudden drop in the air temperature. It was the coolest night since she arrived at the islands. Already her blood was warming and adjusting to the temperate climate.

Jerrod watched her reaction, placed his arm around her shoulders and pulled her in closer to help keep her warm. He didn't have a jacket on or he would give it to her.

Reaching the pure white beach almost glowing in the dark with white frothy breakers gently rolling in, they stopped to take their shoes off. The Captain looked approvingly at her tanned bare legs and held her hand to help her maintain her balance as she kicked off her sandals. He placed them above the high tide line and maintained a firm grip on her hand, not giving her the option of letting it go.

Walking the beach, away from the hotel lights and sounds, they listened to the sound of the waves as melodic accompaniment in tune with their thoughts. They were as comfortable in each other's silence as they were in each other's presence. It gave them both food for thought. A newborn awareness dawned of yet another dimension to share between them.

Boats passed offshore and lights twinkled in the distance where the dark mountainous form of St. John melded into a blur of water and sky. The quiet sounds surrounding them were the sounds of the earth, wind and sea.

The wind rustled through the thick fringe of tree line above them, while the waves beat their constant crescendo of rhythmic pounding surf. Night birds warbled a quiet soulful melody but the sounds of mankind were expunged from the earth.

It was as though they had been dropped off the face of the earth. A pair of people alone. The sky was bright and full of stars. Unshed tears of the night. Each one glowed brighter and larger than they had ever shone in St. Louis. There appeared to be many, many more. Lori searched for the stars that held her loved ones souls. And waited for that special brilliance from them to catch her eye.

Jerrod watched Lori's eyes shimmer a reflected glow from above. Jerrod pulled her closer. He sensed a melancholy yearning in her face. He stopped walking, turned her to face him and stroked her cheek gently with his thumb. "You have no idea how beautiful you are, do you? How many people stop and look at you after you pass, wondering who you are? There is some inner fire within bursting to get out. Some kind of magnet that makes everyone want a part of you or a piece of your heart or both. I can't describe it. I don't have the right words. But I want it, too. All of it."

He lifted her chin to share a kiss that was so remarkably gentle. His hand moved to the back of her head. He deepened the kiss and attempted to worm his way into her heart.

Lori accepted the kiss and kissed him back, amazing herself in the process. She stepped into the kiss and allowed him to mold her body to his, while his other hand slid to her lower back across the sensuous silk of her dress. He tasted of salt from the wind and the sea. She felt the comforting strength in his large back muscles and his bulging biceps when she slid her hands to his shoulders.

Spreading his legs in the sand, he gently pulled her toward him, wanting her to know and feel him. He stroked her back and her hair, almost in pain over his own intense need. Keeping her firmly in his grasp, he lowered his hands to her hips.

She felt her body responding to his masculinity. Her nipples gently brushing his chest were suddenly tender and hard. His kiss was drawing her into a vortex of sensation as his tongue invaded her lips and drew her own tongue into a waltz of dizzying intensity. Her heart rate accelerated proportionally as she felt his broad chest throbbing violently beneath his rippling rib cage.

Jerrod's arms possessively encircled her in a strong clinch, determined that the time was now approaching. He could feel her response. It took all his willpower not to take her right now.

He wanted this woman and he fought to maintain control. Jerrod knew there was fine line she must cross first. He finally came up for air then began bombarding her face with kisses, her eyes, her brows, her nose, her cheeks. God, he was crazy for this woman.

A horn sounded out on the water as a large cruise liner rounded the point, departing St. Thomas for the Atlantic.

Startled, Lori stepped back, withdrawing both physically and emotionally from Jerrod's grasp. Her pulse slowing, she looked up into his eyes and regained control of her senses. She could see the muscles twitching at his temples and the veins at his temples pounding away. Both his large hands were tightly clenched into fists.

Jerrod recognized he had made a tactical error. He should have pressed his advantage when he was in control. And now it was too late.

She stared at him like a stranger, and wondered if it was temper that he was controlling or only signs of frustrated disappointment?

Lori drew a deep breath and let it out slowly, then shook her head wondering at her lack of control. She knew Jerrod had an attractive appeal from the moment she met him, but she had always been able to remain in total control. And she almost succumbed to overwhelming Irish charm and charisma.

What in the world am I thinking? *That's part of the* problem. *You are not thinking, you're feeling. And you know that's gotten you in plenty of trouble in the past. Get a grip on yourself girl. And I mean now.*

The rest of the world instantly inserted itself on that beach when a horn blared and that almost moment of intimacy passed like the sound into the night...

Thirteen

The sun blazed a splendid trail through the blue sky. Lori prepared to give an early warning alert to Jerrod if he again got inside her personal comfort zone. She had allowed him to get inside that space yesterday and almost faced the consequences of her actions. No denying that it was her fault, but she was determined not let down her barriers today. No way.

She packed her bags for Jerrod to take her home after a day of scuba diving. Now she was ready to get back to the lab and get on with her job.

Overnight she neatly packaged her relationship with Hugh and tucked it into a tiny little pigeon hole. Ready to take it out and examine it at another time like a piece of mail. Lori thought she was back on track again. She'd spent most of a long sleepless night reexamining and reorganizing her priorities. She'd shoved the men in her life onto a back shelf. All of them.

This trip accomplished its purpose and cleared the air in her head, not that Lori would ever admit to being an air head. Rather her brain cells were quite capable of making the right decisions and choices. Yep, no longer would hormones rule her head.

After brunch downstairs in the hotel, she departed in a taxi to meet Jerrod at the dock. She wouldn't meet him for breakfast or let him pick her up at the hotel, but had arranged to meet him instead. Lori could tell he wasn't particularly pleased the way the night ended, but he had backed off anyway and she respected him for that.

At the boat, she handed him her bags before climbing on board.

"Thanks Jerrod, for the ride home. I appreciate it." Her intention was to establish a barrier right from the beginning today. No personal contact would be allowed. Put him in his place as a friend and a mode of transportation. Period.

He jerked his head around to peer at her more closely, getting a *different* Lori somehow. He couldn't see her eyes, but her voice was definitely frosty. He squinted at her and stood with her bags in his hands and cursed to himself in silence.

"I apologize for my behavior last night. I should've been... I'm thinking, I was moving too fast. I let myself be carried away by the moonlight or something... I am sorry."

"There was no moonlight last night Jerrod, only stars." She spoke coolly in a matter of fact voice.

"Yeah, um...well, do you forgive me? Am I cast adrift permanently? Can we go back to where we were? Are we going scuba diving today, like we planned? I've got the tanks filled and ready. You've got your suit and stuff, don't you? Or am I to just take you back home?" He wanted to force her to admit she wanted to spend the day with him.

Lori stood, contemplating whether he would be offended if she truly rebuffed him. Besides she did want to dive at his secret dive site. She finally decided to take down her wall part way but only if he remained on the other side of it.

"Yes. No. Yes. Yes. No. I think I got them in the right order. But, please remember what I told you the first day we met. Don't push." Putting her hand up like a stop sign to confirm what she just told him, Lori reminded him quite clearly to back off and please behave.

He put down her bags and extended his hand to be shaken like they had just met and said. "Peace, then?"

She debated for a moment before she allowed herself to touch him, though it was only a quick handshake. Lori shook his hand briefly and was quite pleased to feel no earth-shattering tingle when their hands met. She felt thankful for that. "Peace, Jerrod." Then, turned around and walked mid boat to climb stairs to the bridge.

He shook his head at her retreating back and kicked his scruffy deck shoe on the boat decking like a recalcitrant boy. He wished he had something much more substantial to kick--like a brick wall.

Well, he could play her game too. He had a year to break down the barriers that she erected since last night. Jerrod almost penetrated the fortress last night. He knew that passion was waiting to bubble up from that cauldron of desire she kept buried deep within her.

Sensing her fears, he also knew she *had* responded to him last night like a flower bud to sunlight. He was more than ready to bet that he could elicit that response again, given half a chance. And he'd be damned if he let anyone else get there first. He wished he had more access to her than he did with her isolated on that damned island.

He went about the business of casting off while mentally fuming about his meager prospects today. After spending a restless night, planning with elaborate detail how he would make love to her today, two cold showers hadn't diminished his desire either.

This morning one brief sentence dashed his plans more effectively than a bucket of water from an iceberg. She would be harder to catch but well worth the chase. Yes sir, a fine catch.

They both were less chummy than yesterday. They circled each other like a Mexican standoff, since she was not ready to give in and he was not ready to give up. A distinct chill quivered in the air as they chatted about weather like two strangers at a party. Slowly, Lori relaxed in Jerrod's presence.

Struggling to find a common ground that was not burdened with quicksand, Lori told Jerrod about her dives yesterday with Billy Bob's group, and about the job offer because of her dolphin conquests.

Soon she had him laughing at her description of the other divers' disbelief of her totally unpracticed yet skillful control of the large beasts. How she just happened to swim with them once before and now they knew her anywhere, anytime, whether she was in snorkel or scuba gear. "I just couldn't convince them I wasn't part of the dive. I told them it must have been kismet. Or perhaps the dolphins knew me in another life but they wouldn't buy it. When the Captain offered me a job, they thought that was part of the act, too. I showed them my ID's from Missouri but when I asked them to send me copies of the pictures they were taking to my address on St. Saba, it set them off all over again."

"Well, Lori, I'm thinking, if I hadn't seen it with my own eyes that first time, I wouldn't have been believing it either." Jerrod chuckled.

"Are you up for diving at my secret wreck? That's the plan for today. We can go down through the bottom portal and onto the floor this time. If we swim through the arches of the boat ribs, there's a nice cave where one of the rocks has tumbled part way down on top of another. I've got lights for the shadows the sun casts from the tall rocks ringing the site. There's some interesting species living in there. You'll want to see them, I'm thinking."

He raised a sexy eyebrow in questioning mode.

"Sounds good to me, I'll go down and get ready. But no caves please, I'm claustrophobic of too small places."

The tumultuous sea this afternoon cooled her as she landed on her back in the water. A stiff breeze picked up chilling her more. She had extra gear, since Jerrod provided her with a large detachable light and a big knife besides the weights and camera attached to her belt.

He'd anchored the boat on the leeward side of the rocks this time. She worked harder to stay on the surface and get final instructions.

"Lori, stay close to me. We'll be going around the rocks on a southerly approach and have to swim closer to the surface to get inside the crevice. We'll stay well below the surface until we get there. We shouldn't have any problem fitting in with our air tanks on, but since the waves are rougher today we'll have to time our entrance."

"When I signal you to surface, take my hand at the top so I can lead us in. Once we're inside you can take your time looking out all the peepholes, then we go down to the entrance into the grotto. But be careful. The water is more turbulent today and I'm not sure how long we'll stay down. I need to keep an eye on the weather and I can't when we're down in the grotto or the cave. We cannot surface inside the rocks where the wreck is. We'd surely get pounded to pieces just like that wreckage on the bottom. So no matter what, *do not* surface while we're in there. We can only come back out the same way we go in."

Lori nodded her head at him, put her mouthpiece in, adjusted her mask and turned on her air. She took a few good breaths while listening to his final instructions.

"And keep me in sight today at all times. Don't go off exploring by yourself. I might get an urge to get out of there. So be ready for my signal. Okay?"

He hoped he'd given her enough warnings. There was a storm brewing. He could feel it in his bones. It might not be today or tomorrow, but one was definitely coming. They probably shouldn't dive today, but he knew she would be disappointed. And he wanted to make her happy, since last night's disaster.

They swam to the bottom and she followed his lead but paused to get a fix on direction with her wrist compass and checked the time on her underwater watch. The water depth was twenty-five feet.

Great visibility in the silence of an underwater world with only escaping air bubbles for company, pushed every other thought topside to a distant place in her mind. She allowed herself the freedom to wander in this surreal aquatic portrait of life down under the sea.

She wanted to take off and explore on her own, but instead followed him to the rocks half a mile away. Down here there was no evidence of weather problems. It was as calm as it could be and the schools of fish were busy going about their business ignoring Lori.

She tried to keep close to Jerrod so that he would quit stopping to look back at her. Lori was glad to see the shadow of the rocks looming in the distance and resisted the inclination to explore the pockets of sea life in abundant proliferation beckoning to her.

Jerrod led her around the rock formation and pointed up with his thumb waiting for her to catch up with him before they slowly rose to the surface. He grabbed her hand and searched the sky for any signs of bad weather. Finding none, he waited for the right moment to pull Lori through the hidden crevice and into the small opening in the rocks creating a nice safe pocket. The circling boulders opened only to the blue sky above and the thrashing sea below, protecting the exclusive diving site.

With one last look at the sky he led her down toward the tunnel. He gave her time to enjoy the peepholes on their way down. When they reached the entrance, he went through the tunnel first. Then at the other end he stuck up one finger, then two, then three to signal *'now'* for her to enter the tunnel.

Somehow Lori missed her cue and waited a smidgen too long. She caught the backlash of the waves wrong and tumbled through the tunnel like a bowling ball heading down a gutter. She ejected out of the tunnel in a jumble of arms and legs in forward motion.

Jerrod wanted to put up his hands to catch her but was afraid of ripping her mask or gear off. So she sailed past him and landed on her head on the floor of the grotto twelve feet lower than the tunnel level.

The soft sandy surface moved, constantly in motion from the waves smashing into the rocks through the various openings. Thankfully, there were no rough corals at her impact site to cut her to pieces either. The only damage was her hurt pride. Lori felt herself and her gear to make sure she was all there. Thank goodness, she hadn't landed on the reef and damaged it, too.

Jerrod checked her tanks, gauges, and hoses, and then took her face mask in both hands to pull her face close to him to make sure she was all right. She nodded her head and put her thumb up to signal, okay.

He misunderstood, thinking she meant to rise to the surface and shook his head vehemently pointing his thumb down. Circling her forefinger back to her thumb, she gave him an okay sign. He nodded. His eyes crinkled in a smile through his mask at her.

After such a shaky start, she displayed more caution than she probably would have. Exploring the wreck with fish darting among the corals, she paused to take a picture of Jerrod standing in an arch with his arm outstretched, leaning on it like he would lean on a wall.

The current in the grotto's center was not nearly as strong. The multitudes of small colorful tropicals ignored the rougher tempest at the top and swam lazily in their quest for food. Hundreds of darling little seahorses anchored by their tails wrapped around sea feathers swaying in the motion of the water.

Under a ledge surrounded by bivalve shells hid a small brown octopus with three-foot long legs. Its eyes projected from his body keeping a watch on her so Lori took his picture, too.

She wanted to laugh at a funny faced spotted trunkfish. It maneuvered with most comical movements, its pectoral fins lashed back and forth so fast they almost blurred. For all the fish's elaborate fin waving, it remained in almost the same position.

She watched it swim to the bottom to feed, blowing a stream of water at the sand, excavating a hole to expose small crabs or shrimps. If the trunkfish wasn't fast enough, a slippery dick fish shouldered him out of the way and darted in to capture the yummy meal. The way the silly, funny face kept up its pectoral fin motions reminded her of three Stooges' antics. She expected the slippery dick fish to go 'whoop-whoop-whoop' and smack the trunkfish on the head.

Hundreds of species lived in most reef ecosystems, but today there wasn't enough time to stay down and watch them all. Lori followed Jerrod to the entrance under the ledge that he called a cave. But she didn't go in, since many sharp-teethed parrot fish, several large groupers and spiny sea urchins stayed out of the light and movement, deciding not to invade their territory. Lori spent the rest of her allotted time taking photos of the colorful indigenous population moving within the ebb and flow of this hidden reef ecosystem.

Peeling her mask off once she reached the deck of the boat, Lori lay exhausted on a bench breathing very hard. The dive itself wasn't tough, but the distance from the boat that they had to swim underwater away from the rocks wore her out. Still, it was a heck of a lot easier swimming underwater than if they'd swum back on the rough surface with gear on.

Jerrod's excellent conditioning kept his breathing normal. His fitness level obviously exceeded hers. His massive upper body muscles dominated his torso. She looked him over as her respiration slowed to a more normal rate.

Lori reached for her cell phone to make sure it was still operational and found no indication of any calls. She didn't know whether to be relieved or ticked off at Hugh. And right now her energy level was so doggone low, she was neither.

Jerrod slipped below to the galley to bring up deli sandwiches loaded with cold cuts and cheeses on freshly baked baguettes, huge dill pickles and a gallon jug of cold iced tea. A bottle of wine was chilled down there too, ready to pop its cork. He waffled on whether to serve it, but concluded he had better not push his luck today.

"Time to eat." He announced.

"Thanks Jerrod. I'm always starving after a good swim and that was a bit intense. Don't you think?"

"Are you all right? You didn't get hurt down there in the tunnel did you? You might be sore tomorrow, I'm thinking. Did you bang into anything, besides your head?"

"No, I think I'll be fine. My head's the hardest part of me." Lori said wryly.

"Yeah, it's a good thing, I'm thinking. That was one of the funniest things I've seen in a long time, since you didn't get hurt I mean. You were coming out of that tunnel like you'd been shot from a cannon in a circus act. It's good that you had a soft landing. I was afraid that you had all the air knocked out of your lungs and were going to be in trouble." An irrepressible grin transformed his face.

She responded to that smile in same measure. "Boy, that long swim both ways manages to take it out of you, doesn't it?"

Grabbing a sandwich, she opened it to squirt hot mustard and vinegar on it. She poured a tall glass of tea and began munching away.

"Mmm, good. I might be a little sore later. My shoulders and neck banged a bit on the tunnel." She stretched out one arm, then the other, and then forced her head down to each shoulder and into a circle. "They're a little tight feeling."

"Let me loosen them up a bit."

His blue eyes gleaming, he put his food down and went behind her to place his big warm hands on her shoulders. He began to firmly massage them. Stroking her slender neck, his large thumbs pressed gently on the soft pale skin under her damp fringed hair. He stroked in a downward motion while resting his hands lightly around her neck. His touch was quite tender. He kept up the motion until she shivered and the hair stood up on the back of her neck.

Jerrod smiled to himself because he was enjoying this every bit as much as she was. His hands moved down to knead her shoulders. He traced his thumbs down each side of her spine as far as her swimming suit allowed and with increasing pressure pulled them back up the same path. Placing his palms flat against her back he slowly pushed them outward from the center and lifted them and started all over again from the top of her neck down.

By the time he completed the round one more time, Lori felt like a delicious puddle of molten muscle and bit back a groan.

A clap of thunder way off in the distance interrupted his delicious backrub.

Lori turned out of his reach. Jeez Louise, all her good intentions to keep his paws off of her and out of her space had obviously gone awry.

"Thanks Jerrod, that was great." After putting a definite end to that, she deliberately pulled on a coverup.

"They probably still have horse liniment on the island, if you stiffen up too much. They used to keep horses there before the golf carts turned out so handy. It smells terrible but works well with bruises and sore muscles. Of course, there won't be anyone there to apply it for you, I'm thinking."

Laughing at him she had to say, "And maybe, no doubt you'd be applyin' for the job, I'm thinking?" mimicking his brogue.

"Well, it's a stinky job but *somebody* has to do it." A contagious grin dominated his face again. He shrugged his immense shoulders, spreading his hands out, palm up at her.

"Oh, Jerrod, you are a piece of work. Can't be denying that." Shaking her head and returning to her sandwich, she kept watch on the building clouds and Jerrod in his place. Out of her reach.

Fourteen

Overcast, cloudy days crossed the sky but the rain only threatened. It was the very first time since Lori had arrived in the islands that the constant display of perfect weather was in any way diminished. Until now, the rain fell at night or early morning and the clouds had simply blown away with the rise of the sun. The range of temperature remained in the pleasant sixties, but the lack of sunshine was a bit strange.

Lori found the strange greenish gray skies to be daunting, reminding her of dark tornado weather back in the Midwest. The cloud cover didn't appear as dense as there. But the sun didn't penetrate its barrier. She continued swimming twice daily laps in the lagoon, but kept a constant eye on the sky. She didn't put as much energy into swimming as usual either.

The lagoon lost its lovely azure allure and assumed the same ugly, gray shades as above. Her own spirit tended to mimic them both, particularly when she heard Hugh was back.

Hugh attended the party at Miss Genny's with the wicked witch of the West, which was how Lori increasingly thought of Sheree. How in the world one person could make such a negative impression? Yuck.

Steffan wanted to start sketching her this week but put it off until later in the week. He needed sunshine he said, which was fine with her anyway. She certainly didn't feel photogenic or whatever. Lord knows she needed the sunshine, too.

As usual when she was low, she threw herself into her work. Waiting for Hugh to show his face was not allowed on her daily agenda. She mapped statistical data on the fish normals. Lori tried an overlay of maps on the coordinates where the dead fish sightings had been previously reported.

She recorded facts pertaining to them, time of day, day of the month and week, temperatures. Anything that could possibly relate she fed into her laptop computer. She made charts, tables and graphs and photographed the normal tissue samples to record on CD-rom, and stored everything in her computer.

Lori also kept a backup copy of her work, both in print and in her log book. Daily, she faxed a set of her records back to her computer at the lab in St. Louis. She had learned the hard way over the years that you can't have too many copies of your work. Of course, she had the originals of the work here and all the slides, but better safe than sorry, right?

Finally the preparation time paid off. The signal came a couple days after her return to the island.

A golf cart came flying down the hill to the station with Jake bounding after it at full speed. The driver was a farmer who kept the vegetable gardens and was waving his hat and yelling as he came. "Miss Lori!" he yelled.

"U.S. Navy ship man! To de warehouse, a sighting of floaters! At 40kilom N of 18 degree N and 20kilom W of 65 degree W say man!" He talked so fast Lori couldn't begin to understand his Carib chatter.

He was so excited that they barely could get him to slow down enough to give them the specifics. Luckily, Benjamin was there to interpret. Ben pulled up a chart and told her the location "Approximately 2 miles east of the island of Culebra, Puerto Rico."

In their eagerness, Lori almost tripped over Jeremy's and her own feet in her eagerness to begin gathering the necessary bundles of prepackaged equipment and chemicals.

Jake chased them to the boathouse and jumped aboard. Benjamin piloted the launch while Lori set up for their work down below. The ride was rougher than usual so she left the scalpels and some of the lighter equipment in their boxes. She went back up on deck with her diving gear and the nets for Benjamin to gather the fish while she checked out the subsurface area, in case the fish had drifted too much since they died.

She recorded data, air temperatures, weather conditions, any geographical or topical information that could be pertinent. The floaters were right where reported. No significant tide today and although the waves rolled, there was no appreciable wind on her face.

"Benjamin, drop an anchor. Sound for the bottom and record the water depth. Take a temperature reading here on the surface and check the bottom for anything unusual with the sonar. While you collect surface samples, I'm going down."

"I won't be long and since I am going alone, I'll take a line tied to my waist. If I don't signal you every five minutes, pull me back up slow. I don't think there will be any problems, but just in case. How deep is it here, twenty-five or thirty feet? I'll stay just long enough to look around, see the reef. Do temperature probes. Things like that. I can't believe the time is here!"

She strapped on her gear and checked her tanks. She spit in her mask to keep it from fogging over. As she sank into the depths, the last thing she saw was Jake's silly face, hanging over the edge of the boat watching her. Lori did a number of temperature checks and swam a wide pattern grid on the bottom but didn't observe anything unusual on this small reef.

There were plenty of open and turtle grass patches so she swam in increasingly larger circles. About to surface, her peripheral vision spotted a bright blue something snagged on coral by a rocky ledge. She swam over to investigate and found some kind of torn material, maybe from a plastic tarpaulin. She carefully disengaged it from the branch of staghorn coral, put it in a belt pouch, checked her diving watch for time down and slowly started back.

Benjamin collected an assortment of reef fishes, larger species of parrots, clowns and damsel fishes but also an abundance of smaller varieties of wrasses and sergeant majors. He examined the fish externals and waited for her to begin the actual necropsy.

When she returned to the boat, she carefully examined the samples under the illuminated magnifying glass. "Thanks Benjamin, it's a great start. I didn't see anything down there. Do you think that you got a good representative sampling?"

"Yes ma'am."

"Only a few of the larger fish? Did you find some partially eaten? Were there any observations that seemed odd to you?"

"We need to make sure that our observations are all recorded. Have you started the journal entry on paper or computer? Would you place all the samples that you have examined in that large tub of formalin? Sorry, I'm talking so much that I'm not giving you a chance to respond. Just like Miss Genny, huh? I'll shut up now. I promise." Lori grinned in apology.

"Yes ma'am, to all of your questions. Started the log in the book first. Do you want me to record as we go? Or to examine, then necropsy beside you? We need to keep an eye on the weather, too. The sky looks like bad weather coming."

"Based on what I see here, and the volume we need to get through, let's both get to work. I'll number mine A's. You use

B's. I'll set up the foot pedal recorder to free our hands and when you need to record an anomaly, tell me and I'll tap it on. Each fish that looks normal we'll say then make a transcript later to put in the journal and computer. Let's go, and don't forget to examine each orifice and gill slits, before we begin cutting them. If you have any questions just fire away."

They set to work with a vengeance down in the tiny galley area of the launch, giving every animal a close examination under the magnifier before dissecting and placing them in small prelabeled baggies.

"Benjamin, let's examine them randomly, but add a letter at the end of the number to denote the species, P for Parrotfish, D for Damsel, etc. You know what tissue samples that we need. You've already drawn random serums, haven't you? And placed them in the fridge? I almost forgot them. I'm so excited that we finally get a chance at this."

"Yes, ma'am. As many as we had prepped tubes for."

"Great, I guess that we can't match them to the corpse, can we? I should have made tags to identify them as we work."

"I put an X on their body below their dorsal fin with a magic marker."

"Benjamin, you're the greatest. That'll be a great help. We'll just add an X on the tissue bag, too. Saved again."

For the next couple hours the number of animals floating in the solution continued to shrink and the pile of plastic bags piled up higher. The weather maintained a dismal outlook but nothing ever seemed to precipitate. A couple of times the boat rolled hard enough to get their attention but they looked out at the sky and kept plugging away.

Lori glanced at Jake, who kept watch over them from the top of the stairs.

The only unusual thing that caught their attention was some of the smaller fish had eggs attached or eggs in their mouths. It was spring and time for nesting for many species. There was nothing remarkable about that. Lori collected samples of the eggs anyway.

They returned to St. Saba with a full load of specimens to haul back to the lab for processing. Both were physically and mentally exhausted from keeping balance while the boat rocked to the waves and concentrating on their work.

That night, every time Lori closed her eyes and tried to go to sleep, the sensation of rocking was so great that she immediately opened her eyes to reestablish that she was on solid ground. She finally got up, made herself a cup of hot cocoa and carried it outside to drink.

She blew into her cup cooling it and patted Jake on the head while he sat beside her. "Did you miss me too, old boy?" He had stiuck close to her since her return from St. Thomas, except for meals.

"Good boy, Jake," she murmured.

She sat with her feet pulled up underneath her and watched the dark waves out at sea, hoping to be lulled by the motion and the hot milk. A strange sensation prickled at the back of her neck as though she was being watched. The hairs on the back of her neck stood at attention. Startled, she cast uneasy glances around. She felt very exposed tonight for some reason. She saw or heard nothing. Jake sat calmly beside her so it must be her imagination playing tricks on her.

The lights were off in the cabin and everything in her line of sight was dark and silent. She looked back toward the trees above the station, but she could only hear the soft rustling of the wind in the trees behind her.

The white pointing curve of beach glowed eerily in the dark surrounded by the darker sea inundating it from three sides. Her ears were awash with gentle sounds of the water making its nightly trespass upon the spit of land that was the island's end...

~ * ~

Working hard building up their evidence, they processed the organ samples step by step into mounds of paraffin cassettes. It took three days to embed all the samples and ready them for the next step of sectioning the tissues. Lori decided on a ribboning technique rather than a single section to be mounted since many of the tissues were so minute.

She didn't want to take a chance on wasting any sample. It would mean more slides and lots more microscope work but she thought it would be worth it. On bigger fish, the tissue samples would be large enough for one representative single section per tissue to suffice, hopefully.

Lori was deep in concentration and submerged in work when the door to the lab opened and Steffan walked in. She almost jumped out of her skin. She was used to Jake and Benjamin for company. No one else *ever* ventured into the research station domain before.

Lucky for her, she wasn't operating the microtome or she might have cut herself badly. Her hand flew to her throat and she let out a little scream. Jake stood up, stretched his broad back and walked over to Lori's side before Steffan approached her. The big dog remained silent.

"Hallo. Hallo. Didn't mean to frighten you. Just wanted to see your petite shop in action. I heard you had a chance to work, so I came by to see you. Where is Benjamin? I thought he works with you?"

"Sorry about the yell. I'm not used to company. I sent him to pick up supplies. We've been going through chemicals this week and needed to replenish stock. Yes. Now we find out if we can solve the puzzle. It's very exciting. I've been here more than six weeks and this is the first time we've received an alert."

"*Oui*, that is why I am here. Show me everything you do and why you do it. I am very curious to see you in action. Tell me everything." Rubbing his chubby little hands together, he caught her enthusiasm.

Steffan's portly little figure reminded Lori of a fat rosy-cheeked elf. He only needed pointed ears and shoes to complete the picture. She let her enthusiasm carry her away and gave him a complete tour of the lab, showing him every step in the process. She presented a thorough rundown on what they accomplished so far and what they planned to do. He followed her around, asking intelligent questions and seemed to absorb the technical data Lori tried to generalize for him. He was a good listener.

Lori was pleased to share information with someone as interested as he was. Steffan nodded continually and prodded her on until she had disclosed the anticipated results. By the time Lori finished, he had a general idea of the lab operation.

As he left, he stopped at the door and said. "Do not forget you promised to sit for me. Will tomorrow at four be good for you? I want to use the evening sun, I think or maybe the morning, whichever is more yellow. Let us sketch first in the evening. Then I shall decide which light I would rather use.

"Do you happen to have a large scarf or sari in yellows and browns, a jaguar or leopard print? If you do not, then never mind I will have it sent for. Tomorrow, yes? At four, here on your end of the island. I will bring what I need. You bring yourself, *oui*?"

"Sure, Steffan. Four will be fine. I don't know if I have what you need, maybe a tiger wrap. I'll have to look and see if I brought it. I think I did, but I haven't used it yet."

He must have walked because she didn't hear a cart departing when she went back to work. By the time Benjamin returned, she had made good progress on slide production. He began placing the glass slides into the dryer racks for her.

Stopping to take a break, she watched Benjamin cut tissue sections at 4 microns thickness, then float the sections onto a clean water bath before he picked them up onto a glass slide. He carefully stood each slide on end, allowing the excess water to drain off onto a paper towel before Lori put them in racks to dry.

She kept a vigilant eye on his work but he was as meticulous as usual and needed no further instructions from her. "Ben, you are doing great!"

He grinned his thanks at her.

She told him of the surprise visitor and his interest in their work. Since he was their first and only visitor to the lab since she arrived and she was perplexed at the lack of interest of the rest of the community. So she asked Benjamin about it.

"Well, Miss Lori, it's not you. There's been so many people here doing research over the years the islanders kinda take the station and the scientists for granted. Sometimes there have been two groups a year here. Even two groups simultaneously. Then they are gone. No one has ever stayed a whole year before. If you do, you'll be the first."

"And no one ever came alone before. So you are a little unusual in that respect, too. The researchers studied some weird stuff like micro algae, butterflies, bird migrations, weather and water temperature, to name a few. Most kept apart from the islanders except for Miss Genny's parties. No one escapes those no matter who they are. In fact you're the first ever allowed to miss one."

"Whoops. I've escaped a party. Hope that doesn't blacklist me. She's a wonderful lady and I wouldn't want to hurt her feelings. Maybe I'd better go visit her to make up for that."

"Don't worry. *No one was ever* excluded from her party list. Miss Genny *does* love a party. She loves people and cares about all of us. Even the revolving research station population whoever they are. She loves a visitor, second only to a party. I think she gets very lonely here, compared to her life in France."

"You mean that in all the years there's been a station here, there hasn't been more interaction between the two groups? How strange."

"Not really, just like the tourists on the main island. They come, do their thing, and split." He shrugged his thin shoulders. "The house guests blend more, but then I guess they would. They generally stay longer and are in closer contact to islanders. The painter has been here off and on for many years."

"But Benjamin, I'm making friends here. For life I hope."

"Then *you* are the rarity, Miss Lori. And Jake knows that, too."

"WOOF." Jake added his two cents worth to the conversation while he was lying on the floor, making Lori and Benjamin crack up at him. And they thought all this time he had been snoozing.

"That dog makes my day. He's so funny, aren't you old boy?" said Lori laughing until tears ran down her cheeks. Jake came over to her and put his enormous muzzle up to her and tried to lick her tears. "I'm okay, you silly old dog. I'm just laughing." Lori pushed him away, but not before giving him a hug first.

Fifteen

The next afternoon promptly at four, Steffan showed up at her cabin with his artist case and portfolio to begin sketching her. He fussed and fiddled with her position for almost an hour before he finally began. He placed her on a porch rattan chair with the slanting sunlight casting long shadows behind her.

Jake kept his usual silent watch, and Benjamin watched for a bit too, until returning to the lab to finish work for the day. Lori tried to send him home, but he wasn't ready yet. He was as anxious as she was to get answers.

Steffan was satisfied with a large tiger scarf that Lori used as a shawl. He draped it around her, exposing one shoulder and one arm, artfully arranging it in folds around the rest of her. Finally, he began to draw.

It seemed to Lori he went through page after page of sketches in his book. Modeling was boring, sitting there doing nothing, and trying desperately not to move too much or he would begin yelling at her in French.

Jake came over, slid his big head under her hand that was out of sight and nudged her hand so that she would pet him on the sly. The big goofy dog sat next to her with a silly grin on his face that did not escape the artist's attention.

Steffan's pudgy face contradicted his sharp glance. So one sketch included the massive black and brown head looking up at

Lori adoringly. The artist muttered to himself as he worked and left Lori's thoughts to wander with the winds.

Her thoughts drifted a natural course back toward Hugh. She hadn't seen a sign of him since she returned.

Her uneasiness continued and she still didn't know why. Occasionally, she felt as though someone watched her but she didn't see any evidence of it. She almost felt like she was being stalked, but that was ridiculous on an island of this size. Besides, she didn't feel threatened, just eyes upon her. Once, coming out of the water after a swim, she thought she heard movement over by the lab but she never saw any indication of anyone there.

She thought it must be Hugh. When the apprehension of eyes upon her appeared, the temptation to give him the international symbol of disrespect 'the finger' almost won. But she decided that it was beneath her.

Lori sighed and felt her eyes filling in a blast of anger. She would out wait him and display her ladylike wrath upon him in person. That is whenever the cad had enough nerve to show his miserable face again. *IF* he ever showed up again. After all, it could be another twenty years to see his face with his record. The next time could find her in a geriatric unit. She snorted.

Over a course of days, Steffan showed up to work and drew sketches with an absorption in which only artists can lose themselves. He muttered in French to himself and his pencils. Sometimes he sat motionlessly for long periods. Other times his eyes searched the sky and colors of the sun and shadows, she guessed for inspiration. He stopped and rearranged her now and then, but otherwise he kept busy.

Lori was curious to see his portraiture work. She had seen samples of his work before, but only the lovely pastel watercolor landscapes and seascapes on display or for sale at St. Thomas. Some adorned the walls of various houses here on the island.

172

Two bright tropicals hung inside in her own living room. One landscape portrayed gently swaying palm trees over a sandy beach, the other tropical flowers in a riotous burst of color amid lush green foliage.

Lori sat entranced by the sun's nightly rapid descent from the sky and watched the lighting diminish accordingly. *The closer to the equator, the faster the sunsets, and if you blink, you miss them*, she thought. One moment the sun blazed with a golden red fire and the next, it was gone. Lori enthralled with the sights of sunset, found each to be a momentous occasion of glory.

"Lovely isn't it?" she murmured.

Steffan stared at her. Her hand cupped her chin and her eyes reflected the last golden rain of sunlight. *"Oui,* to be sure, madam. *Magnifique. Certainement.* I am quite pleased with my work today. Saturday, may we begin to paint? I will decide before then whether to use morning gold or evening bronze. Oh, I must decide but I will let you know. What will you do now? It is too late to go back to work now, is it not? Would you like to join me for dinner?"

"Thank you, but I need to swim now, before it gets too dark. Maybe another time. I must make sure that Benjamin has gone home. Sometimes he forgets the time and works too long. I haven't heard him leave yet so I should check on him."

"And how is your work doing? Are you making any progress? Where did you collect your fish from? Where were they spotted this time?"

"Just east of Culebra, a couple miles. There was an enormous amount of the floaters. It was quite amazing to see. And quite alarming."

"How very interesting. Culebra, *oui*?" He displayed a puzzled expression on his face.

"Yes, we've been charting the sighting locations, in case there is any kind of discernable pattern, but so far we can't seem to tie them together. The location is in close proximity to the past sightings and they seem to occur after a new moon. Which is strange in itself and lends a hypothesis of an unnatural occurrence. It's a challenge, but we are digging away at it."

Steffan packed up his work before Lori had an opportunity to casually get over to where he sat and try to get a peek of the sketches. Mumbling to himself, he waddled up the hill into the woods like an overweight porcupine with his case under his arm. Lori shook her head at herself for animating him, but she couldn't help it. He was such an odd little man. Jake stretched and followed him, after all it *was* time for dinner.

~ * ~

Saturday was brighter with more periods of sunshine, but there were storms out in the Atlantic effecting both the weather on St. Saba *and* Lori's gloom and doom. She sat for Steffan again, this time in early morning sunlight, over which he was ecstatic. She felt somewhat better with the bright golden glow doing its best to energize her. Apparently an eastern cloud maker kept sending a gray reminder of some bleak portent to come.

The air was thicker than usual, with heavy, salty humidity. So salty she could taste it when she licked her lips. The wind blew a constant flow over the island, keeping the trees in motion, swaying and rustling behind the station. This end of the island, unprotected as it was, bore the brunt of the Trade Winds. The station's three buildings stood isolated on their curving spit of sand.

The wind blew Lori's hair up and back from her face, making Steffan's pencils and brushes seem to fly with the winds today. He had paintbrushes sticking in both hands, in jars, between his fingers and out of his mouth. He was a whirlwind of motion himself.

He maintained a constant mutter under his breath. Strange little noises came deep from his throat as he worked. Sometimes grunting, sometimes snorting and sometimes he giggled to himself, a silly little "tee hee hee." She half-expected him to rub his pudgy hands together and jump up and down with glee. His appearance did not coincide with his artistic skills. He was amusing to watch, almost like a little cartoon character. Elmer Fudd maybe, after he trapped Bugs Bunny.

A couple hours into the session, Lori had a difficult time keeping her pose for several reasons. But mainly because Hugh quietly strolled up to her porch, dropped down into one of her rockers and casually swung one leg over the arm kicking his foot lazily in circles.

Hugh compared, first glancing at the painting and then staring at Lori.

Steffan frowned at the intrusion but kept working anyway.

Lori had to question his presence. "Mr. Richaud, what brings you on your first visit to the research station? Is there anything that I can help you with?"

She glared in open animosity at Hugh's golden stare. He devoured her with his eyes.

Feeling tension in the air, Steffan looked up expectantly tilted his head like Jake, waiting for the answer. His beady little eyes darted back and forth between their faces and the expressive pair of eyes locked on each other, and watched their interplay.

Hugh looked away first, as he pointed to the palette and paint paraphernalia spread encircling the artist.

"I could not resist seeing the great artist in action. Might want to purchase some of his art work. I enjoy his landscapes and want to see if his portraits also live up to his standard of excellence, he has such a lovely model." He doled out excessive compliments in an attempt to spread oil on the waters he could see boiling in Lori's face.

"Such flattery. How nice," she said crisply and turned back to the painter.

Steffan knew there was an undercurrent he couldn't put a finger on. It distracted him from his work. He could feel JeanPaul's eyes on both him and Lori and he did not like it one bit. He progressively painted slower and slower until his work ground to a complete halt. He took his time cleaning his numerous paintbrushes and set his canvas inside its case to protect it while it dried and to keep prying eyes away from it. JeanPaul had already seen more of his work in progress than he was willing to share right now.

"How about that dinner date this evening, *ma cherie*? Like you promised me, *oui*?"

Looking directly into the embers of Hugh's glowing eyes, Lori was forced to accept if only to aggravate him. "Certainly, Steffan. What time would you like me?" She smiled brilliantly at the artist. "May I help you clean your brushes? Do you need any help with anything else?"

"Eight this evening, if it is not too late? And no, I do not need anything here. I am self, uh...self-sufficient, I think is the word, with my *petite* box." He smiled back at her.

"Then if you two will excuse me, I will swim now."

She swept away from them into the cabin trailing her tiger scarf behind her with both pairs of the men's eyes following her every move. The men sat expectantly as if time stood still. Neither was doing anything but watching the door, waiting for her to reappear. Even Jake sat immobile, waiting with them.

Carrying a hat and towel, she totally ignored the men and the impact that she had on them. JeanPaul groaned quietly at the way the leopard print tank suit molded her body to perfection. Steffan googled as she passed.

The men watched her slender yet firmly muscled legs carry her to the water barefoot. As the sun poked out again, she reached up to place her hat on her head giving the men a fine view of her breasts rounding nicely from each side of her ribs. Neither took their eyes off her as she headed west to the lagoon.

Jake jumped up and followed her, kicking up sand from behind his big feet as he ran to beat her to the water. Not until her body was almost totally submerged as she smoothly stroked her way across the lagoon swimming parallel to the beach did each man's eyes assume a more normal focus.

Jake ran and splashed at the edge of the water keeping pace with her laps, turning back only when she did.

Steffan cleared his throat and began cleaning his brushes again, humming, his thoughts elsewhere, intentionally ignoring the presence of JeanPaul.

JeanPaul stayed in his position, his attention diverted to the little man working before him. He wished to quiz him. Hell, he wanted to third degree the little twerp but wasn't sure he could pull it off at the moment.

Steffan appeared irritated and successfully snubbed him. JeanPaul stared intently and decided that another time would be better, perhaps less animosity would be evident then. The artist was a sticky prickly pear at the moment, not liking his work interrupted. Well, who could blame him? He sure wouldn't like anyone intruding on his time with this lady either.

So JeanPaul sat, planning to delay his departure until *after* the little man left, no matter how long it took. One of them would have to give and it definitely would not be himself. He had the rest of the day to sit there if he had to, so he might as well make himself comfortable. He moved the rocker to better face the lagoon, stretched his legs out in front of him. He crossed his arms on his chest, returning to his former position of watching Lori in silence.

Steffan placed each cleansed brush back inside his case and soon had nothing left to do. He also sat there watching Lori and Jake. After a short period he began fidgeting and could no longer just sit there. He fumed at the intrusion and his only silent adieu to JeanPaul was a curt nod of his head when he stood to leave.

As Steffan left, JeanPaul grinned at his departing back. He sat for over an hour, waiting while Lori gave herself a thorough workout. He too, was fidgeting by the time she came up out of the water like a water nymph, with water streaming off of her in small liquid rivers.

JeanPaul sighed and braced himself for trouble. She was the softest, most giving woman he had ever met. He also knew that she had steel within her as fine and sharp as the pair of Toledo steel knives hidden in his cabin.

She took her time returning to the cabin and when he stood blocking her front door, she sidestepped around him and attempted to walk inside to take a shower and get out of her wet suit. She said not one word to him, so he didn't speak either. Once again he blocked her and devoured her with his eyes searching her face for answers and finding none, searched her body for any telltale signs. Her body gave him the answer he was looking for.

Watching her nipples harden through the wet suit when his eyes stopped at her breasts, he smiled gently. His face lit up like a Christmas tree as he raised his eyes to lock on hers.

Aware of his eyes and their effect, she said. "Trust me. It's only the cool wind chilling me. *It is not you.*" Turning her face away, she marched inside and closed the door firmly behind her.

Jake sat on the porch with his head tilted, somewhat perplexed, either at being shut out or at Hugh's predicament. Hugh didn't know which. He started to put a hand on Jake's head, like Lori always did, but got a growl as he reached his hand out. He withdrew it and put both hands up.

"Okay, you win. I won't pet you, but I am not leaving until I am damn good and ready. So just get used to it, dog." He shook his head. That woman… And that dog!

He began to think the entire afternoon would pass before she'd emerge. Hunger pains started their assault on his senses when she finally appeared, bringing water for Jake but nothing for him.

Lori wore a large T-shirt over cutoff jeans and looked mighty fine to him. She also looked tense, poised to run. Her eyes were a little swollen but that could've been from the salt water since she hadn't worn goggles or mask. It didn't mean she had been crying, he told himself.

She started past him to go back inside when he reached out a hand to her elbow and stopped her. Jake instantly growled low in his throat. He held on anyway and gave the dog a dirty look.

"Lori, we need to talk," he told her quietly.

She looked from her elbow, back up to his face and then down to Jake's upturned face.

"It is all right, Jake. *You, mister* do not have anything to say that I want to hear. I am sick and tired of hearing your words. I see your mouth move and I hear sounds but they have no substance. It's like the adults on Charlie Brown saying 'Wa wa wa wa wah'. Do you know Charlie Brown or were you out of the country? Never mind. It doesn't matter anyway. The sounds could mean anything or they could mean nothing.

"It's all in the interpretation. I hear what I want to hear. Not what you are saying. Or maybe you are saying what I want to hear but not what you mean. Whatever it is, it doesn't matter. I have had it. I've had it up to here." She drew a hand in a straight slash across her throat.

"I refuse to let you hurt me anymore. Enough is enough. I saw you coming off the boat with that witch. I haven't heard from you in weeks. You disappear *again*. With no word and then reappear as though nothing ever happened. For all I know, every single thing you have told me is a lie. Everything..."

She took a deep breath and started again before he had a chance.

"Just back off. I do not need you. I made it a very long time without you and I can do it again. My life has a purpose without you. You know, just like I had a life without you. The world does *not* revolve around you. It never did. And it never will. Do you know that not one single time have you asked me about my son? Or what is important to me? Again. Just you. You. You. Trust only you. Believe only you. Love you. Wait for you. Obey you."

Again she had to pause but pushed her finger into his chest several times to make her point.

"You. Get out of my face. Get out of my way. And leave me alone. Now. I have had quite enough heartbreak in my life, thank you, *and* thanks to you."

She turned sharply and went inside. Jake promptly slid in the door before she had a chance to close it on him. Her heart raced but she was proud of her quiet control. She hadn't raised her voice but succeeded in getting her point across. She went straight to the rocking chair and pulled her feet up under her.

Jake sat at her side, watching her face as cascading tears began a silent journey down her cheeks. She found her chest hurting again with the agony of painful loss, although at least this time it was self-inflicted. And closed her eyes to the hurt.

Hugh stood outside her closed door, momentarily in shock and answered her just as quietly as she had told him off.

"Lori, I left that day because someone came snooping around your cabin after you left. I had to get out. I couldn't get caught here and take a chance on involving you in this deadly game. And it is deadly. One of my men was killed on the docks in Marseilles when an oil tanker from St. Croix docked. A coincidence? I don't believe in coincidences."

"*That's* why I left the island. While I waited for you here, someone came to search your cabin. I couldn't stick around to see who it was because I couldn't be seen. It was more important to protect you. I had no choice but to sneak out a window and I barely made it. I waited up in the trees to see who came out of your cabin but then Benjamin came to the lab and I didn't want him to see me either."

"And yes, I did come back to the islands on a cruise. It was part of my cover. And I told you before that Sheree means absolutely nothing to me. You have to trust me on some things. Is that too much to ask?

"Lori, I will do anything I can to protect you. I am convinced more than ever that I'm on the right track. I am getting close, very close. I came by today to put you on guard. Be extra careful. *Please.* I thought I would slip over while Georges was here and it would appear innocent enough.

"Look, I know that I'm not giving you the answers that you want to hear right now, but when I call you, just get out. We will have plenty of time to talk when this is all over. And remember, I love you. Nothing will ever change that." He spoke softly before he left her alone. Again.

Sixteen

After a few restless days and nights, Lori spent even more time at the lab. She and Benjamin began the final time consuming process of reading the slides, so they could start collating the data they had collected. After dinner one evening she noticed the lights were on in the lab and found Benjamin working away.

So began the habit of spending a couple of hours in the dark room, projecting the slides on the walls, discussing and recording the findings. Although Lori was not a pathologist, she was skilled in reading the slides thanks to extensive training by Dr. Rigby and the medical school. He would do the final evaluations for her.

Finding anything of significance, they photographed the slides with a digital camera mounted on the microscope. They downloaded the pictures into the computer database. Anything Lori found questionable, or needing confirmation, they'd send back to the labs via the computer satellite uplink. They sent back data on a daily basis after they entered it in their log books, both handwritten and backed up on disk.

Lori was concerned at the quantity of male fish in the smaller fish species and wondered at the significance of that. There were almost no females present in the sampling of their selections. It hadn't registered at the time of the actual collections.

She began paying closer attention to the male sexual organs but could find nothing to support a diagnosis on that level. They noted that some gill slits and gill covers appeared swollen and somewhat distended. They recorded visual evidence, per organ, per animal, per species, systematically.

The larger fishes, the parrots and damsels consisted of both sexes and were generally predators of the same smaller fish species that they collected. Nothing other than slightly enlarged mottled livers seemed extraordinary. Lori remarked that commonly happens at death, since livers in all species tend to break down quickly.

Lori suddenly sat up straighter and peered more closely at the slide projection on the wall.

"Benjamin, can you see anything in these eggs? Not in the actual eggs, but look in the medium surrounding them. Something crystalline I think. Do you see it? We haven't noticed it in any of the other egg masses. Can you look up any reference notations on this one that we made when we completed the autopsies? W22B? Was there a serum sample taken of this animal? Do we have the results from the hospitals yet?"

Benjamin went out into the main lab and gathered up the information they already received from the hospital and the autopsy observations. He spread the sheets out for Lori to examine. She spent quite some time studying all the written reports of the initial external and internal examination.

Excited now, Lori pointed her finger at the descriptions that were encoded there. "Ben look here, can you see a pattern? Look, can you see it? Here. There and there. See it?

"There is something showing up in the autopsy reports. I don't know how we missed it at the time. And I don't know what it means yet but it is a start. Can you see it? I'm willing to bet it has something to do with their deaths. Geez, I hope I'm not getting excited over nothing."

Sitting at a desk, she looked up at him expectantly, watching his frowning eyes. Benjamin carefully read through the progression of descriptions over her shoulder. He was meticulous and studied the reports in great detail, displaying a quizzical expression for what seemed like the longest time to Lori. His face suddenly broke into a smile as though a light bulb was turned on in his head.

"The males. Right? The eggs in their mouths? The little ones, they are all mouth breeders? Male mouth breeders? We're seeing something in with the eggs. They're picking up something with their eggs and putting it in their mouths. Do you think that's it? Could we have found it that easily? The first time out?"

She nodded her head at him but needed to caution him. "Whoa, Benjamin. We don't begin to know *exactly* what it is." She held her hand up palm out.

"For all we know, it's sand in there with their eggs. But I do think that sand would have probably washed out of the cassettes in some stage of the processing."

"It doesn't answer the larger fish population's deaths either, unless they're tied together in some finite way. We have a ton of work to do but this could be the break that we are looking for. At the very least, we are doing a good job of correlating the information that we have so far. Before we jump to too many conclusions, let's stop right here and think about what we have found so far."

"This is wonderful. I love this work. Do you think I can be trained to do what you do?"

Lori whirled around in her chair and laughed aloud at him. "Oh, Benjamin, you *are* doing what I do. *And you are great at it.* I have trained lots of technicians and you have caught onto *everything* faster and better than anybody I know."

She stood up and hugged him then danced him around the room like a little kid doing the polka. She led, he followed and soon they were boogying around in the little office space.

Finally, out of breath Lori collapsed back into a chair giggling like a teenager.

"Geez, what will we do when we actually solve this crazy quilt puzzle? Would you want to go to St. Louis and study there? I think I can arrange it for you. You can study with some of the best pathologists in the country. And I can find you a place to live. But there are lots of places for you to train. Of course, you don't have to go all the way to the Midwest. It's such a long way from home for you. Maybe I can get you a scholarship. I'll sure try."

She sat tapping her forehead with a forefinger and thought about his potential.

"Have you ever thought about medical school? Maybe you should be a pathologist yourself and not just settle for being a path technician." She nodded her head. "Maybe we should start preparing you for medical school in our spare time. What do you think about that?"

Benjamin stood in an 'aw shucks' attitude, with his big hands shoved deep in his jeans pockets and shrugged his shoulders at her visionary dreams of his education.

"Okay, it's late. We need to think a bit before we go one step further with this project. Tonight, do me a favor Benjamin. Think about *everything* we talked about here, not just about the fish, okay? You have the potential to be absolutely *anything* that you want to be, Benjamin. I know it, and so should you."

She stood, reached her hand up to pat his shoulder and told him softly. "I believe in you, Benjamin. I believe in you."

She walked back to the desk and turned off the microscope projector light and began gathering the paperwork and slides into an orderly arrangement for the evening storage.

"Take your time and think seriously about your future. You don't have to give me an answer tomorrow or the next day. I'll be around for a while, you know. But I would like a little lead time to get contacts going, *if* you think it's what you want. There's a wonderful six year medical school program in Kansas City that we could get you ready for. Think about it. I won't put any pressure on you. In fact, I won't mention it again until you do, okay?"

Benjamin nodded his head and kept his eyes down.

"It's late. Let's pack it up and go home."

~ * ~

The next morning they spent the first few hours outlining a plan to see how to expand their research parameters on the males and egg samples in question. Benjamin proceeded to make more slides in preparation for extra staining techniques.

Lori called the hospital lab in St. Thomas to see how much serum they had available when they knew what to test for. She decided that they would be backing into an answer based on the results.

"Benjamin, what we are trying to do is prognosticate based on the symptoms that the dead fish exhibited. Which is *not* going to be easy, since there isn't an abundance of signs that are evident postmortem. There may be more that we discover as we go along.

"First, we need to determine what external influence could have caused such an effect on them. When we know that, then we can use the serum analysis to confirm it. Unless we can find an exact sample of whatever is toxic to these animals, we will have to work it out in reverse."

"For instance, we know lead can poison many species. We know it affects the brain and higher functions. And it can accumulate in specific tissues. But we should also find it in the serum levels. Most poisons are detoxified in the liver to some extent or other, since that is one of its main functions. Some poisons are carried through the bloodstream to cause instantaneous cardiac arrest. Like curare for example.

"We have to assume our problem is caused by an unnatural external pathogen since it affects only some specific species. And it does not create a total population wipe out in a certain geographical area, which would happen if for instance, an underwater explosion took place. Am I rambling? Do I make any sense? Anyway, that is why I am leaning toward an external poison of some kind and not just a disease pathogen."

"Some fish species have a very effective way of handling foreign toxicities. Which is why some fish successfully coexist in a symbiotic relationship with the more toxic under water creatures. Like ringed anemones and red snapping shrimp. But other species are more susceptible to exactly the same toxins.

"Pathology is the study of the essential nature of disease, whether it is natural or not. We're playing detective to determine what causes the morbidity of these animals, after the fact obviously. We cannot study any of the sick ones unfortunately, since we don't know how to go about finding them. So we go about it 'bass-ackwards', if you know what I mean."

Benjamin screwed up his face in such a sudden frown that it drew a laugh from Lori.

"Sorry. I forgot that you might not be exposed here to silly old fashioned colloquialisms." After seeing he remained puzzled she countered. "Never mind. It definitely is not important. I suppose you don't know pig Latin?" Now he looked totally confused.

"Pig Latin? Are you jiving me?"

Lori cracked up with laughter. "No. It's not important. Pig Latin is a way of saying things backwards. Well, sort of. Like, my cousin Karen named one of her girls after herself but called her Erin Kay. Get it? My name would be Ori Lay. Sounds trashy, doesn't it?" She raised her eyebrows at him waiting to see if he caught on and finally he starting laughing, too.

"Okay, Miss Lori, I could teach you a new way to speak, too. But trust me, you don't even want to go there. Getting into some of our Carib chatter, you'll think you're on another planet. I could teach you some dances that would give you an education, too."

"Well, I guess that we better not go there now. I don't know if I could handle it. But back to the subject at hand--am I making any sense to you?"

"Yes, but why can't we take the unknown sample that we have and just test it?"

"Test for what, Benjamin? We have an extremely limited volume of material to test. Want to waste it?"

"Uh, well…okay, I get your point. We need to narrow down what to test for, don't we? Until we can come up with something solid."

"Exactly. You know, there's something I'm trying to remember. Something important back there." She tapped her head again. "Something that's waiting to come out but damned if I can extract it right now.

"I'm going to go do some e-mailing and throw out some questions to people I know, and see if we can get any help from back home. You go ahead and complete more sections. Then we'll sit down and do additional charting for the computer to send back. Hey Jake. Been on your rounds today?" She stopped to rub his ears.

She reminded herself to prepare for another sitting tonight. Lori was already slightly tired of the silly business but a promise was a promise. Steffan had been nothing but a gentleman which was a heck of a lot more than she could say about some people. Sometimes he was a little bit nosy about her past but nothing that she could not handle. After all, she was quite curious about life going on here on the island. Not that she'd learned anything of value.

Humph, at least some good was happening here. She was definitely learning to deal with Nathan's loss. She could feel each day was healing her pain and accumulated to the day before. On some days only joyous memories surfaced. And she hoarded those memories like hidden gold.

Even the betrayal by Nick was being pushed further and further into the recesses of her mind and out of her heart's control. She felt the hatred for him dissolving and became more accepting of her share of the failure. It takes two to make a marriage, so it must follow that it takes two to make it fail. She knew she'd married him on the rebound and let him bully her around for all those years.

Who knows? God, divorce was so mental and death so very, very final...

Seventeen

The eerie presence of eyes focused upon her bombarded Lori's senses again. She awoke each morning with an unnatural uneasiness and found herself closing curtains more and more. It was strange to feel totally exposed. She tried to shake it off, but it wouldn't go away. Now she felt fear when she had never before experienced one iota of fear here.

Except for that one night on the beach, thanks again to Hugh. She tried her best to repress a smile at the memory but a small one popped out anyway.

This island seemed so safe, compared to a large metropolitan area, that she hadn't bothered closing her curtains or lock her door, except at night. Now, unless Jake was with her or she was with Benjamin, she spent way too much time looking over her shoulder. An unsettling feeling at best. She didn't like it at all. She considered telling Benjamin but didn't want to sound like a silly goose, since she had absolutely nothing to base it on. Just instinct, or maybe just 'scaredy cat' nerves, she sneered to herself.

At the lab they both were energized now that they were actually getting close to solving the puzzle. It was starting to fit together at last. Lori heard from some of her specialist friends via that wonderful e-mail. Dr. Dana Walker from the San Diego Zoo, had contributed the information that along with mercury, digitalis, methyl bromide, strychnine, and a few other drugs, it was possible for opiates to cause what they'd been seeing. When Lori finished reading Benjamin the message, she suddenly stopped and smacked her forehead with her hand.

"Oh my God, Benjamin have we been dealing with…?"

"Drug trafficking?" He finished for her, excitement in his voice.

"I can't believe it. I mean, I do believe it but…the male mouth breeders must have been picking…"

"It up in their mouths with their eggs." Benjamin completed her sentence yet again.

"And the bigger fish were either ingesting it directly, by eating enough of the small fish or maybe filtering enough in through their gills and mouth to get an unhealthy dose. More important, how did they get it and why was it strong enough to kill? I better get on the line to an investigator I know at the Coroner's office in St. Louis. Maybe she can shed some light on this."

Lori paused, thinking hard.

"Benjamin, we finally have something to test for. This could be it! I'll call Charlotte Amalie and tell them to run a drug panel with any samples large enough. Geez, who'd have thunk it? Fish getting so high that they'd OD. Is this a crazy world or what? Also we will need to determine the actual mechanism that causes the death of the fish." Her mind went off in a million directions at once.

"Miss Lori, do we have to prove how the drug got there? 'Cause that might be hard to do, you know?"

She frowned at him. "Benjamin, what have I told you about my name?"

"Sorry, m…I mean Lori."

"We're partners here, okay? I do not want to have to remind you again. You don't want me to start calling you Mister

Benjamin, do you? No, we don't have to prove how it got there. Just prove that it *was* there and what it did. Geez! That reminds me, what an absolute idiot I've been. I did it again. I *must* have old timers' disease. I will be right back."

Lori ran out of the lab and back to her cabin. She dropped to her knees in the floor of her closet and began rummaging through her basket of swimming gear. She finally came up with her dive belt, and yelled "AHA!"

She tore back to the lab as fast as she could and found Benjamin sitting with his mouth open. Laughing she told him, "Close your mouth before you catch flies." She remembered the night that she met him.

He sat with his head cocked and both of his hands gripping the chair arms, waiting for her next act. The look on his face reminded her of Jake's look sometimes. Maybe it was the soft inquisitive expression in his big brown eyes but she had to hug him, proper or not.

"Excuse me, but what's 'old timers'?"

"Later Benjamin." Holding up the dive belt, she threw it on the counter, muttering to herself. She carefully unsnapped the little compartments, one after another.

"Can't believe I completely forgot this. Bring me two test tubes and a pair of tweezers, please. Remember the day that we made our collection? Well, when I went down to search the area, I found something caught on the coral. I didn't think it was important but I picked it up anyway and then I promptly forgot it. We were so busy with the mass autopsies. No excuses. I *should* have remembered it. It may not be of any value, but you never know. I didn't even record it in my book. I wonder what else I forgot?"

She took the tweezers from him, reached inside and carefully pulled out the fragment of what looked like a blue plastic tarpaulin. Lori placed it in the first test tube and watched Benjamin cork it.

"Now let us see if there is anything else in here. Hmm, turn on that magnifying light over there so I can see better." Lori placed the belt under the light and slowly perused the insides of the compartment.

"These granules might be something or they might be sand. Just in case, we will put them in the second tube for testing. I can pick up the bigger pieces but for the smaller granules hand me a small strip of cellophane tape. Thanks, Benjamin."

She made sure that every tiny particle was placed in the test tube. "Now cork it for me. We will save it for testing later with the other egg granules." She smiled her thanks for his help.

"I am going to the computer right now. We need to upload all of our findings today before we leave. Tonight, I hit the Internet again. I can't wait to talk to Dr. Rigby and the others about what we have found here."

"Don't get so busy that you forget Miss Genny's card party this evening. She'll be upset if you miss another one, you know. What can I do now? I mean what should I do first?" His face glowed with excitement at their discoveries.

"You write the report for today's findings and put a copy in the written log. Make sure you transfer my e-mail from Dana to the file, include anything else of significance. Then send it out ASAP. I'll put these in a safe place and lock them up. While you're writing, I'll call the hospital, then you can use the phone to uplink today's file.

"Oh, then print me a hard copy to take to my cabin where I'll do the rest. Don't worry. I'll tear myself away for the party. I promise.

"I probably won't get to chat with any of them this evening on the Internet anyway. Hmm, this is Friday, what's the time difference? I keep forgetting, St. Louis will be on daylight saving time, and then California time is four hours behind us here, I think. It would be perfect to get them all to a chat room and brainstorm. Would you like to be there, too? Probably tomorrow evening, nine o'clock our time, let's plan for. At my cabin. And I'll send them an alternate time for Sunday. I hope they check their mail before leaving work today. Cross your fingers, Benjamin. This could be it." She pointed a thumbs up sign.

He nodded affirmation and grinned a great big gleaming white smile, ear-to-ear, and went to the desk with pride in his eyes and in his walk.

He muttered to himself. "Cross your fingers? Old timers? Wonder what's next?" He grinned back over his shoulder one more time at Lori before going about his work.

Eighteen

Lori dawdled killing time before getting ready for the party. She went out for a quick swim after she sent the e-mail and followed Jake back to their cabin. Picking up the written daily report laying loose on the table next to her laptop, she nervously laid it back down again. Normally reports were stored on disk or in the log manual back in the lab locked up, but she needed it for reference to think about the queries she sent out. She stood quietly for a moment, assessing her irrational fears.

Her mind was a jumble of questions but she knew she was just killing time because she wanted to delay seeing Hugh again. Face to face. In front of the 'witch'. And any other eyes. It made her shiver just to think of it, particularly his eyes. Well, she would have to pull herself together and get on with it.

Lori folded the report in half, slid it under the computer and disconnected the cell phone from it to put in her purse. Hmm, old habits die hard. She ejected the disk and put it in a kitchen drawer. She was afraid she was getting paranoid or something. It was probably just Hugh watching her. Well, she would put a bug in his ear and make sure he knew what she thought of that. That insufferable man.

"Come on Jake, let's get ready for the party. Tonight you get a shower too, if you're my date."

Lori led him to the bathroom. He stood meekly in the shower while she lathered him up and looked up at her with soulful eyes. He only whimpered once when she got soap in his eyes. She dried him with a beach towel, then her blow dryer and wouldn't let him shake until he was totally dry.

"Good boy, Jake. Now you wait for me to get ready." He went to lie down on his rug and waited patiently for her.

She discarded three outfits before she settled on a plain, straight black dress. She hung around her neck a gold necklace with a large intricately molded gold heart, slipped on a bracelet, one gold heart ring, and black and gold sling heels.

"Going to a funeral, Lori?" She asked herself as she turned around and looked at her backside in the mirror. "Well, if the shoe fits, then wear it woman. I *am* in mourning after all for an abundance of reasons." She grabbed a gold purse and followed Jake out the door.

This time Lori steeled herself and after greeting Marion, made her entrance from the front door through the house with Jake proudly at her side. They went directly to Miss Genny seated in the large spacious living room. It was chilly this evening and the sweet old lady was dressed in a long dark dress with a lovely lace collar and a colorful shawl draped over her shoulders. She had on a long string of pearls and pearl studs in her ears.

"Oh my dear, I am so glad that you could be here with us this time. I missed you. Come sit here with me for a bit before the rest of my guests arrive. How is your work going? I have not seen much of you lately. I see you have domesticated Jake more every day. You will make a gentleman of him yet. We have a good crowd coming this evening. We should have a wonderful time. We will play cards inside this evening since it is so cool."

Lori nodded at Benjamin through the open patio door and sat down smoothly, patting Jake's head as usual. The big dog looked at her with liquid brown eyes.

"Yes, he's always the perfect gentleman. Faithful. Never lies to you. Always comes home. Is always there when you need him. Never demanding. Gentle and loving. All in all, a very good companion."

"Sounds like you speak from experience, my dear. But do you not think a man has *so* much more to offer, and is oh, so much more fun?" Miss Genny chuckled merrily, rolling her eyes, then reached over and tapped Lori lightly on the arm.

"I might be ancient but I have a very good memory. Ah, *amour*. Men, they create many problems but do they not make our lives so much more interesting and worth living? It would be a boring world without them, yes? We need to have a private little chat quite soon, my dear. I think you must need some advice, yes? And I have a surprise for you, tonight. Just wait and see." She clapped her hands together like a cheerful child.

Lori looked at her suspiciously and wondered what in the world she had up her sleeve. She liked this charming lady but she was definitely up to something. She had enough on her plate right now without adding a matchmaker's interference. Right now, her plate 'overfloweth', or whatever.

Lori forced herself to smile as more guests arrived and finally distracted Miss Genny's individual attention to her. She was chattering away when Lori and Jake slipped away to the bar to get a glass of wine and join Benjamin and some of the others outside on the patio. She surely hoped Miss Genny's plans didn't have anything to do with the grandsons. However handsome they were, the pair was *definitely* not Lori's type. Neither of them.

She sipped white wine and grimaced behind her glass as she saw the pair of them zeroing in on her. 'Frick and Frack,' she thought to herself. 'With the wicked witch for a sister.' She almost choked on the wine she pretended to drink when she caught Benjamin watching. He raised his glass and laughed, almost as if he could read her thoughts.

Jon and Gerard surrounded her, started to kiss her cheek on each side, then stopped abruptly and avoided making body contact as they kept a wary eye on Jake.

"Lori, we have missed your presence. Why have you been so busy? You look beautiful, as usual. Grandmere has missed you, too."

Jon effused charm and bowed slightly to her. The men were both dressed in standard island style of crisp white shirt and dark slacks.

"Lovely Lori." Gerard greeted her.

"Well, we've had a lot of work to do." She barely made excuses.

She chose to ignore their flattery and wished that they would both just back up and get out of her space. They were too close. It gave her a claustrophobic feeling even though she was not in a confined space. It made her inch backward from them surreptitiously. Without being aware of it, she unconsciously backed into another conversation group and bumped into a man's back.

Before Lori could turn around and apologize, she heard the catty voice of Miss Sheree laughing shrilly and announcing her presence to the gathered guests. And guess who was at her side? *Well, surprise, surprise.* She told herself bitterly. It must be JeanPaul.

She did her best to keep a frown off her face and turned quickly into the broad shoulders of the man that she had bumped. She was totally shocked to find it to be Jerrod.

"Jerrod, I'm sorry. What on earth are you doing here?"

He turned around eagerly, put his two large hands on her shoulders and hugged her.

"I was tired of waiting to hear from you and finagled myself an invitation from Miss Genny. Of course, that wasn't too hard to do. You've been missing me, I've been thinking, so here I am." That rascals' grin broadened his face.

Jake stood idly by. No growling this time, even at the hugging, as though the dog was willing to share her tonight.

Lori gave him a quick peck on the cheek while he had his arms around her, leaned back and waggled her finger at him. "There you go assuming things again," but not denying it either. It was impossible not to respond with a smile and quickly stepped out of his arms to find Jon and Gerard openly glaring at Jerrod.

JeanPaul advanced on the group with a determinedly grim expression on his face. Oddly enough, Jake made no menacing moves this evening and just kept watch over it all.

Her peripheral vision caught a flutter of movement through the patio door and turned to see Miss Genny waving merrily at her. She watched the whole scene unfold from inside the house on her chaise longue. Lori waved back and smiled at the old lady's maneuvering. *Now what?*

JeanPaul forced his way into the group, nearly dragging Sheree along on her ridiculous spiked high-heeled leopard shoes. She wore the tightest zebra print pants that Lori had ever seen. With a fluffy black jaguar print angora sweater pulled tight over her bosom, Sheree weighed herself down with loads of African looking jewelry.

Humph... Bet she had to lie down to get into those pants or she couldn't possibly get the zipper up. No wonder she never eats.

Sheree's wild windblown hairdo stood out with at least fifty pounds of hair spray. Lori thought her endangered species earrings made from teeth screamed for attention, or something.

Lori forced a most generous greeting to the couple. "Hello."

The men at the party ogled Sheree, tripping over each other to get her a drink.

I'll wager she can't sit down in them either, or they would cut her in half. Yuck. Men are such dumb beasts. Thoroughly disgusted, Lori quietly maneuvered out of the group with Jake to a small table for two on the extreme edge of the patio, while the spotlight remained on the lovely siren.

Jerrod noticed Lori had slipped away. He hurriedly caught up with her before she sat so he could pull out her chair.

"Sorry, I was distracted for a moment. Her charms could never compare to yours, I'm thinking, just between you and me." He leaned forward conspiratorially. "She is one of those empty women. If you know what I mean? No appetite." He raised one eyebrow in a valiant question mark.

"Oh Jerrod, you are so funny." Lori burst into a light peal of melodious laughter.

Everyone within the sound of it smiled, too.

"Jerrod, if you only knew what *I'd* been thinking. But never mind, my mother taught me to keep it to myself if it wasn't nice. So I'll be good."

"Oh, but sometimes it is fun to be naughty." He raised both his eyebrows suggestively this time.

She smacked him on the hand. "Oh be good yourself, goofy. You sound like Miss Genny. Now tell me how have you been? How are your kids? What has your daughter been up to lately?" Neatly changing the subject and steering him into neutral zones, she listened to his monologue.

Ignoring the rest of the crowd, Lori stared off into the distance with the water rippling and sparkling in the moonlight.

She listened to the cadence of Jerrod's rambling about Julie and Joe, not listening to the words, just the musical notes of his Irish brogue.

Peaceful. Calming. Funny. No threat now. It would be easy to give in to his charms. No threatening eyes here, either. She glanced at the mingling crowd of islanders. *Wonder why I have been feeling them lately? Hugh is probably watching me right now but I don't feel it. Or maybe he isn't and that's why I don't feel it. Maybe it's all in my head.* She refused to allow herself to turn around and look at him.

Maybe if I refuse to acknowledge him, then he will just go away. Yeah, right. Dreamer...

The group they escaped from finally noticed their absence and converged upon them.

"Interrupting a little *tête a tête*, are we? Why I do believe your famous doggie date has perfume on, doesn't he?" Sheree questioned sneeringly.

Ignoring the first remark, Lori reached over to rub Jake's ears. "He had a shower and shampoo today, didn't you old boy?"

"Lord. I don't believe it, *bathing with a dog. That has to be a first.* Now I ask you? He has not had a bath since he was a puppy, and a very small one at that. The closest he comes to bathing is swimming in the lagoon. How very unusual. You must be a magician." Sheree's words were loud and shrill and demanding of attention. Sheree's gaze encompassed the group making sure that the men were properly shocked and smirked to see the expressions on their faces.

"Yes, well he *is* remarkable, which is so much more than I can say for some people." Lori calmly looked up from Jake and very slowly made direct eye contact with each of them, watching the men squirm under her level expressionless stare. Of course, the remark went right over Sheree's head. Geez, what a whiff brain. Making fun of a dog with more brains in his paw than that woman had in her entire head.

"Do you let him sleep in your bed, too?" Sheree continued.

"Of course not. He sleeps on a rug in front of my fireplace. *I am very selective about whom I let share my bed.* Not like some people." Lori answered Sheree coolly and crisply, and started to stand up to escape the group before Sheree had a chance to start in again.

Jerrod jumped up to pull out her chair, but Hugh, alias JeanPaul, beat him to it and they each tugged it in two directions glaring at each other. Lori was definitely not amused. She shook her head slightly and ignored them both as Marion called everyone inside to form teams for cards. Lori was happy to escape the bite of the witch's words.

This time she played cards with Jerrod for a partner and spent an amusing hour. His more informal mode of playing cards made it easy to have a great time. He kept her in stitches. She laughed so hard at his antics, her side hurt.

The other tables were seriously staid and silent, allowing no room for chitchat. But before long everyone watched and wanted in on the fun at her table.

Lori caught Miss Genny's bright gaze who nodded her head knowingly at Lori's pleasure in Jerrod's company. Lori glanced covertly at Hugh sitting stiffly, frowning and staring silently at his own cards.

During the dining break at the beautifully laid out buffet, Steffan arrived. Late as usual. He bowed and kissed Lori's hand in greeting as he did to all of the women.

His pudgy lips were cold on the back of hand and made her shiver. She saw both Jerrod and Hugh narrow their eyes at the sight of her reaction, but it was definitely not a shiver of pleasure.

She excused herself and went to powder her nose. Which she never did at a party, powder her nose that is, since she usually didn't wear powder anyway. But she needed to escape the company of those two men. They were behaving like jealous husbands or something. She would prefer to give them a piece of her mind, but then she might not have enough left over for herself by the time she finished unloading on them.

Hugh scrutinized Lori thoroughly, thinking she didn't need to touch up anything. She looked sleekly perfect to him, her hair slicked back smoothly from her tan face. The touch of teal shadow and eyeliner on her eyes and black mascara made her eyes and lashes look luminously enormous. Her golden tan brought out the yellow streaks in her blue eyes, lighting them from within. He wanted desperately to touch her and hold her. He was jealous. He'd admit it, to himself anyway. That damn woman could drive him crazy.

In the bathroom, Lori critically examined herself in an enormous Aztec mirror, and sighed. She looked okay, she guessed. When she rejoined the rest of the party, she found a large group massed in the corner of the room under a spotlight. She couldn't see what was going on because her view was blocked.

"Come here, my dear. We have something to show you." Miss Genny stood off to the side of the crowd and waved her over.

Lori approached suspiciously, her antenna up and quivering an alert. The chatter in the room silenced when they heard Miss Genny's request. She saw Benjamin beaming from the group. *Uh oh, something's up.*

"HAPPY BIRTHDAY!" Everyone yelled at her.

Lori gave Benjamin an accusing glare but he just shrugged his shoulders in response and grinned at her. Expecting a birthday cake, Lori was shocked speechless when the crowd parted. A near life-size portrait of herself and Jake emerged in her view.

She stood with her mouth open until Benjamin nudged her and reminded her quietly. "Close it before you catch something."

She snapped her mouth shut staring at the lovely painting. Steffan stood hopping from one foot to another, off to one side rubbing his hands together. "*Voila!* It is perfection, is it not?" He demanded his share of compliments. "It is one of my best, don't you think?"

Lori was speechless as she examined the portrait. It was lovely, all golds and yellows, browns and black. The portrait mimicked Jake's exact adoring expression.

Steffan had taken artistic liberties with his almost explicit interpretation. Lori had never posed for him quite so provocatively, nor with that love/lust expression on her face, had she? Her body beneath the windblown scarf had never been *that* exposed, had it? Every curve and line was virtually displayed for all to see. And she was absolutely certain that particular mole, where her lower abdomen met her thigh, had never seen the light of day within his presence, had it?

In some unique way the painting was both primitive, priceless and seductive in a very earthy way. *I have never in my life looked like that.* But it was good. Very good, after she got over the initial shock. Certainly this was no wishy-washy pastel watercolor. It had an inner glow of sunshine and light that none of his pastels had portrayed.

"How much are you asking for it?" JeanPaul asked the painter. He stood staring at it and rubbing his chin, his own narrowed eyes lit from an internal fire.

"Yes, I'll buy it, whatever the price." Jerrod jumped in.

"Non, this one is for *ma cherie*. I have three others just as good that I may sell. But not this one, it is for her. My inspiration, you do like it, *oui?*" He eagerly awaited her approval.

"Yes, thank you, Steffan. It is exquisite. I only wish I looked that good. It is the loveliest gift I have ever received." She planted a chaste kiss on his cheek and gave the little artist a hug, blinking back the tears trying to form.

"*Enchanté.* You do not know, but now I show the world what you are." He patted her arms, smiling a Cheshire grin.

Marion, in the meantime, brought out an enormous dark chocolate cake for dessert. Five rich layers with chocolate chips, filled with strawberries and whipped cream between the layers and pounds of white, dark and milk chocolate curly shavings, lined the top of whipped cream icing.

Thank goodness, only one candle lit the top for Lori to blow out. She'd quit counting when she hit forty and in present company only Hugh knew her real age. After a year like the last, she decided to quit celebrating birthdays forever, ha! And she had been too busy to worry about the passing of another year. The generosity of these island people was absolutely the best. At least the majority of them fit that category.

Sheree sulked prettily over in the corner, gnawing on a fingernail, unused to being ignored. She bided her time, waiting for the attention to shift back to her. She was jealous of the painting. She whined. "Steffan, you bad boy, you promised to paint me next!" She grabbed Steffan and forced him into a corner to talk.

Lori hugged Miss Genny and Marion, thanking them for the surprise *and* the sinful cake. She kept an eye on Jake who stared at the portrait, his big black head tilted to one side. He looked back over his shoulder at Lori and quietly "Woofed" his approval at her, making the entire collection of islanders erupt in laughter.

"Perhaps it is time for Jake to have a mate. I am not sure that he does not think the picture is another dog." Miss Genny commented after the laughter died down.

"There is no doubt that he adores you. Maybe we should breed him before you leave the island and break his heart. You will not be leaving us for a long time, will you my dear? Benjamin tells us you are getting close to a solution and that it has to do with drugs? Is that so, my dear? I want you to solve your problem, but I do hope that you will stay here for your full time. I am getting quite attached to you."

"Drugs, did I hear someone say drugs?" Jerrod questioned the group loudly, coming to join Lori with a substantial hunk of birthday cake on his plate.

Heads turned around the room and all eyes swivelled to Lori. Even Steffan looked startled.

Lori frowned and glanced at Hugh's furious face, then quickly shifted her gaze to Benjamin, wishing that he'd had the sense to keep his mouth shut. Damn. *She* should have warned him to keep it to himself.

"Well, we are a long way from solving anything yet. We have a load of work ahead of us before we can make any claims." She attempted to down play the question.

"Don't worry, Miss Genny. I'm not going anywhere soon. I guess you're stuck with me." Lori placed her hand on Benjamin's forearm and squeezed it gently. He looked at her. She ever so slightly shook her head 'no' at him when she saw him about to object and squeezed his arm again, this time more forcefully.

"What do you think of the painting, Miss Genny?" Lori directed the conversation to safer grounds before Benjamin could blurt out any more damaging information. Thinking quickly, she needed to determine a way to apprize him of keeping quiet about work, and without disclosing too much information. For his own good as well as hers. She took Miss Genny's arm leading her back to her chaise.

"Oh, I think it is the loveliest work that Steffan has done, don't you? Quite a surprise for you, was it not? I just could not resist when I learned from Benjamin that your birthday was coming up. I know how depressed you have been. Marion and I were planning a little soiree when Steffan showed up with your finished portrait, so it all fell together. Poof. Just like that." She snapped elegant fingers, and grinned mischievously.

"Yes, thank you again. I cannot thank you enough. You've been like family to me and I don't have much family left anymore. A brother that, if I'm lucky, I see once a year and a plethora of cousins. It was quite a surprise. I had forgotten. I hadn't given a single thought to today being my birthday. It was very sweet of you." Her eyes misted over with tears again. *Geez, where was all the emotion coming from?*

"Now young lady, go and enjoy yourself some more. Let an old lady rest and enjoy watching her guests. Go." Miss Genny shooed her away.

Lori wove her way through all the guests, who wished her a merry birthday and discussed the merits of the portrait. Odd, tonight Jake hadn't growl all evening. Guess he must have known about the party, too.

She knew that she would have to confront Hugh sometime this evening, if only momentarily. She might as well get it over with now in front of this nice safe audience.

Lori walked over to Hugh and put out her hand.

He took it in both of his and stared deeply into her eyes, forcing her to look into the blaze on fire in his own eyes.

"Good God, Lori. What the hell are you doing? You don't know what you're getting into here. I've told you and told you about the danger. What is Benjamin doing talking about drugs?" He hissed forcefully, his anger showing.

"Let go of my hand and quit bullying me. We found a possible narcotic connection. Nothing proven yet. Just a possibility."

"Well, you had better stop him from talking. And why is the good Captain here? What is going on there?" He asked sneeringly.

"Oh, mind your own business. And quit watching me."

Jerking her hand back, she smiled prettily at him as if she were accepting a compliment from him. She glanced around the room to see if anyone was paying attention to them and saw the wicked witch, flying in on a broomstick rapid approach.

"What do you mean watching you? At the party?" Hugh hissed back.

"No. At the station. Dammit, you know where." She hissed back and then said louder. "Thank you, thank you."

She turned away from him rather than watch Sheree's fast attack claim on his arm. That woman probably needed to hold his arm to keep her upright on those ugly obscene spikes, since she was *so* freakin' top heavy.

Meow, she couldn't resist the thought. Lori wanted to sharpen her claws because two could certainly play this game.

Lori hurried across the room to Jerrod. He beamed an absolutely infectious grin at her. She let him place an arm around her shoulders, pulled her to him briefly before he led her back to the card table and seated her.

Jerrod's personality and manners were terrific and she told herself again it would be easy to fall for him. She watched him with speculative intent the rest of the evening and totally ignored Hugh.

Nineteen

All in all, it had been a memorable evening. Not in the least what she'd expected. Jake was already curled up on his rug, fast asleep and already snoring by the time she hit the shower. Must have been too much partying for the dog also. It was very late.

Lori sighed, stretching first to the right then to the left. Doing head tilt exercises and loosening up her stress points, before crawling into bed. She popped her evening vitamins in her mouth, gulping a big swig from the water bottle beside the bed.

Jerrod had driven her home in her golf cart. He'd arranged for Benjamin to bring it back from the boat dock the next day. She and Jerrod had sat with Jake out on the point for a very long time in a pleasant, after party glow. She hoped she hadn't ruined the dress from sitting on damp sand, but if she did, so be it.

Yes, she admitted to herself, it had been a rewarding evening. Jerrod had treated her just right and they had talked and talked and talked. She had left him with a satisfying kiss to end the evening, a kiss with promise, maybe.

She reminded herself, *you never know what life has in store for you, right...?*

Much later Lori was startled wide-awake from a deep sleep. She sat up immediately, her heart beating rapidly in her chest. Hugh? Was it Hugh again? Sneaking in the night like a burglar?

Whatever it was that woke her, scared the daylights out of her. Or was it the remnants of an unremembered nightmare? She shivered and thought she could hear a strange pounding sound and a weird crackling. Was that a *hiss* she heard?

She shook her head groggily, clearing the cobwebs from her brain. Spooked as she was, she shivered again, looking around the darkened bedroom and expecting shadowy eyes or something. She had trouble focusing her eyes and was dizzy.

She only had a few partial glasses of wine the whole evening and knew it was not alcohol making her fuzzy. She *never* drank in excess. Never. The pounding was probably her own heart. It beat so loud that she could hear and feel the pounding behind her ear drums.

A glow behind her curtains lit the outside. Dawn breaking? Already? She stood up and shakily staggered toward the bedroom door to get a glass of cold water from the fridge when she heard Jake barking from a distance. *From outside the cabin.*

Puzzled because she knew he was asleep on the other side of the door on his favorite rug. Hurrying to the door, she flung it open, only to find the entire cabin on the other side of the door engulfed in flames. The smoke was drawing up through the fireplace chimney, because there wasn't any smoke in the cabin, only blistering heat.

She backed up rapidly from the heat and remembered to slam her door closed. Lori frantically looked around for something to put the fire out with, but knew the only fire extinguisher was in the little pantry in the kitchen.

Besides this fire was way too involved for such a tiny extinguisher. It raged out of control. She put both hands to her temples attempting to block the pounding, trying to think.

The sound of an enormous THUD hit the wall behind her. She jumped and screamed. Turning toward the window, she realized Jake was barking frantically and scratching at the window from outside.

She stood for a moment, teetering on her feet, listening to the frightening sounds of the fire behind her. *Think, think.* She told herself. She kicked a blanket into the crack under the door and ran to the closet to get her jewelry box from the shelf. The contents weren't valuable except for immense sentimental value. Her favorite pictures of Nathan were in there and Lori wasn't about to give them up.

Stumbling wearily back to the window where Jake barked ferociously, she yanked the curtains down from the wall. Setting the box down, she tried to unlock the window but the lock would not budge. She had been locking all the windows at night lately. She looked around for something to pry the lock open but couldn't find anything.

Woozy and lightheaded, she looked back at the door and saw flames lick under the blanket and across the wood floor and knew that she didn't have long to get out.

She raised a leg and tried kicking the window out of the frame with her bare foot and saw it bow but not break. Lori kicked repeatedly, until it shot a pain up her leg from her ankle.

Damn! She could swim for miles but couldn't knock that window out, it must be tempered or something strong. Finally in desperation, she lay down on the floor and tried kicking it out with both legs.

"Get out of the way Jake. I'm coming through, one way or another." She screamed.

That didn't work so she picked up the bedside table and swung it in a complete circle before heaving it at the window with all her strength. A loud crash splintered the glass into a multitude of fragments allowing a massive influx of air into the room, feeding the flames and creating a sudden surge of smoke.

Choking, Lori felt the smoke and heat begin to engulf her and blind her. She dropped to the floor, groping for her box, and grasped it tightly in her arms before she succumbed to the fumes.

She thought she heard her name being called from a distance. She was sinking into a deep whirlwind tunnel of heat and darkness, when she felt strong cool hands lifting her out of the tunnel and into the light.

Hugh pulled her from the burning building and carried her toward the tree line. When he saw that she was breathing, he left her with Jake and ran around to her front porch to ring the bell hanging there. He pealed it eight or ten times before the flames backed him away, then ran back to Lori.

Before he made it back to Lori, a small explosion of sound rocked the cabin and the north end of the island. The night breezes died down at dawn and he saw the other buildings didn't appear to be in eminent danger. There wasn't anything more he could do anyway.

Hugh dropped to the ground and picked her up in his arms, pulling her tightly to him. "Oh God. Oh God, Lori. Oh, Lori." He kept repeating, over and over again.

He tugged the box gently out of her grip and pulled Lori tighter toward him, thanking God and the dog for her safety. He ran his hands over her, carefully checking for burns but found nothing but a few minor cuts on her long bare legs.

Her eyes fluttered open wide and round in her grubby pale face. Her teeth chattered like she was in the middle of a Midwest winter and was exposed to the weather in a T-shirt and panties. She croaked one word. "Hugh."

"You're okay, Lori. You're safe now. I have you. It's okay. Are you cold? I'm going to give you my sweatshirt."

He struggled to jerk the gray sweatshirt over his head, leaving his chest bare, his lean muscular body clothed only in sweat shorts. Slipping the sweatshirt over her head, he shoved her arms through the sleeves, gently pulling her cold slender hands out, warming them briskly between his own.

"Geez, Lori. You're in shock. I can't do anything about that until the others get here. I'm not going to let you go. You're safe now. I love you... love you." Quietly, he tried to calm her, affirming his love for her.

He wrapped his arms around her again, holding her in his lap, trying to share some of his body warmth, rocking her in his arms, back and forth. He didn't know for how long. Time seemed frozen. Aware of Jake's ears perking up and alerting him to the presence of someone drawing near, Hugh tensed for trouble. He relaxed when Jeeps and carts raced down the path.

The islanders with one glance at the situation, threw themselves into action. Some ran to a water hose at the back of the lab to begin wetting down the two buildings that were left.

He could see from where he sat Lori's cabin was a goner. The roof caved as help had arrived. The blackened concrete block walls stood but not much of anything else. Standing with the walls, was a chimney shaft, but no windows, doors or porch. Everything wood was either in flame or burning embers or ashes.

The empty shell burned merrily in the emergence of early purpled light. An exquisite dawn greeted the day with the silence of the growing number of spectators. Their focus alternated from the fire to the rocking couple with the silent black dog on guard.

When Miss Genny arrived in her Jeep, she sent Marion over to Lori with a blanket she took off her own shoulders, "Bring them back here."

The islanders moved with one fluid motion, following Hugh when he picked up Lori and carried her to Miss Genny.

Benjamin danced first on one foot, then the other, craning his head to get a better look at Lori.

"She's in shock but she's all right, I think," JeanPaul told them all.

Miss Genny reached down to smooth the hair back from Lori's brow and patted her smudged cheek lovingly.

"Come, we will take her home with us. Jon, you go ahead of us. We should have called before we left. Call for the doctor. Marion, you go too. Get out the electric blanket. Make sweet tea and whatever else you can think of. Put her in the yellow guest room. Get the bed warm. Draw a hot bath, now go... Go." She sent them scurrying to the other Jeep.

"You men know what to do. Where is Emily? Benjamin, where is Lori's cart? Everyone else, please return home. Get some rest. There is nothing to do until the fire is out. Thank you all for coming. JeanPaul, get in with her, please. Gerard, will you drive us home now?"

"The captain left Lori's cart at the dock. He drove her home last night." Benjamin replied.

Miss Genny smiled gently at him seeing his distress.

Jake jumped in and sat in the back beside Hugh and Lori. He kept a soulful watch on her shaking body and reached out his massive head to lick her dirty face.

"Thank you, boy. I might not have gotten here in time if you had not come for me." JeanPaul told the big dog face to face. Nose to nose.

"The dog came and got you? Why wasn't he in the cabin with her? I thought at night he stayed in her cabin? What do you think started the fire? Did you save anything of hers?" Gerard asked JeanPaul.

Hugh kept a firm grip on Lori. The Jeep careened up the bumpy road. He started to answer in a shaky voice, cleared his voice and had to start over.

214

"*Oui*, he came to my place and barked and jumped at the door until I came out. Then he led me here to her bedroom window. He beat me to it and was throwing himself at the glass when I got there. But the glass blew out from the inside. I think perhaps she threw something at it. I reached in and pulled her out. Her room was in flames by then. It didn't start there. Fire was already working through the roof by the fireplace when I came down the hill. *He* saved her. That dog is a hero."

"Well, when it cools down, we will find out what happened. Everything will be all right. We'll take care of her now, won't we, *maman*?" Gerard reassured them and reached over to pat his grandmother's knee.

"Drive faster Gerard and turn up the heat. If I am cold, she must be freezing."

"The only thing she saved was an old wooden box that she had clenched in her arms. I had to pry it out of her arms to put my sweatshirt on her. I don't know what was in it. I left it on the sand. I'd better go back to get it."

"No, I will."

"No, neither of you will. I am certain that Benjamin will bring it along. He won't be far behind us, to be sure."

The road seemed endless to Hugh but in reality they reached the southern end of the island in record time. Gerard drove so fast they'd had to hang on tight.

Lori's shaking seemed to have settled down now but Hugh's concern was evident. She didn't seem to hear him or be aware of anyone else for that matter.

When they reached the house, Sheree was leaning against the open door frame, dramatically dressed in a black negligee with her black hair in a just-got-out-of-bed tousled look. The group entered the house silently and ignored her. Even Hugh brushed past her without saying anything to the siren.

"JeanPaul, what happened? Did she have too much to drink celebrating her birthday, and get careless?" Sheree asked shrilly. She couldn't stand the inattention.

"Hush, child." Her grandmother admonished her.

"Bring her this way. Marion will have everything ready for us. JeanPaul place her on the bed. While we bathe her, you get brandy to add to her tea. Then we shall get her into bed. Now go, so we can undress her. Go. We can do this alone."

Hugh had been in countless situations that had much worse consequences, but he'd never felt so hopeless or guilty. He strode past Sheree into the great room. This time she sat, lounging with a bare leg swinging over the arm of a chair.

She stared at his brown, nearly hairless muscular chest and long strong legs with open lust. She tapped a red painted fingernail on her teeth considering strategy, watching him at to the liquor cabinet.

He poured a hefty glass of brandy for himself, quickly tossing it off. It burned his throat all the way down. Filling another large glass, he hurried back down the hall. Hugh still would not acknowledge Sheree's presence.

He stood patiently outside the door until it was opened by Marion. She gestured him inside. Lori, in a clean white cotton old-fashioned, high throated lace night gown, was propped up on a few pillows and buried under piles of blankets.

Lori drank hot extra sweet tea, grimacing at all the sugar. The smoke and smudges were gone and she had a fresh scrubbed look, but she was still shaking and looked pallid.

Jake sat in a corner of the room watching. Hugh watched her look up at him with huge liquid blue eyes over the cup brim.

"Drink it down now, all of it. It will help. Then drink this one." Miss Genny sat by the bed pouring the second cup half full of brandy before adding hot tea and sugar from a silver tea service. She poured a little bit of brandy into another cup and poured tea for herself. "Marion? JeanPaul?"

Marion shook her head and adjusted the electric blanket setting.

"No thanks. I had a glass out there before I came in. Are you okay, Lori?" Hugh looked wretched.

He beseeched forgiveness with his lion eyes, blaming himself for letting this happen to her. He should have done a better job of protecting her. This was *not* an accident. He didn't know what to do short of kidnapping her, then escorting her to safety. He could sit in the woods on guard duty all night but there was no way he could do that without putting his entire operation in jeopardy.

There was no safe place to hide in the woods anyway, the islanders would spot him in a second, except maybe if he hid in her cabin. That thought made his eyes light up from within. It was a good thing that the old ladies kept their eyes on Lori and not him. They would have been startled to see the feral gleam there.

Or maybe he could convince her to leave the island now. But knowing Lori, he knew there was fat chance of that.

There was a soft knock at the door and Marion hurried over to admit a sheepish pale faced Benjamin, carrying an old beat up antique carved wooden box.

"I found it by the woods, I think it's Miss Lori's. Is she all right?" Ben asked quietly.

Hugh took it from him and stroked its top.

"Thanks, Benjamin, she was clutching it in her arms when I carried her out. It must be important to her. Thanks." He glanced over at Lori, now slid down in the bed, her eyes closed.

"Come everyone. She needs to rest. She is quite all right, Benjamin. The doctor will be here before long to check her for us. She is clean and warm, which is all we can do for her now.

Let us leave her alone." Miss Genny shepherded them from the room.

Hugh hung back with the box in his arms.

"I'll just sit here in the corner. I won't bother her, I promise." He smiled charmingly at the dear lady and won his way.

Everyone else left them alone. Lori fluttered her eyes open, saw that he was there, sighed and went back to sleep.

Gerard and Jon both poked their heads in the door and looked at her. They nodded at him but didn't say anything. There was no sign of Sheree checking on her. The painter hadn't appeared this morning either.

Hugh sat for a prolonged time, his mind a whirling dervish of thoughts and mixed emotions. Finally, to keep from driving himself to distraction and feeling helpless from the inactivity of the moment, he opened the box.

It was an oversized music box. A tiny little ballerina figurine began dancing when he lifted the lid and played a waltz, 'Blue Danube' he thought. He hurriedly found the mechanism to stop the music from waking her, shutting it off, and began sorting through her jewelry and things.

He found a ring that he had given her that long ago summer. It was a huge smoky topaz that must have been forty or fifty carats. He remembered her delight and passion when he gave it to her. Funny, he had forgotten it until now. How could he have forgotten?

There were lots of gold and semiprecious stone settings. Nothing terribly expensive, but quality nonetheless.

Underneath the jewelry was a brown manila envelope. He poured the assortment of pictures and newspaper clippings onto his lap. The pictures brought a smile to his face. They were of her son Nathan in various stages of his development.

One of Nathan, naked in his mom's hat and his dad's tennis shoes, dated age one. The boy playing out in the yard bent over picking a flower, with his underwear on backwards. Priceless pictures. Charming pictures of the fair-haired boy and his wonderful mom. His smile broadened. But the pictures had stopped after the graduation shots. Where were pictures of going off to college?

He started speed reading the clippings, expecting accolades and salutations about her son. He stopped suddenly when he realized what he was reading.

A drunken driver being charged for murdering four teenagers. Oh God, no...

He thumbed through them rapidly until he found the names, when the drunk was actually arraigned and charged. Nathan Sherman's name was listed as critical in a coma. In a later article, many days later, he died.

"Oh my God, Lori. I never knew. I never even asked you about him. I assumed he was off at college. How will you ever forgive me? No wonder you've been so mad at me. So many times that I have never been there for you. I missed so much of your life."

He whispered, sitting in a corner easy chair staring at her. His hands dropped the clippings and sat empty, holding nothing.

Jake watched the papers flutter to the floor and cocked his head at Hugh, before dropping his head back to the floor and returning his gaze to Lori.

Hugh's heart clenched in a tight vise.

His stomach felt like he had been gut punched.

His golden eyes were awash with unshed tears.

"I'm so sorry, my love, so very sorry. Oh Lori..."

Twenty

Several hours later, Jake lifted his head and muffled a gruff bark but not loud enough to disturb Lori. The dog startled Hugh, who was dozing himself. He sat tensely for awhile but since Jake dropped his head back down, so eventually did he. It wasn't very long after that he heard a disturbance outside the room and stood when he heard voices coming closer. The dog jumped on his feet, too, placing himself between the door and Lori's bed.

Hugh bristled when the door burst open and banged the wall as the good Captain launched himself into the room, making a beeline straight for Lori. Hugh bit his lip to keep from making a fool of himself.

Jerrod grabbed Lori's hand on the cover and bent over to kiss her brow. Jake watched, his eyes narrowed, but made no move to interfere. Lori, startled awake from the noise, smiled tentatively at Jerrod's looming presence.

"Lori, whatever in the world happened? I got here as fast as I could. This is the only doctor I could find this morning. The others were on the golf course or on duty at the hospital. This is Dr. Green. Lenny, get over here and see if she is okay."

A small-framed, thin, young man ambled over to the bed. He had red hair with a crew cut, big ears and the thickest glasses Lori had ever seen. They seemed to dominate his freckled face and magnified his brown eyes to enormous proportions. His head perched on such a narrow neck that Lori thought that it couldn't possibly support it. He sat on the edge of the bed and took her hand from Jerrod's and introduced himself.

With a very soft voice he said, "Hello, I am Dr. Leonard Green. Everyone calls me Lenny. Would you please clear the room, so that I may examine her?"

By this time the room was full to overflowing. Miss Genny and Marion had added to the group. As the women turned to leave, Lori reached out for Jake to draw him nearer and to pat his large head.

"Marion, would you get Jake some food? I am sure that he hasn't eaten today and he must be starving. Aren't you, old boy?" She asked in a low scratchy voice, rubbing his big ears.

Marion nodded to Lori, but Miss Genny told Lori. "Of course, my dear. Marion has prepared a superb brunch for all of us. Come, gentlemen, it is time."

She waited by the door. Neither man prepared to leave the room.

"*I'm* not leaving until he does." JeanPaul said, stabbing his finger at .

"Well, *I'm* not leaving. I came all this way to make sure she is okay and I'm not convinced yet. I should be taking her back to St. Thomas with me, I'm thinking. She was fine. Perfectly fine, when I left her last night and now look at her." Jerrod glared at Hugh.

"OUT. Both of you right now." Frail Miss Genny inserted herself between them and pushed them both from the room with a sweeping motion of her hands. "And grow up. Men." She muttered under her breath in an aside to Lori and winked, chuckling to herself at the antics of men. Lori's dilemma was perfectly evident to the old lady.

The doctor examined Lori with a very delicate touch. It almost tickled. His touch was so light.

He saw her laughing and mumbled to her as he examined her. "I'm only a pediatrician but I'm a fully qualified medical doctor. I am not a child. I am older than I look. Don't hold that against me. Kids like me. I am non-threatening to them and *they* do not challenge my medical qualifications. They identify with me. It's not my fault."

"I was not laughing at you. You tickle," she objected quietly.

"Oh, sorry, I'm a little touchy. I'm used to being laughed at because of my looks. I know I don't look old enough to be a doctor. The Captain can be quite forceful. He would never take 'no' for an answer. Not that I tried. I am the doc for his kids although they are almost grown, that's how he knew where to get me." He shrugged his skinny shoulders. "I didn't have anything else to do today. Weekends are quiet for me, except in flu season. Kids are pretty darn healthy around here."

He spent most of his time, after a general examination of her body, listening to her heart, bronchials and lungs, looking for smoke damage. He found no burns, only a few minor cuts on her legs that he treated and dressed, using supplies he retrieved from his little black bag. He spent an inordinate amount of time carefully checking her hands and fingernails for any blue signs of cyanosis. Since he didn't carry sophisticated equipment for measuring oxygen levels, he could only use old-fashioned methods.

He turned her over and listened to her lungs for what seemed like forever to Lori. Finally, he sat back satisfied with his results.

"I think that you are perfectly healthy, but I'd like you to come by my office sometime tomorrow for a chest x ray. I do not hear any rales, crackles or wheezing. I have seen no indication but I want to make sure that there is no residual aftereffect of pneumonia or any other smoke inhalation damage."

"You have no fever, in fact you are subnormal but that is to be expected. It's a kind of shock residual. Are you allergic to any medications? I would like to give you a broad spectrum antibiotic and something to help you to rest. Right now you need plenty of rest and to stay warm. You are very lucky. I do not believe you had much exposure to the smoke or fire. We saw the damage to your cottage when we came in by boat. The Captain circled the island to see it. Do you hurt anywhere? Do you have any pain anywhere at all?"

"No allergies, but my throat hurts a bit. I've a headache, some nausea and the heels and bottom of my feet hurt when you touched them. I tried to kick out the windows, I'm afraid. I guess I must have bruised the soles of my feet."

He gently rubbed the bottoms of her feet.

"Feet are tough. They should be okay in a few days. Your throat hurts, either because you screamed or from smoke. Just do not talk for the next few days, give your larynx a break. I don't see any smoke damage in your throat. It doesn't look too red. In fact, you are a very lucky lady.

"Right now you need a few days of R and R. I am sure that you will be well-taken care of here. Otherwise, I would take you back to the hospital at Charlotte Amalie. Stay in bed, except when you come to see me. And take advantage of the rest. Your body needs it, any questions?"

He gave her an antibiotic shot and to help her sleep. And some 100mg tranquilizer pills of Elavil. "Take one now and one at bedtime."

"Thank you, Doctor Green. I didn't know doctors made house calls anymore. Send your bill here to me. Thank you for coming on your day off. It'll be tough lying around for a few days but I guess I can force myself."

She took his hand and shook it after straightening the long nightgown around her legs, and he'd pulled the pile of blankets back up to her shoulders. She felt like a child being tucked in by another but was careful not to let her humor show. Lori didn't want to hurt his feelings.

Jake had been waiting by the door and returned to her room when the young doctor left. Lori prepared to drift off to sleep but Marion came in with a gargantuan bowl of steaming potato soup with chives and melted cheddar cheese on top.

"Don't tell anyone, it is supposed to be served quite cold, but vichyssoise is much better for you warm. Taste it and tell me if you do not think so."

"Thank you. Marion, it is wonderful. You are a terrific cook. You all take such good care of me. Tell me, who is out there and what are they doing?" Lori asked in a scratchy low voice.

"Well, Bennie is out brooding and wanting to make sure that you're okay. Your two gentlemen friends are staring daggers at each other. Miss Genny has them separated for the moment and is enjoying herself immensely. Steffan just showed up wanting to know what the ruckus is all about. The Captain is trying to convince the doctor to take you home with him, but I don't think it's working. Jon and Gerard are back at the fire, making sure that it is put out with no more damage than necessary."

Wincing at the reminder of the fire, her tender eyes welled with tears. "I don't understand what could have caught on fire or how Jake got outside. I just don't know."

"Hush. You just finish your soup and rest. Miss Genny and Emily Moore will take care of everything else."

"Would you send Ben in for a few minutes? I need to ask him something. Please, I want him to do a couple things for me."

"The doctor wants you to rest and be quiet but I'll send him in for a few minutes. I can see that you won't rest until you see him. But then I will chase him out, okay?" She left Lori alone with Jake, eating her soup.

A frightened Benjamin poked his head in the door and came into her room cautiously, almost tiptoeing. He stood quietly, waiting to see what she needed.

"I am fine. Come in and close the door, Ben. There's a couple of things I need you to do for me. The lab is okay, isn't it? There was no fire damage, was there? Yesterday before we left work, did everything get uploaded to the St. Louis computer? It seems like such a long time ago but it's important."

"Yes ma'am, every report was transferred. Every result we've accumulated so far. Why? The lab building hasn't been touched by the fire."

"Okay, go to the lab and see if our log books are where they should be. See if anything has been disturbed. Give everything a quick check. Don't attract any attention. Act naturally. Go alone and do it quietly. Then come back by here later to give me a report. Do not talk about it or any of our work to anyone. Not anyone, understand? I want you to be very careful."

Benjamin's eyes were wide as saucers.

"Do you think that the fire had anything to do with our work?"

"I don't know, Benjamin. But I *am* sure that my computer and disk were destroyed. And I want to make sure that we don't lose anything else. We've worked too hard to have to start all over. The fire was most likely an accident, but we can't take any chances if maybe it was not, can we?"

"No, ma'am. I won't say anything to anyone. But that means someone here on the island started the fire." Doubt was strong in his voice.

"I don't know Benjamin, not necessarily. At the station anyone could have gotten to us. Just be discreet and do not give out any information. And *do not* mention a drug connection. Okay, not to anyone? I know that I can trust you on this one

Benjamin. Thanks. I will rest better knowing that you will be on guard. Bye."

She put her bowl down and sank back into the bed pillows with a big sigh of relief. It was reassuring to know that he was warned and that their backup procedures gave them a failsafe, even if everything at the lab were destroyed, too.

She knew neither she nor Jake had started that fire. No matter what anyone found out about the fire's origination. They were safe now and with Benjamin alerted to the possibility of danger she could rest easier, too.

She coughed a couple of times and tasted smoke, yuck. Lori shivered at the close call she had and yawned hugely. The medicine must have had a chance to kick in, she thought drowsily, and slid off into the comfort of oblivion.

~ * ~

When next she woke, the room was filled with the solid dark shadows of night. She vaguely recognized it was not her room but could not seem to pull herself out of the sleepy fog long enough to completely wake up. She thought she felt the presence of two darker shadows there with her. But regardless what the shadows were, they represented safety so she sank back down into bliss of restful sleep.

The next time she opened her eyes she found brilliant sunlight decorating the bright yellow room. She stretched her arms above her head and was rewarded with the warm welcoming brown on black face of her favorite bodyguard appearing at her shoulder. He put his head on her pillow and stared into her face.

"Morning Jake." She greeted him with a scratchy voice.

Lori glanced around the room disappointed to find herself alone. She could have sworn that she'd felt *his* presence there with her last night. She needed to go to the bathroom but was not sure where it was. She vaguely remembered having a bath, so she started opening doors, found the third one to be the correct one and Jake followed her in.

While she was in the bath, she heard someone come into her room, but assumed it was Marion hearing her stirring and checking on her. Jake's ears perked up. He went to the door but no one said anything to her and Jake did not bark, so Lori continued brushing her teeth, gargling and washing her face. Everything that she needed was here, all the comforts and necessities, except her own clothes.

She felt much better today, not nearly as weak and shaky, just a little sore and stiff. Her spirit seemed improved, too, in the daylight.

When she went back into her room, it was empty. Jake walked around the room sniffing a little and then settled back down in his corner, expecting her to get back in bed. Instead Lori walked to the hall door, opened it and stuck her head out. She could hear the murmur of voices in the distance.

She didn't have a robe but her gown was modest enough to walk down the hall so she did. Following the sounds and smell of coffee she passed through the empty great room heading toward the kitchen. She found Marion with dimples in her cheeks, preparing coffee and tea trays with Hugh/JeanPaul seated on a bar stool at the counter charming her.

"Lori, what are you doing out of bed? Did you rest well? The doctor says you need to rest. If you are not in bed, you must sit." Marion insisted.

JeanPaul pulled up a chair for her. Jake trotted in behind her and spotting his food bowl, he skidded to a stop on the slippery tile floor and began scarfing it up. The other three, watching the big dog, laughed uproariously.

"That dog is one eating machine." Marion remarked.

"Yeah, and he will probably lose weight, missing his regular daily meals at every house on the island." Lori quietly remarked.

"I think that he will not miss much. He seems to have quite a storage facility, *oui*?" Hugh remarked in his JeanPaul accented voice.

"Well, he is a big dog but I don't think that one single ounce is fat. He is all muscle and heart, aren't you boy?"

Jake finished his first meal of the day and let out a big belch, causing them to laugh again. "Would you mind letting him out? Thanks, I don't know when he was outside last. He has been on guard for long time, weren't you old boy?" Lori asked.

Jake quietly "Woofed" his answer to her. They laughed yet again as he ran out the door lickety-split.

"Would you like a cup of coffee, Lori? Or would you rather have tea or hot chocolate?"

"I think coffee for now, thank you."

"Only if you put cream and sugar in it, no fake stuff, okay? For your own good, the doctor said. Something about stimulants and low blood sugar when in shock."

Stirring sugar and thick sweet cream into her coffee, Lori asked either of them. "Were you in my room right before I came in here?"

"No, we were right here," both of them denied and worriedly exchanged glances.

"When Jake and I were in the bathroom, we heard someone in my room." She tried to shrug it off but didn't succeed entirely.

Hugh strode down the hall toward her room at a brisk pace. He threw back the door and searched the room, the closets and the bath thoroughly. Finding nothing out of place or that should not be there. On his way back to the kitchen he had a thought and hurried back to Lori to confirm his theory. Entering the kitchen he shook his head at Marion and asked Lori.

"Have you put your jewelry box somewhere safe, Lori?" He let Jake back in the door.

"Why no, I haven't seen it or thought about it since the fire. You did save it for me, didn't you? There is nothing much in it but some old jewelry, pictures and private things." She frowned down in her cup and sipped the hot coffee.

"*Oui, cherie*. Actually *you* saved it. You had it firmly in your grip when I pulled you out of the window." He grinned at her, wanting to cheer her up. "I almost had to break your arm to let it go. You held on so tight."

"Thank you. And thank you for saving me. I haven't had a chance to tell you."

Lori told him shyly, looking into his tiger eyes with such trust that Hugh wanted to hold and protect her. She made him feel such guilt. He had never before put an innocent at risk in his work and he felt so damn bad about it all.

He almost wished that she hadn't showed up on this island, but only almost. Now that he had her back in his life again, he didn't know how he could ever let her go. If he was not so damn jealous of that stupid captain, he would let Jerrod take her away back to St. Thomas. He knew she would be safer there, but he could not let her go with that...that pirate. That reprobate had too much interest in her already. Even *he* could be part of this drug ring. No! He could not let Lori go to him.

But someone had shown interest in her jewelry box since it was not in her room. "It is not in your room now. It was last night. Marion, would you mind doing a quiet search around the house, in case someone just moved it?"

Marion nodded her head at him as she went about preparing Miss Genny's breakfast tray and then left them alone.

"Were you in my room last night? I felt you and Jake last night. Were you there all night?"

He nodded his head at her and kept his head averted so she would not see the worry there. He poured himself more coffee and gulped it down, hot, black and strong.

"I didn't want you to wake up alone in the night and be afraid."

She nodded too, but said. "Jake was with me."

"But where was *he* the night of the fire? He came to get me. He woke me up and then led me back to your window. He's the one that saved you."

"I don't know. He is a great dog isn't he? But I just don't understand. He was asleep snoring on his rug when I went to bed, in front of the fireplace where he always slept." She paused. "He never left me at night unless I had company."

He looked up sharply at her. "The good Captain took you home after the party."

Lori put her chin up and stared Hugh in the eye.

"Yes, he did. And he never stepped one foot in my place. We sat out on the point, oh, for an hour or so, until about two, I think. Then he took my cart to the boat dock. I heard him leave. And I went to bed. Alone."

She sat up straighter. "You were the only one who spent the night there, and I think that you know that."

He hadn't realized that he'd been holding his breath until he let it out. He didn't want to get into that here and now. But an enormous burden seemed to lift from his shoulders.

"Lori, you told me at the party to quit watching you. What did you mean?"

"Well, for a while now I have had the feeling that I was being watched. I thought it was you. I never saw anyone but I felt it. Eyes upon me. Made me very uncomfortable. I started closing the curtains, locking up and staying in more. I don't know." She shrugged. "I do not think it was only my imagination. I mean Jake never went on alert, but it was kind of creepy."

"Why in the world didn't you tell me? So I could check it out. Dammit Lori, you need to trust me on this. You know that I have nothing but your best interests at heart."

JeanPaul slammed his cup down and spilt hot coffee over the rim onto his hand and the counter. "Damn." He blurted under his breath. Furious with her but more furious with himself, he tried to keep his voice down and their conversation private but knew that he was getting too loud.

"How do I put my trust in a magician, or an escape artist who says one thing but has the endless capability to disappear into thin air?" Lori asked him wryly. "I do trust you. I don't know why. I shouldn't, but I do. Come to think of it, that's not the first time that Jake got out of the cabin at night. It happened at least three times. I would go to bed at night with the dog asleep on his rug and the next morning I would be alone. I can't begin to explain it. It just happened. Even my front door was locked." She shrugged again.

"I am going to the cabin to look things over. It should be cooled down enough to make some preliminary investigation and see what was going on. I will make sure that Marion or Miss Genny stays with you whenever I am gone."

"Hugh, will you check and see if my laptop burned up on my table? And if my disk was destroyed in the kitchen drawer where the utensils were kept? I put it there Friday before the party. I asked Benjamin to check out the lab and report back to me last night but the doctor's medication must have knocked me out. Did he come back?"

"Yes, he came back. He was considerably agitated when Miss Genny wouldn't let him see you but he wouldn't talk to anyone else. I'm sure he'll show up this morning to see you. I will see what I can find out for you. Keep Jake at your side all day today. Make sure someone else is around you, too. Okay? Promise? And do not go to Charlotte Amalie alone. If I'm not back before you leave, take Benjamin with you to the main island. Do not talk too much, and please, please be alert and on guard for anything else."

Marion returned to the kitchen and cheerily asked. "What can I make you for breakfast, JeanPaul? Lori, for you, I'm making a three-cheese omelet with mushrooms, light but filling then off you go back to your room. To bed. Miss Genny's orders. After breakfast she will be in to join you. She said that you two had a chat coming. Look out. You are in for a marathon." She smiled at Lori. The dog had followed her in.

"JeanPaul, the box that Benjamin brought is in the great room in the corner near the painting behind Miss Genny's chair. I don't know why. I didn't touch it. I thought that you might want to check it out first." Marion nodded her head in the direction of the great room.

"*Oui*, that sounds fine."

Lori's gaze reflected Hugh's mesmerizing golden stare and found it difficult to breathe. She mentally shook herself free of his magnetic pull and cupped her chin in her hand, thinking about all that had happened to her since she arrived. No wonder she had been on such an emotional roller coaster.

Hugh thought how absolutely adorable she looked in that white lacy nightgown thing. She certainly didn't look like forty-three but looked young and vulnerable. Damn, he would give anything to keep her safe.

While the heated glances were being exchanged, Sheree in a bright red peignoir with feathers sauntered in.

"What is all the noise about at this ungodly hour in the morning? And why is that beast in the house? Ah, good morning JeanPaul, how are *you* today?" She asked in her very best sultry seductive voice. "I hope that *you* slept as well as *I* did." Batting her false eyelashes at him, she ran her brilliant red painted fingertips up his arm. Sheree tapped his cheek lightly with her hand and then winked at the room as if she and JeanPaul had shared the night together.

Lori couldn't stand it. She tried not to, but could not help laughing anyway. Of all people *she* knew exactly where Hugh had spent the night.

Marion smiled broadly and turned away to the stove to begin cooking. Hugh smiled at Lori's infectious laughter and placed his hand over his mouth to try to keep his humor private, but it didn't work.

Sheree wondered what was so funny and narrowed her eyes at the other occupants of the room.

Jake got up, stretched and walked over to sit between Lori and the red witch in a display of his own act of defiance.

"What is that dog doing in here?" Sheree asked shrilly. No one answered the question.

Lori could have sworn Jake was smiling his grimace grin, too, which made her laugh all over again. He sure could crack her up. She had to wipe tears from her eyes, from laughing so hard, but reached down to pat his head first. Her grandmother had always said that laughter was good for the soul. At this very moment, hers must be in extra fine condition because of this silly old dog.

Lori inhaled the aroma of the sumptuous steamy omelet Marion in front of her and dug in with a relish. "Yum, it is wonderful, as usual." Taking a big mouthful, she chomped, rolling her eyes in bliss. "I guess I'm hungry 'cause I slept so much yesterday, but I am feeling better already." She made excuses for being such a pig.

Hugh and Marion smiled, watching her eat. Sheree gave her a scathing glare and walked over to a plate of warm croissants that Marion had just taken out of the oven and placed on the counter. Her two long elegant fingers picked up one of the fresh breads. She broke off a teeny, tiny portion of one and bit off an even smaller bite and then proceeded to over masticate it.

Without saying anything, JeanPaul slipped out of the room to check out the 'missing' jewelry box. Someone had obviously shown enough interest in the box to take it out of her room and investigate it at his leisure. And that someone waited until she was out of the room. He knew that nothing but personal things were in there, but someone didn't.

He carefully examined the box and its contents. He didn't have the capabilities here to check the box for fingerprints, but listened first and opened the lid gingerly, feeling around the rim for any signs of tampering or wiring. He sorted through the contents rapidly, finding nothing missing or added and sat silently, thinking for a few more minutes.

The doorbell rang and JeanPaul called out to the kitchen, "I will get it," and opened the door for Benjamin.

He took Ben by the arm and told him quietly. "Benjamin, I want to you to stay close to Lori today, while I go to the cabin and check out the damage to discover what started the fire.

"Lori told me she sent you to check on the lab and report back. What did you find out? Make sure you report to her when she is alone. Can you think of any excuse to stick around here today? I prefer that you go with her on the boat to Charlotte Amalie, too, if I am not back. Is that okay? I do *not* want her going alone. Trust me on this, I know that she trusts you. So I do, too."

Benjamin looked at JeanPaul strangely, but responded by nodding his head at the appropriate times.

"The lab showed no signs of being broken into but the reports were all gone. Both of the daily log books were gone, in fact everything written. Everything. If it was in writing, it is gone. Lists of chemicals, even. It is so weird. *And nothing else is gone.* The slides, the cassettes, the photos are safe.

"But if the fire had spread, the lab could have gone up in smoke because there are very potent inflammables present. It would have been like a bomb, a giant Molotov cocktail. Alcohols and xylene. Gone lab. Just like that." Benjamin snapped his fingers.

"None of the locks looked tampered with? No scratches on the smooth surfaces? No pick marks, or unusual digs?" JeanPaul asked.

"No. Not even on the drawers where the paperwork was kept locked up. It was as though no one had ever been there. Phantom intruders."

"Thanks for filling me in, Benjamin. Avoid the lab until Lori is ready to go back, can you? And stick here with her today, please?"

Hugh led Benjamin back to the kitchen, stuck his head in and said. "See you later."

Halfway to the station, Hugh smacked the steering wheel three times, realizing that he allowed himself to step out of role. No wonder the kid had looked at him so strangely. He had forgotten to use his accent. Damn! So much for JeanPaul.

He had never been so distracted on a case before. *She* came first, not the assignment. He almost wished that she would leave this place but he knew that was a purely wasteful wish. She would be part of a team but never, ever be controlled. Maybe that was part of his fascination for her. She was so damned independent.

He loved her. He'd loved her most of his life and if it meant he had to sit out in the woods every night watching her sleep, he would.

Of course, he would rather be *inside* with her.

Twenty-One

The trip to Charlotte Amalie was unremarkable except for the fact that Lori had both Jake and Ben as escorts. Jerrod had done everything in his power to keep her on the St. Thomas and she had been tempted. She knew whatever had caused the fire was no accident, and maybe everyone would be safer with her out of the way for a while. But then again, she never could resist a challenge. Besides she had work to do and would get it done. Period.

She didn't have pneumonia or lung damage. Lori knew that long before the trip back to town, but no one would let her out of it. She was not burned and the stiffness would fade with time. Lori was antsy to get back to work and didn't think that she could take much more of sharing a house with that witch. No matter how pathetic she was.

Miss Genny and Marion were great and the guys were nice, but she needed her own space and would explode if she had to stay there much longer. She chafed under all of the well-meaning attention. Her smile had become irrevocably glued in place. At least Jake never made her feel so doggone crowded.

Everyone hovered, waiting for her to collapse like some damsel in distress. *What's the matter, do I look like I'm made of glass or something? I am surely not that helpless, am I? I don't think so.*

Lori knew that she would be pinned down here for a few more days at least. Miss Genny, that sly thing, intentionally restrained her from getting any clothing, therefore, doing an excellent job of keeping her pinned at the West house.

Captain Jerrod would bring her a shipment of some clothes from town on his next delivery run but there was bound to be someone closer to her size on this dang island. It had taken them an hour to come up with a windbreaker suit for her to wear to the hospital. The sucker had hung on her like a tent from St. Louis Tent and Awning Co. You'd have thought she was a shrimp, or something. Her size was not *that* unique a size.

She hated being the center of attention and treated like an invalid, but resigned herself to live with it a little while longer. A constant stream of islanders stopped by to check on her.

Benjamin reminded her of the computer and cell phone loss and of her inability to contact her friends via the Internet. She knew that they would be worried when she didn't hit either of the specified chat times and they could check to see when she last logged on.

Since there were apparently no other computers on the island, she asked if she could use a phone. She was informed that the only off island phone line was at the main house. So Lori sent Benjamin to call Dr. Walker's pager and Dr. Rigby to leave a short message that Lori would be contacting them for a chat no later than Tuesday or Wednesday. Lori did not want them freaking out when no one could reach her.

She also told Benjamin to call Jerrod to ask if he could please bring her a new laptop computer with the specifications she needed and the software programs loaded for her and also a new cell phone. She carefully wrote down her requirements so it would be compatible with all the necessary hookups. "Tell Jerrod I can pay for the items with grant money but I'll have to get new plastic to replace the destroyed credit cards or transfer money from my account on the mainland to pay for it. Whichever he prefers."

"Something else. JeanPaul told me to stay with you today. But Miss Lori he had no accent! It was gone! He talked as plain as me or you!

Lori made a face and told him. "It's okay. Don't worry about it. And please, Benjamin, it is important to keep it to yourself."

She could see the questions in his eyes but he didn't ask. Maybe this would all be over soon, and they all could get on with their lives. But she was definitely not yet ready to leave this lovely place. Not yet…

She wanted to cut her downtime losses to a minimum, and was determined to recoup all her files and necessary paperwork. Ha. Thank God for all the backup precautions. Whoever had cleaned out her lab, just *thought* that they shut her down.

She was ticked off at the loss of all her written work. Benjamin had been surprised at her fury when he told her. Well, maybe the intent had been to scare her off, but whatever, it was *not* going to work. *I can be as tenacious as a tick on a hound if necessary.*

As soon as she had the chance, she would have to see that her personal files in St. Louis were placed in a more protected database, too. She had not originally planned for them to go to mainframe storage, just the redundancy of her own PC back in Missouri. She damn sure did not want to lose the only hard copies remaining of her work. Her PC at the lab was not the Pentagon and even that had been broken into by hackers.

All day she waited for Hugh to come back and tell her what he found back at the station. She was anxious to find out the cause of the fire. It seemed like everyone here took it for granted that she had started the fire. That is, everyone but Ben and Hugh.

JeanPaul returned to the West house as gregarious as ever that evening, but Lori didn't have a chance to speak alone with him. Upon his return, she sent Benjamin on the phone call mission and managed to survive the flow of well-wishing islanders.

Except for the wicked witch who was in her usual, ever pouting jealousy mode.

The inactivity was getting Lori down. She could feel fat accumulating on her butt. She had not been able to swim laps in what seemed like days. Every time she tried to get up and swim or even walk on the beach, Miss Genny threatened to call the doctor on her and made her promise to rest.

Geez. How could anyone rest in a place like this? It was like Union Station in St. Louis. People were coming and going all the time. Miss Genny and Marion were in their prime, tending to the influx of guests, feeding the flock.

Lori chuckled at that, finally giving up, and returned to her darkened room with Jake at her heels. She slid into bed with a pounding residual headache. Probably due to all the fuss and stress, she told herself. She quickly drifted off into a dreamless, but restless nap.

The door opened quietly. Hugh slipped noiselessly inside the room. Lori woke instantly, totally, wide awake now but with a blasting headache.

"Turn on a light Hugh."

"Why? Afraid to be alone in the dark with me?" He asked her teasingly.

"After running into you on the beach that night, I don't think I could ever be afraid of you again." She retorted. "I'm afraid a body can only be ravished like that once in a lifetime. It couldn't survive more than that."

He turned on the lamp on the corner table and watched Lori flinch at the light. "What's wrong?"

"A headache, Hugh. I have had one most of the time since the fire and some nausea too. You know, I've been thinking about it and I think that someone drugged me the night of the fire."

"What!?" He stood and started pacing the floor. "What makes you think that?"

"Well, I normally drink a whole bottle of water at my bedside before I go to bed when I take my nighttime vitamins. I didn't drink it all that night for some reason. When the fire or some noise woke me up, I could hardly navigate to get out of bed to get to my bedroom door. It was like I had no control over my body. I was dizzy and weak."

"And when I got the door open, I couldn't see smoke in the cabin. It was drawing up the chimney just like a good fireplace fire. There was heat, plenty of heat, but no smoke to make me light-headed and woozy. I should not have collapsed like that after I broke out the window. I am strong as a horse and my lungs are in great shape from swimming, which by the way they won't let me do now." She almost scowled.

"Lots of things could have made you crash then. Did the doctor take blood samples today?"

"Felt like he drew about a quart, at least."

"I'll call and ask him if he can test for a drug panel."

"Okay. Well, spit it out. Tell me what you found out."

"The fire looks like it started in the living room in the fireplace. Then a log rolled out and set the hardwood floor on fire. It was made to look like an accident. But we know you did *not* start *any* fire. It would have worked, too, if Jake hadn't come to get me in time. Some things don't make sense. There was no sign of your computer, phone or your disk. I'm no expert, I guess it's possible they could have burned up if the fire was hot enough but I'd expect to find some residue or something from them." He stopped pacing the floor, sat back down, then leaned forward, putting his elbows on his knees and clasped his hands together.

"Benjamin tells me that all your reports and paperwork are missing from the lab with no signs of forced entry. That tells me that someone has keys or other means of gaining entry to the lab. To all the buildings, most likely. So what are you thinking?" He saw her eyebrows drawn together in yet another frown.

"Something someone told me but for the life of me I cannot quite remember it yet. But I will, I will. Something important, I think. I hate it when I cannot remember something that I want to."

"Just relax, don't force it. It will come to you. Tonight I'm going back. Do you think you will be okay alone here for a couple hours? I want to slip out after the island goes to sleep. I hope to poke around under your cabin.

"They already started clearing out the burnt debris. That's why I stayed all day. I was afraid I'd miss something and I didn't want them getting rid of anything that might be important. So I helped them clear. Emily Moore has ordered a shipment of lumber and shingles, coming out shortly. The men on the island will stop their work until the cabin is back in shape. A matter of days they tell me."

"You are kidding, that quick? Boy, that's amazing. They do not mess around here, do they?"

"No, they don't. You need to be thinking about whether you want to move back into that cabin or the other one. Miss Emily has ordered the other one prepared for you. Or you can move in with me." He put a hand up, halting the objection he saw in her face. "Either way, I will be spending nights with you from now on. No argument."

"Oh Hugh, for god's sake, don't start."

"I'm not going anywhere. We've got a lot to talk about, honey. I went through your things. I know what happened to Nathan, and I want to tell you..."

"*Stop*. I *cannot* talk about that now. Please. Not now." Tears welled up in her eyes and she grabbed her head in pain. "Please Hugh. I am just not ready."

He couldn't stand the defeated look in her eyes. It made him want to crush her in his arms but he respected her wishes and backed off. He wiped her eyes gently with his thumbs and felt her quiver beneath his touch. Hugh forced himself to back away from her and continued.

"I'm either staying with you openly, or you are staying with me. Or I am sitting in the woods. Or sitting on your front porch at night. So you decide. I'll be back later tonight. Sleep on it. Remember. I love you. But now you better come out from hiding. It's time for dinner. Or you might be cornered into another chat." Grinning, he watched her groan and pull a pillow over her head.

"I'm coming. I'm coming. Give me a break. I love her dearly, but my head hurts way too much for two in one day. My head is spinning a Kansas twister right now. Thanks. You have definitely added to my peace of mind. Now get out so I can put on a robe or something." She threw a pillow at him as he went out the door, sighing as the door closed.

Much later when the household settled down for the night, he whispered to her in the dark. "I am leaving now Lori, lock the door behind me. I am going out through your patio door. Try to go back to sleep. Jake will stay here with you. I am walking all the way across the island so it may take me awhile. If I'm not back by dawn send out the cavalry." He told her casually.

"Don't joke Hugh. Be careful, please." She whispered back. Lori locked the door behind him, listening for the sound of his footsteps but hearing only the silence of the night.

She tried to stay awake but the tranquilizers worked their magic spell. She drifted off to sleep with a swirling pattern of questions and answers, bouncing around and around in her head like the black eight ball toy, waiting for the right answer to emerge...

~ * ~

She tumbled free fall off a cliff in a blitz of adrenaline and forced herself out of a deep sleep when her ears registered a scratching sound at her door. Jake stood up in his corner and shook himself but didn't show any obvious signs of tension. It was nearing dawn and she knew it must be Hugh. Trying to slow her heartbeat, she went to the door to let him inside.

"Lori, let me in. Sh. Be quiet." He scratched at the door with a fingernail.

She opened the patio door, held the curtains back, let him in, then dropped the room darkening curtains back into position.

"Do not turn on the lights until we get inside the bathroom. Then close the door and turn on the light. Do not make any noise." He mumbled to her.

When she flipped the bathroom light on, she was startled to see dried blood on his face. "Good grief, Hugh what in God's name happened to you? Did you fall down?"

Seeing a purple swelling at the base of his neck, she gently wiped her hand over it and brushed the sand off him.

"No, when I got there, I heard some noise down inside your cabin where I was planning to explore. Before I knew it, someone put my lights out. I didn't have a chance to get out of sight. There must have been more than one of them."

She set him down on the toilet seat lid, wet a washcloth with warm water and washed the blood off his face and neck. There were no marks on his face. The blood had trickled from the wound on the back of his neck. She shook her head at him.

"Obviously, you should have let me go with you or at least you should have taken Jake."

"Yeah right and leave you alone. Forget it."

"Well, you damn fool. You let someone sneak up on you and club you on the head." She hissed at him, angry at his injury and held a cold wash cloth to the bump on his neck.

"Yeah, well someone was quiet as a mouse. I never heard him coming. One was on guard. And the other one was doing whatever, probably hiding what I was looking for."

"Are you hurt anywhere else?"

"Only my pride, Lori, my love. Only my pride. It took forever to get there. I was so quiet crossing the length of the island. I stayed off the roads and never saw or heard anyone along the way. When I got to the station, I could hear sounds like a shovel or rake on sand. I didn't see lights but the walls could have hidden any small lights.

"Before I stepped out into the open, WHAM! When I finally woke up, all I could hear was silence. I didn't get to do what I planned. I lost my flashlight when I went down and couldn't find it in the dark. What a waste of time."

"Do you think there is any chance of concussion?"

"Not on my hard head. Now I'll have to be back to work in a couple of hours and try to find what was going on while we are working today. Without anyone being the wiser. Will my collar cover the bump?"

"No, but a turtle neck would."

"Okay, no sense in advertising it. Either they know who I am or they do not." Hugh shrugged his shoulders.

"Too late to worry about now. I will go back to my place to change before I go to help the men at the station anyway. Is it all right if I lay down here a little while and rest before it is time to go? I do not want to leave you alone any longer tonight, or rather this morning, until the household is awake here. Do *not* stay by yourself today. Keep someone around you all the time and Jake of course. Can I?" He pointed at the bed.

"Go ahead. I will watch *you* this time."

"No. I want you to lie down beside me, please?" He kicked his shoes off, stretching out on the bed with his outstretched hand palm upward for her.

"Please?" He repeated until she gave in and lay down carefully beside him, making sure to leave space between them. Which he immediately erased by pulling her into his side. Rolling over on his side, he tucked her into him like two perfect fitting spoons. He wrapped one arm around her, preventing any escape, burrowed his nose into the fresh lemon scent of her hair, sighed once and was instantly asleep.

Lori smiled to herself in the darkness and said, "Men." She snuggled her way back into his warmth and closed her eyes.

Twenty-two

Several hours later, Lori found herself alone again. Except for Jake, of course, a constant in her life. She put her hand behind her on the bed and found the sandy spot where Hugh slept, was now cold. She hoped he was more careful today, that fool. Lori needed to get out of here, if only to sit outside on the patio today. Maybe if she was lucky, she could coerce Benjamin into taking her to the station.

The day passed excruciatingly slowly for her, after doing everything but count sheep to pass the time. She wanted to sneak outside to swim laps but most likely would have sunk to the bottom of the pool in the baggy sweats that she had on today. No one seemed the least bit interested in providing clothes that fit. She ground her teeth in frustration. Benjamin came to get lunch for the men, working at the station. Lori and Jake slipped out of the house, hoping to escape unnoticed, and sneaked into the Jeep while Marion and Miss Genny were occupied. But when they came outside and found Lori determined to see the damage, Miss Genny decided to go along and check the progress, too.

The freedom of the open air felt wonderful to Lori, which made her feel guilty for not appreciating the thoughtful care provided her. They could have blamed her for the fire, and treated her considerably different than they had.

Her spirits lifted under the brilliant blue sky that created such a balmy ride across the island. She hugged Jake in response to her emotional high. The high didn't last long, though. Only as long as it took to reach the sight of the research station.

She came crashing down at the destructive display of evidence. Like a sore thumb blighting this end of the island. Her beautiful white cabin stood like a big black smoky, empty shell. On this side, large gaping windowless eyes stared blindly at the empty pit of nothingness. A jumble of blackened wood had been piled outside the cabin. The men had spent hours, clearing out the debris.

The two other buildings stood brilliantly white against the darkened shell, already freshened with a coat of whitewash. The men were busy as bees, readying the cabin for the load of lumber on its way.

Lori shivered, realizing how close she came to being a part of the very ashes being disposed of. It was a wonder the other cabins had escaped from the blaze.

Miss Genny caught Lori's shivering and fussed at her. "You should have stayed at the house, you are cold. You did not need to see this now. It could have waited until later."

Lori leaned forward from the back seat and kissed her on a soft wrinkled cheek.

"Miss Genny, I'm fine. I needed to get out of the house. I needed to feel again. I need to get busy again. Oh, I need so many things. I also need to thank you for how wonderful you have all been to me. Over and over. But I need to get on with things. You understand, don't you? I just can't sit around doing absolutely nothing. It's driving me bonkers."

"I know, my dear, just for another day or so. Then you can be about your work." Miss Genny patted her hand. "I do so enjoy having you around. You do not mind an old woman being selfish, do you? The Captain will be arriving before you know it. Then you and Benjamin can get back to business."

They sat in the Jeep and watched Benjamin carry the food baskets to a trestle table set up under the shade of a large tree. Miss Emily sat with the reconstruction floor plans spread out on a table while she directed the workers. No wonder everyone appeared so competent. The men quit working and washed their hands with the outside hoses used to battle the fire, before ambling over to the table for lunch.

"They are so efficient and organized. It is amazing."

"Not really, my dear. We have had disasters before. Storms, hurricanes, and yes, also fires." Laughing at the dismay written all over Lori's face, she tapped her arm.

"It is simply a matter of practice. We have learned to be self-sufficient over the years. We could use our own wood if we had to but that would mean drying the lumber. This way we save time. The cabin will be back to normal in a week or two at the most. If the weather holds for us. My boys went back to their work on St. Croix but all the other men will divert their energy to restoration until it's complete."

"Remarkable."

"Yes, is it not? Besides their regular jobs, almost everyone here is multi-tasked. They are trained in a number of other fields, carpentry, plumbing, electric. Practical things like that. They have built any number of houses, either here or on the big islands. They enjoy it. We give them the time off to do it whenever they want. Gives them a break from their regular work and a feeling of satisfaction I think, when they have completed their project."

"Do you mind if I walk around a little?"

Miss Genny laughed at her. "Of course not, dear."

She gingerly stepped out of the vehicle onto the sand, her feet a little tender on the soles and slowly walked around her cottage.

It looked like complete devastation to her. The wooden veranda and steps were gone leaving an ugly hole in the sand in the front of the cabin. She took a deep breath and walked around the other side. A small four foot gap in the concrete block wall appeared where the small gas tank for the stove had exploded. Otherwise, the concrete block walls looked sound. No roof, beams, ceiling, flooring, or interior walls remained, just a big black empty shell.

It was depressing as Hades, Lori thought, as she scuffed her sandals on the sand. It took all her will power to ignore the lab when really she wanted to run inside and guarantee her work wasn't compromised. She knew better. She would just have to trust Ben on that one, but it took a bit of will power.

The men joked, cutting up with each other while they stuffed their faces. Jake investigated the possibility of food for himself until Emily Moore placed a plateful of food on the ground for the big dog to greedily wolf down. The men watched him eat and poked fun at him but he was impervious.

Miss Emily waved Lori over. "Miss Lori, tomorrow we begin reconstruction. Are there any changes you might like to recommend? You saved me a trip. None of us have ever lived in one of the cabins with your design. I wanted to know if you see a need to modify it in some way?"

Lori thoughtfully scrunched up her face, staring off at the lagoon. "Well, I think the plan is practical. But the glass in the bedroom window was so strong, it wouldn't kick out. I almost didn't get out because of that. I had to throw the night stand through it to break it."

"Oh dear, but why didn't you open the window?"

"It would not unlock. It was stuck."

"But there is a backup safety window in each room that swings out. Were you not shown them? I am afraid we have been derelict in our duties to you. The windows are strengthened to protect them during the hurricane season. But three windows in each cabin can open like a door in an emergency, since there is only the one door." Emily frowned at Lori.

She pointed out the windows on the floor plan. "Here, see them? There should have been a card on the back of the bedroom door showing the exits clearly. I am so sorry."

"Like on a hotel door? Hmm, well I am sure I would have seen that. Thank you for asking my opinion about the plans."

She drifted off toward Hugh, hoping it wasn't noticeable she was seeking him out. What the heck, the secret was most likely no secret anymore. Or it wouldn't be for much longer if he planned to guard her bedroom every night. After shyly greeting the men, she stood around self-consciously until Hugh finished eating. Then he detached himself from the group to escort her back toward the Jeep.

"How's your head? Discovered anything today?" She wasn't able to keep her eyes from the dismal scene. Besides it was better *not* to look at him.

"Fine. Maybe. No one seemed interested in me today. Everyone seems natural. Either someone is a good actor or they are *all* innocent."

"Hugh, did you know there were emergency exits posted on the back of the doors in the bedrooms of the guest cabins? There *never* was one on my door. Was there on yours? I never had any idea that three windows swung on hinges, like a door, besides sliding up and down. Whoever heard of such a thing?"

"No, I haven't seen a sign like that either. I wonder if you can use them to get inside from the outside. Or if the lab has any windows like that? Go on back and don't make an issue out of the window thing. We'll figure it out one way or another. I'll check out the windows at my place when I clean up. Stay with the others and I'll see you for supper later. Love you, Lori. Jake, where's Jake?"

Lori checked behind her and saw that Jake finished eating and was running to catch up with them.

"Don't worry he'll beat us to the Jeep. I don't think the windows in the lab are the right size to use as a door. They are only half windows to begin with. I'll ask Ben."

Lori reached out and touched his arm as she climbed up into the back seat. *It was just to stabilize me*, she thought making excuses to herself. *Yeah sure,* she mocked herself, *and the Pope is not a Catholic, you silly fool.* She was not going to spend the day arguing with herself. Surely she could find something more important to do than that.

Never would she be more thankful to get clothes that fit and out of this confinement. *Ungrateful wretch,* she told herself. *Get a grip and thank your lucky stars. Yeah, yeah, yeah. Just zip it, bimbo lips...* muttering disparagingly to her lusty other self.

~ * ~

After another boring nap Lori resolved to swim laps. She could feel herself getting flabby, from inactivity. She marched out onto the patio with Jake trotting along behind her and confronted Miss Genny.

"Look, I know that you only have my best interests at heart but if I don't get to swim or exercise soon, I'm going to explode, or whatever. If I have to go skinny dipping, I am going to swim, okay? Do you think that you could find me something to wear, please?"

"Oh Lori, my dear, you are so funny. Why, that would be a sight." Genny chuckled louder and louder.

"I do not think that will be necessary. I have another surprise for you. While you were sleeping, the Captain came by and brought you some rather large boxes. When he found you asleep, he went over to check the progress but he will be back for dinner. Maybe there is a swimsuit? Why don't you go see my dear?"

Miss Genny was laughing merrily. "Oh Marion, quick, come here and listen to this." She repeated what Lori had said.

She flew into the house and threw things out of the boxes that contained clothes until she triumphantly came up with a swimsuit. "AHA! Finally, someone with sense." Holding it up and checking the size, she was satisfied to find it should fit her. She rushed out to the patio area and would've passed right on through to the lagoon until Miss Genny gently wagged her finger at her and shook her head, reminding her of caution.

"I do not think so, my dear. This pool is heated and much safer for you now."

Lori surrendered, gratefully slipping into the warm pool and started with a few stretching exercises before laying back in the water and slipping into the regimen of swimming laps. Ignoring her surroundings, she lost herself, engrossed in the exercises.

Stretching. Breathing. Stroking. Reaching out, reaching down deep. Turning. Pushing and pulling herself, back and forth through the water. When finally she reached the mindless limit of her exhausted body, she slowed, rolled over on her back and swam slow motion backstrokes.

Decelerating her metabolic rate, she put her other functions of sight and sound back into gear. She gradually became aware of her surroundings and found the afternoon had lengthened into evening and the patio was filled with spectators.

She suddenly stopped stroking, sunk into the water and instead of gasping for air, her mouth filled with water. It forced her up and out of the water, sputtering and choking to the sound of catty clapping. She quickly swam to the edge of the pool and lifted herself out of the pool.

Jerrod jumped up from his lounger to get to the edge first and offer her a dry towel. Hugh, Marion, Miss Genny and, of course, the wicked witch were watching.

Lori stood poised at the pool's edge, rubbing the towel briskly on her hair and suspiciously eyed the group gathered at the cocktail tray. Jerrod appeared comfortable in a blue denim shirt and well-worn jeans.

Hugh wore a black polo shirt and black jeans. She watched him raise his glass to salute her. Lori glared at him, sitting on a settee next to 'guess who?' dressed in a skin tight black catsuit.

Since revenge could be 'oh so sweet', Lori leisurely dried her legs and arms, patted her chest dry and said. "Why, I did not have any idea I had an audience or I would surely have performed for you all." Lori added a slight southern drawl to her Midwestern accent, batting wet eyelashes on her cheeks, and smiled ever so sweetly up at Jerrod.

She wrapped the towel around her body, and reached over to hug Jerrod. She wrapped both arms tightly around him and kissed him firmly on the mouth.

"Thank you so much, Jerrod. How did you know I was so desperate for clothes that fit me. Everything here on the island was just *way* too big for me. However did you get the size right? And thank you so much for bringing my other gear. I didn't expect you until tomorrow. You're a lifesaver."

"I knew you'd be anxious. Once Julie and I had everything gathered, why wait until my regular run, I was thinking? Julie supplied the size and most of the shopping. She thought you were probably one size up from her. I can see she did a great job of fitting you. Must be a woman thing. She said it was great fun spending someone else's money. I picked up all the electronic stuff for you, too. So here I am." Jerrod looked pleased as punch.

"Excuse me while I get dressed. Thanks again, Jerrod." She smiled brilliantly at him, blew him a kiss and waltzed past the others with Jake on her heels.

She was both furious and elated at the same time. *Must be an endorphin high, never mind, what do I have to wear?* The boxes had been moved to her room and the clothes were hung in the closet. Not a big selection to choose from but she had been in baggy clothes way too long. Silently thanking Marion for unpacking, she swiftly sorted through them looking for something. Something different. Something special.

"Yes." She found what she had been looking for. She'd give them the chance to compare apples and oranges, by golly.

By the time Lori walked back to the great room, she found that the group migrated indoors with the addition of the painter, Steffan. Needless to say, attention was focused on her entrance, so she made the most of it. Playing a femme fatale was something she hadn't done in a very long time, if ever. *Just let it come naturally, go with the flow, Lori.*

She didn't swing her hips or exaggerate her femininity in any way but taking a deep breath she entered the room with all the aplomb of a princess of the realm. She had chosen a simple mock turtleneck ivory sweater dress, which was form fitting, brushed and dried her hair into a bashful Lady Di do, then added a touch of eye makeup.

The men sat up and took notice, like dogs on point.

Hugh thought the dress was neither too long nor too short but set off her elegant legs to perfection.

This was going to be so easy, it was almost laughable, she decided. She went over to an easy chair, seated herself as gracefully as possible and crossed her legs.

Miss Genny asked her "Lori, my dear, would you like a drink? Assuming it will not interfere with your medication?"

The three men in the room moved toward the bar in one motion without waiting for her response, stumbling over each other in their haste.

"Seltzer with lime please, a tall one, is all I need."

Short little Steffan managed to elbow the others out of the way by a sneaky approach between the taller men. He successfully poured her drink and carried it to her.

"*Voila, mademoiselle.* And may I say that your speedy recovery has left you more beautiful than ever."

"Thank you, Steffan." She answered him quietly with lowered lashes, then staring at him she hoped with wide-eyed innocence.

He sucked in his breath and stomach in a most comical manner and said with a wide smile in his chubby cheeks, "I haven't had a chance to see you, or to find out what in the *sacre bleu* happened to you. I can very well see that you are fine now, but tell me what happened."

"I just don't know."

Looking around the room at the others, she saw Sheree smoking a cigarette with a long skinny holder with a massive pile of butts in a crystal ashtray beside her.

"All I can tell you is that a fire broke out in the cottage. I woke up and finally broke a window out. JeanPaul pulled me out of the burning cabin. I can't remember much more than that." Lori shrugged her shoulders at the thought.

"But Steffan, I am so thankful the portrait was here. It was so lucky that I did not try to take it home that night. I want to thank you again for the portrait. It was certainly quite the most memorable birthday that I ever had."

She got up to hug the little painter and watched Hugh squirm and narrow his eyes at her. "But I am fine now, thank you for asking."

"We were waiting for you for dinner. Now Marion, I think that we may begin." Miss Genny smiled mischievously at Lori's actions. She directed the table seating arrangements and placed Lori between the painter and, across from JeanPaul seated between Marion and Sheree. Seating herself at the head, Miss

Genny watched the complex interplay of sexual tension in the room.

Lori flirted.

JeanPaul scowled.

Jerrod beamed.

Steffan ate as voraciously as Jake did at his plate in the corner.

Sheree stirred the food in her plate endlessly.

Miss Genny kept up a constant stream of chatter. Marion listened and nodded at the appropriate places, which would not have mattered anyway.

Lori thought the evening would never end, since her main objective at this point was to get Hugh alone, all to herself in her room. She had announced to the others that she planned on moving back into the other cottage at the station. She wanted to get back to work as soon as she could.

Miss Genny tried to dissuade her but Lori was adamant. It was time. She was ready. She was appreciative but she just didn't need any more coddling. Of course, she didn't tell Genny that.

Miss Genny was no fool. She knew exactly what Lori needed. Privacy. Her eyes sparkled at the thought.

Lori finally bid them all good night. She kissed them all on the cheek, even the witch, saving Miss Genny's sweet-scented cheek for last, then led Jake down the hall for her last night here in the West house.

YES! She yelled silently.

Twenty-three

Tap, tap, tap sounded on the patio door. Lori had almost given up on him tonight. Jake made no aggressive moves, so she turned out her light, pulled back the curtains and opened the door to admit Hugh. Soundlessly, she pulled him into the room.

When Hugh turned to her, he grabbed her roughly, pulled her to him and hissed at her. "What kind of game are you trying to play? Trying to make me jealous? Okay, it works. I am jealous. *You are mine.* And I do not want those other men putting their filthy lips or paws or anything else on you, got it?"

Lori tried her best to loosen herself from his hold but succeeded only in Hugh's grip tightening. So she tried the reverse and wriggled her body in closer to his.

"Oh Hugh, their lips are *hardly* filthy and they *most definitely* do not have paws. Besides, you hardly have room to talk. Every single time I turn around, *you* are in the clutches of that skinny witch." She hissed vehemently back at him.

Which made him relax his grip on her and chuckle quietly. "Guess you've got me there. It is hard to keep her at arms length." He pulled her in for a bear hug.

"You don't even try." She snuggled in provocatively to his body. "You wretch." Lori smacked him with her fist on his shoulder at the same time.

"Hush woman. And keep still, I need to think. Come here, let me sit here in this chair." Pulling her into his lap, he sat in the corner chair.

"Anyway, *you* are the witch. You have bewitched every man on this island. But sit here quietly. We need to talk. I think that I found something. I said *sit still.*" Her squirming distracted his natural thought processes. He nibbled on her earlobe and breathed heavily into her hair.

Hugh simply couldn't stand it any longer. He stood up, straining with her in his arms, and dumped her unceremoniously onto the bed. Alone. He paced the floor and began talking softly again. He needed to warn her. "Woman. You stay where you are." He pointed at the bed. "The framework around the windows in my house that opens like a door? If the latch is left undone, it can be swung open from the outside. The latch is concealed easily. I never noticed it before. I thought it was part of the frame to hold the screen in place. Anyway, if it is unlocked, you can get it to open, relatively easily, from outside with a knife or something thin.

"And in the sand underneath your front porch, there was something strange. I didn't get to examine it because of all the workers around, but there was an area of sand that was a totally different color than the rest. When I tapped it with my foot, it sounded hollow. I think that there is a door or something wooden under there. I am going back tonight to find out for sure, before the porch is rebuilt and I can't get to it."

"And get clobbered on the head again. Hold on. I'm going with you."

"No! You are not. Forget it. You are staying right here with Jake, where I know that you are safe."

"You need me to help."

"Lori, I have an excess of experience in this spy game. I cannot do my job if I am worried about you. Then I am putting us both at risk. Do you understand? You wait for me, and I'll be back before dawn again, I promise. Okay? Trust me. Don't you leave here, and come after me either. Promise me?"

"All right. But if you are not back by dawn, I'm coming after you. *That* much I promise." He laughed and said. "You've got a deal. Now go to sleep and I'll wake you when I get back. By the way what is your new cell phone number? And kiss me goodnight, my love."

She jumped up from the bed and went to the closet, turned on the closet light, picked up the phone and read the number to him. "334 474 2721."

Lori proceeded to give him an exceedingly thorough 'curl his toes', eye-opening, take-his-breath-away kiss, her hands on both sides of his face.

"Just you remember that, Mister JeanPaul whoever you are." She said triumphantly, closing and locking the door after him, and jumped back in bed with a smug expression on her face.

"Maybe he will be a little more attentive now, Jake. Good night."

Tonight she took vitamins but not the tranquilizer. Lori didn't need it anymore. She needed to think. There was a memory attempting to surface, somewhere firing away at the neurotransmitters and hitting a wall.

She tossed and turned for hours, trying to recover that random memory then got up. Jake lay in his corner and watched her pace. Geez, she must have picked up the habit from Hugh. She tried reviewing every single conversation that she'd had since she reached the island.

Lori knew that it was something that she heard. Words and thoughts, memories and phrases tumbled round and round in her head, and the darkness outside her window was getting lighter when it finally popped free and hit her right between the eyes.

She must find Hugh and tell him what she'd finally remembered. Lori threw open the closet door and looked for a sweatshirt and pair of tights to put on. It was only an hour or so until dawn so she would not worry about dark clothes now, but she wanted to catch Hugh before it was too light to test her theory.

She put on socks and tennies, opening the door to leave, before she realized she'd forgotten her cell phone. She reached into the closet for it when she remembered it had never been activated or the batteries charged. She sat back on the floor, opened it, punched a few buttons, receiving nothing for her effort.

"Damn. Where is my brain? I should have done it already and all I was worrying about were my stupid hormones." She took a flashlight from the nightstand drawer and put it in her pocket.

"Come on, Jake. We have to get to the other end of the island without making noise. We are going to walk up the east side on the beach, okay old boy? Hope it's not a high tide." She mumbled to him.

"Come on, let's go." Slipping out the door of the patio she crept noiselessly along the patio with the dog padding silently.

She cut straight through the woods across the island to bypass the guest cottages at the West house. When she reached the smooth sand, she opened her stride into a strong power walk. She was not much of a jogger but could cover ground pretty fast this way with Jake loping along beside.

Surely Hugh would not be mad at her when he heard what she had to contribute. She couldn't believe it took her this long to remember. It was right in front of her face from the very beginning.

Her breathing was deep and slow and she was anxious to find Hugh. If anyone saw her, they would just think that she was out for an early morning exercise. She thought this was much better than sneaking through the woods, besides being faster.

Determined and enjoying this predawn calm, she lengthened her stride, drawing in the fresh salty morning scent. The air felt a little cool on her face but the exercise kept her warm. She could tell that Jake was loving this walk/run by the silly grin on his face. He kept pace with her by splashing noisily along in the edge of the water, leaving deeply puddled tracks as the tide went out.

The eastern sky hadn't yet assumed its purpling predawn hue but was a lighter shade of dark. The stars were beginning to fade.

The pair slowed down when they reached the lower level of rocky beach below the cliffs, then picked up their speed as they hit more level sand again. The trees above the shore settled to a quiet murmur as the wind died away to almost nothing.

It was a lovely time of day that Lori usually missed because she was much more of a night person than a morning one. It seemed to her that most normal human beings slept their soundest at this time of day.

She recognized the landscaping as she drew nearer the north end of the island and began slowing. She didn't want the pounding of their feet heard and needed to cool down her breathing anyway.

As they reached the curve that led to the station, she stopped and grabbed Jake's collar to hold him back, too. She and Jake stood for a long time with their heads atilt, listening for any sounds that did not belong. They only heard the lapping of the waves. Quietly approaching her old cottage, they walked around to the front.

A large hole gaped where the porch had run across the front of the house. Seeing no sign of Hugh, she slid down the sand into the pit. Jake stayed at the top, peering down at her with his front feet hanging over the edge. The pit sank six feet deep and was extremely dark. There were four stacks of concrete blocks for support of the porch when it was rebuilt.

Taking the flashlight out, she switched it on, pointing its narrow beam over the bottom of the sand. Three walls of the hole were packed with damp sandy dirt. The back wall was the bare foundation of the concrete block structure with a two foot by two foot access hole under the cabin. She shined the light in the hole but only saw more of the dirt and pipes in the darkness.

The sandy bottom was covered with footprints but there was no obvious sign that Hugh had been there. She saw no marks where he would have been digging. No sign of sand displaced or rearranged that she could see.

She started tapping her feet on the sand, listening for hollow or different sounds. Lori thought maybe there was a distinct muffled sound in a certain area but couldn't be sure. Mostly it sounded like somebody stomping on sand. She didn't have any tools for digging, so she kicked at the sand with the sole of her shoe but was getting nowhere fast.

Convinced she had missed him and he was already long gone, she climbed back out of the hole, and headed for Hugh's cottage, hoping to catch him there. She knew he would be mad if he returned to West house and found her missing. She should have thought to leave a note, but she was positive she'd find him.

Her anxiety level rose quickly. It had seemed so simple. She tried to convince herself that she must have passed him on the way.

She and Jake trotted south toward East house while the sky continued to change its hue and ever so dimly began to brighten the night sky. Each minute the darkness changed as the shadows of the woods began to turn from black to darker shades of gray and green.

Lori and Jake slipped silently into those woods like wraiths through the misty quiet of the predawn night.

Hugh's cabin stood, quiet and dark, forbidding and alone, in its clearing of whispering pines. The pine needles crunched softly beneath their feet as they made their way to his door.

Lori tapped on the door, waited a few minutes, then tapped again. Getting no response, she went to the windows and pressed her face against each glass, trying to see inside. She switched on the flashlight, shining it through the window, trying to see better. But found the curtains closed on the front of the house. She tapped again, going around to the bedroom side of the house, assuming his floor plan was the same as hers. Perhaps he was in the shower and couldn't hear her knocking.

Lori knocked harder on the window, shining the light into a bedroom that was a disaster zone.

"What in the world happened?" Lori asked Jake as if he could answer.

It looked like everything in the room had been tossed up in the air and left where it landed, clothes, mattress, bedding, furniture, everything.

Clasping her hand to her throat, her heart lurched in alarm. She realized his room must have been ransacked to be in this mess. She ran back to the front door and tried to open it. It was locked. Trying to calm down, her mind raced off on another tangent all its own. She bent over at the waist and had to make herself get a firm grip on her emotions again.

She was afraid that he was inside and hurt, or worse. Recalling which of the windows opened outward, she tried two of them without success. The third, she felt it give a little bit.

She didn't have anything to slide between the frames, so she resorted to using her fingernails. After breaking off three nails until they bled, she finally got the frame to slip out far enough to get her fingertips on it. Then she slid the frame outward making an opening big enough for her and Jake to step through.

Glancing over her shoulder at the awakening sounds of the forest birds, Lori shivered. Afraid of what she might find, she stood and listened for a few minutes before she got her nerve up enough to go inside.

Jake would have barked if there was anything wrong. She was sure of it. It would be safe. Lori took a deep breath and then let it out.

They stepped carefully over the window frame into the messy room. She didn't turn on a light, instead turning on the flashlight. She looked around as cautiously as she could. She entered the bathroom, the closet, the kitchen, the living and dining area.

She didn't know what she was looking for but at least Hugh was not here. Relieved there were no signs of blood. And she didn't see the black clothes he had on when he left her or any wet towels, signs of him cleaning up.

Simple reasoning convinced her that he hadn't been here to clean up yet. Most likely he didn't even know this had happened. He was bound to be back at her room at West house and that was her next course of action.

Running as fast as she could, she and Jake sped down the western beach to beat the dawn. She knew there was a chance of being seen by the villagers, but at this point she simply did not care.

Right now the most important thing was to get back to safety and find Hugh there.

Approaching the West house, she moved as stealthily onto the patio as she could. Lori knew that she was breathing as stertorously as a horse but wanted to get inside quickly. The only house light visible was the same one on when they left--the kitchen's night light. Just maybe, they could slip in unobserved.

She went straight to her patio door, which she had left unlocked, and prayed. "Please, let him be here safe and sound."

Entering her room, she found it deserted. Exactly as she left it.

Lori locked the door behind her. When she let out an enormous exhale, it was like all the air had been let out of her lungs. Now she didn't know what to do.

If he was not here and had not been back, then where could he be?

What should she do now?

She raked her hands through her hair repeatedly and dropped down onto her bed. Defeated, she kicked her shoes off. She had no idea what she was doing. God, she felt so helpless.

Lori was inept and totally inexperienced at whatever was going on here. Flopping backward on her pillow, she groaned aloud. A cold wet nose sniffed her cheek, his massive head on the pillow next to her.

"Oh, Jake, what in the world is next? Is he gone again? Is this a repeat of his last disappearing act? Or is something much more sinister going on? Can you help me, old boy? Do I sit here and wait as if nothing is going on? I guess I don't have much choice do I? I must be deep in trouble asking a dog for answers. Even if he is a super dog."

He responded with a big lick to her cheek. She rolled over and placed her face nose to nose with his. "So I remain here doing nothing? Okay, you win." She threw the pillow in the floor, grabbed a blanket, got in the floor beside Jake and pulled the cover up to her chin.

She was too exhausted to do anything remotely intelligent until she received some rest. Determined to shed no tears and try to be rational, she closed her eyes to the gloom and doom of her black thoughts.

As daybreak became a dazzling new day, she surrendered to the safety of sleep next to her constant, ever faithful buddy.

Twenty-four

Midmorning, the old lady's curious face partially opened the door, determined to find out why Lori was sleeping in so late. She saw the pair, curled up on the floor, both heads on the same pillow. She chuckled, shaking her head, and softly closed the door on the sleeping duo and bustled off to tell Marion what she'd found.

Aware of stiff and sore sensations, Lori woke up feeling like she had slept on a board. Which, of course, she had. Geez, what had she come to?... Sharing the floor and sleeping with a dog. She groaned, getting up on her knees before creaking to an upright position.

"Jake, I am way too old for this."

She put her hands on her hips doing body tilts and twists, wondering at her sanity. Today the only alternative was to go forward with her plans.

First, she would get her phone activated, move into the other cottage and do a 'wait and see' for as long as she could stand it. Twenty-four hours, tops would be the most she could wait. Perhaps, there was a perfectly good explanation for this. If not, she would take matters into her own hands.

At least she would be doing something, even if it was wrong. She took a long hot shower, washing away the sweat and worry stains, both inside and out. Hoping, in the process, she could iron out the miserable kinks in her body.

Neither Marion nor Miss Genny mentioned JeanPaul today so she didn't either. Luckily she wasn't subjected to the wicked witch before she moved out.

Thank you, for small miracles. She presented a wan smile to the sky in gratitude.

She discovered she could put on a normal face, just as usual and get on with things. Ha. Maybe she had missed her calling and should've been an actress.

She hugged both Marion and Genny fiercely and kissed them goodbye like she was leaving them for good before loading up her new belongings. They had taken her in like family and she loved them for that.

Lori argued like the devil with them when she found out that everything that she was loading and all that needed replacing had already been paid for. She protested but after being heavily overruled, threw up her hands and surrendered as graciously as she could, then kissed her friends all over again.

"Benjamin, stop at the main house on the way to the station, so I can call and get the phone set up." They found the big house locked and silent. There weren't any workers on the grounds, either.

"They are probably busy with the reconstruction." Ben informed her.

Upon reaching the station, she was astounded at the progress made today. The men were in the process of building the roof trusses and putting them up. Some worked on framing the windows. Piles of lumber were strewn everywhere. Windows in frames stood stacked against a tree.

Once again Hugh wasn't present, which made her chew on one of her few remaining fingernails, debating whether to make an issue of his absence or not.

At this point she decided it would be more conspicuous not to ask. Lori approached Miss Emily directing the work force. "Miss Moore, I need to use the phone at the big house to activate my phone. Could you tell me when would be a good time to do that?" Before receiving an answer, she smiled at the imperious woman, glancing around at the workers and casually asked. "Where is JeanPaul? Isn't he working today?"

"After I am finished here, we can go to the house if you like. I have not seen him yet today. Maybe he is working on his book. When he does that, he tends to lose time, or so I am told."

"I understand that you are moving into the other cabin today. Are you well enough and ready to live by yourself again Miss Paige? I do not think it is appropriate for you to live out here all by yourself. I was against it from the beginning, you know. A lone woman should not endanger herself." She replied a little primly, pursing her mouth.

"I will be all right." Lori answered distractedly. But she had made the decision with Hugh's comforting presence in mind... *Not* his alarming absence.

She wandered toward the construction to see how it was coming along and found the hole at the front of the house already covered over with a wide veranda of treated wood decking. A small latticework door fit unobtrusively on the side for access under the porch, which she hadn't noticed previously.

Wonder what else I missed? I need to be more observant, she told herself, returning to the Jeep to help unload her things.

It didn't take very long to unpack her meager belongings after she sent Benjamin back to work. She gave him his choice, the lab or the construction crew. He chose the lab. He was as anxious to get back to work as she was.

Lori wasn't sure how much work she could generate today but she needed to keep her hands busy. Unfortunately, work would only occupy her hands, not her brain. She would rather go over and pick up a hammer if she thought they'd let her. Instinctively, she knew she wouldn't be welcome there.

Burying herself in work did nothing to alleviate the tension that was mounting inside her. She couldn't correlate any data, work on reports or communicate with her peers on the mainland without a phone and computer data. So instead, Lori forced herself to sit and plug away at the day to day lab histotech work that she and Ben had ignored lately.

She couldn't call the hospital lab at Charlotte Amalie to get their report. It was frustrating as heck but not nearly as frustrating as the disturbing quality and quantity of unknown factors rotating aimlessly in her head.

Good thing the work at the microtome was routine and uncomplicated once procedures were established. She had repeated those exact procedures literally thousands of times, probably hundreds of thousands if she took the time to add them up. Whew. Scary thought. Nevertheless, she kept cranking them out, producing the slides one at a time. Over and over.

Benjamin worked beside her, prepping the slides for staining. He was happy to be back at work. Before they started, they had spent a couple of hours doing an exceptionally thorough search of the lab. They covered every inch of the place but discovered only what they already knew. All recorded data were missing. Nothing new was added. Just as Ben had reported to her days ago.

She couldn't understand why all the real evidence remained. It just didn't make sense. *Unless it was all meant to burn, too.* Chilling thought, but she doubted she was the first to think of it. While they worked, she discussed the ramifications of their findings in a vague way but Benjamin was too sharp for such generalities.

His keen mind easily figured the fire *and* stolen lab papers were somehow interconnected, and he warned her about staying alone at the station. Lori remained inflexible on the subject. She did not want to get him involved any more than he was. If the lab was supposed to burn up with her cabin, then it might not be over and he could be in danger, too.

Before it was time to meet Miss Emily at the main house, Lori planned a quick trip to the village warehouse to stock up on fresh food. She locked the lab behind her and drove away with Benjamin and Jake in attendance.

Jake had been staying in close proximity to her. She didn't think the big dog had been on his regular chow trail in days. Poor baby had probably even lost weight.

She didn't want to make it a big deal and spark Ben's interest, but asked him casually what he knew about any caves or tunnels here on the island. He didn't have anything new to contribute and when he started quizzing her back, it was time for her to shut up.

Again he was too smart for his own good. After forcing Benjamin to remain behind in the village, only by forbidding him to come back with her to the station, Lori drove straight to the Main house and knocked on the front door.

Emily Moore, again dressed in a forbidding looking black bombazine special, greeted Lori at the door with only a slight bow of her head for acknowledgment. Lori followed her stiff back through the immaculate interior to the kitchen where Emily pointed dramatically to the white phone on the desk. Then she walked all the way across the huge room to give her privacy. She made Lori feel uncomfortable, like it was a great imposition to use the phone.

She picked the phone up anyway, placing it to her ear and heard dead space. Nothing. No dial tone. No signal of any kind. Lori looked at the phone quizzically and put the receiver back to her ear. Taking her forefinger, she depressed the button on the phone several times, receiving no tone for her efforts. She held the phone up and shook it several times at Miss Emily.

"Doesn't work No dial tone."

"Are you quite sure? I have not used it today." Emily returned from the window where she had been looking out and took the phone from Lori then listened herself.

"It worked fine yesterday. Perhaps the storm brewing in the east has affected the underwater lines. Sometimes a tropical depression interferes with the service. It should be okay in a few days. I will let the Captain know. He will report it for us. I will let you know when it is working again. Now if you will excuse me. I should hurry if I am to leave word."

With that Emily quite competently shut Lori down and out, and led her to the front door.

Temporarily stymied, Lori sat in the cart a few minutes, collecting her thoughts. She was beginning to get paranoid about the situation here. No outside communications pretty effectively shut down the island. *Could be coincidence*, she thought, *could be?*

Her analytical mind did not find a lot of confidence in coincidence. She had a higher regard for her own capabilities than someone else manipulations, too.

Damn. She was getting sick and tired of being a victim, of any kind.

She called to Jake, who had run off around the house to eat. He was smart enough to know he would never be allowed to step one foot in *that* house, so he might as well get fed. Smart dog, he knew when to take advantage of a good thing.

She had not heard of any storm brewing. Then again, she seldom listened to news or weather reports. There hadn't been that much variation here. The weather was not like St. Louis where the temperature could change forty or fifty degrees in one day. Back home they had "just wait" weather. If you didn't like the weather, just wait a minute and it would change.

The weather that she'd seen so far in the Caribbean was much more reliable, but a storm could be out there somewhere, she guessed. Clear skies now, but it was possible. Lori looked around at the fading light.

"Jake, come on."

She yelled at him and started the motor, thinking he'd hear the sound and come running, but he didn't return. She turned off the motor, got out of her cart and ran around the house to where the food bowl usually sat on the patio and found it empty. The dog was gone.

Lori was puzzled but not overly concerned. He'd hardly been out of her sight in days. Maybe he needed a little freedom. She could certainly understand that. She eyed the patio, viewing the back of the house, the landscaping and surroundings a bit more thoroughly than she would have if Jake had been by her side.

Lori made up her mind. She was not going back to her cabin right now. She was going to Hugh's, right or wrong. From now on she was following her gut instincts. Maybe a more thorough search would reveal more than the one in the dark last night. It seemed so long since she'd seen him last.

Alone, she drove her cart to his place and nestled it in close next to the building, so anyone would have to be right up on it to see it there. She parked next to Hugh's cart. Had it been there the night before? She didn't remember it being there but she had run in from the beach and could have missed it, she guessed. She *should* have paid more attention. Lori would *now* and hoped it was not too late.

She immediately went to a window where the curtains were open and peered inside, and was utterly shocked to discover the room in front of her was neat as a pin.

"What the…?"

Either he had maid service. Or he had been there. Or someone did *not* want it to appear the way it had in the middle of the night last night. She went around to his front porch and plopped down heavily on the first step. Now she didn't know what to think. If she'd been talking, she undoubtedly would have been speechless.

"Now what?"

Apparently she would keep running into blank walls. She slowly walked up the steps to the front door, almost afraid to approach it. Afraid of what she might find. She reached out her hand to knock but for some reason pulled her hand back and tried the knob instead.

It opened easily in her hand.

"Uh oh, here we go again. Whatever is going on here, has more twists and turns than a maze."

She muttered to herself and wished again that Jake was with her. Lori was definitely afraid to go inside the cabin alone now but didn't know what else to do. She needed to find out anything and everything that she could. Taking a deep breath, she willed herself to calm down and entered cautiously, tiptoing a few feet into the living room.

The room was totally silent, with not even the sound of a clock ticking. She stood silently, absorbing the sounds, or lack of them, and smells.

It smelled clean like lemon. Pledge, cleaning stuff maybe. Sanitized.

She sniffed the air and smelled nothing of food or signs of habitation. It smelled like a clean empty house where no one lived. She ran across the room to the bedroom and threw the closet door open.

It was empty. Totally. No clothes, no shoes, nothing.

Feeling sour nausea at the pit of her stomach, Lori mumbled to herself. "Lord, not again. Please not again. Has he disappeared from my life all over again?"

Dammit, if he was going to leave, she wanted to be the one to send him away. She dropped to the floor when her knees gave out on her and placed her head in her hands.

She'd never felt more cut off from the rest of the world than right now, at this very moment. She thought she was going to throw up and tried to shake off the nausea. *Think, Lori, think. Use your head.*

She felt very vulnerable and totally alone. It was so quiet she could hear the sounds of her own heartbeat pounding in her ears. She squeezed her eyes shut and listened for a few moments trying to decide what to do. She took deep breaths to stabilize her stomach.

It wouldn't do to puke all over the place, so straighten up, she told herself.

What if it was meant for her to think that he is gone?

What if she was being manipulated?

After all, if he had left the island, someone would know, wouldn't they? *Emily Moore kept so tight a rein on this island that she surely would have known. She seemed to know anything of consequence and she had just told her that he was probably working.*

So... unless she was in on this, too, he could not just walk off the island. He had to leave by boat or else he is here. That is all there was to it. So if he is present on the island, then where in blazes is he? Oh Lord, haven't I asked that question before?

Feeling like she was plagued with a convoluted Chinese riddle, she forced herself up off the floor and proceeded to search anyway. She didn't know what she was looking for but she was looking.

Originally she planned when she left the main house to look for his cell phone. She knew he had one, but first things first. Was there a flashlight in the nightstand by the bed, like the other bedrooms on the island? Yes. She claimed her first success and placed the light in her pocket.

"Okay, let's be rational about this. If he has not left voluntarily then he is here on this island and I refuse to believe that he would leave me again. Blind spot? So what? So where would he be and what would he have left behind? A gun maybe or some kind of weapon. Surely in his business he carries a gun, though she'd never seen one on him. But he had always been in control when she saw him and could have placed it somewhere safe." She reasoned with herself out loud. "So where would it be?"

She assumed anyone cleaning this place would have searched the obvious, under the mattress, toilet tank, etc. She went into the bathroom and stood there. Lori tried to slide out the medicine cabinet from the wall, but it wouldn't budge. She opened the little linen closet and felt the bottoms, sides, backs of the walls, shelves and found nothing.

She pressed on the small square of the ceiling. Standing on the closed toilet lid on her toes, she strained to reach up to the circulation vent in the ceiling. Struggling with it, she couldn't get it loose.

Lori jumped down and ran to the kitchen to the tool drawer, which contained a small variety of tools exactly like her cabin. She selected a multi end screwdriver and a little hammer which she slid into the waist line of her jeans at the small of her back substituting it for a pocket. She hurried back to the bathroom to unscrew the vent, dropped it down and reached as far as she could reach, both directions inside it. Frustrated, she found nothing but smooth sheet metal ducts.

Moving into the bedroom, she looked under the dresser, behind it, pulled out each drawer and looked at the bottoms and backs before replacing them. Again she was not tall enough to reach the ceiling fan from the bed but got a couple chairs from the dining room table to stack and stand on. Lori slid her hands over the tops of the fan blades and the top of the fan housing but found nothing, not even dust.

Before she had a chance to move the chairs underneath the bedroom vent, she heard Jake bark and an answering boat horn far in the distance. Well, at least Jake must be okay.

Then it struck her, "Jerrod." Should she involve him in any of this? Would he know anything about Hugh leaving the island? Could she put him at risk to help her hunt for Hugh? No. No more than she could involve Benjamin. But would she be able to get to the main dock in time to ask the Captain to make some phone calls for her when he returned to St. Thomas. Or use his radio on the boat? And get help?

In a quandary of indecisiveness, she finally decided to at least have him get her phone activated and place some mainland calls for her. She ran out of Hugh's front door, closing it behind her, when she stopped suddenly. She quickly reentered the cabin to unlock one of the windows, so she could get back in if she found the door locked the next time. Then she ran to a kitchen drawer to add a small paring knife to the odd assortment of weapons and tools she was collecting.

When she went around the side of the cabin, an eerie feeling engulfed her yet again. The hair on the back of her neck stood up. She knew she was being watched again. She ignored it and drove the cart as fast as she dared, bouncing it along toward the dock. Maybe if she was lucky, she would be in time *and* Jake would be there.

Luck was not with her. The boat was already heading out through the lagoon opening through the coral when she pulled up with a screech to the dock. His boat was leaving the lagoon, far enough out he couldn't possibly see or hear her. Jake was nowhere in sight either. Boxes were neatly stacked on the edge of the dock. No one was in sight.

The sun was setting in the west, getting ready to dip its final red glow into the water. 'Red sunset tonight, a farmer's delight' one of her grandmother's quotes that meant rain was headed their way in the Midwest. Lori had no idea if that applied to weather here and couldn't be bothered to worry about it. She retraced her path back to the East cottage to continue her search where she left off. *I am not ready to give up yet.*

The cottage clearing was enveloped in rustling dark shadows and gave Lori the creeps. Goose bumps rose on her arms. The wind in the pines picked up instead of dying down and sang a whistling tune that preyed upon Lori's nerves.

She parked back in the same niche, thoughtfully alert on her approach vector. She halfway expected the front door to be locked when she reached for the knob and let out a sigh of relief when it turned easily in her hand.

Lori entered and closed the door silently, leaning wearily against it for a moment. Motionless, she stood for an eternity it seemed. Waiting for, she knew not what, but something. Anything. She listened for any extraneous sounds that didn't belong, relieved to hear none.

She returned the chairs to their previous position before she ran off on a wild goose chase, climbed up and searched this vent. She carried the chair to the ceiling fans and vents in the next rooms. In the kitchen she was ready to pull her hand from the venthole when the tip of her fingers brushed something just out of reach. On her tiptoes, no matter how hard she strained, she couldn't reach it, whatever it was.

She pulled the screwdriver from her back pocket and tried again. This time she definitely ran into something bulky. It wouldn't move, though, in either direction. She was just too damned short.

She glanced around looking for something to elevate her that little bit more that she needed. She couldn't put another chair on top of the other two. Her position was precarious enough as it was.

There were no phone books here to stack, but there were some books in the other room. She stacked six on the chair and then returned to the drawer for a spatula that would help extend her reach. She climbed back up on the chair, very carefully this time, extending her arm into the vent.

The darkness grew inside the cabin, but she didn't turn on any lights. The books elevated her enough to touch the cool hard metal of a gun. It appeared to be taped down. She pushed the spatula in under it and with a little extra effort, pried it loose, using the spatula to slide it close to her.

Lori carefully gripped the gun, making sure that her fingers were clear of the trigger, and jumped down from her perch on the chair. She situated the gun in her pocket, replaced the chairs to the table and sat down heavily on one. Pulling the gun from her pocket to examine it in the waning light, she discovered it was loaded but the safety was on. She removed the clip, laying it on the table. The gun was a 9mm Sig Sauer P239, a small lightweight powerhouse only six inches long.

She blessed her dad for teaching her gun ethics although she was 'just a girl'. Because of that, she wasn't afraid of guns. When she was small, they'd spent many weekend mornings on the Mississippi river bank. They'd hiked down the railroad tracks, cooked breakfast on an open fire, shooting rifles and pistols at driftwood.

She'd been an excellent marksman, as long as the weapon was not too big or it didn't have too big a kick. She could take a gun apart and clean it faster than her left-handed brother could ever dream of doing. And she could out shoot 'Lefty' any day of the week.

There were eight shots in the clip, no spares. "Would have to do," she mumbled matter-of-factly. Lori had never pointed a gun at any living thing before but she always believed she *could* defend her own, if she had to.

Scary thought, but what the heck was she doing here if she were not willing to fight for Hugh? *If* she could find him.

Finally, it fell into place. He had *not* willingly left her again. He was definitely here somewhere on the island. Unless someone had transported him off island, but Lori refused to think of that possibility. Since she found the gun, she knew he had not left of his own volition. The gun must have been his backup and they were satisfied with finding only one. Whoever they were. Which meant they were not professionals, professionals would have done a better job and found the gun.

Good. It was obvious she was far from being professional either, she admitted ruefully. She felt better about it. In fact she felt much better, considering. Made her more on equal ground with whoever had Hugh. Two against two. Maybe...hopefully. *Up rises the eternal optimist,* she smiled to herself.

Now she was hungry and needed to do some heavy thinking before setting out tonight to rescue Hugh. She was going home, and maybe Jake would be back. But when she returned to the research station, she found herself alone. This end of the island was quite empty.

She went about her business as normally as possible under the circumstances. She turned on all the lights to cook something to eat. Lori needed something filling, not sumptuous. Rooting in the pantry and refrigerator, she settled on a broccoli, ham and cheese omelet. She made toast with butter. "What the heck," she splurged and added strawberry jam to toast.

Lynda LaPorte

Twenty-five

Her head hurt from trying to figure out what was going on here. There must be more than one person involved. The night Hugh was knocked out there had been more than one. It would take more than luck to find what she was looking for and get out without being spotted. What made her think she could do something that Hugh couldn't do, or didn't do? Whatever. Didn't matter. She would.

Well, she knew what she was looking for. He didn't. In addition, she would be prepared, as ready as she could be anyway. She placed the assortment of tools, weapon and flashlight on the table in front of her, after drawing the curtains that provided much needed privacy.

Lord, she wished Jake was here with her. But no matter, she was going. It was late now and time to get ready. *Think this through, Lori, Hugh's life may depend on it,* she told herself.

Fact one: Hugh had to be here on the island.

Fact two: She was going to find him and either escape with him or get help, if she had to leave the island to do it. Period.

In order to do it, she'd start at the beginning. If he thought there was a door under her front porch, then there must be. She would find it and follow that tunnel to the cavern of the legends.

She copied his clothing style wearing a dark T-shirt and black stonewashed jeans and tennies. Now what else could she possibly need? A shovel. She had spotted a shovel over at the lumber pile and planned to appropriate it.

A small light remained on in her bedroom. She checked all the windows to make sure they were locked, turned a low volume on the radio in the bedroom and cleaned the kitchen. She added a dark lightweight jacket and commenced loading her pockets with duct tape, paring knife, screwdriver, flashlight and wire. Snapping the clip into the gun with the safety on, she slid it in the small of her back next to the small hammer. Both held in place by her waistband.

All she needed was gum and matches to be mistaken for MacGyver. For several minutes she stood going over a mental list. Matches weren't such a bad idea. She grabbed a handful, placing them in a plastic baggy.

Opening the front door, the wind howled in her face. Whew. Bad weather was brewing but she was going underground and ignored it. After one last look around her cabin, making sure that she hadn't forgotten anything, she locked and closed the door.

Lori stood immobile on her porch listening again but only heard the sound of wind and crashing waves.

Creeping first to the lumber pile to pick up a shovel, then over to the side of her old cabin, she bent down and pulled open the new latticework door. She slid down under the porch into the sand pit. Safely inside, she turned on the flashlight and checked the bottom surface.

Comparing her position to where the sound variances occurred before, she started tapping until she found them again and started digging. She only dug about six inches, before she hit something with a thump. Scraping sand away with the shovel and her hand, a wooden door, two feet by three feet appeared.

"Yes." She hissed, encouraging herself, and trying to discourage her fears.

At this moment all she could think of was her own fear, overwhelming claustrophobia. Lori almost hyperventilated at the thought of what could be waiting for her down there. It was the darkness that freaked her.

Scuba diving didn't bother her as long as she could see light through the water. Night time diving would be an entirely different story. In daytime she knew the sky was present. It was closed in spaces with no light that brought out her worst fears. Exactly where she was going now, the black windowless pit scared her spitless. Her mouth was dry and she was breathing too fast. She hadn't brought a paper bag for hyperventilation.

Darn, she forgot something, trying to make herself laugh and relax the mounting tension. But it wasn't working.

With the screwdriver's help, prying into the door's edge, she lifted it back to reveal an aperture to total darkness and total silence. It was an ominous yawning black hole in the universe. She shivered at the thought.

She closed her eyes and tried slow deep relaxing breaths. When she opened her eyes again, she flashed light around the hole and saw that if she moved around from the side where she was standing, rungs led down into the opening.

It took all her effort to start down into that abyss. She stood, at war with herself for a few more minutes before she won, or lost, depending on one's perspective and started down into the pit of nothingness. Step by step.

Down, down, down into the dark. She put the flashlight in her pocket with the beam pointing up so light emitted from the pocket. Otherwise, she was climbing backwards into complete darkness.

Lori was scared silly.

The intense quiet was spooky down there. With each step the surface sounds receded into the distant world of the living. She reached the ladder bottom, taking the flashlight out to shine in a circle behind her, before she stepped off. She would never have been able to get Jake down this ladder anyway. But Lord, she'd give anything for his presence.

The walls were dirty rock. The ceiling was six feet above the floor. At least she wouldn't have to stoop. A tunnel veered off into the distance as far as the light beam reached. Thank goodness, there were no cobwebs, she *hated* spiders. And snakes. Yuck. Shivering again, she moved forward slowly, one step at a time into the darkness, forcing herself to breathe with each agonizing step.

"Hugh, I'm coming," She felt better whispering into the silence. If only temporarily.

The tunnel felt moist and clammy or maybe *she* was the moist and clammy one. It felt like she'd been walking for days. When she checked her watch, she had been down there for half an hour. So far it was an endless tunnel, no sign of anything or anyone. Eventually she reached a branching of the tunnel.

Oh great. Three choices to select from. The center, I'm sticking to the center. It does appear a smidgen larger. Besides, the floor appears more worn in the middle.

In the silence she could've heard a pin drop. She should be able to hear any movement in the tunnel but there was nowhere to hide and it was a long way back to the end. A long way.

The walls and floor changed to a different color rock. The air reeked with dampness and humidity. She stopped, flashing the light back the way she came, and saw that the floor behind her had a gradual rise to it. The tunnel was dropping her deeper under the island. She dug the screwdriver into the wall to see if she could tell what kind of rock it was. It crumbled easily. Limestone, perhaps?

Lori had to force herself to quit shivering and keep breathing. Not an easy trick, considering her state of mind.

She had a hard time keeping her eyes off the tunnel ceiling, expecting it to fall down at any moment onto her head. Lori's labored breathing sounded loud to her ears. It was not because of exertion, but because of fear.

She reached a tight bend in the tunnel. Before going around the curve, she turned out the light and cautiously stuck her head past the wall to make sure there were no hidden surprises. Flashing the light back on, she noted that the tunnel widened around the bend. Maybe it was an illusion but it appeared to be brighter, too. She turned off the light, letting her eyes adjust to the darkness. Yes, there is some kind of light ahead.

She turned the flashlight back on and into a jacket pocket, this time with the lights head pointing down, creating a soft glow of light. Her nose filled with a dank musty odor. The tunnel opened into a large cavern at least twenty feet high, more than fifty feet across.

Dropping down in a crouch, she turned off the flashlight. Pulling the gun from behind her back and holding it carefully in both hands, her vision slowly encompassed the cavernous area. The walls, ceiling and floor were natural rock formations. Definitely not manmade. Five enormous dark boulders were sprinkled randomly around the floor. Stacks of boxes obstructed her view.

The sound of water trickled, dripping off to her left into a small pool of water. The entire area was backlit by a single light bulb on the opposite side of the cave, which couldn't begin to erase the shadows from such a large area.

Hearing no other sounds, she decided to explore the area first from the periphery of the cavern and then proceed around the room keeping her back to the wall. There wasn't much to see; just a couple more tunnel entrances and a very old wooden door. The door reminded her of a barn door. Closed and locked with the sturdiest padlock she'd ever seen. It would take the jaws of life to break that sucker open.

After completing one revolution around the room, confirming the fact that the cavern was empty, she replaced the gun in her waistband again. It was uncomfortable there, but the discomfort also made her feel safer. Probably purely an illusion, but a necessary one she needed to hold on to right now. Finding herself alone, she breathed a little deeper and calmer, trying to settle her jumpy nerves.

Curiosity urged her to find out what was in the boxes. She warily crossed the room to get to them. The plain brown cardboard containers were unmarked with no labels. She lifted one and found it to be a manageable weight. The boxes were sealed shut with brown sealing tape. Lori didn't know if she could open one without showing it had been tampered with. She didn't want to leave any evidence of her presence. Twenty-four cartons in a pile, were stacked six deep in four stacks. Three separate piles. A load of loot.

Lori planned to take one from the top of the pile, open it and replace it on the bottom underneath the others. Hoping it stood a better chance of going undetected. Taking one, she sat in the floor in the middle of some large boulders, turned the box upside down and used the paring knife to slit open the bottom seam of tape.

"Bingo." She'd opened the two halves of the box bottom and revealed a blue plastic tarpaulin type material wrapping a square shape. Stabbing the knife into the bright blue package, she pulled the blade out with a white powdery residue on it. She sniffed it and licked it and felt a tingling numbness on her tongue. Since she didn't know exactly what taste or smell to expect, she wrinkled up her nose and shrugged her shoulders, assuming the worst. What else would be stored secretly underneath an island.

She knew what it *was not.* It was not flour or sugar or any of the multitude of acceptable legal powders. So it must be drugs or illegal contraband of some sort.

Odd though, it was not in the brown raw form that she expected. She thought it would most likely be a form of raw opium straight from the poppy fields. And that this island would be merely a transition point of transfer from point A to point B.

Replacing the blue package back into the box, she taped it with a short section of duct tape to keep it closed. Then moved the stack out of the way to put this one on the bottom and replaced the others on top of it. She stood back and checked to see that all the stacks looked alike. Satisfied with her work, she sat back down next to the boxes but her eyes kept drifting back toward the locked door.

Behind door number one must be a lab of sorts. Had to be where they refined it. Could it be where they have Hugh locked up? Curiosity drew her back to the door, shining her flashlight on the floor in front of the door where fresh wet, reddish brown spots dotted the floor. Surely not blood. *Please*. A sense of urgency overwhelmed her.

She stood and padded over to the light fixture illuminating the room to see where the electricity came from and where it went. An electrical romax cable led to the fixture from the tunnel beyond it and then another electric wire ran the length of the wall to a small hole above the giant door. She followed the wire to its end and stood there by the door.

Assuming no one but Hugh could be in there since it was locked from this side, she called softly to him. She scratched at the door and said.

"Hugh. Hugh, it is me. Are you in there?"

The sounds magnified and echoed around the big chamber causing her to jump into the air. It scared her into shutting up. She continued to make scratching sounds at the door but heard absolutely nothing in return. The thickness of the wooden door would most likely deaden any sounds from being transferred, so she stopped making the noise. It wasn't helping and only frightened her.

At a loss for what to do next, she checked her watch and saw it was just after one o'clock in the morning, the witching hour.

What to do? What to do? The only thing left that she could think of was to follow the power source and keep her fingers crossed. She approached, with great trepidation, the end of the tunnel with utterly no idea where she was.

Above ground she had a great sense of direction but down here she felt absolutely helpless. For all she knew she could have gone in a circle, she'd made so many turns.

The tunnel ended at a door, a regular looking door on hinges. No trap door at the top of a ladder like at the other end of the island. She turned off the light, adjusting her eyes again to darkness, saw no light shining under the door. Putting her ear to the door, her hand on the knob, she prepared herself to enter whatever was on the other side.

Almost expecting a locked door, the knob turned in her hand and she pushed it open. And found herself in a small unfinished basement area with a sandy dirt floor. A lightning flash illuminated the area through tiny shuttered air vents on the sides. Her stomach dropped to the floor when she saw personal things sitting on top of boxes in the corner.

She was dismayed to confirm that they were all Hugh's things…jacket, shoes, cell phone. Even her own cell phone and her computer! She started shaking all over, suspecting his clothes were in the boxes, too.

Telling herself to look at the bright side, at least it corroborated her theory. She had to assume he was on the island. Since she couldn't find him, now she *had* to get help.

She drew in big gulps of air trying not to cry. It wouldn't do anyone any good to break down now that she had come this far. Neither of the cell phones worked. Dead batteries. The phone line off the island was down.

She had to believe he was here on the island and alive. *Blood drops or not. He had to be.* And she was the only one to help get him out. The *only* one. No matter what happened she must get out of here and off the island to get help. The only way to do that is to take a boat. *Now,* before it was too late to help and while it was still dark outside.

Lori searched the basement area for a way to get out. No way did she want to retrace her steps. The only door was the one where she came in from the tunnel. There were no stairs like she expected. She had to examine the entire area with the flashlight beam before she found a set of rungs leading to another trap door.

She drew in another deep breath. Fear had no place either in her heart or her mind. She had to put all that baggage aside to accomplish what was ahead. Taking no time for tears or fears or to give herself an opportunity to back out, she put out the light and crept up the rungs.

At the top she pushed the trap door up extremely slowly.

From the size of the area of the basement, she assumed it was under a cottage but the question was, *whose?* Where was she going to find herself in the middle of the night?

With the door pushed up only an inch all she could see was pitch black. Her eyes adapted, finding the dark quite solid. The noise level increased dramatically. The storm outside had not lessened but had instead intensified. She could hear wind shrieking and thunder crashes, but couldn't see lightening flashes. Lori surmised, she must be in a room without windows. Pulling herself from the opening, she stifled the sound of dropping the door back in place.

Flashing her light in a tiny circle on the floor and cautiously scrutinizing her surroundings, she saw a broom and a mop leaning in the corner of the floor.

"A closet. I'm in a closet." She whispered to herself, pointing the light at the trap door, and found it hard to see. Lori ran her hand over the wood to feel the border of the door. Very fine carpentry. How many more doors would she have to pass through?

Opening the closet door with the light out, she tiptoed into the room on guard. With the aid of lightning flashes, she could see a kitchen of a guesthouse. She wouldn't know until she was outside which one it was. She knew it wasn't hers or Hugh's place. The floor plan was a mirror image to them.

Moving stealthily through the living area, she saw something leaning against a wall and heard snoring through the closed bedroom door to her left. Curiosity grabbed her once again. Before she could think about consequences, she uncovered one of the canvas wrapped rectangles, gasping aloud to discover the portrait was herself. Nude! Why she had never posed nude for him or anyone else. She quickly discovered they were *all* pictures of her.

"Good God! Steffan, the painter."

Grimacing when she realized she said it aloud, she hurried as fast as she could to get out of there. Hearing the snoring in the bedroom stop, and change to snorting sounds, she picked up her pace.

Opening the front door, she ran through it so fast she tripped over a large lump in her path and slid across the front porch. Picking herself up, she heard loud stentorian snores from the dark mass she tripped over and realized it was Jake.

In a single lightning flash she saw a partially eaten bowl of food sitting there floating with rain. Not a normal sight at all.

She never saw him waste food. Not ever. And he had hardly budged when she tripped over him.

She went back to the dog where the wind and rain slashed at him and tried to wake him. Lori shook him and hissed at him.

"Jake, wake up." She had to give up when a light went on inside the cabin. Jumping off the porch, ignoring the steps and the heavy rain, she dashed for the boathouse. Thankful at least to be on the right end of the island. She was worried about Jake.

The weather had brewed itself into a tizzy of a storm and she dreaded taking the boat out in this, but could see no other options available to her. Stumbling her way amid wet sloppy sand and drenched plants, she was soon soaked all the way through to her skin.

She was cold and she was wet but she kept running.

Before she reached the open beach in front of the boathouse she heard repetitive pounding, splashing sounds behind her and looked back over her shoulder to see a familiar form close to the ground chasing her.

"Come on Jake!" She yelled over her shoulder at him and kept running. Her side began to hurt and she could feel oxygen deprivation before she reached the door.

Throwing it open, she ran down the decking to the launch. She leapt onto the boat and flipped switches, turning on the blower to clear fumes, and checked fuel level dials. Immediately, she jumped back on the dock and lowered the boat on the lift into the water. When the boat settled into the water, she turned off the lift and boarded again, this time getting the engines started. Lori hoped that the storm would block the sound of the motors from anyone on the island, but wouldn't bet on it.

The door blew open with a slam and made her heart jump up in her throat. The bright lightning lit the inside of the boathouse, showing Jake running toward her. He ran and leapt, almost falling into the boat beside her, staggering to a halt at her feet.

She didn't have time to check him over, but was immensely grateful to have him beside her. She'd never taken a boat out to sea in this kind of weather in daytime let alone night and was more scared than she wanted to admit. Even to herself. She wasn't certain she could reverse the boat out of the slip by herself, but she had to try.

She put on a life jacket, and with that sick feeling in her gut almost a stabbing pain, she slipped the ropes loose from their mooring posts. She reversed the throttles, said a little prayer and told Jake.

"Hold on boy, we're gonna get outta Dodge!"

She bounced the boat off the slip walls several times before the boat exited and backed into the thrashing sea of the lagoon.

Using the light of the storm to visualize where she needed to go to pass through the reef opening, she slung the boat in a wide arc to head east to St. Thomas. She knew she'd need to navigate strictly by instruments because when she hit open water, she would lose most of her visibility.

Tonight the storm blew in gale force and the sea was the choppiest since she arrived. The powerful boat had trouble staying on top of the waves until she opened the throttle increasing speed. Lori did not like the feel of the launch dipping in the troughs and felt like she was on a Six Flags ride. The boat bounced up and down, taking on too much water between the downpour overhead and rough action of the sea. The bilge pumps worked in full force. She hoped that it could keep up with all the water.

Jake whined beside her. He looked pitiful, deluged with water and was having trouble keeping his balance wedged between her and the boat side. She wished she'd taken the time to put a life vest on him too. There was an extra vest under her seat but she needed both hands on the wheel to control the boat.

The coordinates for the big island were due east, and with the compass, she couldn't possibly miss it. She was much more concerned about any small islets or rocks between here and there. She would need all her powers of concentration to stay alert for danger signs.

Now she had *three* lives at risk. She should have left Jake behind. They were both shivering in the cold driving rain and wind.

Scared *and* cold. Too late to worry about that now…

Twenty-six

Lori and the dog, Jake, are safely hidden inside the standing stones after escaping St. Saba

Sore, stiff, and bone weary, Lori had spent the remainder of the night remembering this adventure in paradise. She must have finally crashed. Mentally assessing their situation, she knew they were still a long way from true safety. Physically, she barely identified her own back. It had grown ice cold plastered against the frigid rock. Her left side had gone totally to sleep, numb until agonizing pins and needles began stabbing her into a conscious reality. Her front was fairly comfortable where Jake's body heat kept her warm.

The rain stopped sometime in the night, yet she could hear either another storm moving in, or maybe the first storm was moving out. From the sound of the waves crashing against the outside of their rock shelter, a storm *was* still moving their way.

The sky brightened to gray. Dawn was approaching. It was not bright enough to read her watch. She tried the flashlight, flicking it on but it wouldn't work.

"Too bad." She tossed it into the water. No need for dead weight.

Well, at least in her head, she recognized where she was and why she was here. Survival. Hugh's and hers and she couldn't forget Jake. Talk about jumping out of the frying pan and into the fire. So much for uninvited Midwestern advice from her dear departed grandmother.

When Lori tried to move to an upright position, she groaned in pain and received a sloppy lick of commiseration from Jake. She patted his big head. Her throat felt scratchy.

"Morning, old boy. Did you get any rest? I sort of did. Maybe it was all in my head. But ouch. This rock is hard. It sounds like another storm is rolling our way, so we better try to make it to land before it hits and before high tide. Think we can do that? Hmm boy?"

Jake yelped an affirmative. She hung her feet over the ledge after she sat up.

"Ow. My poor butt is trying to wake up. Stop licking me, silly dog. My circulation needs to start working, that is all. I need to think. My mind is as foggy as the sky. I need to go out and look around before we leave, so I guess I better put your life jacket on you before I go. No, then I can't get you through the crack. Damn, I don't know if I can manhandle you into it once you are in the water."

"Well, I don't have many options. I can't leave you in here. All I seem to do lately is talk about options, options, options," she mumbled to the dog.

She threw her jacket into the pool of water encircled by the rocks. The other jacket floated there already. She slid down off the ledge into the water.

"Stay, Jake. Stay there for now. I will be right back."

The big dog started running back and forth along the ledge and whining at her. "Stay." She repeated one more time then slipped through the crevice and swam out of their hiding place. This side of the rocks, the island side, the water was quieter. The other side was blasted by crests at least five feet higher, crashing and spraying around them. Lori spotted the gray outline of the largest islet of the cluster, by the white line of the surf breaking on its shore. She remembered the distance to be less than a half mile, give or take.

Looking toward the eastern sky, a second storm followed the first. Treading water nervously, she searched the surrounding sea for signs of boats.

"Just do it." She muttered to herself, swimming to slide back in the crevice. Where she found Jake pacing, wagging his big rear end when he saw her again.

"Come on down, Jake. Jump. Come on, just jump. You can do it. Come here, boy!" Finally the dog took the plunge and jumped in almost on top of her. A huge splash filled her mouth.

Teach you to talk to a dog, she thought as she sputtered and choked. He paddled over to her when he popped back up to the surface. Lori slipped the life jacket back on and fastened it, leading Jake over to the entrance, and tried to shove him through it while keeping the extra vest on her arm. It took several attempts to force his square barrel chest into the narrow groove in the rocks.

An extraordinary wave passed by, sucking him through the opening, and jerking him from her hand and out into the open water before she could reach him. She went after him as fast as she could but lost maneuverability with the extra vest in her way.

She was frantic. The big dog was yelping.

"Jake!" She screamed. "I'm coming."

The gap widened between them. The current carried him further away from her by the second. He tried to keep his head above water but was not always succeeding. She couldn't hang onto his vest any longer. It created too much drag, so she tossed it away and planed her body perpendicular to the water to get more power behind her thrusts.

She started making headway toward Jake, when she saw him floundering. He went down under a particularly big wave and she was afraid the dog would not to come back up. The water continually grew rougher. When she reached the spot where she thought he had gone down, and with her heart beating fearfully in her throat, she again cried.

"Jake. Jake. Where are you?"

He rose to the surface ten feet in front her. Quickly closing the distance, she had to swim around his big powerful feet, desperately pawing the water, and approached him from behind. It was light enough that she could see the fear in his eyes. And knew that her own eyes reflected that same fear.

With no experience in towing a man-sized dog at any lifeguard class, she could only assume that if she hooked her arm under both his front legs across his chest, it would be the same. If he didn't fight her, it *should* be okay. Throwing a look over her shoulder dimmed by the briny saltwater, she began towing the huge dog toward the islet.

She was fortunate. With amazing grace, he accepted her awkward embrace and laid back for her to pull him along. The problem was his size. He was such an enormous beast. Lori had not gone halfway when her legs and arms felt like lead.

She wasn't sure how much more of this misery she could take. She was out of breath but afraid to go slow because the storm returned with fervor. The waves piled higher and the wind and rain were back in full force.

Her vest helped keep them afloat but wasn't made for the weight it supported between them. Their buoyancy was borderline. And she had to exert all her energy to keep them heading in the right direction.

Some big waves bombarded them. By the time their heads were out in the air again, they were hit again. It was beginning to look hopeless. The waves were so tall, she couldn't determine what direction they were heading. If they missed this islet, they were done. She didn't know how long she could keep them both afloat.

She was struggling, and struggling hard. It seemed as though she was kicking in slow motion. Her lungs hurt. Her eyes burned. Her legs felt as if they were about to fall off. Her right arm felt like someone else's. She didn't dare switch arms in these treacherous waves or she would lose him again.

She had heard before about the agony of defeat and felt she was about to be completely overwhelmed by it. Her own salty tears blended with the sea.

Just in time, as she was about to give up, she felt a gentle nudge at her shoulder. At this point she didn't know what to expect. The sea to open up and swallow them, maybe.

But miraculously, her chirping, chattering dolphin friends surrounded them. With elegant ease the big fish took turns, ignoring the building storm, and pushed them closer to the islet.

In almost no time, she knew they'd almost made it when she heard the louder surf sounds that were music to her ears. The rolling breakers were a good indication of the shallowing water before the beach. The wonderful animals pushed them into the shallows. Then leapt and frolicked their way back to the deep, leaving a totally exhausted, but mighty thankful duo behind.

Lori struggled into an upright position, the tip of her toes barely touching that wonderful solid feel of land but Jake still couldn't touch bottom. They were close enough that she turned him loose, at the same time pushing him to catch a ride on top of a wave rolling rapidly toward the beach. He rode the crest, making a mad scramble to get to his feet, as he tumbled and then beached on his belly like a whale riding the surf.

She laughed when she followed him in, almost slap-silly hysterical. He jumped out of the water, barking and running up and down the beach while shaking the water and sand from himself. He was excited, but then again so was she.

The new storm intensified, forcing her to pick herself up off the sand, where she had collapsed when she made it to land. She called Jake to her side, heading for the interior of the islet to search for some kind of cover under the trees.

The best location on this tiny islet after searching the high ground, was a fallen palm tree trunk along a bank that should protect them from the wind coming from the east. She took off her life jacket, throwing it down.

She scooped out sandy dirt, with her hands from around the bases of several palm trees and palmettos along the bank partially exposing their roots. She planned to make the depression deep enough, like a narrow cave of sufficient size to shelter both of them.

A few larger trees grew on the same side of the little islet but they were big old mangroves in a low swampy area. They definitely didn't need any more wet tonight, thank you very much. Enough was enough.

She would do her best to keep them drier now. On her discovery journey around the island, she'd gathered up every loose palm frond that had come down in previous storms and would place them over the opening.

There was nothing to eat or drink but if they could stay out of the weather and get some more rest, they would be okay. She was afraid Jake would dehydrate. She'd read somewhere that dogs needed more water than humans. In addition, he'd been sick when she found him. It seemed like days ago instead of just hours. This night dragged on forever. Almost.

She dug deeper until she was completely satisfied. Looking around one more time at the storm and sea, she pushed Jake into their hole in the ground. Then wove the pile of fronds into a fairly efficient roof/wall. Lori backed herself into the opening beside the dog and embedded the fronds ends into the dirt overhead.

As long as the wind didn't change directions on them, they were protected from the wind and rain. Pleased with her efforts, she snuggled in next to Jake, using her vest again as a pillow. She sighed as she wriggled her wet jeans into the sand and explored her pockets for anything useful.

Lori wished she had brought some candy bars. She would give anything for a bar of chocolate, or food of any kind right now. She thought she'd burned ten thousand calories tonight. Although she was tired, she was more hungry. But it would *not* do to think about food now.

It might be hours before they got off this islet, refusing to admit it could possibly be days instead of hours. Her pockets yielded nothing of interest. Most of it wet and useless at the moment.

The storm crested overhead, making Lori feel smug and snug in their latest little hideaway. Jake hunkered down close beside her and was soon snoring again. Lucky critter.

Lori was past sleep and watched the storm pass through the makeshift roof/wall. It effectively funneled water off them. Their body temperatures were actually warming up their nest.

Her thirst overwhelmed her, wondering if she dared take the dry matches from the baggy and use the plastic to collect rainwater. But then her matches might not stay dry. For right now they appeared dry but she didn't know whether to waste one now to see if they were.

She *could* go back out and explore for something to catch rainwater in, but couldn't bring herself to do anything but simply contemplate what else to do. The storm rumbled around them and the questions in her brain tumbled with it.

What happened to the boat? Where was Hugh? How were they going to get out of this mess? How was Hugh?

She sighed again.

Where was the cavalry when you needed them? What is there to eat on this godforsaken place? Who was going to help her find Hugh? Where are her shoes? You know, all those mind consuming critical brain teasers, that defy all rational thought and can be quite impossible to turn off sometimes...

~ * ~

Sliding in and out of reality in a dreamlike state, Lori was aware of the passage of time and the storm moving westward. The sky lightened considerably and the morning breeze had freshened the rain swept landscape.

Slowly, it turned into day. The morning light was bright enough to create shadows but they remained in their shaded hollow. She merely couldn't get up the energy to emerge. Like a cocoon, she thought. She felt like she was in 'la la land'.

Drifting, ever drifting...

She could have sworn that she heard her name being called. Nah. Couldn't have been. It was only her overactive imagination kicking in for the umpteenth time. She eyed Jake when he lifted his head and 'woofed' a hoarse woof, then laid his head back down beside her.

She closed an ultra heavy eyelid to match the other one. It was easier to lie here, all warm and cozy next to Jake and succumb to nothingness.

Maybe she was sick. Couldn't move. Didn't need to yet anyway.

There it was again. Lori. She definitely heard her name being called. Maybe she was hallucinating or something. Then she heard it, a motor. She started to sit up and bumped her head on the dirt overhang, knocking sand in her eyes and wiped them with already filthy hands.

Jake lifted his head and ears, appearing alert. He barked louder this time.

"Sh. Jake. Quiet now. We need to stay here and be quiet. We're going to be very careful about with whom we leave this island."

He sat up and Lori put her arms firmly around his neck, making sure he remained with her in their hiding place. She laid her forehead against his big head, receiving a lick in return.

"Silly old dog. I smell like wet dog, don't I?" She squeezed him.

She heard a boat circling the island and had a hard time keeping Jake at her side. She was certain he recognized the sound of the boat but he obviously couldn't express that to her. He made mewing sounds in his throat and little muffled barks here and there, but stayed put under protest.

She knew she might regret it but held onto him tightly. Fear kept her there. Their position would not be terribly secure in the light of day. She had little choice but to keep Jake reined in.

Lori listened intently, thinking the sound of the motor diminished as it rounded the island. She wanted to creep outside and look but knew she couldn't control the big dog if she did. It was better to remain hidden.

"Lori-i-i-i" whistled on the morning wind back to her ears for a while longer. Then the pervading tones of wind blowing through the trees, birds twittering and other island noises dominated the surf sounds and allowed her to relax at last. Lori hadn't realized how tensed up she'd been.

Her stomach informed her of a clamoring need for food and she was wondering what to do about it. If she were this hungry then surely Jake was too. She was mired deep in thought about what their next step could possibly be.

Lori considered crawling out of their hiding place to explore for food when she heard the sound of approaching footsteps on the island. At least that's what it sounded like to her. She felt the black dog's muscles tense up again beside her. She shook her head and put her finger to her mouth to shush him again. He tilted his head at her but remained quiet.

"Oh, Lori-i-i-i." She could hear the underbrush of the island moving as someone moved through it and straight toward them!

Twenty-seven

She froze, holding Jake perfectly still. Both hands on his collar held him tight, while he growled deep in his throat. A shadow fell over their hollow hideaway. Sounds of shifting sand and clods of dirt slid down the bank next to them. A loud thud bombarded them as the weight of a large person hit the ground.

Before Lori could say a little prayer for them, the palm branches that had protected them from the storm had been pulled back to expose them to the Captain.

"Lori. Why didn't you answer me? Are you all right?"

He reached a hand down to pull her up and out of their pocket hideaway and into his arms for a great big bear hug.

"Uh hm. You're feeling mighty good to me, I'm thinking."

He hugged her again, picking her up off the ground, and leaving her feet dangling before he set her back down. Jake leapt out, prancing and wagging his big rear end and added his usual happy "Woof!"

"Oh, Jerrod. How did you find us?" She hugged him back after she got her breath.

"Miss Genny called me this morning after Benjamin could not find you. The boat was missing so they have boats out searching for you. She called me to help with the search. Why are you hiding? Why didn't you answer me? Couldn't you hear me calling you?"

"I found boat debris on the beach and I found a vest wedged in the crack in the rocks. I knew you had to be here somewhere. Your friends are out there, circling the islet. They did everything but put up a sign to tell me that you were here. I don't think they would let me leave if I tried." He was chuckling.

"They saved our lives last night, pushing us to the shore. They were wonderful. Weren't they, Jake?"

"Woof! Woof! Woof!" He danced around them in circles.

"Oh, a triple woof. He *is* getting excited." Jerrod laughed with her. "You didn't tell me what happened? Are you sure you're okay?"

"Before we get into that, do you happen to have anything to eat? Jake and I had a very strenuous night and we are starving. It seems like our stomachs have been growling forever."

Jake quit dancing, skidding to a halt at Jerrod's feet with an even bigger "WOOF!" and sat there panting.

"I'm thinking, he's hungry too." He looked down at the enormous hungry Rottweiler at his feet. "Come on. We have to get him into a dinghy on the beach. I couldn't bring the big boat all the way into the shore. Too shallow. I didn't know if you were injured or what. There's plenty of food on board, but you haven't answered my questions. Why in the world were you out in that storm? You've got more sense than that. And why were you hiding and not answering me? What is going on here?"

He grabbed her hand, leading them back over the hump of the little island toward the opposite shore with Jake at their heels. Jerrod took his jacket off, placing it over her shoulders.

"I don't have any shoes for you. I just don't understand why you are here." Shaking his head at her, he took her hand again in his.

"It's a long story, Jerrod. Do you have a way for me to call St. Thomas? A radio or something?"

"Yes, but don't you want me to let Miss Genny know you're safe so that they can call off the search?"

"NO! I mean, not yet. First, I *have* to communicate with St. Thomas. Do you have a cell phone or what?"

"Short wave radio." He scrutinized her with a quizzical expression on his face.

"Just trust me on this Jerrod. I will explain everything soon. I...I'm going to need your help. Thank you for coming to look for me. I know you have other responsibilities and I do appreciate all that you have done for me. It means a lot to me." She squeezed the large hand holding hers.

"Had to rescue a damsel in distress." He shrugged off her thanks.

She watched, when Jerrod tried to coax Jake into the little rubber dinghy. The dog would have no part of it. Nope, the dog was not interested in the least. Land looked very good to him. Even after Lori crawled over the boat wale, he still didn't want to participate in a boat ride.

Finally, she told him. "Look Jake, we are going out to the big boat over there and then we are going home. So come here."

That didn't work, so she pointed out to the boat anchored on the eastern side of the island but away from the big rocks.

"And there is food on that boat."

That did it. Jake's ears perked up and he scrambled to climb in by himself but Jerrod needed to lift him up and in over the boat wale.

"Umpf." Jerrod grunted, lifting the heavy dog into the boat. He was mumbling about big feet with claws.

Jake cooperated fully the moment he realized food was involved. He sat like a meek little lamb, while Jerrod pushed and shoved the small craft out into the gentle surf. It was a little lopsided with the big dog weighing down one corner of the raft, Lori in another corner, and Jerrod rowing toward his boat.

The friendly bottle nose dolphins soon circled the little craft, chattering away at Lori where she and Jake were hanging off the edge of the dinghy watching them.

"I hope you have plenty of fish for them. They deserve a gourmet fish meal. Thank you. Thank you all. Thank you fellows! I'm going to see that you get lots of yummy fish for a feast. Speaking of food, Jerrod, we are famished."

"We'll take care of that. Talk to me Lori. I need to know what in the world is going on. You owe me that much." The rippling muscles in his back and arms strained as he rowed them to safety.

"I owe you more than I can ever repay." She reached over, gently touching his firm shoulder.

"Jerrod, I am not sure where to begin. Some of it started a long, long time ago." With a far away look in her eyes, she had to shake herself back into the reality of here, today and now.

"I was hiding here on this island because someone wanted me dead. That boat was tampered with. I don't know how. But the next time I took it out, it was meant *not* to come back. The radio was damaged. All systems went out. *After* I was safely away from St. Saba, that is. They gave me time to get this far."

Jerrod rowed the two oars faster and faster, his mouth open in shock.

"Are you sure it wasn't an accident? It could have been an accident you know. Couldn't it?" He asked her beseechingly.

"Jerrod, if *every single system* on a boat shut down at once, would it explode? Could it explode by itself? Is it realistic to assume it could happen by itself? Spontaneous combustion maybe? I don't think so. The only reason we are alive today is because I had the sense to abandon ship. The boat headed for the rocks, so we escaped...*before* it blew."

"But why would anyone blow up your boat? Why would anyone want to kill you for god's sake?"

"Because I know too much. I don't know a lot, but I can tell you one thing. It blew up *before* it hit the rocks. There were multiple explosions."

"Too much about what, Lori? I don't understand. Tell me." He did not break a sweat in the fresh morning air.

"We discovered that someone on the island is part of a drug conduit to France."

"What? You've got to be kidding. No. You're not kidding. That's what this is all about. Drugs. Money. It always boils down to money, I'm thinking. Why I left Chicago. And now it's here. Hard to believe. The island. I know every one of those people. *Every single one.* Who is it?"

His brown face showed his disappointment but he grew tense and alert.

"I need to call for help to Charlotte Amalie, before anyone has a chance to hide any evidence. I need to get back there, as fast as we can. While they think I'm out of their way. They followed us last night and searched the wreckage. We spent part of the night on a ledge inside the rocks. We have to get back to save a life. Hugh, I mean, JeanPaul has been captured. He is a prisoner on the island. I don't think they've had time to get him off the island, yet. I hope." She muttered getting quieter as the story progressed.

"But where? Why?"

"Caves. Tunnels. The island is honeycombed with them. There is a stockpile of processed opium in a cave. A lab, too, I think. Raw comes in, processed goes out."

"*Who are you*, Lori?" He gave her an even stranger look.

"Don't look at me like that. I'm just a technician from St. Louis, Jerrod. That's all." She sighed.

Reaching the boat at last, he helped her onto the boat first, so she could help him get Jake up there. It was hard to do, but they managed it between them. He pulled the rubber dingy on board and led them both to the galley.

"I don't have fish food for your friends today. We'll have to give them a rain check for a thank you feast. There is hot coffee in the thermos and ham sandwiches in the fridge. Help yourself. Oh, and there are clean socks in the drawer by the bunk. That will help your feet get warm. Take anything else that you need."

Smiling his wonderful contagious wide grin, he leaned over to touch her. The boat rocked. When she wobbled on her feet, he accidentally touched the gun in her pocket. "Jesus, Lori." He was startled again, and raised that questioning eyebrow at her.

She thought he must have practiced that eyebrow rise thousands of times in front of a mirror to get it that perfect. She patted her pocket and shook her head at him.

"It's not mine. I borrowed it. Turns out I didn't need it. Yet. Don't worry. I'll tell you more when I come topside. First things first. Water, then food. We worked up quite an appetite, didn't we Jake?"

Jake had followed them down to the galley and was sniffing around. She poured him a large bowl of water, which he immediately began lapping, and drank two full glasses of water herself. Her stomach screaming, she hurriedly yanked a couple of sandwiches out of the fridge, one for each of them, putting his on a plate on the floor. She ran up the short set of steps back onto the deck, munching all the way and chasing Jerrod topside.

"Mmm. This is fantastic. It really hits the spot. God, we needed this."

Jerrod was already fiddling and talking into the radio.

"Thank you again, before we get too involved here. Jerrod, this could get dangerous. Do you have a gun on board? You may need it. I need to hold on to this one. Let me see, how does this work? Can I call anyone on this? Like on a telephone?"

"Well, yes, but there has to be a middle man to patch you through to a phone line. I called Dumond at the office. He works for me, watching the office when Julie or I can't. She's in school today. But are you sure that you don't want to let Miss Genny know that you're safe? He could call the island for you."

"NO. I don't want anyone on the island to know yet. *It is imperative, Jerrod.* Got it? No option. Now tell me how this thing works."

"You talk to Dumond and tell him 'out' when you're finished. He calls your party and repeats exactly what you say. Speak slowly and distinctly, so he can understand. Just don't talk too fast. That's the worst thing that you can do."

He delivered the microphone handset of the radio to her, stepping back. He gave her space but not so far out of range that he couldn't hear.

Swallowing the last bite of her sandwich, she cleared her throat. "Hello, Dumond? Can you call this number for me 774 1829 there in Charlotte Amalie? It's Hotel 1829. Ask for Charlie, say it is important and that it is Lori Paige calling."

She thought for a second then added, "No, just say it is an emergency. No name. Uh, over." She felt like a dummy and stood impatiently tapping her foot, waiting for the connection to be completed.

"By the way Jerrod, can you head us back to St. Saba? Now, please, so we don't waste any time?" Then she turned back to the radio again. Dumond reported that he had called and was waiting for them to get Charlie.

Lori surveyed the surrounding seas, considerably calmer since last night's storms. Scanning the sky, she noticed less wind, fewer big waves, and minimal clouds. The water churned in a gray tossed turbulence, green seaweed roiling to the surface. No high breaker whitecaps unless the water neared the shores or rocks.

She was impatient to get back to St. Saba and get on with things now that her own hunger was temporarily assuaged and her thirst was quenched. Once more fear dominated her thoughts. Not fear for her own survival, but fear for Hugh's.

Trying to organize her thoughts for Charlie to understand her cryptic message, Lori was afraid to speak too frankly on open air waves. You never knew who could be listening. She was learning to be much more circumspect and less trusting of this crazy world.

Absentmindedly, she pulled the gun out of her waistband, opened it up and wiped it down with the towel around her neck with which she'd dried her hair. She promptly broke it down into its separate components, making sure that each piece was dry and free from salt and water. Ejecting shells from the cartridge, she rolled each of them dry in the towel before reinserting them. Then she quickly reassembled the gun.

Making sure the firing mechanism moved properly, she snapped the loaded clip back in and slid the top slide back and forth several times. She pointed it, aiming it at a rock in the water then fired once. The bullet hit the rock, splintering off a chunk. Lori waved it in the air a few times to cool it and slid it behind her back again into her waistband.

It could stand oiling, but she thought it would be adequate for now. She couldn't anticipate really using it. Satisfied with her progress, she glanced at Jerrod, shrugged her shoulders then smiled sheepishly at the open dismay on his face.

"A regular Annie Oakley, I'm thinking. You have been making a fool of me. Are you sure you're who you say you are?" He turned her around to face him with both hands on her shoulders, forcing her to look him square in the eye.

"Of course I am, Jerrod. Just because I can handle a gun does not mean I'm not whom I say I am." She snapped the testy answer at him.

Dumond told her. "Go ahead. The party is present on the other end."

"I need your help. The subject we were discussing the other day has done it again. More than twenty-four hours ago. Over."

"Go on. Over." Dumond told her.

"I have found what Hugh was looking for. Over. It's there on the island or was nine hours ago. Please come for it. Over. I am going back there now but I need help. As soon as possible. Over." She waited impatiently for a response.

Dumond reported back to her. "They are on their way, whatever that means. He has already hung up the phone. Miss Lori, anything else I can do for you?"

"No thanks, Dumond. You have been a great help. Out."

Jerrod nodded his head at her. "Now hang up the mike in the clip there and turn it off. And tell me what in the world that was all about. What do you mean you have found what you were looking for?"

"Not you, *Hugh.* I told you. It's a long story."

She climbed up in the chair behind Jerrod, watching him steer the boat, and pulled her feet up underneath her to get them warm. She hadn't taken the time to put on dry socks and was feeling the chill of the morning.

"You see, JeanPaul Richaud is Hugh Richmond, who I knew in college a zillion years ago. He is here undercover. He has been captured and we have to go back to find him. We *cannot* wait for reinforcements."

"It was the cavalry that I just called out. Or whoever. You see, Charlie was my contact in case anything went down. I am afraid he won't thank me for blowing his cover, but I didn't know what else to do. He was my only contact. I was supposed to go to him when this happened, but I can't. *I* am the only one who can save Hugh now. If you will help me, that is."

"Hugh. JeanPaul Richaud? No French Canadian? But shouldn't we get you to safety first."

She shook her head firmly, putting her hand on his arm.

"Get it out of your head, Jerrod. I am going back if I have to swim back."

At which Jake looked up with alarm from his snooze on the deck. "Don't worry, Jake. I have a plan. We need to get to the island as quickly and quietly as possible. I particularly *do not* want the whole island alerted to my return. I must get to Miss Genny first to get her cooperation. She'll help. I should have trusted her before."

"Actually my instincts told me to trust you too. I tried to get your help last night but I missed your boat. Now, I need her to call all of the people of the island together in one location. *And* keep them there. That's where you come in. Ringing her bell I think, should cause them to assemble."

"If you can hold all of them there with her, then I can go in alone and release Hugh. I am sure I know where to find him." Lori's eyes focused on the distance, her mind racing ahead as they approached the island.

Jerrod stood bewildered by what he'd heard, and shook his head at her. But she knew he would help her. He had to.

"By then Hugh's backup cavalry or whoever they are, should arrive to take over the whole island for a search and seizure, I think it's called. Do you have a gun or any kind of weapon?"

"I only have a flare gun and a pretty wicked fishing knife."

"Take them both. Now, how can you get me to Miss Genny without one single person seeing me? I can't let anyone see me but her. Do you think you can take your boat to the boathouse? Then get Miss Genny there to talk to me? Or would I fit in a box that you could carry into the house? What do you think?"

"I don't know if I am strong enough to carry you in a box all the way to West house from the boat house. You'd probably break my back." He grinned ear to ear.

"Oh. I'm not that heavy, you beast. You're strong as a bear. You have carried lots of heavier boxes." She hit him on the shoulder.

"Now if I could put you in a sack and throw you over my shoulder like a sack of raw potatoes, no one would notice."

"Stop it. You clown. This is important. People could be in danger, including you. Besides, potatoes get delivered to the warehouse first."

"Oh, you're too practical, I'm thinking."

"And you're too silly. Come on now, think. This is so important. Which is the best idea? Come to think of it. It definitely wouldn't be normal for Miss Genny to go to the boathouse, would it? In fact, I've never seen her anywhere but West house except for the fire."

"Would it be very unusual for you to go to the boathouse instead of the main dock? Would that alert someone on the island that something was up, do you think? We need it to appear as normal as possible."

"No, I think the box idea is the best one, although I am supposed to be out looking for you. Even if they headed for her house thinking I'd found you, by the time they got there I'd have you inside. They would think it was special supplies I was delivering, maybe. That would be as good excuse as any to use the boat house."

"I'd carry the box in and ask to speak to her in private. Then you could explain your plan and put it into effect. But I do not like the idea of you going in any tunnel alone. I'd rather be with you."

"NO. I don't know who to trust but you and Miss Genny. I need you to watch all the islanders and keep them in the house until the police or whoever show up. Besides I am *not* going alone. *This* time I'm taking Jake with me. The entrance to the tunnels under Steffan's cottage is level. I just have to get him down a few rungs below a trap door in his pantry to the basement area. After all we've been through, that should be a cake walk, right old boy?"

"Woof!" was the dog's quiet answer.

"Should I let her know I am coming to see her?"

"No. I don't think so. Don't need to put anyone on guard. Just take your boat in as quietly as possible and get me to her ASAP."

She kissed him on the cheek and gave him a quick hug when St. Saba came into view. Lori led Jake below. After Jerrod docked, it was time for her to get into a wooden crate with rope handles on it. They would leave Jake in the boathouse until it was time for Lori to make her way to the guesthouse. She didn't want the dog's abrupt appearance causing speculation about his whereabouts for the last nine hours.

Twenty-eight

The box wasn't terribly comfortable, but she fit in easily. She'd had to take the gun from behind her back and hold it in her hands though. Lori was thankful for Jerrod's strong broad back, when he lifted the box with a single grunt. He kicked the boathouse door closed on Jake, trapping him inside. She thumped along inside with each step he took as he carried her across the sand to the West house.

So far so good, she thought. Lori heard him ask Marion to see Miss Genny alone. The beat of his feet padded on the bare hardwood floors, heading toward Miss Genny's small sitting room. Listening to the murmur of voices and the sound of a door closing, the box settled on the floor.

"Don't be startled, Miss Genny. It's Lori, I found her and she is okay. But she wants to talk to you alone. I'm going out for coffee with Marion while you talk. Call me when you're ready."

Jerrod helped Lori step out of the box. Looking back as he left the room, he saw the two women engrossed in a tearful hug. Smiling, he closed the door securely on them. He sought Marion in the kitchen, both to occupy himself and to find out the latest news today on the island. "Marion, I could use a cup of your coffee."

All the boat slips had been empty. He hoped no one would show up prematurely and let the dog loose. Listening to the soft cadence of her chatter about the hunt for Lori that had been ongoing since early morning, he saw speculative questions in Marion's face but ignored them for now.

The news was what he had expected. The whole island was abuzz and had been thoroughly searched. The search had been expanded to the sea when they realized not only Lori, but the boat was missing, too. Ben was frantic.

The Captain quizzed Marion about who took the boats out this morning. She told him, "Steffan, Miss Emily and Sheree are searching in one boat. The Laurent men and Ben are out in the other big boat. The Coast Guard, Navy and Rescue teams are on the lookout too. I am positive they will find her."

But obviously, Jerrod knew no one had reported the wreckage he'd spotted on the little island. And someone must have known about that wreckage from searching it the night before.

After the bell for the West house rang, and the islanders were gathered in the great room, Lori slipped out a back door at the far end of the house. She stayed hidden in the foliage as much as possible, only exposing herself on the quick trip across the dunes to get Jake out of the boathouse.

She'd put on clean dry socks, a sweater and some stretch slippers on her feet, since Miss Genny's shoes wouldn't fit. Lori prepared to take on the world if necessary.

Jerrod had coerced her to add his flare gun to her arsenal. He said it wouldn't be any good in the house. He had no intention of pulling his knife either. He couldn't imagine anyone trying to escape. How could they?

She broke into Steffan's cottage. Everything was locked up tighter than a drum. Lori didn't have any inhibitions about bashing in the glass in the front door and unlocking it. In fact she rather enjoyed it. She led Jake rapidly across the cottage to the kitchen pantry and opened the door.

Getting him down that primitive ladder was going to be a little harder than she thought. She considered pushing him in, wishing he'd land okay, but wouldn't take that chance. Besides that seemed abusive. She went down the ladder first and coaxed him to her.

Jake hung over the square opening with his front legs and head. She pulled him down to her. He yelped and she almost fell the rest of the way when his weight bore down on her. But she rapidly managed the last few steps until his weight bore her backwards.

She landed on the floor on her rump with a thump, where Jake landed on her lap making her feel like a Dr. Suess character.

"Ouch. Come on Jake. We have to hurry."

Lori was pleased to see that Hugh's things were in the same place. Good sign. She hurried to the tunnel door. Lori found it locked this time and went to work with her screwdriver to undo the latch, leaving the lock intact.

Throwing the door open, she started running down the tunnel with Jake at her heels. She turned on a boat's flashlight. She'd added a spare light from the house, in case this one conked out. The tunnel seemed endless and she had to stop once to choose which fork to take, but remembered to follow the wiring from the cavern.

She took out her screwdriver and scraped an arrow pointing in the direction of the cavern, showing the police the way when they got there. They scurried down into the black void of the tunnel like half-blind moles into the musty darkness.

When they finally reached the big cave, she made sure that the room was empty before turning on the only light switch, pocketing the flashlight. The boxes were stacked right where she left them, which indicated that they must not be in too big a hurry to get out of here. More good news.

"Please let me find him." She mumbled, making her way across the room to the massive locked door. Lori knew the enormous padlock would be tough. It wasn't going to open with just a screwdriver. In her mind she went over available tools but decided to beat on the door and yell to see if he would answer her.

It wouldn't do any good to get in there if he was somewhere else on the island or in another cave. But she could not leave with the door unopened either. Anyway, supposedly the island had already been searched when they looked for her.

"Hugh! Are you in there?"

Lori beat on the door with both hands because this time she wasn't afraid to make noise. She was only afraid that he might *not* hear her or he could not. She pounded on the door until her hands hurt. Lori stood for as long as she could with her ear pressed to the door, straining for a sound, any sound to come through the wood.

She thought maybe she heard scratching sounds on the other side, and looked down to see if Jake reacted. His nose was pressed to the floor under the door making snuffing noises and then he began scratching with his big front feet.

That was all it took for her to pull out Hugh's gun and take the safety off.

"Back up, Jake. This could ricochet. Get behind these boxes here. Now stay. STAY!"

She went back to the door with the gun held tightly in both hands, and fired into the padlock, effectively destroying the locking mechanism. She had to pry the lock off using the screwdriver as a fulcrum. The sound of gunfire echoed through the cave, bouncing off the solid walls. When the lock came loose with a loud thunk landing on the floor, Jake poked his head from behind the big rock.

"Come on Jake."

It took all her strength to pull the heavy door partially open. She and the dog prepared to enter the darkness. Lori needed to get the flashlight out, turn it on and keep the gun handy. Tricky but she managed. With her left hand, she turned the flashlight over, shining light out of her pocket, keeping the gun in her right and led them into the dark room.

Jake took off like a bolt across the room barking. "WOOF!"

Her left hand flashed the light pointing to see where the dog had gone. The light slowly traversed the room. The big dog had circled a large crude lab bench. It was what she had suspected. In the back of the room, Hugh was chained to a bolt in the wall.

"Good God! Hugh you look terrible. Are you all right?"

She took a filthy old rag out of his mouth. He had dried blood on his forehead and dark wet bloodstains on his left pant's leg. No socks. No shoes. Both arms manacled, chained together and held over his head.

He looked sick as a dog, pallid and gaunt. After running her hands over the lumps on his head, Lori tied the rag tight above his thigh wound. Holding his head in her hands, she made him focus his eyes on her.

She repeated. "Oh God, Hugh. Are you okay?" She hadn't thought to bring bandages or a first aid kit. *Dummy*, she berated herself. But the bleeding had mostly stopped and crusted over long ago.

"Water. Do you have any water? I'm dry."

Hugh had never in his life seen a sight more welcome than his woman. He croaked. He reached for his throat but couldn't quite make it. The chains on his wrists restrained his reach. He watched Lori use the flashlight beam to find a bottle marked distilled water on the counter and pour a cupful.

She located the light switch. When she flipped it on the brilliance from the lights hurt his eyes so much that he squeezed them closed.

She tasted the water before she held it for him to drink. He gulped it down too fast, then retched and shivered.

"Drink it slower this time." She refilled it, this time only letting him drink a small sip at a time. "You didn't answer me, are you okay? Do you have a fever? How am I going to get these chains off you?"

She felt his forehead with her other hand, but couldn't tell if he were as hot as she thought or if her hands were just too cold. Putting her cheek next to his, she could feel his hot dry skin. She put her hand to his throat and felt his pulse racing fast and furious.

"No, I don't know, Lori. Slight concussion, maybe. How long have I been here in the dark? Seems like a week. I ache all over. You alone? You have to get out of here." His voice creaked weaker.

"About thirty-four hours, maybe more. Hugh, are you strong enough to stand? Can you walk? I am not going anywhere without you. Besides Jake is here with me. Is there a key to these?"

"Yeah, see if there is a key over there somewhere." Hugh shivered convulsively.

She shined the flashlight in his face, watching his eyes, and saw that each eye didn't dilate the same way. He looked ghastly and she was worried sick. He most definitely had a concussion.

There was no way they could stay put and wait any longer for the rescue party. No way. She had to get him to medical help *now*. She took off his belt, using it as a tourniquet around his leg to prevent the wound from breaking open and bleeding when he put his weight on it.

"Too tight?" She received a mumble for an answer.

She rummaged through piles of stuff on the counter top. This lab was a shambles. It would be a miracle to find anything in this mess, she thought.

322

"Are you sure that there is a key here? This place is disgusting."

His only answer was "Umm."

She expanded her search area to another cluttered counter top and finally found a large black iron skeleton key.

"This? It looks like an antique. If this thing works, I bet I could have used my screwdriver." Hurrying over to him, she inserted it in the first lock, then with a twist and a clank, it dropped loose from his wrist.

"*Voila! Mon chere.* See? I will have you out of here in no time."

He grinned weakly at her cheerful demeanor, and with his free hand reached up to stroke her cheek. He peered at her face more closely for the first time.

"You don't look so hot yourself, woman. What have you been doing? And by the way, don't give up your day job and do *not* try to pass yourself off anytime soon as a French mademoiselle. Your accent stinks. Here give me that key. I am not totally helpless. Do I smell wet dog?" He talked slowly, sniffing at her hair while fumbling to unlock his other hand.

"Thanks a lot, you brute. I was just trying to cheer you up. So suffer, you insufferable man. Yes, I smell like wet dog. It's another long story and right now we have to get you topside. Or whatever they call it. And to a doctor."

She helped him get to his feet and watched him grimace in pain.

"Can you walk and put pressure on your leg? It won't bleed?"

"I think you already asked me that, or else my brain is in a feedback loop." He stumbled, attempting a first step on his own. "Let's go."

"Here, lean on me and we'll take it very slowly. Let's get moving. Come on Jake. You lead us out, but don't get too far ahead, okay boy? I guess we've got to go back the way we came. Out through Steffan's. Ready Hugh?"

"Steffan's?" Puzzled and perplexed.

"Yes, of course Steffan. Isn't that who put you here?"

"No. It was a woman. I think. A tall woman. I didn't see her face or hear her voice. Only felt her gun. On my head. Several times. Then in my ribs. Vindictive bitch. Got me good. I let my guard down because it was a woman. Shot me in the leg so I wouldn't run off. Won't make that mistake again for a long time."

He spoke in disjointed sentences, shaking his head and wincing with pain for his effort. He shambled along like an old man, and was beginning to scare Lori.

She shifted him to her left side, allowing her right arm freedom for the gun. It should be safe now. Surely the good guys had already arrived. Leaving the lights on, and the door open she steered him toward the tunnel on the right side of the cave. She stopped him when they got to the entrance of the tunnel and handed him a flashlight.

"Can you carry this for me?"

"Sure, anything else sweetheart?" He answered in a lousy Bogart voice.

"Well, you may be fluent in five languages but don't waste your time trying out for any Hollywood parts. Come on, let's get out of here."

"You sure this is the right way?"

"Just shut up and walk."

She helped him step by step through a long dark tunnel that seemed interminable. Thank God, he walked, mostly bearing his own weight but leaning on her, too. She felt like she'd been run through the mill in these last few days. Jake trotted a few steps in front of them but stayed within the light's range.

Before making it to the branch in the tunnel, noises reverberated toward them in the dark. Jake skid to a halt and stood, his ears pointed forward. Lori stopped, needing to make a decision immediately.

Should they turn around and run back the way they came? Was it the rescue team?

Hugh didn't seem to notice they'd stopped, let alone give any indication that he heard anything. He was breathing hard.

Oh God, he must be out of it, she thought. In a split second decision she shoved the Sig Sauer pistol into Hugh's hand. Taking the flashlight from him, Lori carefully eased him to the ground, leaning him against the wall.

"I am going to leave you alone for a few minutes while I see who is coming. I have another gun." She whispered. He didn't need to know it was only a flare gun.

"I will be right back. Maybe it's the good guys. Jake you stay here."

Jake took one look at Hugh and followed her anyway. Lori hurried toward the tunnel fork. She kept the flashlight in her pocket, face down this time, keeping the light as dim as possible.

Somehow, in all this mess, she'd managed to forget her claustrophobic fears. They had receded into inconsequential recesses of her mind. Her heart pounded madly in her throat and her adrenaline had kicked in to record dimensions.

When she reached the branch in the tunnel she stopped again to listen and could hear someone running down the tunnel toward them. The sound of the footsteps didn't seem heavy enough to be military boots to her untrained ears, but it sounded like more than one person.

Whoever it was, came so fast Lori backed into the other section of tunnel that went who knew where, holding Jake back by his collar.

"Quiet. Stay boy, stay." Lori hissed to Jake. She switched the light off when she saw a dim light growing brighter as it approached them. Lori felt the tension in the big dog's neck as she held him back.

A pair of black women's shoes abruptly appeared in the downward light cast by a flashlight exactly like the one she was carrying. She also could hear another rapid set of footsteps, pounding and gaining on the woman that ran past Lori's hiding place in a blur.

"Damn." Cursing under her breath, she didn't want anyone running into Hugh and his position wasn't very far down the tunnel. So she took a chance and yelled at the top of her lungs.

"Stop! Police!" Letting Jake loose when a man ran past the Y, Lori flashed on the light when she yelled and blinded the running man to a halt. He threw his hands up over his eyes to protect them. In that same instant Lori saw it was Jerrod, the ugly fishing knife glinting in his hand.

The running woman stopped and aimed a shot toward Lori and her light. The woman was either a lousy shot or it was rotten luck, but the bullet plowed into Jerrod's arm, spinning him and knocking him immediately to the floor.

Identifying the light as a source of trouble, Lori tossed the flashlight back up the other tunnel, away from them. The woman continued firing, but at least she didn't have Lori's light to aim at now. Hopefully, she'd reduced their chances of getting shot. By now everyone had changed positions in the dark. The sound of gunfire reverberated through the tunnels.

"You okay?" Kneeling by his side, she tore off a strip of her T-shirt to tie on his arm to stop the bleeding.

"Where is your gun? Pick up the knife for me. I dropped it." Jerrod whispered in the dark.

"I left it with Hugh when I heard someone coming."

She showed him the flare gun in the dim light. They were not backlit since they had backed off into the deeper shadows of the side tunnel. Lori felt around on the floor for the knife, handing it back to him. She couldn't see Jake and didn't know what he was doing although she could hear him.

~ * ~

That nosy bitch. She is no police. She should have blown up in that boat! I'll get her this time. I'll get them all. I know I hit someone. She didn't know how many people were down there but she recognized that little troublemaker Lori's voice. The woman huffed from running, slid to a stop and shot a couple more times. Bullets ricocheted off the walls. She turned her own light off, using the illumination of the flashlight on the floor to see by.

Nothing will stop me now if I have to kill every one of them. Her chest heaved and she began to creep closer to take her chances before firing again.

~ * ~

Jake's growling, not a little grumble this time became a serious growl. Before Lori could do anything, Jake jumped out of the darkness at the woman. The woman had the gun poised to shoot but Jake leapt at her knocking her to the floor before she fired.

Lori's intent was to distract the woman. She aimed the flare gun over everyone's heads, shooting it down the tunnel and praying it wouldn't hit Hugh. The light, tracking the flare, startled the woman enough that Jake's teeth got a ferocious grip on her gun arm. He pushed her flat to the floor when she tried to rise, knocking the gun from her grip. The dog held her down while she tried to dislodge him by kicking and screeching obscenities. She was frothing at the mouth in her anger.

Lori threw the flare gun down and ran over to pick up the woman's gun, checking to make sure there were still bullets left in it. The whole tunnel area was lit by a diminishing red glowing light when the dark form of a man began to take shape. He limped up the long tunnel from the cavern with a gun in his right hand, his other hand on the wall.

He came onto a scene he would not soon forget.

Lori stood with her legs spread, holding a gun in both hands aimed at the screaming woman in the floor.

Who in turn was held down by the big dog.

A wounded man lay prone on the floor in the shadows.

All in the glow of a flashlight and a fading flare.

"Lori, what's all the ruckuses about? You sure know how to get my attention. I heard and saw the shots. Then I get a flare shot at me, but I guess you've got everything under control here." Hugh spoke slowly and slid even more slowly down to the floor, using the tunnel wall for support again.

"That is an understatement, if I ever heard one, I'm thinking." Jerrod added and smiled a big roguish grin, holding his hand over the wound in his arm.

"Captain, tell me, who's the screamer?" Hugh mumbled to him, recognizing Jerrod's voice.

"It's Emily. Emily Moore. Hard to believe."

Jerrod shook his head in the growing darkness as the flare burned itself out. He lifted his head when he heard the pounding of heavy boots coming their way.

Twenty-nine

Lori and Jake were allowed to walk out of the depths on their own. The men were carried out on stretchers, under the care of paramedics. She kissed both their cheeks before they left. The woman, screaming shrilly, had been sedated and carried out by guards after the paramedics tended to her arm. Jake's teeth had penetrated the black cloth of her sleeve in a couple of places. She had been screeching an unfathomable vocabulary until the medicine took effect and finally silenced her.

Lori had pointed in the direction of the cavern. One of the police nodded first at her, then at the others, and the rest of the troops disappeared down the tunnel. They had brought some kind of bright lighting with wiring strung out behind them. The tunnel now was brilliantly illuminated.

The soldiers or policemen were dressed in dark clothing, with all kinds of pockets, gizmos, gadgets, and guns. It was odd. Not a single word was exchanged. All orders were transmitted in some kind of silent verbalization with gestures. It was as if they knew what to do by osmosis.

Strange, Lori thought. *Bizarre, even.* Kind of in a dreamlike funk, she and Jake trotted back up the tunnel alone.

When Lori and the dog reached the end of the tunnel, Jake looked at her as if to say now what? She knew she couldn't get him up the rungs of that ladder by herself, so she poked her head up into the pantry hole and yelled. "Hello. Can anyone help me here?"

A young man in a uniform of some kind came over to her and politely asked, "Ma'am?"

"I need help to get my dog out of here." She placed the gun on the cabin floor and pointed back at Jake looking up at them. "You might need this for evidence, too."

"Yes, Ma'am, will you come on up out of the way? I will bring him up."

"Okay, but you don't know how hard it was to get him down."

He looked at her as if she must be kidding him and went down the rungs quickly and efficiently.

She shook her head and waited for him. He grunted, groaned and strained, huffed then puffed. Anxious as she was to get out, she tried not to laugh aloud at the young man's efforts to get the dog up into the house. But by the time he finally succeeded, silent tears of mirth were running down her cheeks before Jake's head finally emerged above the trap door.

Thanking the young soldier or police officer, whoever he was, she opened the door and led Jake out of the cabin and saw all the activity on the outside. Her guys were side by side on stretchers on Steffan's front porch. A MEDIVAC helicopter was landing on the beach.

The clearing around the cabin was filled with wide-eyed islanders. Marion and Benjamin were on each side of Miss Genny, who was holding up quite well. Lori waved to them, dropping to the ground off the porch to check on the men. Hugh's brow was hot and feverish and his skin felt like paper. He was still shivering.

"Hey. Annie Oakley. Shoot anybody else since we left?" Jerrod grinned ear to ear.

"Oh, stop it. I never shot anybody, did I? How are you two feeling? I'm going to have to report to Miss Genny, in a minute."

"I'm okay. Flesh wound. Been hurt more with fishing hooks, I'm thinking. Will you call my kids for me, so they don't hear about this and get worried?"

"Oh, Jerrod, you are so full of blarney. Of course I will." She shook her head, kissed both the men's cheeks and walked away when paramedics set up IVs for both men. She walked into the group of islanders and was instantly surrounded by them. They reached out their hands to touch her in some way.

She put her arm around Miss Genny's waist and wearily leaned her head against the old lady's shoulder.

"I am sorry, Miss Genny. Hugh has a concussion and a gunshot wound in the leg. He's feverish. Infection probably. Jerrod's been shot in the arm, not too serious, I think. "

"It is not your fault, my dear." Miss Genny patted her arm. "None of this is your fault. You have done nothing wrong. I am very proud of you. I should have known what was going on here. It *is* my island. *I* should have known."

"Where is Steffan?" Lori searched the crowd with her eyes.

"The police have already taken him into custody. They found him running up the beach on the back of the island. He had a boat hidden to escape with. Bah. Such a coward. The island is simply crawling with police. It is very exciting, is it not?" Miss Genny's eyes twinkled with excitement. "I have called for Jacques. He is on his way from Paris. Jon and Gerard are here."

"The phones are working again? The Captain wants us to notify his children that he is okay and to meet him at the hospital. And I am way overdue with calls back to St. Louis." Lori's concern showed in her voice and her face.

"The phone, it worked all along. Evidently, Emily did not want you using the phones. One of the men discovered the line had been disconnected this morning when they searched for you. I'll call Jerrod's children for him."

"Thank you. Damn, I forgot. It was a satellite phone, not an underwater cable. Another mistake I made." Lori yawned hugely, shaking her head at her own stupidity.

An official pair of men marched over, introduced themselves as detectives and sent the islanders back toward the West house. They separated Lori from the rest, holding the gun she had abandoned that was now in a plastic bag.

Acknowledging the gun with a nod, she said. "It was Emily's. Emily Moore's. At least we took it from her."

"We?"

"Jake and I."

"Who is Jake?"

She pointed silently to the big black dog, then knelt beside him and hugged him.

"He took her down for us and knocked the gun out of her hand." She informed the pair.

"Yes, ma'am. We need to talk."

She watched over her shoulder, as Hugh and Jerrod were carried to the waiting chopper, pointing at them. "Can't I go with them and talk later?"

"No ma'am, not now. You are the only one that can fill us in. Can we go inside and talk? We have some questions for you. We can take you to them later."

She sighed, leading them back indoors with Jake at her heels, past the stack of original paintings, where a full cabin search was in progress. The police officers searching through the stack had recognized her from the paintings, elbowing each other and nodded their heads at her.

Lori knew she was in for a long, long session. She plopped down in a chair next to the dining table, yawning again and pointed pink slipper-clad feet straight out in front of her, she asked. "Do you think you could find some food for us? We've been on the run for so long. Jake and I worked up quite an appetite."

"Yes Ma'am. But could you start at the beginning. I'm recording this, all right?"

"Well, JeanPaul Richaud, I mean Hugh Richmond disappeared from the island. And I couldn't find him anywhere. Then I remembered hearing when I first came to the island that there were rumors of pirate caves here, so I decided to search underground when I found an entrance to a tunnel under my burnt out cabin's front porch." Lori hurried and spoke fast, thinking it would get her to the hospital to see the guys quicker.

The two men exchanged looks and one of them said. "Whoa! Wait a minute. Stop! You need to back up. Can you please begin at the beginning. What is your name? Why are you here?"

Epilogue

Three months later at East House

"Hugh, have you seen my sunglasses?" Lori asked.

"They're probably where you left them," he answered her grumpily.

She studied him surreptitiously. She did not want him to see her examining him from across the room. He had fine lines in his face now but his coloring was slowly beginning to return to a healthy tanned glow.

Hugh was not a happy camper since he'd been grounded, and absolutely despised having to use a cane to get around on. He'd gone through a long serious stay in the hospital, getting over the concussion and infected gunshot wound in his leg. And, like most men, he'd been a lousy patient. He'd never been hurt seriously before and the long slow recovery was definitely *not* his strong point.

He'd been back on the island with her for a week. The Laurents had insisted on his complete recovery there. They both were invited to stay for at least the rest of the year. The East house was theirs to use as long as they wished

Lori prepared to go pick up Hugh's physical therapist at the dock. She and Hugh had been gingerly dancing around each other all week. She did not know if he blamed her for his injuries or what the heck was going on inside that stubborn head of his.

She knew that she could have done things differently and it could have made a difference. If only she had blasted him out of that freaking cave earlier, the severity of his illness resulting from his injuries might have been reduced. It was her decision to leave the island and go for help. She should have rescued him sooner. Whatever it was, she wanted to shake it out of him. She was tired of not knowing.

They hadn't talked much either, since his injuries. And she hated it. They'd been perfectly polite strangers. Sometimes she felt as though she was dealing with a contrary child instead of a grown man. Humph. Perhaps a spanking would do him some good. It certainly couldn't hurt.

Well, for now she had to go meet the boat. Jerrod brought the therapist on his mail rounds and Lori already heard Jake's bark and the answering boat horn. Which reminded her, she needed to find where Jake was spending his time.

The puppies had been born but no one had seen them yet.

Jacques had arrived from Paris with a young female Rottweiler for Jake's mate. When the litter came due, the dogs found a place secluded from people on the island. Every single one of the islanders had searched at one time or another but no one had been successful yet. The adult dogs showed up for food, one at a time and then just as quickly disappeared.

Deep in thought, driving a Jeep this time, Lori appreciated how these last months had flown by. After 'the day', which is how she thought of it, apparently everything happened all at once.

Dr. Rigby arrived, concerned over her disappearance from any communication. Miss Genny's cousin, Jacques, had arrived to deal with the crowd of legal beagles. And everyone on the island had been endlessly interviewed and questioned.

The wicked witch had been sent back to France in disgrace. Sheree had been solely responsible for bringing Steffan to the island where he had joined forces with Emily Moore. Actually, the not so benign little man had addicted Emily Moore to the opium, so he could manipulate her to help him. *As far as I'm concerned, he overdid it with her. She was scary.*

Steffan had been the brain, the moneyman, who supplied the drugs to a distribution network in Marseilles that funded a European terrorist group. Emily had been a willing watcher, a lab assistant and a vicious general helper. But it was Steffan who had been creeping around in Lori's cabin at night, moving belongings and letting Jake in and out.

Whew. Such a scary man for an innocuous looking character, she shivered.

She and Benjamin successfully completed her research and submitted their findings for publication. Ben had decided to take the medical school exams and Lori spent a lot of time prepping him.

She had stayed on full time at the hospital in Charlotte Amalie until both Jerrod and Hugh were well on the road to recovery. Which for Hugh had been complicated by a concussion, pneumonia, infections and several corrective surgeries repairing the gunshot damage to his leg.

It had frightened her to see him on the respirator with that horrid machine breathing for him. It had reminded her too much of Nathan. She could finally think of him with less pain.

Somehow she had physically and emotionally distanced herself from the trauma of losing her son. The pain would always be there, but bearable now. The healing had truly begun.

Sighing, she shook herself, putting a fake smile on her face in time to greet Jerrod and Fanny DeClue. What a name, Lori almost giggled. Regardless of her name, that woman was an absolute godsend, with infinite patience and a fine strong will to deal with onerous patients. Fanny was a pretty petite brunette, with soft brown almond doe eyes, and had an enormous hidden strength in her hands.

A widow with great calmness of spirit, Fanny could coerce her patients with relative ease. Fanny had given Jerrod physical therapy for his arm. Lori had watched Jerrod fall like a rock for Fanny. Lori didn't know if Jerrod knew it yet himself, but she was sure that Fanny would let him know, when she was darn good and ready.

It was amusing, watching Fanny manipulate Hugh into doing exercises with his leg that he was just as determined not to do.

Today, after she had reviewed his exercise program with him, Fanny released him. She told him he didn't need to see her for a month *if* he would start walking at least an hour a day and doing his exercises himself. From now on it was up to him. He didn't need her anymore.

Hugh was shocked. He'd been paying more attention to Lori, who'd been busy watching Jerrod and smiling secretly to herself. Hugh was oblivious to the fact that Jerrod in turn had been staring the entire time at Fanny.

Hugh withdrew with a sour face and limped over to an easy chair where he'd been spending most of his time since he'd arrived back on the island. He grunted, barely acknowledging the couple's goodbyes, when Lori drove them away.

When Lori returned, she was determined to get him up and moving. One way or another. Before she entered the house, Jake trotted around the corner of the house toward her with a two-week old pup in his mouth. Lori dropped to the patio to hold the wriggling puppy he placed in her hands.

From inside the house, Hugh watched the glow of love on her face as she nuzzled the tiny black dog. Jake immediately disappeared around the corner. Lori sat on her heels, waiting and petting the pup to sleep in her lap. Before long, her lap was full of black mewling pups. Then Jake and Momma Dog were bearing the final two pups of the litter to her. She stroked Jake and Momma Dog. (That was the only name anyone had called the young female since she arrived. No matter what her impressive pedigree was.) She bragged to the pair about the handsome litter.

"Look Hugh. There are seven pups. Aren't they absolutely beautiful?" She held one of them up by her cheek.

A random ray of sunlight penetrated the trees overhead and streaked down on her golden shining head, illuminating her face. An intense pain stabbed directly into his heart at the thought of giving up this woman. But he would. He had to.

Lori saw his face wrenched in agony and jumped up from the floor of the patio with her arms full of wriggling puppies. She carried them into the house to set them in a circle of pillows before kneeling at his feet. She settled her hands directly on his knees. The first time she had actually touched him since he'd returned home except for a passing pat here or there.

"Are you all right? Do you need pain medication? Did you hurt something in your exercise?"

He told himself that he would never be all right again. He shook his head and cleared his throat.

"Lori." He stopped and then started again. "Lori, I have seen the way that you look at Jerrod."

"But…" she tried to interrupt him.

"Wait. I saw how he came to rescue you. And how you spent all that time at the hospital with him."

How would you know? You fool, she thought. *I spent ten, no, more like a hundredfold more time with you.* She withdrew her hands from his knees and sat back on her feet, calmly waiting for him to get it out.

"*He* is a whole man. He is capable. A good man. He doesn't need a cane to walk or therapy or anything, to get on with his life and take care of you." He watched her staring at him, her eyes large and luminous, her lips twitching.

She forced herself to remain silent. *So. This is what you have been brooding about, you fool.*

"And most of all, I found out that you are due a reward, a substantial reward from the French for solving this case. Seven figures. Very healthy. Can make you totally independent."

She sat in silence, smiling inside. After this last year and all that she'd been through, Lori had finally found out who she was and what she needed in this life to be whole, and it was sitting right smack in front of her.

No longer was she on the edge of paradise. She *knew* where her paradise was. Now, here with him or wherever that might be.

Finally, she stood up. She took his cane from the arm of his chair and calmly walked away from him, tossing it out onto the patio through the open door. Jake and Momma Dog both quizzically watched her performance.

"You are a fool, Hugh Richmond. You are a fool, if you believe that anyone is better for me than you. *Or* if you do not know that the *only* reason I came back and put *everyone* on this island at risk was for you."

She slowly unbuttoned her blouse, watching him lick his upper lip.

"You are a fool if you do not know that Jerrod is in love with Fanny DeClue."

Lori threw her shirt on the floor, unhooking her bra from behind her back, and enjoyed watching his discomfort as he swallowed.

"You are a fool if you think that reward means that I do not need you. Why I've been aware of that money for months. And surprise, I'm still here."

She slung her bra across the room, and observed his eyes begin a golden predatory gleam.

"And, you are *definitely* a fool if you think that I am going to marry a crippled, helpless old man who feels sorry for himself!"

After slithering out of her shorts and panties, and dropping them on the floor, she hooked one finger at him and headed down the dark hall, quite, quite sure that he would follow.

And somehow he managed to do just that!

Meet Lynda LaPorte

Lynda's career path has encompassed biological and chemical research science, a real estate agent and broker, talent agent, photographer, and a homemaker. She is a member of Romance Writers of America, member and past officer of Missouri Romance Writers of America, Member of Society of Children's Book Writers & Illustrators. She has been writing stories since elementary school. Lynda has written and illustrated dozens of children's musical e-books (soon to be published) and is currently working on a second suspense. Her hobbies include swimming, snorkeling, landscaping and angel crafts. **Edge of Paradise** is her first novel. Lynda, her husband, son and extended family call the St. Louis area home. Her website address is www.lyndasburch.com.

Look For These Other Titles

From

Wings ePress, Inc.

Romance Novels

An Exaltation Of Larks by Megan Hart
Edge Of Paradise by Lynda Burch w/a Lynda LaPorte
Silver Wings by Amanda Kraft
The Secrets Of Hanson Hall by Allison Knight
Ties by Roberta O. Major
Under The Mulberry Tree by Margery Harkness Casares
Where The Firethorns Grow by Marilyn Nichols Kapp;
Wrong Side Of Love by Diana Lee Johnson

General Fiction Novels

Juno Lucina by Amanda Hager

Coming In July 2002

Romance Novels

A Change Of Plans by Ann B. Morris
Dark Legacy by Christine Janssen
House Of Cards by Savannah Michaels
Last Resort by Cheryl Norman
Monster In The Moat by Fran Keighley
Serendipitous Rose by Sue Thornton
Southern Pride, Northern Honor by Sandra Dugas

General Fiction Novels

Bloody Captivity by Linda Suzane

Be sure to visit us at http://www.wings-press.com
for a complete listing of our available and upcoming titles.
